Praise for *Good Things Come and Go*

'With an expert eye for light and shadow, Shapiro traces the contours of sorrow, regret, and the luminous moments of bliss we hold close. Poignant, redemptive, electrifying.'

— Catherine Chidgey

'A tender, tough story of loss and renewal, love and rage, the promise of youth and the aching regrets of middle age, Josie Shapiro's *Good Things Come and Go* pays careful attention to lives that on the surface look broken at worst, at best, ordinary enough. The reward is a powerful reminder that inside every one of us is a dream worth chasing, no matter how much time or talent has been laid to waste. The writing is carefully understated, at times brilliantly, blazingly physical: I love reading Josie Shapiro describing bodies in motion, bodies at rest, bodies that hurt.'

— Noelle McCarthy

Praise for *Everything is Beautiful and Everything Hurts*

'*Everything is Beautiful and Everything Hurts* plunges the reader into the gruelling world of the long distance runner — every pleasure, every pain. Shapiro deftly weaves the coming-of-age story of Mickey Bloom into a gripping account of adult Bloom running the Auckland Marathon. This is compelling storytelling that exposes the sacrifices — physical and emotional — demanded of our sporting elite. Chilling, yet ultimately heartwarming, it celebrates success without flinching from staring down its brutal costs. A sophisticated debut that will capture the racing hearts of its readers.'

— Sue Orr, *Loop Tracks*

'Josie Shapiro's accomplished debut novel has the compulsive forward motion of a world-class race. You don't have to be a runner to get the high, just read this book!"

— Kirsten McDougall, *She's a Killer*

'This is THE novel that allows us to understand this very special sport. We were caught up in the beauty of this text about a young sportswoman, who runs without us knowing whether she is running or chasing something, but who feels she exists in this effort. It quite simply fascinated us.'

— Constance Trapenard, Editions JC Lattes

'Mickey Bloom is a loner — shy, dyslexic, awkward, with a life full of insults and regrets — until she discovers running which turns out to be the one thing that she can do, and ultimately it saves her. As an avowed non-runner, it's remarkable that I loved this as much as I did, which is a testimony to the power and quality of the writing, which won the inaugural Allen and Unwin Fiction prize. Mickey Bloom stole my heart and this is truly a book to love.'

— Joan's Picks, Whitcoulls

'*Everything is Beautiful and Everything Hurts* is a rollercoaster, heart-in-the-mouth read that deposits you in the pain, ache and joy of both running and living. Mickey Bloom is a memorable character that will get under your skin, with her doubts and her struggles, her recognitions and her learning leaps. This book will linger with me for a long time.'

— Paula Green, *Kete Books*

'The journey of underdog competitive runner Mickey Bloom is one of ambition and catastrophe before it comes sweet with recovery and growth. In this commercially appealing, carefully held book, the author is doing something subversive. I clung to this story in a way that both surprised and, at the risk of sounding schmaltzy, healed me.'

— Claire Mabey, *The Spinoff*

'Much of the book is about long-distance running but it won't matter if you are not a runner — Shapiro's fine writing makes the detail of training, the absolute focus, and the punishment on bodies (and souls) completely riveting. A deeply affecting and absorbing novel from a writer to watch.'

— Jane Arthur, *The Dominion Post*

GOOD THINGS COME AND GO

GOOD THINGS COME AND GO

JOSIE SHAPIRO

ALLEN&UNWIN
AUCKLAND • SYDNEY • MELBOURNE • LONDON

First published in 2025

Allen & Unwin Aotearoa New Zealand
Level 2, 10 College Hill, Freemans Bay
Auckland 1011, New Zealand
+64 (9) 377 3800
auckland@allenandunwin.com
www.allenandunwin.co.nz

83 Alexander Street
Crows Nest NSW 2065, Australia
+61 (2) 8425 0100

EU Authorised Representative: Easy Access System Europe, Mustamäe tee 50, 10621 Tallinn, Estonia, gpsr.requests@easproject.com

A catalogue record for this book is available from the National Library of New Zealand.

ISBN 978 1 99100 670 7

Cover design by Christabella Designs
Text design by Carla Sy
Typeset in Miller Text, 11.2/17 pt
Printed and bound in Australia by the Opus Group

10 9 8 7 6 5 4 3 2

MIX
Paper | Supporting responsible forestry
FSC® C001695
FSC www.fsc.org

For Lee

Hurting now does not mean your future holds pain

Whangamatā skatepark graffiti

PENNY

AT THE TAIL END of an August night in Los Angeles, Penny Whittaker sits alone in the studio behind her house. The room smells of mint and lanolin, and a single lamp gives the blank canvas on the wall in front of her a subtle glow. Slick with sweat, Penny turns and stares out the open door. Dawn is still an hour away, but she can't sleep. It isn't the heat keeping her awake. Riggs has been gone for five days, and she can't paint. When she thinks about it too deeply, she finds it difficult to breathe.

The buzz of backyard crickets wafts in, and from further away the yipping of a coyote, followed by a long, howling whine. It isn't the first time Riggs has disappeared, though this is the first time he's been gone longer than a day or two. She looks at the untouched canvas and feels the sting of a disappointment so intense it burns inside her chest. In three weeks, she'll be forty. She's acutely aware that the years she might have created her best work are probably behind her and her fiancé is an addict who can't keep a promise. Riggs will eventually come home, yet she's tempted by a strong, shameful desire to get in her car and drive somewhere, anywhere, to live some other kind of life, instead of fixing the one she has.

She won't do it, of course. If she ignores Riggs's tendency to vanish, and the grief she works hard to hide, her life isn't bad. The lovely house and studio he bought in Woodland Hills, a pearlescent-blue swimming pool nestled between the two buildings. She'd be an ungrateful idiot not to see how good she has it. And all of it — the house, the studio, her being in this city — it's all thanks to Riggs. After Rose died, and Penny wanted to quit her part-time job at Sketchy's Art Supplies so she could try one last time to succeed as a painter, he'd said okay, I'll support you. When they'd left New Zealand, and she had no money, no education, no plan, he said he'd take care of her. He asked only that she stick with him. Which she has done, on the whole. After they left New Zealand, once they were on the plane, it was only him. She has been loyal and true. Perhaps that makes her a fool.

She opens a sketchbook, takes up a stick of charcoal and sketches outlines, ideas, shapes, movements. Page after page, scribbling and sketching. Eventually she slides the paper away in disgust. Offers up a prayer to Catherine de'Vigri in desperation. I'll do anything, give me one more chance. For me, for Rose. Let me do this.

Before she could walk, before she knew what other things life might hold, Penny was given a pencil and encouraged to draw. And then, from pencil to pen, from felt-tip to crayon, from pastel to paintbrush, seeing the joy it brought her parents, feeling a pulse-rushing pride in her developing talent, she knew she would be an artist. As a child, she painted the way she breathed: in a way that suggested she could not live without it. And that has not changed. Now, in fact, she isn't entirely sure she can live without it — not after Rose. If this too is gone, what is there worth living for?

She repeats the prayer, feverish and quick. Desperation makes you do crazy things, doesn't it? She opens her eyes. The paintbrush is over there. Still can't use it. The prayer, like everything before, hasn't worked. Why did she bother, anyway? She doesn't believe in god, or saints, or herself.

Where has her talent gone? All this time and freedom, this glorious studio, and she can't paint. All these years of work, tears and thankless effort, and no gallery or art collector wants her — what a useless waste. Can't call herself an artist, not anymore. An embarrassment, definitely that. Her father would be horrified. Used to be she couldn't stop with the ideas. Saw the whole world in colours and shadow, line and shape. That's gone now, along with Rose, and gets worse every time Riggs takes off. As though he steals it from her. Well, she wants it back.

The tantalising dream of driving off, burning this all to the ground, strikes her again, and she smiles at the absurdity of it. As if talent and inspiration would be on the roadside somewhere in northern California. Besides, how would she survive without Riggs? She has no qualifications. They left New Zealand before she completed her final year of high school. The only job she's ever had is that one at Sketchy's. Not exactly in-demand work experience. She was born with a brush, her father liked to say, and she'd had no formal training, unless living under the same roof as Sir Damian Whittaker could be considered an education. Watching him. Imitating him. Outclassing him. She will have nothing if she leaves Riggs. She has to stay.

But — the next time he disappears she might not stay. Next time she might leave.

She turns away from the canvas and her sketchbook and gazes out toward the house. Creases of pale peach have settled into the eastern sky. The day has begun. She gathers up her notebooks and her sadness and walks across the paved courtyard to the main house. The air is laced with the bitter edge of smoke. There must be a fire close by. She takes a deep breath. She's always liked the smell of burning.

JAMIE

LATER THAT WEEK, ON the other side of the world, Jamie Flannery carves long, loose arcs on his board at the skatepark near his house in Grey Lynn. It's not long after dawn, and low dark cloud holds the best of the early-morning light at bay. Jamie looks as though he's straight from a vintage edition of *Thrasher*: long arms extended graceful as wings from his long lean body, blond hair curling around his ears. At this hour, the skatepark is all his: the box, the rails, the half-pipe, the vert, the bowl. Hard rough ground, sculpted and staged for magic. The forecast rain hasn't come, and the dry ground crackles under his wheels. It is, he concludes, an omen. It will be a good day. He's owed a few of those.

He keeps his mind on a tight leash, focusing on the board, on the sensation of the cold air biting his cheeks, on the exact movements he needs to make to execute each trick. And it is a trick — a trick played on the mind to distract it, to keep it here, in this moment, and not lost in the past. He needs to be in the moment, or he might hurt himself.

He finds it difficult to see in darkness and the dim light at the edges of the day, so skating at this hour is risky. He's been hurt before, badly, and he's not keen to repeat the experience. Only he needs to skate, visibility be damned. Coffee isn't enough after a night like that, awake every hour, dreams haunted by people he can't forget. When he's strung out he goes for a skate — your mind can't wander when you're flipping the board up onto the slick steep line of the rail or taking a leap from the crest of a staircase. Let your thoughts trickle somewhere else and your destiny is disaster.

Skateboarding has forever been an escape for Jamie. So what if he has a job he doesn't find fulfilling? So what if he has little time to paint anymore? So what if he's single and is starting to suspect he's never going to find what he's yearning for? So what if he doesn't have kids, and doesn't see his mother as much as he should? When he's skating, none of it matters. The physics of skating don't change, and his belief in himself on the board is mostly steady, and those two things are pretty much all you need to skate. Those, and a desire to risk it all.

He's had that desire his whole life. Maybe that's why he's lost so much. Didn't hold it close enough, though he's certain he didn't give Madeline up without a fight. Other things, other people — who knew? Maybe he could've tried harder. Maybe if he'd been there that night, his dad might still be alive. Or not. There are so many things he could've done different, and the passing of time hasn't made them any easier to reconcile.

His watch alarm buzzes. Work awaits. Only he wants one

last trick, so he tacks the board around to face the park. No matter what, there's time for one more trick. A kickflip backside lipslide on an A-frame rail — you can't think about your dead father when you do that. 50–50 grind nollie shuvit — can't get angry at Madeline for leaving when you perform that trick. Skating fast and leaping down a ten-step staircase — can't steep in regret about Penny and how you pushed her away when you do that. You'd break your neck, or worse, if you let distraction get in the way. Skating is freedom from the past, a refusal to consider the future, an entry to being entirely present.

He wheels around the park at pace, hurtling toward the box. He shifts his feet in tiny increments. Prepares for the trick. Shadows lurch and haunt every bend, and he reins in his focus. One more push to gain some momentum and he hits something unexpected. Something hard and unforgiving. It lunges in from nowhere, snatching at the edge of his board, clipping it out from under him. He's a grommet again, tumbling to the ground. The impact jangles through his body, hip, shoulder, elbow. Adrenaline surges, and his heart skids too fast for a few seconds before it returns to a calm, regular beat. He sits up and realises he's hit the rail. Nothing's broken, thank Christ; it can still be a good day.

The board's in one piece too. He's not sure how. There's no lasting damage, though his hands tremble as he slips his board into the back of his ute and don't stop shaking until much later in the day.

By the time he leaves the building site that evening, he feels grim as the reaper. The sharp outlines of a headache that lingered all day in his temples expand into a killer migraine, and he's not sure he's safe to drive. He's suffered these headaches about once a month since he hit his head as a teenager, though recently they've been coming more often.

That evening, back at home, he takes some codeine and ibuprofen to keep the headache at bay, then he mopes about the house for a while, unsettled. Later that night, when he's watching television, the dog beside him, a Domino's pizza box warm on his lap, he's struck with a sudden recognition of what has actually upset him. Why he's still feeling so ill at the thought of his fall that morning.

Because it wasn't the fall exactly. Falling was the price you paid for standing on that deck, thinking you had any chance in hell of controlling those four wheels. No, it wasn't the fall; it was the fact he hadn't seen the rail before he'd hit it. He runs the memory over in his mind, and he realises he hadn't been able to see his board or his feet either. He'd been looking down, and all he'd seen was a narrowing tunnel of black.

RIGGS

AT A SKATEPARK TWENTY miles from his house in Los Angeles, Adam Riggs rolls toward the lip of a skate bowl, a goofy smile plastered on his face. He's worn the same clothes for six days, hasn't shaved for five, and he's slept no more than three hours each night he's been away from home, curled up beneath a motorway underpass or, if he's lucky, on a lumpy mattress in his dealer's apartment. It's noon. The sun is high and caustic overhead. Sunburn blisters his nose pink, and his body is rank with sweat.

He's been skating for hours. It's been months since he's been able to skate this long — his back would normally be screaming in agony after an hour. Today he can't feel anything: he's high on painkillers. Faster and faster he skates, and then he drops into the bowl, falling into the hollow like he has nothing in the world worth living for.

Rose. He pumps around the bowl and thinks of his darling Rose. That soft hair and the particular way she'd smelt, like peanut butter and glitter. He pumps his knees and swoops up to the lip of the bowl and hovers, the board balanced precariously on the coping.

Penny. He's going to lose Penny. It seems inevitable, given his behaviour. Down into the bowl again he falls, almost too fast, kamikaze. Hell, he can't lose her too. Come to think of it, how is he going to tell her the show's given him the boot? *Roll With It* no longer want him. Maybe no more skating either — at least that was the advice from the doctor. His back is truly fucked. 'I recommend surgery,' the doc said. Surgery? He can't afford surgery now he's lost his job and his benefits. Spent too much money on drugs, and at the casino, and now he will have to tell Penny all about it.

There seems no way to tell her that won't humiliate him, so instead he thinks about that look on her face when he wakes in the night and she's sleeping. The calm beauty of her in those quiet moments. The only time she looks content. It's been years since he's seen that expression in the daylight. Back home, maybe? When they were kids? She had that bloody look on her face every second of the day when they were living in New Zealand. It had been the three of them in those days: her and him and Jamie. And it was that look that sent him over the edge, caught him, snared him. A smile as enigmatic as Mona Lisa's and he was a goner. Would've done anything for her, anything at all, and in the end he did.

He can't lose her, that's the truth of it. The very idea is inconceivable. He'll fight for her, bloody tooth and nail. He's a fighter, always has been. Doesn't mind taking a punch, certainly doesn't mind throwing a few. Never hit Penny though. Never. He loves that woman.

Overcome, his eyes fill with tears, and in that same moment he swings up the side of the bowl, loses his footing and slips from the board. It rolls away from him and he lands hard. The impact is worst on his hip, though his face takes some of it too. He lies on the concrete, blood thick in his mouth, his shoulders shaking with wasted laughter, aware that his back will charge him dearly as soon as the pills wear off. He'll go home then; he'll be good, he will. Tomorrow. He'll get some Vicodin, lots of oxy, stock up to get through the next few weeks. Figure out a plan. He'll tell Penny about the show, and they can figure out where they might go from here. Tomorrow he will go home.

PENNY

THE CITY IS ENGULFED in a late summer heatwave. The canvas hanging in the studio remains untouched, and a large spider is taking up residence in the window frame. Rather than dusting the web away, Penny watches the spider progress with its work, methodically creating a thing of beauty from nothing. If only her work, her life, were so simple.

She goes to the shop to pick up bread and milk, juice and ice cream. She pretends not to see a neighbour in the aisle beside her and idles in front of the cooler for a long time, both for the respite from the heat and because it calms the urge to cry. Riggs has now been gone for eight days. With each day, the temptation to leave grows stronger, and with it the guilt for even considering the idea.

At home, the temperature hovers above 101. Hot, and extremely bothered, Penny opens her phone and scrolls social media sites. She hates social media, the intense fakery of it, the angry bitter righteousness of it, but when she's trying to avoid reality, she can't keep away. She snoops on artists with thousands of followers, her heart bitter with an envy she wishes she was too generous to feel. She closes the app, opens Facebook. Her feed is full of photos of people having a great time: friends on the Brooklyn Bridge in New York; an acquaintance on holiday in Lake Garda, eating gelato, the sun glinting on the water. It appears from here that none of them have ever suffered pain. Never felt a loss so sharp it cuts flesh from bone. She slides her finger up and the screen is filled with an image of someone's baby. A mutual friend has shared the photo with the comment: My gorgeous niece!

The baby looks a bit like Rose. Something in the shape of the eyes, the fullness of the lower lip. Penny pinches the screen and pulls her fingers apart to zoom in. Those cheeks. Penny remembers the feeling of kissing Rose's unbearably soft face, her full round cheeks. Can almost taste it, the rush of it pulsing through her as she looks at this stranger's child. With a stab at the screen, she exits the site. It's insanity, spying on this unknown baby, and now it's made her think of Rose. She doesn't want to think about her daughter. Not now, not now; not ever.

A call comes through even before she can put her phone down. The number on the screen is unfamiliar. But she recognises the New Zealand calling code. Her parents.

'Mum?'

A woman laughs. 'Not your mother. Although I suppose I should take that as a compliment.'

'Shit, sorry.' Penny shifts the phone to the other ear and

stands up. Sitting down and speaking with a stranger she's called Mum feels too casual.

'No need to apologise,' the woman says. 'I'm calling to speak to Penelope Whittaker?'

'That's me.'

'Kia ora, Penelope, I'm Sally Trubridge. I'm the director of a small gallery in Parnell, Auckland. Stonewall Gallery.'

There's a pause, perhaps for Penny to express her acquaintance with the name; when she doesn't, Sally Trubridge carries on with only a vague note of pique.

'Anyway, Penelope, I recently grew familiar with your work, your series *The Art of Falling*, and, to be candid with you, I was blown away.'

The art of falling. A series of seventeen paintings from the perspective of a bird, or a drone, replete with a strange sense of drama, each piece designed to make the viewer feel they're falling towards the ground at great speed. When it became impossible to deny that Rose was close to the end, Penny had sequestered herself in her studio and worked all day and all night until her feet swelled from the long hours standing, until her fingers grew calloused where she held the brush, until she finished.

That summer had been almost as hot as it was now, and in the heat and the sorrow she'd felt possessed in some odd way, and happy, despite the certainty that Rose was going to die. And it was this unexpected happiness that gave her the feeling that painting might be the very thing to save her when the world was crashing down and taking everything, everything, with it. In those weeks, with Rose slipping from her and the sense that nothing would ever be the same, it seemed possible that her life might still have some meaning and that the meaning would be found through her old friend, creating art.

She was shocked when she saw the completed paintings. They were inspired in a way she'd thought no longer possible for her. When Rose was a newborn, Penny hadn't painted much: she was sleep deprived, too scared of her previous failures. Her fears about having children and continuing to create good work had seemed realised, and she'd considered her dream over and done with. But these were good, and she was sure she didn't think that only because she was desperate for it to be true. No, it was obvious. There, in the bold and panicked energy of the brushstrokes, in the way the eye was drawn into the work, giving the unsettling sensation that you were falling, like one of those bad dreams that slammed you awake. There was something there. Penny had hoped the paintings were good enough to get what she'd always wanted: critical success, as well as sales. She wanted to be everything her father was and everything her mother wasn't, and, because the world was falling apart, she wanted it more than she ever had before.

Only no one had wanted to show them. Submissions to over thirty galleries that accepted unsolicited proposals went mostly unanswered. Rachel, her former colleague from Sketchy's who sold her pastoral watercolours for good money on Instagram, suggested she ask Sir Damian Whittaker for an introduction.

'It's all about relationships,' Rachel said. 'If you let him, your father could help.'

Penny refused. 'I didn't move halfway across the world only to stand on his shoulders,' she said.

Rachel was unimpressed by her principles. 'I think you

should consider it,' she said. 'He's one of the greatest realist painters of the twentieth century, but I mean, hey, it's your call. You could come to the dark side, you know, and join me on Instagram. Best thing I ever did. No more gatekeepers.'

Did it make Penny a snob because she didn't want to sell her work on Instagram? It probably did. Honestly, it was pathetic how much she craved the prestige of a gallery and the validation that someone with power had chosen her.

Sally Trubridge is speaking again: 'I was hoping you might be interested in a solo show, maybe first quarter 2024? I understand you're currently living in the United States? It would be ideal if your schedule allows you to return to New Zealand for the launch. I understand you have family connections in the Auckland region?'

'A solo show?' Penny says again, to be certain.

When she'd left her parents' house twenty-three years ago, when she'd boarded that plane with Riggs without telling Jamie she was going, her fingers were still taped together, her father's best brushes were in her backpack, and smuggled in her suitcase were some of his best paints. She'd taken the seat beside Riggs, the pressure in her chest building not only from the plane's acceleration for take-off but also from all the things she was leaving behind and didn't want to think about. This was what she'd left for. This was what she'd waited all those years for. It had happened. Finally.

'That's correct,' Sally Trubridge says, and later Penny won't recall the rest of the conversation: what she said, what Sally Trubridge said. What she will remember is the feeling of her heartbeat racing in her sternum, the satisfaction of a dream realised, and the wretched ache she tried to push aside: the stinging realisation she would give up all of this to hold Rose one more time.

It isn't until much later still that Penny also realises she hasn't submitted to any galleries in Auckland. To any galleries in New Zealand. Her surname is too recognisable there. But it doesn't matter. This woman likes the work. Blown away, she'd said. Blown away.

After the call, in the hours until dark, she plans the trip. She will stay with her parents. She will swallow her pride, endure their passive-aggressive pettiness, their outdated views, their dismissal of her feelings, their smirking condescension. The next thought comes with a frisson of exhilaration: she will go without Riggs. She could leave in less than a week. In the coming days, she will arrange shipping of the paintings. They will require careful preparation for travel, and she'll need to figure out what to do with the house while she's gone: who knows when Riggs will return? What will happen when he does come home, only to find she's no longer there? He's made threats before. About what he would do if she left, what he would do to himself.

Don't think about that; don't think about that now. A single swipe on her phone and she's searching one-way flights, Los Angeles to Auckland. A list flashes up: Qantas, Fiji Airways, Air New Zealand, United. Six hundred dollars for the cheapest flight, US dollars; eleven hundred for another: a queasy sensation overtakes her.

Riggs looks after the money. It makes sense. He earns it, mostly, and she's no good with numbers. Her Sketchy's pay cheque went into his account, and he'd given her money, a decent amount, each week, to spend as she wished. 'You don't need to worry about money, babe,' he'd said, his hand on her knee, her shoulder, the back of her head. 'You need anything, you can ask me.' She's never even had a credit card.

It's only now she understands how this has been a form of control. She taps her passcode into her banking app, and it's as if the floor has slipped away beneath her. The last allowance was due three days ago and it seems that wherever he is, doing whatever he's doing, he isn't concerned with her bank balance. The screen shows she has a total of $30.65 to her name.

If Riggs doesn't come home, she can't book a flight. And she will not ask her parents to help her. Anything but that. They'll hold the debt over her forever and a day.

There is no good option. She calls Riggs.

'Hi, this is Adam Riggs, not available right now. Leave a message and I'll get back to you when I can.'

At the sound of his voice, her mouth fills with a strange mixture of salt and bitterness, fear and resentment. Damn you, Adam Riggs. Damn you. She hangs up without leaving a message and dials another number immediately. This time she calls Los Angeles Medical Center, then Cedars-Sinai. Martin Luther King Jr Community Hospital, then UCLA West Valley Medical Center. Waits patiently when she's put on hold for ten, fifteen minutes, 'Are You Lonesome Tonight' playing down the crackling line. She almost throws the phone across the room.

This song was playing while they waited for their first urgent appointment with the pediatric oncologist at the Children's Hospital. Three years ago feels like yesterday, like an eternity ago. Time does this now, like it runs and slips, out of order and jumping ahead. She'd sat beside Riggs in the waiting room, watching Rose play in the corner with a set of wooden blocks, Elvis crooning from the corners of the ceiling. Rose was lethargic and quiet, her cheeks shocking white with tiny purple crescents deepening under her eyes, her strawberry-blonde hair glinting under the thin electric lights like a warning signal. Penny remembers feeling that her life had come unstitched, that the path her life should have taken was drifting away, leaving her marooned somewhere she didn't want to be. Riggs held her hand in both of his, and she clung to him, and he clung to her, both of them terrified. She feels the same way right now, waiting for someone at the hospital to answer her call, to tell her whether Riggs is there, whether he's still alive.

'His name is Adam Riggs,' she says when they come back on the line. 'Adam Montrose Riggs. Brown eyes, five foot eight. A tattoo of a rose on his right forearm.'

Very sorry, they say in turn, crisp and decidedly unapologetic. He's not listed as a patient here.

She wipes at the sweat coating her forehead. He's gone for good, or he's dead, or he's a bastard: maybe all three are true. Only she needs him here, and that realisation makes her sick. To think she needs him to release her. She considers calling the police. She can guess what they'll say: your boyfriend isn't missing. He's chosen to leave. He's done it before, gone away for a while without telling you, don't get too excited. They'll have that look on their face, like the one Riggs gives her when he says she's overreacting. Eyes warm with pity, lips pressed together in a sad smile. They will suggest she's irrational. Riggs likes to describe her that way too, and though he never says the word hysterical, she knows he wants to. Is calling the police after eight days irrational? She's finding it harder to tell what's normal behaviour and what is indeed over the top.

What she needs is a drink. The crisp coolness of a white wine on her lips. The oblivion that might come with being completely drunk. It's been a long time since she's been wasted. After the devastating final appointment, when the oncologist explained Rose was no longer strong enough to qualify for stem-cell transplant and there were no other options they could consider for treatment, Penny had stopped drinking. Riggs seemed to find her sobriety a personal insult. It was, in a way, though her abstinence really had nothing to do with Riggs, and it was typical of him to feel as if it did. She stopped because when she drank, she couldn't sleep, and in those loose, unhinged hours between midnight and 5 a.m., when the world slowed and the ghosts emerged, what she had been avoiding all day chased her down. When she couldn't sleep, she thought about the past, about the way she wished things were. She thought about Rose.

But, honestly, what does it even matter now? Sleep: who needs sleep? She's getting precious little of it these days. Between the oppressive heat, Riggs's disappearance and the roiling sense of despair that she can't afford to leave even if she manages to secure the courage, she can't see the harm in adding a bit of alcohol-induced insomnia into the mix. She sets her phone down on the floor of the studio and walks to the house. Inside, the air is thick and musty. A noise from down the hallway stops her short of the kitchen: a rustling sound, body against bed sheets. The skin on the back of her neck prickles. For a moment she thinks she spies a flash of strawberry-blonde hair, a small head racing around the corner and out the door ahead of her.

'Riggs?'

Her voice sinks into the house, and there's no response. She steps further down the hall and calls his name again: 'Adam?'

Whatever she'd heard, or thinks she heard, doesn't sound again. The bedroom is empty. No one's hiding in the bathroom. Rose's bedroom door is closed, and she doesn't open it to check. Can't bear to see the room as it is, as it was: the Minnie Mouse bedspread, the lilac tutu, the six-inch soft-top skateboard Riggs gave her for her third birthday. She can't open the door, she can do no more than rest her ear against it and listen to be sure, to be sure, and she's sure, there's no one there. The house almost throbs with absence and she doesn't know whether that makes her want to laugh or cry.

The light inside the fridge doesn't flick on when she opens the door, and the interior is uncommonly warm. She leans in and listens: silence. The cooling system must have failed. Worn down by the heat, probably, or simply a victim of time. There's a bottle of wine, still cool to the touch, cool enough to drink, though it won't be long before the food begins to spoil. Great, just great. The new tub of ice cream will melt, the fresh bottle of milk will sour. She knows she should eat as much as she can, discard the rest and call a technician. Only the thought of food makes her guts twist, and she can't pay a technician for the work. She takes the bottle of wine and lets the door close. Fuck it. It can wait until Riggs comes home. He will be home soon.

In ordinary circumstances, Riggs would be the one to deal with a broken refrigerator. The things he can't handle are more emotional. Practical household problems? He's on it. Groceries? He's at the store. Talking about his anger? Can't fix that with a Phillips screwdriver, so it's off the table. The fact they haven't had sex in almost two years? Hell no, not to be discussed. Hasn't always been this way, but after Rose got sick, the dynamic shifted. Before Rose, it had been clear he needed her more than she needed him. And now? She pours a large glass and drinks it quickly, as though quenching an intense thirst, then pours herself another, even larger glass. She carries it and the bottle outside and dangles her feet in the pool. Takes a long, slow sip and closes her eyes. Now, well, they might not need each other, but they haven't yet found another way to survive.

Evening settles in. She downs the wine and refills the glass. Thinks about Sally Trubridge's phone call. Blown away, she'd said. Blown away.

The water is cool and refreshing on her legs, and she slips into the pool in her clothes. She floats on her back, letting her tears merge with the water. The haze that sat over the city for most of the week has lifted, and she can see the pale-yellow moon rise over the Santa Monica mountains.

It's difficult to swim with clothes on, so she strips them off, letting them sink to the bottom, feeling the water soft on her body. She hasn't swum naked in years. Not since that night in Rocky Bay. One of those bonfire nights when she was a teenager. The wine twists in her blood and the moon flares in her vision, and she thinks about the girl she'd been then, so full of wonder and hope. How on earth had she ended up here? A childless mother, an artless painter.

She doesn't enjoy dwelling on the past. Never has. She hates the feeling that her life is now nothing more than a few fluttering images, no more real than a story. No more real than a painting. But with Riggs gone, with Rose gone, she finds herself thinking about her past, her parents, Waiheke Island, Jamie Flannery, and the choices she'd made.

Later that night the heatwave abates. A cool northerly wind picks up, lifting the surface of the pool into a series of glittering frills, and she hears, from far in the distance, the deep roll of thunder. At seven minutes after midnight, she's woken from her half-sleep by a knock on the door. While it's a relief to know he's home, she also feels a wave of resentment. If he is going to leave, he should stay gone. She peers through the window for a few seconds, letting him wait for her for once. The silver light of the moon picks out the first few grey hairs in his beard, and she can see a large dark stain on his tee-shirt. When he notices her at the window, he taps on the door with a knuckle and smiles. Penny can't help but flinch at the sight: his front left tooth is missing.

She opens the door a crack.

'Hey,' he says. 'I'm home.'

She presses her foot into the corner of the door to stop him pushing it open. The sharp scent of his body wafts to her: women, whiskey, dirt. He smells of cigarettes and that sharp, profusive sweat of users. A thick stubble shrouds his gaunt cheeks. She doesn't want to look at him. She wants to shut the door, but she doesn't. She wants to go to New Zealand.

'Come on, Penny,' he says, quiet in the night's darkness. 'Let me in.'

She hates him as much as she loves him, and despite this, and possibly because of this, she lets him into the house.

JAMIE

ON A CLEAR THURSDAY morning in the first week of September, ten days after his fall at the skatepark, Jamie sets his tools in the back of his ute. He's packed lunch today: a peanut butter sandwich, two chocolate digestives, a banana. Without someone else to help with the rent and bills, without Madeline, he's trying to curb his spending, even though he much prefers a Pita Pit or a Subway when he's on the tools. He's working up in Long Bay, a kitchen renovation for a retired couple. Their house has a spectacular view of the Waitematā. Two days he's been there already, and both days he's been dumbstruck by how much the place reminds him of Penny's parents' place on Waiheke.

He doesn't particularly want to think about the last time he was at the Whittakers' — that night when the police dropped him and Penny at the door at two in the morning, her hands still wet with red paint, his lips still smarting with the feeling of that kiss. Christ, the staircase in this Long Bay house is almost identical to the one at the Whittakers' place, the one Sir Damian had stormed down that morning in his pyjamas, apoplectic, screaming at Jamie for being such a deadbeat, screaming at Penny for wasting her talent and his time. Jamie doesn't like to think about that man holding Penny's hand, holding her hand so tight her pink skin went white. He feels sick when he remembers that man. The look on his face when he twisted her hand, turning it so hard she squealed, the slick hiss in his voice when he said he wouldn't let go until she promised not to hang out with Jamie again or she'd be sent to London, to some Royal college of art. Jamie doesn't want to think about what he did while this was going on, because he did nothing but stand there for far too long. Should have stopped him the minute he touched her. Useless, pathetic, cowardly.

Nah, he doesn't like to think of that night at all.

He reverses the ute into the street in a rush. Is that the time? He's late again. Another terrible night, another awful sleep. When he'd gone to bed, a throbbing, thumping headache reverberated through his skull and progressed to a full-on migraine as the hours ticked by. He must've slept at some point, because he didn't wake at the sound of his alarm. When he did, the headache resumed and now, dammit, he's late. What he needs is another coffee, a triple shot, black, strong enough to turn the devil blue. Something to dull the throb not just in his head but in his bad ankle, the one he'd hurt at the Alley-Oop competition same day he'd bumped his head bad. He turns left out of his street and heads towards Three Lamps.

Time slows strange and weird on the way down Kent Street.

Picket fences whisk by one post at a time; uniform grey villas stand pale and gaunt on either side. Above him, the washed-out blue spring sky is streaked with the thinnest ribbons of cloud. He's hypersensitive to everything and his head whirls at the overload. His favourite Pearl Jam song comes on the radio: he turns the volume up and sings along. Twists the words up, laughs at himself. He feels shit but he's determined to make the day a good one. It can still be good. Coffee makes everything better.

He presses his foot down on the brake, riding up to the intersection with Lincoln Street, and he notices a car then, a rusted-out green station wagon with roof racks parked up on the left-hand side. His father had driven that exact make and model, and for an instant Jamie could've sworn the number plate is the same and it isn't just a similar car but it is in fact the very same—

The sound of metal on metal is indescribable. His body expands and the seatbelt burns tight across his chest. He coughs: sees her face, a white light, then nothing.

A man's at the window of his car. He taps on the glass. 'You all right, mate?' Jamie can't speak. His chest's too tight and his mouth is filled with a sticky bitterness. He's not certain his teeth are where they should be.

'I live over there—' the man points to a house up Lincoln Street – 'and I heard the smash. Pretty nasty. I've called an ambulance, don't worry.'

Jamie runs his tongue along his teeth. All accounted for.

'I'm fine,' he says to the man. Not entirely true, though, is it? His head feels as though it will burst open from the migraine. He needs that coffee. He needs to get to work. He needs to throw up.

'You're bleeding,' the man says. 'Wow, okay. There's actually a lot of blood. Let me see if I can get you out of there.' He tugs on the door handle. It won't budge. It's stuck like obsession, and the man says they'll have to wait for the fire appliance. 'They'll cut you out no worries.'

Jamie's lips are wet, and he wipes his hand over his face. It comes away streaked with a violent red. 'Shit.' He glances up at the window, then turns away – panic clots his throat. The man at the window: his face is cloudy and indistinct, and daylight is burrowing away in a narrow tunnel. Jamie covers his face with his hands and starts to cry.

In his statement to the police, Jamie doesn't mention his headache. He doesn't mention his eyes. Christ, you can't say he lied exactly; he tells the truth, half of it at least. He clutches the other half, the part that scares him, close. He hadn't been distracted, he says. He tells the police about the blue station wagon, no, green, sorry, it was green, he tells them, how he'd noticed this car. Doesn't mention why. Tells them about it to prove he was alert and that his ability to recall clear details without confusion demonstrates a driver of great caution. 'I paused,' he says, his voice shaky as the migraine creeps further around his forehead. 'I paused at the intersection. I looked both ways.'

Full concentration, he's certain of it. He'd looked right up the hill of Lincoln, then down on his left, and he tells the police officer he took the obligatory second glance to his right before pulling out. There was no car. No car! His hand grips the rail along the side of the hospital bed. What he wouldn't give for some pain relief, Christ almighty. He'd even take a general anaesthetic if that was on offer. Something, anything, to take this feeling away.

'Eyewitnesses indicate the other driver was over the speed limit, so at this stage we don't consider you to be at fault.' The officer wants to look him in the eye, and it takes all Jamie's energy to focus on his face. Details smudge and reform, and Jamie's nausea grows worse. 'But we'll continue our investigations and be in touch.'

As soon as the policeman has gone, a nurse comes in and says he needs to settle down, take it easy. 'We'll have you here a few hours yet. You've likely got a concussion.' She checks some boxes on a clipboard and stares at the monitor beside his bed for a few seconds. 'We'll run a few tests, observe you, and if there's nothing obvious you should be able to go home this afternoon. Do you have someone who can pick you up?'

Jamie wants so badly to go home, and yet he doesn't want to go home. He doesn't want to be alone. So he suggests his mother, though she'd have to come over on the ferry. She lives at their old house, the one he'd grown up in, next door to Riggs. The same house he'd come home to one night, aged seventeen, and found his father two hours too late.

Trish doesn't answer the nurse's call.

'Is there someone else we can call?'

There is no one else, not really. Can't call Madeline, no way in hell, and he doesn't want to bother any of his mates:

they have jobs, young kids, other priorities. Plus, he couldn't keep from his mates the other half of the truth if they were to ask. Because he hadn't been distracted. Truth is, it was like the accident at the skatepark when he hadn't seen the rail. He hadn't seen the car coming down Lincoln Street because his vision had constricted to a simple, thin tube of light.

Trish calls the next morning while he's throwing a ball to the dog in the pocket-sized backyard of his Grey Lynn rental. 'I'm sorry I missed your call. Is everything okay?'

'Yeah,' Jamie says. He explains the accident in simple terms. Fast driver, big collision, bad concussion. Doesn't mention his vision. She'll only worry. 'My car's written off. I can't work. I'm in one piece, so it could be worse.'

'Last thing you need is another bad concussion. You know what happens to those rugby players with repeated head injuries. Would you like to come stay with me for a few days, recover together? And how about money? Are you okay while you're off work?'

He'd rather wait until hell freezes over before he goes back to that house, but he can't say so. Nah, not just the house, he doesn't want even to be on that island. Every day he'd have to drive past Rocky Bay where the bonfire burned that Saturday night. He'd have to drive past the butcher's. Witness the phoenix fading and eventually vanishing altogether. How fucking depressing that would be.

'I've got a doctor's appointment this week, so I should stay in the city,' he says. 'And ACC are covering me for two weeks off work, with the concussion.'

‘Let me know if you need anything. Anything at all.’

‘I’m fine, Mum.’ Jamie’s voice is hard and he wishes it wasn’t. He doesn’t feel hard. Inside he’s melting, soft and unformed. He’s terrified. He swipes to end the call and puts his phone on the table. Outside, the dog barks. A siren wails. The clock above the kitchen sink is wrong; it’s slowly losing time.

The appointment with the doctor gives him no easy answers. The GP peers into his eyes with a small light, the flickering brightness slipping and popping between them. He feels the glands under Jamie’s jaw, bony fingers pressing into the yielding softness of his neck. Jamie stands on the scales and consents to the blood-pressure cuff being placed around his bicep. When it inflates, Jamie feels the tightness not just in his arm but over his entire body.

‘Could be nothing, but let’s err on the side of caution,’ the GP says. ‘I’ll make a referral to an ophthalmologist, Dr Sobhani. Best in the eye business.’ He tips his head. ‘Do you have health insurance?’

No, is the answer. Jamie has no rainy-day fund, no back-up. Christ, insurance is expensive — life is expensive and getting more expensive every minute — and because he’s had no serious ill health since the Alley-Oop accident, it’s seemed overkill to throw money into the insurance ether when he could use it for more tangible, immediate, rewarding things. Such as that holiday in Noosa with Madeline or a new set of wheels for his board, or a set of paints. It’s a brutal turn of events now to realise he’s made a serious mistake. He could wait on the public list, but waiting times, the doctor tells him, are over eighteen months. After Covid, the doctor says, as though this two-word sentence is enough to explain the dire state of things. He recommends Jamie goes private and pays for it himself, if he can make that work. 'You want to get on top of things like this,' he says. 'Waiting only leads to more heartache, in my opinion.'

And so it's decided. Credit card will take the burden and Jamie will figure it out somehow.

Dr Sobhani's receptionist accepts the request for an urgent appointment, although Jamie still has to wait two weeks. Fourteen days of greeting each dawn with a whimper and a prayer. Please let me be okay. Please let everything go back to how it was.

As the appointment pulls closer, he stops leaving the house. Supermarket delivery guys drop bags of two-minute noodles and bananas on the doorstep — the only food he can stomach and afford. He contacts no one, and no one contacts him, and he begins to feel like he's fallen off the face of the Earth. Would anyone even notice if he disappeared? In this murky and uncertain time, an unexpected thought starts to visit. He wonders whether Madeline was right. Maybe he is damaged. Maybe he's more like his father than he has ever wanted to admit.

'Rest your chin here.'

Dr Sobhani indicates a small plastic shelf on the machine between them. Jamie leans forward slightly and allows his face to settle onto it, although what he truly wants to do is storm from the room and never come back. Nothing feels good right now. His chin, clammy with sweat, sticks to the plastic. The seat is hard and uncomfortable. The air too warm. Dr Sobhani lowers the lights in the room until it is almost completely dark. Jamie presses his knees together and takes in a breath. In the gloom, he can see very little and it's taking an immense amount of energy to remain seated and calm. He imagines his foot on the tail of his skateboard, holding it fast to the coping, imagines his body suspended above a deep superpipe, knowing that if he can't hold it together he's going to drop into deep empty space and smash to the curve below. Maybe, if he can hold it together, he can drop into the largest superpipe he's ever experienced and it will be all right.

'I'm going to have a look at the back of your eyes.' Dr Sobhani moves the machine around Jamie's face. 'I'm going to shine some lights and take some photographs. If there's any discomfort let me know. Look up, please.'

Look down, look left. Right. Straight ahead. What can you see. How many can you see. What is brighter, what is clearer? With every question Jamie is more convinced he's giving the wrong answer. He's contradicting himself and proving there's no issue. It's all in your mind, Dr Sobhani will say. You're making it up; you're going crazy.

After more tests and flashing lights and eye drops that make him feel woozy, Dr Sobhani tells Jamie to relax, and then he says, 'I can't tell you too much yet, but what I can tell you is that we will need to do some more testing. There are some indicators here that things aren't quite right, though it's not time yet to worry. We'll order an MRI, a blood test, a genetic test. First, though, tell me, have you suffered a significant head injury in the past?'

'There was one time,' Jamie says. 'When I was seventeen.'

He doesn't want to tell that story. When he looks back at

his life, he imagines everything that went wrong started that day, though sometimes he thinks, no, it started a few weeks before that, the night they painted the phoenix on the side of the butcher's.

The ophthalmologist leans back in his chair, folds his hands into his lap and says, 'Please, tell me about what happened when you were seventeen.'

There's no getting out of it. Jamie tries to focus on the light pooling under the door from the hallway, on the sounds of the receptionist's phone ringing, the splash of water in the pipes outside the office, tries to centre himself in the moment, as he would on his board, and then he starts to tell the story of the one and only time he entered a skateboarding competition, the Alley-Oop.

THE ALLEY-OOP

THE DAY WAS SCORCHING hot and bright as a firecracker. Jamie, Riggs and Penny caught the dawn ferry from Waiheke to downtown, their skateboards tucked behind their backpacks, just $20 and a fistful of luck between them. It didn't matter – the three of them were high on the thrill of anticipation. They were young, they were brilliant, they were invincible, and they had each other, which was the most important thing. They were in this together, and today they were going to watch Jamie change his life.

From where he stood on the deck of the boat, the ocean spread out before him, burnished like steel under the rising sun. The sky was stained a deep blush and there was no rain on the forecast. Perfect conditions for skating. He was excited about the competition, of course he was, and as much as he wanted to think about nothing but that, he was distracted by Penny standing further along the deck. Her swollen and bruised fingers were taped inexpertly, and her pinkie finger had assumed an odd, cracked shape. Sunlight sparked on the ends of her hair and lit the sharp lines of her cheekbones, as if she were spotlit on a stage, so although he tried not to look at her, it was a lost battle. He was moth to flame.

The ferry pulled in late, so they cut through downtown in a mad rush. When they reached the edge of the park, Jamie's heart seemed to fill his throat. There were the grey curves of the skatepark in the far corner, in the shadow of the motorway overpass. He'd skated there a couple of times with Riggs in the last few months. They'd wagged school, heading off on the ferry instead of to their classrooms, exchanging the hush of study for the rush of the city. Those days passed too quick — a few hours of gingersnap and 540 flips and nose slides and indy grabs and it would be time to catch the ferry home.

Today was different. This was the Alley-Oop. The skatepark was heaving with people and the sound of wheels rolling, scraping, rolling. It was the first competition in the newly redesigned plaza, and a thrilling yet volatile atmosphere pervaded the course. A glistening new tag of bright red graffiti blazed on one face of the pyramid: Skateboarding is not a crime.

Around the edges of the concrete plaza were yellow and blue gazebos. A long queue had formed in front of the tent set up with the registration table: a bunch of young kids hoping to take out the under-13 comp; some other bigger teens for the under-17 title; then — there they were — the older guys who looked rugged and ready for action. They had scars and tattoos and their boards weren't any fresher than they were, scratched up from tricks and risks taken long ago. These hulks were Jamie's main competition in the open category. They looked battle-hardened and ready to scrap. He felt his optimism flag. Riggs squirmed in the line behind him. Penny crossed her arms over her chest and said she was going to find a spot to stand and watch.

'Where will you be?' Jamie said.

Her eyes didn't meet his when she answered. 'Dunno. Over there somewhere.'

She was still angry with him. Didn't blame her, really, when he'd pushed her away and said he couldn't. Shouldn't. Because. You know. Riggs. He liked her, Jamie had said, he did. But. Riggs liked her. Bros before hoes, Riggs liked to say, and Jamie was trying to uphold that sentiment. Christ, he was trying.

She wandered away and he turned back to the registration. Stop thinking of her. Focus. He wanted to win, wanted it more than he'd wanted almost anything before. The first prize was more than bragging rights, otherwise he wouldn't bother. He could do the run any day of the week if there was no more reason than to say he'd done it. He wanted the prize and the life it offered. Two thousand dollars, flights for two to Los Angeles and an entry into a competition, Temerario, at Pedlow skatepark, where reps from skate brands might offer you a contract that would set you up for stardom. Because, in truth, he wasn't doing this for himself alone, he was also doing it for her.

If he won, they could leave. They'd tell her father to go fuck himself, grab their passports and leg it out of town. If he won, Riggs would understand. He'd do the same if it was him — winner takes all. He'd hate it, but he'd get over it, eventually. Bros before hoes, right?

But first Jamie had to win. It wouldn't be enough to do a good job, a tidy execution of some mediocre tricks. It was essential he explode the judges' conception of what was possible on this blazing Saturday morning in Auckland, Aotearoa New Zealand. To this end, he'd planned a run crammed full of technical and ambitious tricks. He'd manipulate as many of the elements as he could: the wedge, the quarter-pipes, stair grind, pyramid funbox and banked ramps. The last week, he'd spent every waking minute running it over in his mind, finessing the order, visualising success on every trick. He didn't have long to accomplish this madness. Two minutes, that was it, to flip his world around.

Registration complete, Riggs and Jamie headed to watch the smaller kids and the younger teens compete. After they'd finished up, the loudspeaker announced a short window for the open category to warm up. Jamie pushed around the park and watched the competition. A man with orange suede skate shoes flicked up on to the rail. His speed was perfect, and he landed on a boardslide, with his back truck hooked on the rail. Near the end of the slide, he shifted his weight to his front foot, balance undisturbed, and popped off back to the flat. That was similar to what Jamie wanted to do at the end of his run, the grand finale to cap it off, only he wanted to roll up to the round rail, the trickier rail, then he planned to slip his back foot into the pocket of the board between the hardware and the tail, toes slightly over the edge, and pop down, do a reverse circle with his back foot, and wrap the board around his foot in an impossible ollie. He'd lift his feet to pop high, the graphic of the board visible to him and the crowd as it flung around, then he'd land, nose heavy, on the round rail to finish with a nose grind. There was no room for error; he needed to lock it in good. It was a winning move. Ollie impossible nose grind. All the way to LA.

The open category started amid the day's swampy heat. The crowd was hyped. Jamie stood in the marshalling area and watched the first skaters roll in. Some of these dudes had impeccable timing, a flair and a bravado he didn't think he could match. They knew the perfect pressure for each trick. It was clear he couldn't afford even the smallest mistake if he wanted to be in with a chance. He lifted his cap, pulled his hair and replaced the cap on the back of his head. His name blasted from the tinny speaker system. Jamie Flannery, from Waiheke Island. This was it. His turn.

He stood and turned to grab his board. It wasn't there: it had vanished. Only a few minutes ago he'd seen it next to him, propped on its side. He turned, spinning a circle. Gone. His name over the speaker another time. The crowd cheered, and when the noise died down he heard one lone voice calling out his name in support. Penny. He ran the tip of his tongue along his upper lip and swore. Where the fuck was his board? They called his name again, and one of the volunteers recognised him. 'That's you,' she said. 'Get up there.'

'I can't find my board.' He didn't know what else to say, how to explain it. The volunteer stared at him blankly. His legs went weak as sin.

Another competitor, a white guy with dark freckles and baggy navy Dickies pants, called out, 'You can use my board if you want, mate.' It was an eight-inch Blind board with red wheels. The underside was ugly, the grip tape dirty and worn, the trucks tinged with rust.

There was nothing he wanted less than to ride someone else's board. He needed his board. The one he knew intimately. He knew the exact shades of its balance. It was an extension of his body — at least that was how it felt. At times, when the riding came smooth and he could do no wrong, he felt certain he could ride with his eyes closed. Never dared try it, though it spoke to the confidence he felt. The trust. He needed his board.

'Thanks,' he said. 'I think I'll try to find mine.'

The guy shrugged. 'Whatever.'

The volunteer said she'd help him find it. Jamie searched under the tables in the gazebos, through the stack of boards supplied by the sponsor. Started grabbing the other skaters' boards to be sure they weren't his. He kept at it, though he knew it was hopeless. The board had disappeared. He would have to pull out of the Alley-Oop.

He sat on the steps on the side of the skatepark and held his head in his hands. There would be no winning. He wouldn't save her. There would be no Los Angeles. Before this event, he wouldn't have described himself as super-competitive — he'd prided himself on embodying the pure ethos of skateboarding that he'd grown up worshipping: there was no competition, there was only camaraderie. There was only the grind. Turned out he coveted the glory same as everybody else.

Time started to droop, elastic in the heat. The crowd grew restless, and Jamie knew it was his fault. The moment he'd been waiting for was here and he'd messed it up. His board was his responsibility, the only thing he needed to have on hand, and it was gone. The man on the loudspeaker was talking with one of the volunteers. They glanced up at Jamie, and he could tell what they were thinking. Bloody amateur. Cut him, they were saying. Go on to the next competitor.

'Bro.'

Jamie looked up. Riggs.

‘I’m out, mate,’ Jamie said. Tears smarted at the corners of his eyes, and he wiped them away with the heel of his hand.

‘Nah, bro, you’re not out.’ Riggs held out a board. ‘I found it.’

His board. The sparkling grip, the clean lines of the green and red and white geometric design Penny had painted on the underside, the blue Bones wheels.

‘Christ, Riggs. Thank you.’ He gripped the board under his arm and ran to the drop. The loudspeaker announced his name one last time to a weak response from the bored crowd. He’d win them over. Ollie impossible nose grind. He set the board on the coping, held it firm with his right foot. Inhaled, set his tongue against his teeth, leaned his shoulders forward, and dropped down into the run.

The first sixty seconds were pure spectacle. Elegant, daring. He was peerless, every movement effortless and timed to perfection. Not a wobble or a misstep. He rolled down the incline, wind in his face. His arms out from his side, and he pushed, gaining speed, rolling up the edge to a fakie, before flicking around and coming around to the pyramid. He took a quick angle, kicking the board around, feeling his body as though in slow motion, his ankles and feet pointed, the board rotating, his body hanging in the air angel-like. Then quick up to the top, rolling down and over the drop, landing low and unimpaired, absorbing the impact with soft knees, landing neat, rolling out regular. He pushed now, to pick up speed, toward the rail.

This was it, his pièce de résistance, his winning trick. Lord knew how hard it was, how many hours he’d spent perfecting it, how many bruises and cuts and laughs in the making of it. It was glorious to watch, he knew it, and the judges would melt. He swept up to the rail, pushed his left foot into that specific pocket, his right leg lifting and moving out of the way. Then he executed the impossible ollie, rotating the left foot anticlockwise, Penny's design flashing quick, and he was up, up, up to land the tail on the rail. He was up on the nose, the board sliding slick and smooth down the round rail. The crowd went mental.

Time for the dismount, the chance to win it. He wasn't going to drop off the way he'd thought he would. No, he wanted to do more. He would come up clutch. As the board came off the rail, he let his heel catch the back edge, spinning it like a galaxy spiralling out from the Big Bang before hitting the ground.

The sound of the crowd crying out hit him with the same crushing thud of the concrete. He must've gone out for a bit, 'cause next thing he knew there were people clustering close and making so much noise he felt as though he was drowning in it, and it took him a second to realise most of the noise was in his head. His ears were ringing loud and sharp. Everything felt hazy. Nothing made any sense. Paramedics were there, and he caught sight of someone, she was familiar, with dark hair heavy over green eyes, and next thing he was in the back of the ambulance, cold and crying for no reason that he could make heads or tails out of.

Later, he'd discover that one wheel nut had been loose, so when he'd landed, the wheel had slipped free of the worn-down axle, rolling away on its own agenda. The board then tipped on an unlucky angle, and he was a goner, lurching to the ground. He'd fractured his ankle. Saw it on the x-ray. It was the thinnest hairline crack, a non-displaced fracture of the fibula. Six weeks in the moon boot. Absolutely no skating. He'd hit his head in the fall too, knocked out cold for thirty seconds at least, maybe longer. The doctors were worried about long-term damage to his brain, but they reluctantly let him go home three days after the injury when the swelling reduced and the headache fucked off.

It wasn't until he got home that he found out Riggs had won the competition. He didn't want to admit it to his best mate, but he hadn't thought Riggs had it in him. Jamie was gutted, but he was practical. If he couldn't do it, then the next best person should have the wildest ride instead.

It took a bit of adjustment getting used to the moon boot. It was heavy and hot, annoying as all get-out. The cut on his head healed up nice, though the bruising on both his leg and his head took its sweet time to clear off, shifting from deep purple to blue to yellow and brown before vanishing completely. As the days went by, he supposed he was lucky the consequences weren't much worse. Could've sprayed his brains out on the concrete if he'd fallen different. Broken his leg in a way that would've needed surgery and caused him lifelong mobility issues. He was gutted, 'course he was. What he'd thought he might do with his life was now a mere dream, but there was plenty to look forward to. Like the bonfire that next weekend down at Rocky Bay beach.

RIGGS

THEY SIT OPPOSITE EACH other on matching armchairs in the lounge room. Riggs is exhausted, thoroughly and utterly bone tired. The bedroom is mere metres away, and he wants to crawl there, curl up in the soft, clean linen and sleep. Can't do that, though. He's too dirty, beyond dirty — he's bloody filthy, and he's aware of this now because he's sober. He's off the pills. He isn't high on anything else. The last beer was hours ago. And he knows he can't go to bed until he's talked to Penny.

Funny, it's his house and his bed, yet she has all the control. It's important he gives her a chance to speak. He gets it. He might not want it this way, but he knows she deserves to be heard. He's not a monster. Doesn't want to silence her, for crying out loud. Only there's a lot he could say and he wants to say it, he aches to say it, but he knows that even if it's true she won't think it's kind or necessary, and it will likely make things worse than they already are. So, he's got his trap shut and he's doing his best not to comment on her hair. She's got it clipped up behind her ears when she knows she looks better with it loose and hanging down. Telling her to unclip her hair would go down like the proverbial cup of sick. No talking, then. Keep it quiet. There are so many things he's fucked up in his life, a long, long list of them, and, really, she's the last good thing. He can't lose the last good thing. But the way she's looking at him now, or really the way she won't look at him, he's afraid he's too late.

He leans back into the cushions, waiting for her to speak, and within seconds an immense and full-bodied pain in his back bolts him upright again. Holy hell. He wants to punch someone, or kick someone. Unleash his pain and pay it forward. He could do with something pricked into the vein right about now. Might help him relax. They could both do with something to help them relax. He can see she's held tight as a spring. Gonna hurt when that recoils. He smiles to lighten the mood, pulling his upper lip down to cover the space where his tooth should be. Penny's face pulls tight in displeasure. No, not displeasure. Maybe rage, or contempt. Either way, he's fucked.

He opens his mouth and closes it a few times before he figures out what to say: 'I'm sorry, babe.' Useless. He's a complete and total waste of space.

'You're going to have to do better than that, Adam.'

He shakes his head. Adrenaline and cortisol race ragged and hot in his blood. 'I know, I know. It's just ...'

It's just what? The truth hovers there, ready to be spoken: *Roll With It* is over — well, the show itself isn't over, he's been turfed out, they've hired someone else to host it, someone younger, some Swedish skater with perfect English and no fear and a smile that melts the hearts of the youth, and it's about the youth, they told him this with a straight face, they told him they want to engage youth in the show and Riggs, well, he isn't a good fit for that demographic anymore.

True, he's getting on a bit. There are a few lines around his eyes that weren't there a couple of months ago. He doesn't think he looks too old, but. He certainly looks younger than most guys in their forties.

It doesn't help his back is buggered. The producers had asked how could he present the show if he can't actively engage in the skating. He'd been shocked when they said this. When he has enough painkillers in him he can do it all, no one can even tell he's injured. He didn't think it would help his case to tell them surgery had been recommended and the doctor had suggested Riggs should accept his days of skating were limited. 'At least, not the big stuff,' the surgeon said at the last appointment. 'A little bit of riding around on the streets, that shouldn't be a problem. But take it easy.'

Dude didn't understand. It most certainly is a problem. Riggs doesn't do easy. This is his job, his livelihood. He loves *Roll With It*. Can't give it up like that. Tony Hawk is older than him and he's out there doing the big stuff still, the real stuff. Now Riggs isn't saying he's Tony Hawk but—

'Adam,' Penny says. 'It's late. I'm flying back to New Zealand on Monday and I really need some sleep.'

'You're what?' Riggs sits up, hands on his knees. Home? Aotearoa? Land of that long, long, long, long white cloud? He's gone back a few times over the years, seen his olds. Penny's had this weird thing about it, so he often went alone. And now she's going back? Unless. It worked?

'I'm going to New Zealand. On Monday,' she says.

A burst of car headlights lights up the room and it's as though he can see her more clearly than he has in a long time: pale-lilac rings under her eyes (like Rose, like Rose), her skin wan and lined. How quickly they've changed, grown old, fallen apart. How the days piled on top of each other, seemingly unimportant, yet when you added them up, it was their lives slipping away.

Penny speaks again: 'I've been asked to show in a gallery in Auckland next year and I've decided to stay with Mum and Dad for a while.'

Who cares about *Roll With It?* Surgery can wait. Where is his passport? Where are his togs? It's happening!

'What time's our flight?'

Penny looks up at the ceiling. 'I'm going by myself, Riggs.'

He moves quick to sit beside her. Takes her hand, holds it tight, so tight. Her fingers are long and cold, and he places them on his lap. Tethers her. 'Don't be silly,' he says. 'I'll come with you.'

She turns away from him but doesn't withdraw her hand. There's the hope — in the touch. Can't deny it. Hold them tight and hold them close, that's the way. He pulls her hand and holds it even tighter.

'We can stay with your olds,' he says, 'or maybe with my parents, or find a cheap place to rent maybe, close to them, and you can work, and I can—' He stops here, uncertain what to say. What will he do? Anything. That's what he'll do. Anything she wants him to do.

'I'm going on my own, Riggs,' she says.

Her hand twists in his and he grips it hard.

'No way.' He shakes his head. 'No bleeding way.'

'I'm not happy,' she says. 'I haven't been happy for a long time. Let me go, Riggs.'

'Penny.' He licks his lips. 'Don't be so dramatic.'

'I'm not,' she says. 'I'm tired, Riggs. I want to go to bed.'

He laughs, gentle though, so she'll know he's laughing with her. Not at her. She can be so sensitive about these things. 'You're overreacting,' he says. 'I'm so happy for you. I don't think you understand how stoked I am to hear about the exhibit. I want to come with you. We can make this work, I swear.'

'Riggs.'

'I need you, Penny. If you leave me ...' His voice catches. 'I don't think I could go on.'

'Don't say that, Riggs.'

'I'm being honest with you,' he says. He paws at her hand, desperate-like. 'I can't live without you. I can't lose you too. It would be too much.'

And it's true: she knows it. Her hand falls limp in his and he rubs her palm with his thumb in wide, slow circles. 'Penny, don't do this.'

She says nothing.

'How are you going to pay for the flights?' he says.

'I'll ask my parents for the money.'

He can tell by the way she says it she's not sure this is what she wants to do. I know you, he wants to say. I know you inside out.

'Don't embarrass yourself,' he says. 'You're forty years old.'

'I'm still thirty-nine.'

'For what, like, four weeks?'

Penny's voice, when she answers, is clipped. 'If you come, you need to get clean.'

'What do you mean?'

'No more drugs. No more pills. Nothing.' She squeezes his hand — the hope. 'I mean it, Riggs. You get clean and I'll give you another chance.'

Clean. Hell's bells. Twelve hours on a plane with this back and no relief. They'll land and he'll be homicidal. Only there's no other option, is there?

'I'll get clean,' he says. 'I'll get clean, and then we could get married.'

Penny laughs. It's quiet and small but there's no doubt what it means. 'Don't get ahead of yourself,' she says.

'You're still wearing the ring.' He touches her left hand, presses his finger into the diamond.

She prises her hand from him then, and stares at the ring.

'We can do this,' he says. 'Come on, Penny. You can't give up on us now. For Rose's sake. Let's make this work.'

She stares at him for a long time. A line of sweat beads up along the nape of his neck. It's too hot, still so damned hot, and she's taking too long to give in.

'I don't know if we can make it, Riggs,' she says.

'Let's give it a shot,' he says. 'New chance, New Zealand.'

He loves Los Angeles — the sprawling concrete beast of a city, traffic for miles, everybody a hustler, the Hollywood sign white on the brown dry hills. The centre of the world. Dogtown. And New Zealand? The bottom of the world. He'd never wanted to go back, not full time. Going back felt too similar to failing, like saying, I can't hack it out there. It's a concession that you've misfired and been unable to launch yourself properly into the world. But if this is what it takes, this is what it damn well takes.

'What about *Roll With It*?'

'It's over, Penny.' Saying it out loud isn't as bad as he'd imagined it might be. In the dark night, coming down from the cocktail of drugs and drink, now she's agreed to stay with him, it isn't that bad at all.

'What do you mean?'

'I'm out,' he says. 'They've found someone else. Alex Alexsson, or whatever the fuck his name is. Scandinavian kid. Big on TikTok apparently. I'm too old, Penny, too bloody old and wrinkly and boring.' He plays it up, rubs his eyes as though he's about to cry. She hates to see him cry. Eventually he drops his hand from his face. She isn't moved by his tears this time.

'Well, I guess there's no reason why you shouldn't come then.'

'You look stoked,' he says, teasing. 'I'm saying I'll follow you to New Zealand and you look like I've smacked you across the room.'

'I'm happy, Riggs, truly. I'm tired.'

He screws up his face. 'What's that stink?' he says. 'Smells as if something died in here.'

'The refrigerator is broken,' Penny says, and then they sit there for a long time in the dark, aware that what he's said has once again reminded them of Rose. Riggs glances at Penny. Here's the real truth moving between them like a ghost: she blames him for their daughter's death.

She'd deny it if he ever came right out and said it straight, but he knows. The rest of it even he can only ever think about slantwise. That he believes it's his fault as well. That bloody skateboard, those bloody bruises. Another parent would have noticed there was something wrong much sooner. A better parent would have said those bruises can't all be from falling. Penny said that, didn't she? The better parent. She'd said the bruises looked strange and he'd told her she was overreacting. 'This is what a skateboarder's body looks like,' he'd said. 'Like you're in Fight Club. She's fine.'

Penny didn't get it, he'd told himself. She hadn't spent her life staring at her naked body every day, marvelling at the new grazes and bruises. Too busy pottering away with her paintbrushes as though she was Amy March. Too precious to understand the bruises were medals of honour, badges of recognition. Truth was, he'd been proud of Rose's body. Stoked that she'd wanted to join him. Four years old and she could ollie like a champ, kickflip like a pro. She wore a tutu to skate, and everyone started saying she was a ginger Rayssa Leal. At every skatepark they went to she was a superstar, the centre of attention, and dudes would ask, Is that your daughter? Yeah, he'd say. She's mine. They'd watch her, obviously in awe of her skill, slamming their boards on the edge of the coping in applause when she pulled off an incredible trick. It made him feel good, it did. Almost as good as when he'd do a move so insanely beyond, namely skate over a twenty-step staircase, flip the board mid-air and land it smooth as snakeskin. She gave him that same feeling. And the bruises, he'd told Penny, were the price you paid for skating. And Rose loved to skate.

Christ, he's a stupid bastard.

Riggs knows a lot of people grieve for lives they haven't lived, for the roads not taken, but he wonders if those people feel as much regret as he does. At his insistence, they'd left it too late. They did all the treatments available, clinical trials, even the woo-woo homeopath shit when the rest failed. They tried everything and nothing worked. It was his fault. She'd been kind enough not to say it out loud, but he heard her loud and clear nonetheless. When you're together twenty years, you tell each other a lot more in your silences than you do in your words.

A helicopter buzzes somewhere over the city. Penny's breathing settles soft and regular. He picks her up, one arm under her legs, the other under her arms, and carries her to the bedroom. He used to carry Rose like this. Penny doesn't wake either. The sound of the helicopter recedes, and he lays her on their bed. He stretches out beside her, eyes burning yet wide awake, and he thinks about New Zealand and what he's promised Penny.

The last time he went home to New Zealand, Penny was eight months' pregnant. He was a couple of months off starting to film *Roll With It.* Stepping back from competition skating had been a tough call, but it was time. The younger ones coming through — hell, they had no fear. He couldn't keep up, much as he hated to admit it, so the offer to host a series about skateboarding around the world was perfection. Travel, a bit of online fame, skating with interesting people, what wasn't to love? Those were the glory days.

Now he's going back as a loser. A has-been loser, a mid-life dead loss with no daughter, a dodgy back and a fiancée who isn't ready to say I do. But all is not lost: if he knows how to do anything, it's how to get back up after he's fallen down. He's good at that. Has a knack for finding the weak spots where he can press and work his way back up. They'll be happy in New Zealand. They'll return together and start again. He will give her everything she wants. Hasn't he always done that? She'd wanted to leave New Zealand when they were kids, and he gave that to her. Bought her the ticket, got her on the plane, built her a life, built her a home. He could do it again.

By the time he falls asleep, light is creeping around the edges of the curtains, the northern mockingbird's night chorus has faded away, and a new day is about to begin.

Surprising how easy it is to fold up a life: aside from dealing with the stinking broken refrigerator, there was very little to do but book the flights and find the passports. Penny sorted the shipping of her paintings. A mate of his offered to stay in the house while they were gone, and when Riggs told him to make himself at home, just not that one room opposite the kitchen, the guy had taken it in his stride, posed no awkward questions. It had felt almost too simple. Was this all it boiled down to? A closed door, an identity booklet, a ticket to another hemisphere?

The flight itself is torture. Every time Riggs dares move in the stiff, narrow seat, zags of lightning-bright pain are unleashed in his back. If there has ever been a time he's hungered more for pills, he's forgotten it. His skin itches with the craving. He rages inwardly at Penny, at her insistence that he give them up cold turkey. He should've secreted a stash for moments such as this, when it's treacherous to live without them. He can't concentrate on any of the films, and the food makes him nauseous. Thirteen hours of pure, unadulterated hell, but he's doing it for her.

When the seat belt sign flashes on for the descent he's awash with relief. Flight attendants swarm the aisles, clearing food trays and opening window shades, helping seat backs return to the upright position, and soon the cabin is prepared for landing. Riggs runs his tongue over the rough edge of the crack where his front tooth should be, burrowing into the damage. He leans over Penny's sleeping body to look out the window, and when he spies streaks of whitewash where the dark teal ocean rolls up onto the coast of Aotearoa he almost cries with relief.

The plane dips its wing and soars over the city, the grey mass on the isthmus stretching beyond sight. Auckland. The Sky Tower. Sunlight twinkles on the Waitematā, over the frilled sail boats moored in the marina. He thinks of the dolphins he'd seen out there as a boy, fishing on the old tin dinghy with his dad, Trent. From here, he can even make out a thin slice of Waiheke. The plane flies lower and lower, hunkering down over south Auckland, rounding back toward the Manukau and the runway and then, with a bump and bang that causes a few passengers to call out in fright, the plane careers toward the terminal, slowing with every passing metre.

In a jetlagged daze, they roll their bags through Biosecurity. The beagle sidles up to him in a way that makes his skin prickle. Can the bitch sniff out his secrets? He touches his tongue along the cracked tooth once more, anxious and alarmed, scooting away from the dog, and Penny looks at him out of the corner of her eye.

'What?' he says. She shrugs and looks away. In a few seconds they'll come through the doors into the main arrivals hall. His hands shake and he wonders what his parents would say if they saw him like this. His sisters too. Lord knows he's let them down so many times, it would go unremarked. Despite everything he's achieved, his success, they all still see him as the ne'er-do-well skater. Living in sin, a child not just born out of wedlock but dead before she was christened. Well, they're wrong, and he's going to prove it to them. It's not over for him yet.

Penny guides him to the exit, toward the rental cars. She takes his bag awkwardly, as though deliberately avoiding his hand, and puts it beside hers on a trolley. 'You all right?'

'Yeah,' he says. 'I'm good.'

'You sure? You don't look so good.' Is she smiling? Does she think this is some sort of sick joke? He wants to pick up the suitcases from the trolley and launch them into the oncoming traffic. He isn't a psycho, only he needs to let it out, all this anger. His whole body is tight, and he hurts, my lord he hurts. She gives him a look and he knows what it means: push the trolley and keep yourself under control.

This is it, she'd said to him before they'd left the States. Clean up or it's over. And here they are. If he can't make this work, then he truly is nothing but a piece of shit.

Penny says, 'You okay with the trolley?'

'I'm good.'

It's mid-September, springtime here, yet a blustery wind blows hard from the south. Despite the cold bite of the wind, he's sweating bullets. Pushing the trolley is agony for his back. Only there is nothing else he can do, so he follows her to the waiting rental car. He'll drive them into the city, where they'll board the ferry, and then, finally, they'll be home.

PENNY

ON THEIR FIRST MORNING back in Aotearoa, Penny wakes slightly breathless, consumed with thoughts of her upcoming solo show. A lifetime, moving toward this. A distinct pressure rubs in the sides of her jaw, and she knows she's not going to be able to fall asleep again.

Riggs lies beside her, his head tossed back, mouth slightly open, his broken tooth stark and vicious. They'd not drawn the curtains before bed; now the room is filled with a golden light. She loves this — what's better than lying in bed, sunshine warming your cheeks, clean bed linen — until she sees the time. Downstairs, her parents will be furrowing their brows and making light but pointed jokes about lazy millennials. They view sleeping in as a moral failing and even jetlag isn't an excuse. 'The early bird doesn't just get a worm,' her father used to say when Penny was a child, 'the early bird gets the juiciest worm.'

A worm was still a worm, Penny replied, and nobody wants a worm. Damian would smile, touch Penny's head with a hand so light it was almost as if no part of him touched her, and said, 'It's about motivation, darling. Dedication. I thought you wanted to be the best?'

She did want to be the best. Which was why they'd left Los Angeles. And now she's in the same room she'd slept in as a teenager, though you'd be hard pressed to guess. All evidence has been meticulously erased. The walls are a tasteless shade of cream, no sign of her posters or artwork. Her books — *The Golden Notebook*, *Gravity's Rainbow*, *The Wind-Up Bird Chronicle*, *The Secret History* — have vanished from the shelves, replaced with ornamental vases and stylish earthenware, two brand-new Jo Malone candles and a set of coffee-table books about European artists of the late eighteenth century.

She has been replaced with banal, *House & Garden*-worthy decor. Depressing, yes, but honestly, not that surprising. Her mother never wanted kids — an unspoken family understanding — and her father warmed to her only as a student to whom he could impart his knowledge and who would grow up to be a prodigious talent. Unable to make that come true, Penny isn't shocked that they moved the detritus of her existence out of sight. She thinks of Rose's things in the small room in the Woodland Hills house. The tutu, lilac, the soft-top skateboard, her bookshelf with her picture books, *The Gruffalo*, *Hairy Maclary*, *The Very Hungry Caterpillar*, all the beloved soft toys. Will she ever be ready to clear it out? They're just things, so it shouldn't be such a big deal. Only it is, it is.

She sits up in bed. Riggs groans, turns over, folds his tattooed arm under his head. Penny stands in front of the window and takes in the world. Beyond the house, the ocean pours out blue and thick. How could she have forgotten this view? This wondrous, wild view. The house, bought with the rewards of being one of the greatest living realist painters of the twentieth century, sits high on a cliff overlooking a wide arc of beach, a beach called Rocky Bay. This was the site of the Saturday night bonfires she went to with Jamie and Riggs once upon a time. Gangs of teenagers burning whatever they could find that wasn't bolted down, who drank whatever they could get their hands on that wouldn't corrode their insides, and hooked up with whoever was willing and able; she remembers the night of the final bonfire, Riggs dashing naked into the water, firelight dancing on his skin, the whooping shout he made as he hit the cold water, and Jamie, quiet in the scrub of the dunes, hair long over his ears, with his moon boot and spray paint and beer.

The skatepark is down there too, and that's where she first met Riggs — and Jamie. In fact, she met Jamie first, even if Riggs liked to tell the story his way. Doesn't like to lose, that man, even when it doesn't matter. Second place, in his opinion, is nothing but the first loser.

Beyond the beach, the timeless depths of the ocean stretch out, the hazy range of the Coromandel peninsula looming high in the distance. If she were to paint the scene, the range would be rendered with Ultramarine Violet mixed with Terre Verte. Maybe she will paint this for the exhibit. Some new work alongside the old.

The urge to paint heats up in her chest. Riggs is back, and when Riggs is back, it feels less like Rose is gone, and maybe, just maybe, she might be able to paint. She'll talk to Sally, get the okay to include some new pieces. Start on them today. Damian might let her use some paint. He'll be gagging to help her, to finally set in motion the Whittaker dynasty of great artists. 'Tell me what I can do,' he'll say. 'Tell me how I can help.' He'll be frothing to help, even if the works are slightly abstract and not traditionally realist. At least they aren't graffiti. She holds her hand and examines her pinkie finger, the one that has curved inwards ever since the night Damian broke it, after she'd been caught spray painting on the butcher's shop with Jamie.

She leaves Riggs sleeping and walks downstairs to find coffee. Her fingers twitch and she holds her hand tight as she walks through the entranceway — it was there, right there, he held her hand and broke it.

The kitchen has been renovated since Penny last visited. The entire space is a severe and caustic display of white. White marble kitchen island, white tiled splashback, white walls. Even the espresso machine pressed into the corner of the far bench is white and immaculately clean. Her mother, Meg, sits on a white stool at the island, drinking coffee and reading a newspaper. She looks up when Penny comes in, and smiles. 'I wondered when you would wake up.'

'Sorry,' Penny says. 'I forgot to set an alarm.'

'I'm just glad you're here,' Meg says, and she lays the newspaper down on the bench. 'Is Adam still in bed?'

Penny can tell Meg is disappointed. Because Adam's still sleeping? Or is it because of his chipped tooth, or his newly shaved head, or the fact that he's been made redundant, even from a job as inane as hosting a YouTube skateboarding show? It could be the new tattoo — Rose's name in a thick, gothic font, accompanied by an intricate rendering of a rose blooming on his right forearm. Even Penny hates the tattoo, and she likes tattoos generally. Honestly, it could be all of those things and none of them. Her parents had never warmed to Riggs — they had thoughts about skateboarders, and they had thoughts about what sort of person their Penelope should marry — and Penny, without thinking, falls into her usual habit of defending him.

'Yes,' she says. 'He's shattered. I told you last night, he has a bad back. The flight was torture for him. He needs to rest.'

'I've got some tramadol, if that would help get him up and about,' Meg says. 'Best thing for bad backs is to keep moving.'

Penny closes her mouth and nods, hoping her mother will forget to offer the pills to Riggs. Meg and Damian don't know about Riggs's problem with painkillers. Penny had often joked with Riggs about her parents' preference for floorboards in their houses, considering how much they loved shoving everything under the carpet.

'So, you must be thrilled,' Meg says. 'Stonewall Gallery.'

'Yes,' Penny says, her hesitation seeping through.

Meg puts her hand on Penny's arm. 'Are you okay?'

Was she okay? How could she even begin to answer that question?

Around the time Rose stopped eating, and the end was drawing near, Penny had concluded that life was essentially meaningless. One day we are born, and one day we will die. In between, we eat food filled with microplastics and fuck up the planet, even as it continues its never-ending orbit, slowly and now too quickly warming. War, it seems, will never end, but will shift from hot spot to hot spot, and thousands will be mindlessly slaughtered. People, people you know and love, they will lie, steal, murder. Her daughter, for no reason, no reason at all, was taken from her. What is the point of it? Penny, in the time after Rose's death, discovered she didn't know. She thought she'd known and now she didn't. She could no longer understand what the point could possibly be. Knowing this, she found it difficult to let joy or indulgence into her life. What was the point?

And now she wonders if this is the point. Creating. Painting. The only thing she's ever been good at. But is that, too, a lie? Maybe Sally Trubridge will call, explain that there's been a misunderstanding. 'Sorry for the confusion,' she'll say. 'It was someone else I was thinking of.' The excitement Penny feels is tenuous, fragile and undeserved. Because what sort of woman could lose her daughter and then go on to be happy?

There's no easy way to explain this to her mother, and now Damian is here, slippers tapping on the floor. Meg pulls her hand away from Penny.

'Darling, you're awake,' Damian says. He leans in and kisses Penny twice, once on each cheek. He smells of cologne and mint toothpaste. 'That's quite a sleep-in.'

'Good morning,' she says. The bait is there but she won't bite. 'Thanks again for having us stay.'

'Ah,' Damian says. 'Mi casa, su casa, mi hija.' He claps his hands together and looks expectantly at Penny and then at Meg, who stares into her coffee cup. Damian pinches his eyebrows, 'Well, where's Adam? Should I make you a coffee, Penelope?'

'I'd love a coffee,' Penny says. 'Adam's still asleep.'

Damian makes a clicking noise with his tongue. 'He's missing the best part of the day!'

He switches on the espresso machine. He's a slight man, long torso over short legs. She's aware it's been a couple of years since she's last seen him, but he looks much older than she remembers. They'd visited her a few times in Los Angeles, mostly after Rose was born, though they hadn't made it over for the funeral. Covid, they'd said, though Penny had felt this was a convenient excuse.

Damian glances at her over his shoulder, milk jug in his hand, and asks, 'So, I know you probably mentioned it last night, but remind me: how long are you staying for?'

Penny glances at her mother, who is absorbed again in her newspaper. 'A couple of months?' she says. 'I'm not sure exactly.'

Her parents exchange a quick glance.

Damian fiddles with the coffee grinder and selects mugs from the cupboard. 'Tell me about the collection you'll be showing,' he says.

She sits on one of the stools beside her mother. Meg is humming a nonsense melody, off-key, as though the conversation isn't happening. 'It's a series called *The Art of Falling*,' Penny says.

'That's quite a title,' Damian says slowly. 'What's the theme? Are they new pieces?'

'I painted them when Rose was diagnosed,' she says. This answers both questions, though she doesn't know why she bothered saying anything. They will pretend she's said something else, anything else.

'Right, right,' Damian says, his voice loud. 'I'm so pleased for you. Thrilled, actually. I'm so pleased you never gave up on your dream.'

'I really did these to stop myself committing suicide,' she says. It's only partly a joke, but neither parent reacts. Her mother doesn't stop humming; her father slides her coffee across the bench with a smile. She takes the mug and fingers the handle, refusing to be the one to break the silence this time.

'Well,' Damian says. 'It's taken you longer than expected but I'm not surprised you've found a gallery to take you on. This is what you were born to do. Oils, I hope?'

'Of course,' she says, then she pauses. 'I was hoping to do some new pieces while I'm here.'

'New work?'

'Yes. Something more hopeful. About what happens after you fall as far as you can.'

Meg flicks the newspaper in an exaggerated fashion and Penny bites her lip.

Damian says, 'Are you certain you have time to do new work? Do you need me to ask Sally for an extension?'

Penny's heart falters. 'Sally?'

'You know,' he says. 'Sally Trubridge. From Stonewall Gallery.'

'Yes, I know who Sally is. Do you know Sally?'

'Of course, I know Sally! We go way back. God, she's got an eye, that woman. Knows her stuff. When I showed her some of your work, wow, she was impressed.'

The air in the room grows thin and Penny touches her hand to her mouth. No, no, no, this can't be true. 'What do you mean?'

Damian looks affronted, and his voice is unnaturally high when he answers: 'What do you mean, *what do you mean?*'

Penny looks to her mother for help. Meg sits silent and completely still. Penny remembers this dynamic. She remembers it so vividly and still she's shocked. Why is she shocked? This is her father through and through. Slow to praise, quick to criticise. A man who's never apologised for anything and who demands apologies for the slightest wrongs. She holds her hand and feels the bend in the broken finger, and her heart aches.

'I mean,' she says slowly, 'what do you mean when you say you showed her some of my work?'

Even as she says it, Penny understands exactly what he means. The exhibition wasn't Sally Trubridge's idea. It was her father's.

She turns to her mother. 'Did you know about this?'

Meg inclines her head towards Penny but does not look her in the eye. She says, 'Know about what, darling?'

Penny can't disguise her fury, her voice is hot. 'Did you know that he set this up? To humiliate me? Calling in some favour? Did you know?'

Meg folds her newspaper neatly in half and places it on the bench beside her empty coffee cup. She stands from the stool, every movement elegant and graceful and removed, and her face is hard when she looks at Penny. 'I think, my dear, that whatever it is that goes on between Sally Trubridge and your father, well, it's really none of my business.'

Meg leaves the kitchen. Before Penny or Damian can speak, Riggs comes in. He hasn't showered, and he's ripe with sweat and sleep.

'Good morning,' he says. 'Could I get a coffee? I'm feeling pretty average, to be honest.'

Penny stares into her coffee. She hasn't taken a sip and it's growing cold. If only she had the courage to tell her father what she wants to say. She wants to tell him she never wanted him to do this. That she'd moved to the other side of the world to avoid this exact situation, to prove to her parents that she could do this without any help from them. To prove to herself that she was good enough. And here she is, almost forty and still naive enough to believe that someone might have seen her work and fallen in love with it for what it was, without any association with Sir Damian Whittaker, greatest living national treasure or whatever it was they wrote in his profile in *Art News* last year. In the end, all she's able to say is, 'You're fucking Sally Trubridge?'

Damian frowns. 'Don't be so uncouth, Penelope. She's a dear old friend. It's true we've been spending some time together, and yes, if you want the guts of it, I have grown quite fond of her. I didn't ask her for a favour. I showed her your work – no more than a few pieces. I'm a proud father, you know that. Perhaps I mentioned what a shame it's been that your career hasn't blossomed in the way we would've wanted and that you'd suffered a terrible loss, but it was her suggestion, *her suggestion*, to do the show. Her suggestion!' Damian slaps his hand on the benchtop for emphasis. *Her suggestion.*

Blown away, Sally had said. Something was blown, that's for sure. Nausea sweeps through Penny's stomach and up into her mouth.

'Should I make it myself then?' Riggs says. He presses the power button on the espresso machine, and it whirrs back to life; he rattles in the cupboard to find a mug. Penny isn't sure if Riggs is deliberately trying to annoy her or if he is simply too stupid to know when to leave things alone.

'Adam,' Damian says wearily. 'Back me up here. The exhibition is a good thing. Tell her she's overreacting.'

Riggs shoots a glance at Penny and says, 'Hm. Well. I'm not sure.'

Damian's face falls either from disappointment or exasperation, she can't tell.

'If I'd wanted your help, Dad,' she says, 'I would have asked for it.'

Damian looks at her. 'Then why didn't you?' he asks.

'What? Ask for your help?'

'Not just that. Why didn't you want it?'

Penny feels suddenly too heavy, her body weighted down with dismay and something else, something more catastrophic. She finds herself pushing her stool away and telling Riggs he can have her coffee. She takes the staircase to the bedroom one slow step at a time. At the top she pauses and turns behind her, certain someone is there, certain there's a flare of yellow hair, only there's no one. Not even a ghost.

When Riggs joins her, because she knows he will, she'll tell him to pack his bags. They can't stay with her parents, not now. She sits on the bed and soon she hears her father and Riggs come up the stairs. They're talking about her, she can tell. Riggs, his voice honeyed with a tone meant to impress, is talking about how important this trip is to both of them, and Damian remarks that his daughter is too sensitive, and sometimes, sometimes, he says, she's made some bad choices. Penny can't hear what Riggs says in response, but it must've been amusing because they both laugh. She hears Damian's studio door close and then Riggs comes into the bedroom. He stands next to her, hand on her shoulder.

'What's wrong?' he says.

She screws her face tight. 'How could I have been this stupid?'

'You're not stupid,' Riggs says. 'You're making a big deal about something that's not that bad, but you're not stupid.'

'It's over,' she says.

'It's not over. Come on. Don't overreact.'

'I've dedicated my life to this,' she says. 'And if I was truly good at it, I would have succeeded already. I'm what, forty, and ... this. I'm this.' She gestures to show him her pathetic, miserable self.

'You're not forty, not yet.'

'Adam.' She puts her face in her hands. He doesn't understand. 'We have to leave.'

'Penny,' he says. 'What the fuck? We just got here.'

She knows he doesn't want to leave. He loves her parents' house. It's a rich person's house, and Riggs prefers the finer things in life. Expensive champagne, designer clothing, fancy restaurants, class-A drugs, beautiful women. Couldn't tell that by looking at him, that's for sure, especially now with the tooth and the gaunt face and the ugly tattoo. He's a man of contradictions, of incredible soaring highs and terrifying, devastating lows, and for a long time that was what she'd liked about him. He's a risk taker, a recalcitrant boy who refuses to grow up. You had to be to have done the things he'd done on that skateboard. Never says no, always says yes. Doesn't want to listen to her when she tries to talk reason. It had made him fun to be around, at the beginning at least. That spontaneous trip to Puerto Rico when he won his first skate competition in Portland, for instance, and the wild weekends in Las Vegas where they didn't sleep for days on end. Never listened to her voice of reason, not once, and that was fine, until one day it wasn't.

'I can't stay here,' she says.

'What about the exhibit?'

'I'm not doing it.'

Riggs sits on the bed beside her and takes her hand in his.

'Are you sure? I thought this was what you wanted.'

'I never wanted him to pull the strings,' she says. 'I wanted to be good enough on my own.'

'Your dad has good intentions.'

'I don't think he does. I think he does it for his own ego.'

'He knows how much you want it. I think it was a nice gesture, actually.'

She makes a low, snorting sound.

'You're quite tough on him,' Riggs says. 'You're quite tough on people.'

'I'm tough on him? He's the one who broke my fingers.'

Riggs looks confused. 'No,' he says. 'He didn't do that.'

Penny laughs. 'Yes, I've told you this story before. See?' She lifts her hand, shows the crooked little finger. She remembers the night in graphic detail: the police appearing from nowhere, no time to hide, the phoenix on the side of the butcher's shop almost complete, her father's fury when they dropped her home and told him what she'd been doing. After they'd gone, he'd grabbed her hand, wrenched it around. She'd felt the pull through the fingers and the wrist, the pain a vibrant palette of incompatible colours, heard Jamie behind her, moving forwards and pushing her father to the floor. Damian, crimson-cheeked and out of breath, had hissed, 'Piss off, you little shit. Leave Penelope alone or I'll get them to lock you up next time.'

'I don't remember you telling me this,' Riggs says.

Penny presses her hands together between her legs, as though to hide the evidence that divides their memories, divides their experiences, and says, 'I don't want his help.'

'It's called being a nepo baby,' Riggs says. 'Like Dakota Johnson. Make the most of it, I reckon.'

'I can do it without him.'

Riggs lets out a long deep sigh. 'Really?' he says. 'You're going to keep painting?'

'What's wrong with that?'

He opens his mouth to speak and then seems to change his mind. After a minute, he says, 'I don't know. It seems to me you don't even enjoy painting.'

'I do enjoy it. I love it.'

'Really? You're miserable when you don't paint, and then when you do paint, you're even worse. Come back from the studio groaning and complaining that nothing you do is ever good enough. It seems to me you like the idea of being an artist more than you actually like making the art.'

'Why would you say that?'

Riggs licks his lips and places his hands palm up on the bed between them. 'You're a brilliant artist, Pen. A brilliant artist, a beautiful woman. But if it was going to happen, don't you think it would've happened by now?' He inches his body toward her. 'You know what I was thinking? We could have another baby.'

Another baby. Imagine: her stomach swelling, a child growing inside, the fact it would not be Rose. There is no way to replace her. The possibility, the attempt, feels almost repulsive to Penny, and the air rushes out from her lungs as she gasps, 'Oh—' One quiet, uneasy sound that couldn't possibly capture every wash of feeling that sweeps over her: terror, sorrow, anger. Another baby. The loss of her dream.

Riggs bristles. 'We could do it right this time,' he says.

She speaks before she thinks. 'I don't know if you're ready to be a father again.'

He stares at her, lips parted slightly. There's a look on his face that she doesn't recognise, and a hot flush races over her chest and neck. He rubs his hand over his newly cropped hair, and laughs, the sound breathy and cold. Her cruelty has shocked them both.

'I'm sorry,' she says. She touches his leg. 'You know what I mean. I'm not ready either.'

'Fuck you,' Riggs says, his voice shaky. 'I'm here cold fucking turkey, losing my shit, back in New Zealand, all for you, and that's how you say thank you?'

His neck is blotchy red, and it strikes her that he could leave and she'd be stuck at her parents' house with no money, no plan, no friend. Nothing. He doesn't even look at her, and she panics. She says, soft and gentle, almost believing herself when she says it, because it's true even when it's not: 'I love you. Adam. I'm sorry.'

He nods and looks away out the window to the blazing sky and beyond, and all she can see when she looks at him—

All she can see is her daughter.

JAMIE

THE OPHTHALMOLOGIST OUTLINES HOW there are several possible explanations for what's going on with Jamie's vision. Whether it's the paralysing grip of fear or simply because he's dog tired, Jamie finds it difficult to pay attention to what the man is saying.

'At this stage,' Dr Sobhani says, 'I wouldn't want to make any assumptions. When the results of your blood tests and the other scans come back, we'll know a lot more. Call if there's any sudden change.' He suggests that perhaps it's all a delayed result of his head injury at the Alley-Oop, and that his eyesight might settle as it is: foggy at times, clearer at others, worse at night. Whatever way the dice rolls, there are a few changes Dr Sobhani says are non-negotiable: no more driving, at least for now; no more work, at least no more building; and he mustn't, unless he wants to break his neck, get on a skateboard, not for love or money.

'We'll be in touch,' Dr Sobhani says as he ushers Jamie out of his office. 'Take care, Jamie.'

Back home, Jamie knows he can't put it off any longer. He calls his boss, Clem, and says he's still sick from the accident and he doesn't know when he'll be back, which is true. Building sites are no place for someone who has trouble seeing his tools. Clem is kind but clear: 'The work still needs doing, Jamie. You're out of annual leave and sick leave, so for now consider yourself a free agent. Let me know when you want to come back, and I'll see if we've got anything you can do.'

So that's it. He's unemployed. Can't hold it against Clem, really — he has a business to run, kitchens to build, houses to re-clad, mouths to feed, bills to pay. Jamie gets it, he does. But the loss of income fills Jamie with alarm: the ACC payments from the accident have ceased, his rent is due, he's put another three hundred on his credit card for the specialist visit, and there's an MRI to pay for. His ute was written off in the accident, so he can't sell that, and the insurance company refuses to pay out until the final police report comes in. Jamie needs cash now.

And if the police figure out he lied about the accident? They could charge him with reckless driving. Fuck the insurance, he might go to prison! But then; is that any worse than the torture of waiting for an answer about what's going on with his eyes? If there's something wrong with his brain and he's going to die, maybe prison wouldn't be so bad.

By the time he's scraped up enough for the MRI, he's on to his last few dollars and his credit card is close to its limit. He rings the Ministry of Social Development and waits on hold for fifty-five minutes. It's wasted time: the outcome is as unhelpful as a dog's turd. They won't consider the health and disability benefit without a formal diagnosis, and the results from blood tests, the MRI and the CT scan aren't likely to come through for another week at least, Dr Sobhani's receptionist tells him without much sympathy.

'The Jobseeker Support might work,' the MSD woman says, 'but there is a stand-down period. Perhaps dip into your savings?' Statement, or question, he isn't sure, so he says, no, he couldn't do that, he's already done that, and the savings were nothing much to begin with. He swipes red on his phone, ending the call without saying goodbye.

There seems to be only one option left. He cradles his phone and considers chucking it across the room. He'll have to give up the lease on his place. Return tail between his legs to the family home. Forty years old and back with his mother. What the hell has he done to deserve that? And then he catches himself. He doesn't believe in karma, or spiritual retribution; life simply is what it is. So he picks up and calls his landlord.

Without too much fuss they agree on a date to end the tenancy, week after next, and Jamie will forfeit his bond to cover the unpaid rent. His home of six years gone just like that. He wouldn't have minded some fuss. A thank you for looking after my house, at least. If anything, the landlord seemed pissed off. As though Jamie's situation is an inconvenience to him.

The next call won't be any easier. It takes him a while to explain to his mother what's happening with his eyes, and what that means — no job, no licence, no home. She isn't quick on the uptake — never has been — so he has to ask straight out.

'Could I move in with you?' he says. 'Just for a bit, you know, until I know more about what's going on.' It's an effort to keep the disappointment out of his voice.

'Oh hun,' Trish says with a sharp inhale. Is she going to cry? He doesn't think he can take that. He's balanced on a very, very thin line and that might well tip him over the edge. But she does him a good one: 'Of course, of course,' she says. She pauses, and the moment stretches out, bloated with a comfortless tension. He knows she's also thinking of him in that house, seventeen years old, home late with one too many beers sloshing around in his guts, smelling of sex and smoke, a goofball grin on his face and Penny on his mind, and his father, waiting, waiting, waiting, body slack in the passenger's seat, shrouded in the grey gas of car exhaust, waiting to be found by a boy who had no desire to find such a thing.

He takes the ferry back to his mother's on a rainy Saturday. As the city fades away in a low haze of cloud, he wonders if his life there had been a hoax and he's been a dimwit for believing it could've been for him. The dog sits at his feet, her face resting on her paws, seeming to understand the cheerless reason for their trip. That life, as they knew it, is coming to an end.

Trish is welcoming but wary. She gives him space and leaves for work each day with a sad smile, which serves to infuriate him further. He can see enough to get on with things, only there's nothing to get on with. He's a man with no job, no hobby, no life. He takes to staying in bed as late as humanly possible, getting up only to use the bathroom and make coffee; evenings he feels a strange obligation to sit in the lounge with Trish while she clutches a cup of tea and watches *Britain's*

Got Talent or *MasterChef Australia*. Beneath him the garage throbs with memory; beside him the Riggses' house looms, and he hates it all.

The garage. He remembers wandering home that night after the bonfire down at Rocky Bay. The streets dark and still, his moon boot scraping loud on the gravelled road verge. High as a bloody kite with lust he was, his skin tingling with the feeling of her hands. The pain in his ankle and the humiliation of losing the Alley-Oop all but gone. He thought he might be falling in love.

There's no better feeling, is there, than love. Nothing better than knowing someone wants you, needs you. Is waiting for you. It's terrifying as well, if he's honest. Feels a lot like dropping in. Like you might not land it and there's a lot of hurt in your future. You're fucking scared, only you want it so bad you do it anyway. Because there's the chance you might get it.

It was well past midnight when he arrived at his house. The security light in the Riggses' carport blinked on when he came up the driveway, and for the first time since he'd left the bonfire he felt something other than elation. He would have to tell Riggs about Penny. A white panic creeps on his neck at the thought of it.

At the top of the steps to the front door he saw a dim light through the small, cobwebbed garage window. His father must have forgotten to turn the light off. He kicked off his sneakers, hung his backpack on the hook near the kitchen bench and opened the internal door to the garage. He was thinking about Riggs and Penny, so it took him longer than it should have to notice the garage was cloudy. It took him longer than it should have to notice the clotted white air stank of burning petrol.

Then he felt the buzzing rumble of the car engine deep in his gut and his legs went weak. He moved stiffly towards the vehicle. Bent to look in the window.

Dad.

After that, things blur. He remembers Trish holding him. She was saying no, no, no, repeating the word, rocking him until Maureen Riggs arrived. She took him from his mother. Made up a bed in her basement. He buried himself under the covers and berated himself for not being home. If he'd been at home his dad would be alive. If he hadn't been with Penny his dad would be alive. It was his fault. It was her fault. A dreadful rush of guilt and shame mixed with thoughts of her body filled him, and he sat up, gasping. Through the blinds Jamie saw the lights of the ambulance. There was no siren. They weren't in a rush. His father had been dead for hours.

The days pass in a drawn-out haze of near intolerable boredom. He's not sure he can continue this for much longer. But how can he contemplate anything other than continuing? After a week, Trish starts to deflate when she sees him. He doesn't blame her. He's quite the insult. A grown man with no hope, and a reminder, no doubt, of Paddy, a reminder of their shared grief and disappointment.

Two weeks he's been there when there's a break in the tedium. They're eating dinner together, and Trish says abruptly, 'I talked to your Uncle Martin last night.'

'Right,' Jamie says. He has an odd feeling about where this conversation might be heading.

'He mentioned his place in the Coromandel. The kitchen

needs a bit of work, he said, and wondered whether you might be up for it. Might keep you busy, a bit of time to figure things out? Bit rundown, he said, no one's been there for the best part of eight years. Gotta be better than hanging around here, though? I know I'm not much company.'

The Coromandel. He remembers the long, hazy blue ridge of it hanging over the horizon when he was a kid. Look east and there it was. He'd never gone there when he was young; holidays were spent in Hamilton, where his mum's sister Clare lived. When he was older and living in Auckland, he'd gone there with mates, camping in Matarangi or Opito Bay, fishing in Amodeo Bay, surfing in Tairua, skating in the small towns that had skateparks. Madeline's olds even had a place in Pauanui, a monstrous modern build they had the temerity to call 'the bach', where they'd celebrate Christmas and spend more time in the swimming pool than the ocean. He'd bickered with Madeline about preferring the smaller bays, the creaky hidden places, more than the flashy gentrified summer spots, though if he's honest, it was all pretty sweet.

His Uncle Martin's bach — he can't picture it. Maybe he's never been there, or visited too long ago to recall. One thing he knows. Whatever condition the place is in, it will be preferable to the haunted domesticity of Trish's house. Besides, who could be sad in the Coromandel? Golden beaches, quiet isolation. Maybe he can get through this if he's in a place like that, all on his own.

The police call the day before they're due to drive to the Coromandel. The officer's Scottish accent is difficult for Jamie to parse, though he gets the gist: they'd completed their investigation. The other driver is at fault: twenty kilometres above the speed limit, blood alcohol over two hundred. 'Mental behaviour,' the cop says, 'seriously mental.'

So he's off the hook. He can hardly breathe for the relief of it. The officer assures him his insurance company has been sent a copy of the report and that he should expect payment soon. Oddly, the thrill of relief is short-lived. He isn't guilty, yet he doesn't feel particularly innocent either.

He glances out the window. There's Maureen, taking shopping from the car boot, and Trent in the doorway, hands out to take the bags from her. He knows what Riggs would tell him about the way he's feeling: that being innocent and feeling guilty is the domain of the Catholics. Jamie's beginning to understand what Riggs was going through all these years.

Riggs. Wonder where that bastard is now. God, what a pair they were. Unleashed, dirty, ferociously independent. Outside from sunrise to sunset. People don't let their kids roam that way anymore — a shame really, 'cause some of his best memories are of him and Riggs out in the world, no one supervising. Seven years old, eight, ten, haunting storm pipes on cold winter afternoons or scouring beaches for unwanted treasures. They found a dead sheep propped up on the high-tide line like a trophy and shrouded in a haze of blowflies. One of them — Jamie never could remember who, though he guesses it was probably Riggs — found a sharp-edged mussel shell and sliced the ewe's bloated stomach open, releasing a swamp of guts and a stench as ripe as their worst dreams.

When they were older, they swapped out the beach for the skatepark, a piece of crap which had been built on an old rubbish dump and was incrementally sinking into the marsh. Didn't matter to them though, not at that young age. After that first drop in, Jamie was hooked. And whatever Jamie did, Riggs did too, of course. They wasted so many hours — maybe too many, practising trick after trick, heads down, jaws firm, failing and falling and falling and failing, but doing it together. Those days, Jamie thinks, watching Trent and Maureen carry the last of the groceries inside and shut the door, those days are long gone.

They leave for the bach early the next morning, taking the first car ferry to the mainland, then pushing on around the Firth of Thames in silence. The dog sleeps in the back seat. Trish wants to stop at the second-hand shops in Paeroa and 'find a bargain', so they go the long way round. In the car while she browses, Jamie stares at half-seen shapes through the window, sure his phone will buzz. The police again, saying, Sorry, we've made a mistake, please could you come into the station, right now, and for a moment he almost wants it to happen.

When they get back on the road Trish tells him about the good deal she got on a set of Crown Lynn swans at the SPCA Op Shop and her regret at not also picking up the mid-century mirror with the bevelled edges, only the man at the shop wouldn't budge on price. Jamie wants to share her excitement, but he's irritated by it all: the shopping, the way Trish sprays the windscreen to clear her view, how slow she drives around the snaking turns along the coast north of Whangamatā, the way she puts one hand on the gearstick as she drives, even though it's an automatic. Go faster, he wants to say, though he keeps his expression blank to avoid an argument.

'I forgot to tell you. I saw the Whittakers the other day,' Trish says. She looks over at him. 'Apparently Penny's coming back soon. A gallery is going to show her paintings. Fancy, huh? Takes after her father, I suppose.'

Penny Whittaker. Even the name makes Jamie feel strange. Good-strange, and also bad-strange. He hasn't thought of her for a few days. That deserves some kind of celebration. After she'd left with Riggs, he'd worked hard to get her out of his mind, and eventually he thought of her less and less. Months began to pass without a thought of her to disrupt him, then years, though in the last few months of his relationship with Madeline he fell into the habit of closing his eyes when they were having sex and thinking of Penny instead. It seemed immature to him, and disloyal, except that it made him relax, and it felt good. Not much was good in those days with Madeline, so the temptation to find that feeling was irresistible. He saw Penny's long hair spread out beneath him, her milky white shoulder. The softness of her body, the hard corners too. Shoulders, collarbones, ankles.

It was around the same time he also noticed how often he thought about Penny when he wasn't having sex. He was both sad and lonely, the loneliest he'd ever been, and that was saying something. This was during the first lockdown, and he and Madeline were financially crippled and stuck together every second of every day. The atmosphere inside their small house in Grey Lynn grew tight and oppressive. The fighting was near-constant and seldom about anything vital. How to stack the dishwasher; where the house keys should be kept when they were both at home; the correct way to place their shoes in the storage cupboard by the door. They fixated on these small things, afraid to examine the real reasons behind the misery. Madeline was cruel in her heartbreak. About a week before they split for good, she arrived home from a lockdown walk and immediately started downing a bottle of rosé. Six drinks deep, she sat down beside him and explained why she thought they shouldn't have kids. You'd be a terrible father, she told him, before saying more clearly: 'I just think when you have a parent who commits suicide, it sort of taints you.'

Christ, it still makes his breath catch in his throat when he thinks of it three years later. It wasn't a surprise they broke up, even if he was, is, inexplicably sadder and more lonely than before. He no longer feels disloyal when he thinks of Penny, just intensely pathetic. What if he never feels as strongly for someone as he did for Penny Whittaker? Is he truly, utterly fucked? What he needs to do is tell himself: I can still live a good life, I can make this life a great one. I don't need anyone else to live a good life.

In the car with his mother, all Jamie can say is, 'Penny Whittaker? She's an incredible artist.'

He remembers the night they met at the skatepark, her cans of spray paint and no clue except an eye for it and a yearning for something different. Then for six months they were inseparable. During the day she watched him skate, or they'd sit in his bedroom listening to music. Talking about art. Parents. School. Life. What they wanted to do next. Then, when the sliding lavender evening drifted into the indigo dark of night, they were covering Rocky Bay's set of shops in colours and shapes and spectacle.

Trish says, 'I wonder if I'll see her around the place. It's a pity you fell out of touch with her, you two were thick as thieves for a while. The phoenix you two did on the side of the butcher's shop is still there, you know. A bit worse for wear now. Did you see it when we drove out?'

The phoenix. The last thing they'd worked on together, the final masterpiece. They'd planned the work for a few weeks, trading detailed sketches and resolving issues with compromise and innovative ideas. Penny had certain demands about how the feathers should look (feathery and soft), and he had certain reservations about how to pull that off (the problem of how to make such subtle and delicate work with a blunt medium). The sketches mutated and the image split open and rearranged into new shapes: a phoenix from the flames, from the flames a phoenix, until at last they found a way to create the image that would satisfy them both.

They started working on it around nine-thirty one Saturday night in late October. The moon was bright at their backs, making their torches almost redundant. It was spring, though the night felt closer to deep winter, and Jamie's hands soon felt as though they were gloved with frost. Neither spoke much. They usually enjoyed talking while they painted, but this piece was more complex, and much larger, than anything they'd attempted before. It would take longer to do, and the longer they were there, stark in the moonlight, exposed in their crime, the more likely it was they'd be caught. Besides, both were hungry to see it complete. Ravenous, even. Though Jamie enjoyed the process, the finished work was the ultimate. An artwork that was in their minds and now made real. Christ, he loved it. There was an ease to it all, a warmth. Different from the things he and Riggs did together. Like the skating, which was often flavoured, or tainted, by an almost undetectable current of jealousy and competitiveness. But the artwork he made with Penny? It was never competitive. Never. He felt equal with her in some way he wasn't sure he'd ever felt before.

By twelve-thirty, the phoenix was near done. Penny put the can of black spray paint on the ground, pulled the mask from her face and said they should take a break. The Rocky Bay shops were unearthly silent. A slow breeze kicked a Snickers wrapper along the gutter, and Jamie's arms speckled with goosebumps. He felt sure they were being watched, though when he sat down, Penny beside him, the glory of the work they'd created pacified his nerves. The moon had dipped below the horizon by this time, yet, even in the dim, yellowish glow provided by the streetlight twenty metres away, their work was radiant, and brilliant.

And then she'd kissed him.

Jamie, face to the window to avoid his mother's eye, says, 'The phoenix. No, I didn't see it.' Deliberately turned his head to miss it each time he'd gone through the shops.

'Wonder what she's been up to all these years.'

'You could ask Trent and Maureen,' Jamie says.

That kiss. Hard to forget the thrill he felt in that moment. Or, what he'd said when he'd pushed her away. Riggs, he'd said. We can't do this to Riggs. They'd struggled to get back into the painting after that, and then, what would you know, the cops showed up.

'That's right. I forget they're together,' Trish says. 'Wouldn't have picked it, that she'd end up with Adam. But you never know how these things will work out.'

Trish slows the car to take a winding turn. She says, 'I actually caught up with Trent and Maureen yesterday. They were clearing out their garage and they found one of your old skateboards. I've got it in the boot.'

'Mum.'

'What? What have I done this time?'

He lets the silence hang in the air between them for a while, then says, 'Say thank you to Maureen for holding onto it for all that time. I wouldn't have blamed them if they'd chucked it.'

Trish indicates and slows the car to make a right-hand turn. 'They've always looked after you.' She shifts her hands on the wheel before nosing the car down a narrow gravel driveway bordered on both sides by a thick forest of pines. 'I suppose some people might say they looked after you better than I did.'

The Riggs family had looked after him. After his dad died, Adam and his family basically adopted him. In those first few days, it was comforting to be at the Riggses' house, away from his mother and away from Penny. Maureen and Trent enveloped him into their routine, feeding him all his meals, making up a bed on the floor of their basement rec room. Every couple of days, he'd find a stack of newly laundered, neatly folded clothes on his bed. He'd pick up his school shorts from the pile, press his face into the creases and silently scream, thinking of his mother in the house next door, pickled by noon, stumbling through the days blurry and sodden with grief.

All this put pressure on his friendship with Adam. Riggs didn't say anything outright, but Jamie knew him well enough to see the resentment lurking beneath his chill façade. Riggs, the youngest of three children, had always felt he was the shadow behind two brilliant sisters, and now here was another person stealing his parents' attention. And Maureen and Trent treated Jamie different, that was true. They didn't judge the way he behaved in those confusing, terrifying days after he found Paddy in the garage. He wasn't proud of how he'd behaved — he'd been belligerent and rude — but it wasn't surprising, was it? He was in shock. Mostly, though, he wasn't proud of what he'd said to Penny. The cruelty of it. Maybe he should forgive Madeline for what she'd said to him. Maybe even good people say things they wish they could take back. Still, there was no excuse for what he'd accused her of, what he'd blamed her for. No excuse. Only his dad was gone, and he couldn't help thinking that when his dad was taking in those last toxic breaths, he wasn't with him to save him. He was with Penny at the bonfire.

'Here we are,' Trish says.

He can't see anything. The pines along the driveway, Trish tells him, were planted in the nineties by a forestry group who not long afterwards went into receivership. Their landholding was subdivided — the entire beachfront plot, what should've been a goldmine — but the timing was wrong and no one was interested. Uncle Martin bought his section from the liquidators for a song, and for even less a house for removal from Waihī. He trucked it in and then promptly left for Norway and a job in the oil industry. He rarely comes back. No one else lives in the bay, and each end of it is blocked by steep, rocky cliffs, so there are no day trippers, no tourists. Just the bach and the beach and the sand and the sea.

'You'll be on your own,' she says. 'Which makes me a bit nervous, but something tells me being alone is exactly what you're looking for.'

They drive into a small clearing beside a small fifties-designed shack, and it's clear the place hasn't seen any love in decades. The berry-red weatherboard exterior is matted with a lavish coating of dust and dirt and sand. The roof is mottled with the flaking deep orange of rust. Pine trees hug the walls, and the gutters must be choked full of needles. To the side of the house is a shed that has seen better days: the door hangs from the upper hinges and the small south-facing window is smashed to shards. Trish stops the car between the shed and the house.

'I've heard people call the bay here Pākarukaru,' she says. 'But Martin calls this place Desire.'

She unlocks the back door and goes into the house. Jamie stands on the threshold and calls, 'Come on, girl.' The dog doesn't need telling twice: she runs up the step with a gassed-up yelp and streaks inside.

The back door leads into a small laundry. An open door to Jamie's left allows him a glance at an ancient toilet with a metal pull chain; through another door he spies a curtainless shower cubicle. They wander through the hall to a small lounge. The carpet underfoot is thin and crunchy, with sand or Christ-knows-what. He sees his assignment then, tucked into the far corner of the room: a worn-out, outdated mint-green abomination of a kitchen. It'll take a bit to make this look good.

He is starting to assess his options for the renovation when his attention is diverted by his mother sliding open a floor-to-ceiling glass door in the lounge. It crunches open and then sticks, leaving a gap scarcely big enough for them to slip through. He stands beside her on a kwila deck, the boards rotten and soft beneath his feet, and understands now why this place might be known as Desire: from where he stands, you look right down onto a stretch of golden sand and, beyond that, the water, the blue-grey chop pulling out to the horizon, the lug of Slipper Island Whakahau loping heavy to the right, and then nothing, nothing at all between him and Chile. Tufts of tussock grass combed over the top of the dunes bristle in the breeze. Ribbons of cloud thin as gossamer trill across the sky. Two lonesome white birds sweep over the water. Desire.

The dog runs out the doors behind him, leaping from the deck onto the dune, and without pause scurries onto the sand to race in ever-widening circles. Two oystercatchers lift into the air and float, black and brilliant orange. Jamie's sight is uncannily clear. He doesn't even want to blink in case he messes it up. Wants to look forever on the perfection of the dirty turquoise water and the sky melting into a pale wisteria-purple where it kisses the ocean. The old pain in his bad ankle twinges when he steps further toward the high-tide mark. Rain on the way. He'll need to clear out those gutters.

He turns to speak to his mother about a ladder, only she's back inside the house. There's the sound of her, opening cupboards, turning on and off the taps. She's talking in there, her mutters lost in the walls. He squeezes back through the sliding door, and she says, 'Should be most of what you need in here for a few days. I'll get Roy Avery to drop some groceries to you each fortnight. He's a good bloke, won't mind doing me a favour. Might take your rubbish too, if we ask nicely.'

Jamie looks around the lounge. Musty furniture surrounds a dusty, darkened fireplace and a wall made of books. A mix of classics and titles he doesn't know. Next to the hearth, a pile of sun-faded puzzles and board games — Monopoly, Scrabble, Trivial Pursuit.

'No TV,' he says.

'Nope. No internet and very patchy cell reception.' She pulls her phone from her pocket. 'I'm not getting any inside. Last time I was here I could get a bit down on the beach. Maybe try that if you need to get in touch with me — you know, in case of an emergency.'

Down the hall are two bedrooms, side by side, each with a view of ocean through the pines. Jamie sits on the bed in the bedroom nearest the lounge. The dog leaps up to join him, sniffing nonstop. The mattress is lumpy and damp in the cooling evening air. Christ, even though it's late September, technically spring, he can tell it's going to be bloody cold in this place.

As if she reads his mind, Trish opens a cupboard door in the hallway outside the bedroom and rolls a small oil column heater into the room.

'You're going to need this,' she says. She sighs, pushes her hair away from her eyes. 'There's the fireplace in the lounge but no firewood. I'm sure you can sort that out. I've left your tools in the shed and I'll ask Roy to drop off the things you'll need for the kitchen.'

For a moment neither he nor Trish speaks, and the dismal silence is filled by the slap and slam of a wave. Through the windows, the light dims as the sun droops. The shadows of the pines deepen, another wave slashes to the shore, and Trish says it's time she got on the road. Jamie's eyes worsen in the gloom, and he runs his hand along the walls as he follows her through the house and out to her car.

'Careful with the tank water,' Trish says, 'though it's been a wet winter so you should be right for a while. Martin said there's surfboards and probably a wetsuit you're welcome to use in the shed, though God knows what condition they'll be in.' She opens the car door and hesitates. 'Are you sure you're going to be okay out here by yourself?'

Jamie lifts his hand in a wave, a gesture that belies his frustration. His fear. He is ready for her to leave, to take her sweet concern and piss off. He doesn't want to cry, not today.

'I'll be fine,' he says. 'I'll talk to you soon.'

The dying light pulls the forest in closer still, and from this distance he can barely see her face. He hears the car for a long time after it has disappeared from view, and when the sound has evaporated fully, he goes inside the house to confront whatever it might be that waits for him there.

RIGGS

RIGGS PUSHES THE DOWNSTAIRS bathroom door shut, careful not to make a sound. Damian and Meg are already in bed in the room next door. For a long moment he stands, unmoving, bare feet cold on the marble tiles, heart rushing fast in his throat. He wants to believe he's no more than a man in a room, but it's not true. He flicks on the light and is shocked by the sudden brightness — and by his reflection in the mirror. Like death warmed up, that's what he looks like. Grey around the gills, his dad Trent would say. Peaky. It's there in his face, all of it. The fear. The grief. The loss. The love. The anguish.

The bathroom is immaculate. Riggs doesn't know anything about tapware, but he recognises quality when he sees it. He turns the lever on and off to test the feel of it. Heavy to the touch. Responsive. His fingerprints muddy the shiny finish, so he takes a handcloth from the rail and wipes it clean. He was never here. No one can prove a thing.

Two navy Turkish cotton towels hang on a heated rail next to the shower. Above that is a blond ash shelf with a fern and one of those enormous candles that smells like candy or bergamot. He'd half expected there to be a wall-hung mirrored cupboard that he could click open to expose an array of small brown containers with white lids, their labels prescribing myriad pharmaceuticals to Sir Damian Whittaker and Lady Meg Novak. But there's only the drawer under the basin. He pulls it open. He isn't planning to do anything, isn't going to touch a thing. He just wants to look, to see, to pretend.

In the corner, between a new box of toothpaste and a set of hotel toiletries, are several white boxes with that label he'd imagined: the pharmacy logo on the top, the black text, alternating in lower and upper case, detailing dosage amount and frequency. A box of amitriptyline. No thanks. A strip of laxatives. Not today! Under that, though, the motherload. Not quite the same as oxy, but it will be good enough: a box of tramadol.

Then he breaks his first rule and picks it up. What's wrong with a little bit of curiosity? Horniness is basically curiosity and horniness is never wrong. The medication is prescribed to Meg Novak, Penny's old lady. He checks the expiry date, for interest's sake. He isn't going to take any. To be honest, he isn't concerned what date it says. If risks were pills, he could say with all sincerity that he eats them for breakfast — he's a skater. Hell, it would take more than a calendar to scare him off. The expiry date is more a worry for Meg. November 2025. Safe as houses.

A box of tramadol. His hands shiver, and the pills rattle. It would mean nothing to look inside. Just a man looking in a box. To see how much is in there. Doesn't mean he's going to take any.

The box opens like legs, smooth and tempting. Three blister packs, all accounted for. Penny's old lady must have nerves of reinforced steel, all this and not one downed. For a second — possibly two — he wonders if he might return the box back where he found it. The chance, it's there, only he skirts past, shutting the drawer with his knee, the box still in his grip.

Not going to take any. No no no. He's stronger than that. It's good to simply have them in his hand. The silver foil covering the pills puckers over the indents where the pills reside, little silver houses for little white miracles, and he presses his nail into one, testing the foil and his own resolve.

Then his back contracts and bursts. The pain is always there, all the bloody time, a poky wee friend who stays long after the other guests have left. He's bored of it, the way it zings and aches and robs him of his life. Who could blame him for getting addicted to the pills? They helped. They helped with the grief too, and two birds one stone, who can argue with that? The pills dull it all, numb it, fuzz it. We need what we need to get through, right? Alcohol takes the edge off but it isn't as good. Not nearly as good. Penny doesn't understand what she's asking of him.

His nail cuts into the foil and he snatches his finger up. It would be better to have them in his pocket. He's promised. No more. He slides the pills into the box and then puts the whole thing in his pocket. Immediately the full-body shivering ceases. Maybe that's all he needs. To have them near. Knowing they are there will bolster him, and he can motivate himself with his incredible willpower. See, look, he has some with him now and he hasn't taken any. He's strong. Able to withstand the allure and the pain. He'll stay clean, they'll get married. Maybe they could try for another kid. It isn't such a stupid idea. Look at him now. Strong and able to resist.

The way she'd flinched when he'd mentioned getting pregnant again. Hell, that hurt almost as much as his back. Mostly because he knows she's right. Rose's death was his cross to bear, and quitting the pills is the price she has asked him to pay. That's why he won't swallow any of Meg's tramadol. Having them with him is enough. A back-up plan he will never need to enact.

Before he switches off the light, he takes one last look at himself in the mirror. Lifts his lips and bares his teeth. The remaining teeth are yellowed and the space from the missing tooth is ominous in its darkness. Occasionally he has the feeling Penny is frightened of him, and right now he can see why. It's honestly terrifying to see himself as he really is: an addict, a liar, a fraud, a fool. He knows they don't say addict anymore, or junkie. It's person with substance-use disorder — only for him that's too clean, too hygienic. A hot, hard force hits up behind his eyes and he kills the overhead lights.

Riggs had been a boy of steel. A little Superman, that's what his mother liked to say. Never sick, not once, not even for a minute. An immune system designed to withstand the plague. When he was a baby, she said, she never even knew he was teething. There was no crying, not a drop of redness in his cheeks. Unlike his sisters, who wouldn't sleep and grizzled and fussed and drooled and whined. Not Adam, Maureen said, he was a cheery wee thing. She said she felt stupid getting him vaccinated — a kid like him didn't need it, did he?

When he was learning to walk, he fell as much as any toddler, maybe more, because he was trying to run before he could even stand steady. Falling didn't upset him. He took the hit, stood up and carried on. Hardly any days off school, either: the only days he can remember missing primary school were when Trent took him fishing instead. Secondary school there were admittedly a few more missed days. Only they were truancy, not illness. No one said Adam was an angel. Far from it.

Before he was twenty, he'd never even taken paracetamol. He never got so much as a cold. His sisters both had chickenpox and sat around contagious and miserable and fretting about scars on their foreheads, and he never caught it. Four years into this damned pandemic and he's yet to even get Covid. Has a pain threshold higher than anyone he knows. Can slam his body nasty and then stand up with nothing more than a grimace. That's what gives him the edge over the other skaters. At the very least, he knows it's given him an edge over Jamie.

They spent so much time together when they were kids that even some of their teachers got them muddled up. But there was one major difference between them. Jamie felt things more than Riggs did. Physical things, on the whole, but emotional ones too. Jamie would cry over every trifling thing. He'd cried when they'd found that dead sheep on the beach. It washed up on the high-tide line, eyeballs bulging and wool darkened near black with seaweed and sand. Riggs couldn't stand the tears that day, and he'd taunted Jamie by prodding the bloated stomach with a stick. 'Stop it,' Jamie had said, and Riggs only laughed. He wasn't doing any harm. Damned sheep was already dead. He hadn't meant to do more than give it a poke and scare the shits out of Jamie, only he pushed too hard and the stick went straight through the water-softened skin. The stink that came out with the guts made Jamie wail even harder. Riggs felt a bit queasy too, though at no point had he felt he might cry. In fact, he still feels proud that he hadn't been upset that day. He was a tough kid. He could handle hard things. It would take more than death to knock him from his feet.

So that's why it confuses him: how has this tough-as-guts boy turned into this weak and pathetic grown-ass man? Or maybe it doesn't confuse him. Maybe he doesn't want to admit grief has shattered him so magnificently he no longer understands himself or the world around him. He'd thought he was tough. He'd thought he was brave. He'd thought he had the ability to do things no one else could do. Turns out he was wrong.

'I can't stay in this house any longer,' Penny tells him the next morning. 'We need to leave.'

It is dire being at the Whittaker mansion, he agrees with her there. He'd gone downstairs earlier to get a coffee, and Meg was sitting on the stool at the island, silent as a glacier and definitely as icy. Damian refused to speak to him, wouldn't even look him in the eye. Riggs takes some responsibility for how it all went down, but Damian is overreacting. Like father, like daughter. Riggs would love to stay, if everyone could sort their shit. He loves the Whittaker house. But between Penny's sulking and her parents' silent treatment, and no sign of a truce, Riggs too thinks it's best they leave before any more shit goes down. The blister pack crinkles in his pocket.

'Why don't we go stay with my olds for a few days?' he says. 'Maureen is hanging out to see us.'

'I want to leave Waiheke.'

'Car ferry's booked up for two days, babe.' A quick lie won't hurt her.

'Honestly?' she says.

'True story. I'll tell Maureen we'll be there soon. She'll be thrilled to have us.'

He eases the rental car down the Whittakers' driveway and takes a left onto the main road. The speedo loiters above 70, which is too fast for the narrow roads, only he can't help himself. He's bored silly – he hasn't skated in nearly two weeks. He's itching for movement, for adrenaline, and although driving sets his back to scratching it subdues his thirst for action. That's what most of us want, isn't it? To have our needs met, at least most of the time?

Maureen opens the door before he's even put the car into park. Penny unclips her seatbelt. Out of some strange impulse he grabs her leg and says, 'Wait.'

That face, when she turns to him: those eyes. Rose's eyes. The same sorrow in the depths of them, the hurt that warms them up from the inside and makes them glow, and he cannot bear to see them for a second longer. He shuffles in the seat and brushes his pocket with a stray hand. Just checking they're there. Just checking. And with that movement, a twinging spasm shoots up through his back.

'Riggs?'

His hand is still on her leg and now Maureen's at the car window. She knocks on the glass. Everything's too rushed. He wants to sit for a minute and wallow in the memory of the last time he was at the house with Penny. His eighteenth birthday party. A lifetime ago. They were kids. He'd had long hair, and she'd been what, sixteen? Seventeen? A child. He can't quite see inside the carport, where he'd kissed her for the first time. The feeling of that kiss — hell, he can still conjure it up. It's entirely possible he'll never forget how insanely wonderful it had felt to hold her face, and pull her close, after months of dreaming about that very thing. Shame that it was — and still is — tinged with the knowledge she'd been looking for someone else.

Maureen tugs at the car door handle, then leans in to embrace him. 'Adam, darling,' she says. 'You're here!'

'Mum, hi.' He puts his arm around her and pats her shoulder. She's thin as a chicken bone, a skeleton walking. Christ.

Penny's out of the car, hugging his father in the doorway to the house. 'Shall we go inside?'

'Of course, darling,' Maureen says. 'I've got the jug on, and I picked up some biscuits from the supermarket when you said you'd be here for morning tea.' She wipes her eyes, clearly overcome, and he's ashamed his first instinct is to feel irritated.

'Sorry,' she says. 'I'm so happy we can all be together. Really. Come inside before I put on a show for the neighbours.'

Only two steps inside the door and he's hit hard, assaulted even, with the past. It still smells the same in this house, the distinctive Riggs family scent, that mix of cinnamon and tobacco and ash and eucalyptus. His school photo from Standard Three hangs beside the portraits of his sisters at the same age, all framed in ugly brown wooden frames. The row of creepy, tiny ceramic owls his mother collected from various op shops on the top shelf of the bookcase in the hall, themselves now the collectors — of dust and cobwebs and children's hopes and dreams. It gives him the shivers to be confronted with his past as though nothing has changed.

'I've done up your old room,' Maureen says. She holds his arm with both hands and leads him down the hallway.

'Thanks, Mum, really appreciate it,' Riggs says.

His father is leaning against the kitchen bench. Kettle steam roars up behind him. He's gone completely grey, his short-clippered hair white against the tanned, weathered skin, and Riggs has that classic realisation of every adult child when they see their parents for the first time after a break: they're getting older, and your time to be with them is finite and shortening with every breath. You'd think losing your daughter would prepare you for loss, give you some idea of how to comport yourself in the face of its impending return, only he finds it doesn't. A cloying hack presses in his throat and he starts to cough to stem the tears. He's not sure his parents have ever seen him cry. Now is certainly not the time to change that.

'The house is looking good,' Penny says.

Trent nods his head slowly, and when the jug clicks off, he turns around to pour hot water into the cups. 'We've done a few things since last time you were here, Adam,' he says. 'New washing machine. We replaced the windows in Belinda's old room too.'

He hands cups of tea to Maureen and Penny, who walk down to the lounge together. He offers another cup to Riggs. 'Come,' he says. 'I'll show you the windows.'

Riggs takes a sip of the scalding, weak tea as he follows his dad to Belinda's old room. Trent begins waxing pretty darn lyrical about joinery and double glazing, and he's still sipping the unbearable tea when Trent leads him to the bathroom, where he describes in intricate and dull detail the tiling work he did last year. Riggs can't focus on his father, doesn't care an inch for the tiles or the grout or the men who installed the windows. It takes all he has to leave the pills in his pocket and remain sober — for her. For her. All for her.

The lounge-room doors are open to the upper deck. From where he sits, Riggs can see Jamie's old house. Knows that place almost as well as he knows this one. That there — that window with the curtains drawn — is the window of Jamie's childhood bedroom.

'Is Trish still living next door?' he asks.

'She sure is,' Trent says. 'Don't see much of her, though we had a good chat with her the other day when we were clearing out the garage. We'd found one of Jamie's old skateboards tucked in behind some old bits of wood I'd kept for who knows what reason. She said she'd get it to him. Don't know if he's still skating, do you?'

'No,' he says, hot in the face and the neck all of a sudden. 'I don't know if he's still skating.'

Trent looks over at Penny as if to save his son from the shame of not knowing about his oldest friend. God, they'd sat on that deck out there, legs dangling into the fresh spring air of November, their whole lives ahead of them, closer than twins — or at least that was how it had seemed. And now this. Like strangers.

'He's a builder, you know,' Trent says. 'He was staying with his mum for a few weeks recently. I saw him coming and going. Didn't come over and say hello, which your mum thought was a bit odd, but I told her he's a grown man now, doesn't owe us anything.'

'How was he?' Riggs asks. 'Did he seem okay to you?'

'Well, I mean, I told you I didn't talk to him. He kept to himself. Seemed quiet, I guess, but maybe he was always that way.'

Riggs nods and stares at his feet. Jamie is doing all right then. Alive, walking, talking, hanging out with his mum. He's a good man, a good son, visiting his mother on the regular. A builder. Nice steady work. Doing better than Riggs, it seems, in almost every way. Maybe in the end the accident at the Alley-Oop has damaged him more than it hurt Jamie. He hates keeping secrets, but really it isn't the keeping of a secret that turns out to be so pernicious: it's the knowledge he could be that sort of person. Shit like that, it eats away at you. Try as you might to debunk it, you are that sort of person.

Then he sees Trish in the garden behind her house; she's wearing a wide straw hat and carrying a spade. At the corner she stops, sets her feet wide and begins to dig. Riggs can see Jamie in her — the graceful long arms, the wavy blonde hair, the quiet watchful face.

'Where are you going, darling?' Maureen says, her voice high.

He's standing at the door. He can hardly remember getting up from the couch.

'I'm going outside,' he says.

'Outside?'

'I'll be back,' he says in a hurry, and he's through the front door, down the steps two at a time, the sound of Trish's spade filling his ears. She looks up at the sound of him coming up the grass towards her.

'Adam,' she says.

'Mrs Flannery.'

'Call me Trish, for goodness' sake,' she says. She presses the tip of the spade into the ground, leans on it and wipes her cheek with her arm. 'I heard you were coming back.'

'Right, I suppose Maureen told you.'

'No, actually.' She shifts her stance and looks down. 'I was talking to Penny's mother. She said Penny's got an exhibit. I'm thrilled for her. Tell her I said that.'

'Oh, right, well.' He glances up at his parents' house and sees his mother watching him from the window. 'We're only here for one more night.'

'Leaving so soon? That's a shame. I know how much your parents miss you.'

'We were staying with Penny's olds, but ...' He doesn't finish the sentence, and Trish looks him directly in the eye.

'Yes, I've heard some things about her father. I'm surprised she wanted to step foot in that house again.'

'What do you mean?'

Trish laughs and lifts the spade again. 'Nothing, nothing, pretend I didn't say anything. Is there something specific I can help you with, Adam?' She looks down at the half-dug hole and he's aware he's interrupted her. He's not even asked how she is. His mother would be appalled at his manners.

'I wanted to ask after Jamie,' he says. 'Is he in Auckland?'

'No,' she says. There's a pause. 'He's gone up to the Coromandel for a while.'

'Okay,' Riggs says. 'Do you have his number? I'll give him a call.'

Bloody oath, the Coromandel. He could go surfing, drink some beers, let Penny cool off a bit. They both deserved a holiday.

'Fine,' Trish says. 'I suppose I can do that.' She says the

number slowly, and Riggs types it into his phone. 'Reception's a bit spotty out there, so don't be surprised if you can't get hold of him.'

'Sweet, thanks,' he says. 'Sorry for interrupting.'

She waves him off, her head tilted away from him already and when he's back in his parents' lounge, no one asks what he's been doing. His father pats the couch beside him and Riggs sits. The blister pack rustles.

'How's Penny doing, by the way?' Trent says.

'She's good,' Riggs says slowly. Slow talking sounds more confident. Like you're telling the truth.

'Look.' Trent turns to him, his voice low, as though to ensure he doesn't attract Maureen's attention. 'We know we've said it before, but your mum and I, we wanted to say it again, in case it wasn't clear before. We're sorry we didn't get to meet Rose. Bloody Jacinda.' Trent takes a sip of tea, then holds his mouth in a straight line. 'Glad to be rid of her. Election in a few weeks. Not too late to get yourself enrolled and vote for change.'

'I know,' Riggs says. 'I know.' He doesn't want to get his old man started on that shit. Covid conspiracies and closed borders and quarantines, he's heard it all. His father was a Labour supporter when Riggs was a kid. Missing out on meeting Rose had soured him. Riggs knows his father is angry, at least as angry as a Catholic man can be, but he doesn't really accept that Jacinda was responsible for Trent not meeting his granddaughter. That honour went to Riggs himself.

'God is mysterious in his ways,' Trent says. 'He called your child to him much earlier than we were prepared for. He knows what you're going through. He too was a father. And God, he knew there was a plan for his son, and he never fought it, so we must trust in his plan for Rose—'

'Okay, Dad.' He glances over at Penny, who's seated on the couch beside Maureen. She's staring at Trent. It's clear she's heard it all. Bugger.

'God's plan?' Penny says.

'Yes, dear,' Trent says. He stretches out his legs and crosses them at the ankle. 'I understand how you must suffer, but there will be a plan. The Lord gave and the Lord hath taken away.'

'Fucking Christ,' Penny says.

Maureen cries out and puts her hand over her mouth.

'Penny,' Riggs says. Don't start, he means to say. These are his parents. And what he doesn't say: Let them blame God. He doesn't need them knowing the awful truth of it.

'I understand how bereavement can turn your head,' Trent says. 'Which is why I'll forgive your blasphemy this time. But listen. I know that you'll find solace in my words if you listen carefully to their meaning.'

Penny stands, eyes blazing. 'Riggs, it's time to leave.'

'Don't go,' Maureen says. 'I've made up the bed.' She stands and takes Penny's hand.

'It's okay, Mum,' Riggs says. 'We aren't leaving yet.'

'Riggs!' Penny is aghast.

Maureen touches Penny's engagement ring. 'Maybe you two could get married before you have any more children,' she says.

'Are you saying Rose is dead because God was punishing us for having her before we were married?' Penny's cheeks are blotchy pink and white.

The pills in Riggs's pocket are heavy as rocks. Christ.

'Of course not,' Maureen says. 'I just thought a wedding

might be a nice thing to look forward to.' She sighs and pulls one hand through the other, her mouth pulled tight so her lips shrivel to a narrow point.

'We were thinking we might get married,' Riggs says. 'We thought we might do it soon, right, babe?'

'That's wonderful,' Maureen says. 'I'm so happy for you both. Pauline was telling me the other day about a florist she met who said she'd do your flowers for a reasonable price.' She wipes her eyes, and laughs, the sound so melodic Riggs is transported to his seventh birthday, at that table he can spy now through the door, the cake set before him, the shape of a swimming pool filled with jelly, chocolate fingers standing sentry around the sides, and that sound, the laughter, floating high above it all, making him warm and safe and happy inside.

'You can text me the florist's number,' Riggs says, standing to join Penny, who's moving to the door. His parents follow them down the hallway, and he feels as though he's in trouble for leaving when they've said he ought to stay and that punishment is imminent.

They pause on the doorstep, and he can see Maureen's trying hard to keep it together. Her eyes are red and she's clinging to Trent's arm. 'There's quite a few new places being built in Rocky Bay,' she says. 'You might see them when you drive around. Some very unusual architectural designs.'

'Lots of bloody Jafas with too much money building bloody eyesores, that's what it is,' Trent says.

'Nothing wrong with that, is there?' Penny says. Riggs can almost feel her eyes rolling.

'I'm not complaining,' Trent says. 'I hate seeing the locals having a hard time getting a rental, that's for certain, but I don't mind change. Sometimes you hold on so hard to something, hold it tight so it stays there with you and stays the same, and you can get all worked up about it when, really, you have no choice but to let it go.'

Riggs hugs his parents, mutters assurances he'll be back soon, yes, soon. He heads the car down through the Rocky Bay shops. Penny sits silent beside him. Out his window, the primary school he went to with Jamie, the field and the creek where they'd spent those loose, easy after-school hours. There's the skatepark. He can still recall every inch of that place, even after all these years. Seared into his brain. The half-pipe, where Jamie had taken his first ill-fated turn when that older kid dared him to try.

Around through the shops. The bakery. The fish and chip shop has gone, replaced with Luigi's Pizza 'n Pasta. She doesn't look back, but he does — he takes his eyes from the road for a second, flicks them up to the rear-view mirror to spy if it's still there.

He wants it to be gone. Painted over, or simply vanished, leaving just dusty and overgrown brickwork. It looks like he might get his wish. The side of the shop is in sight and he holds his breath — he can't see the bird.

And then the car veers right, and it's there. That bloody phoenix. A bit worn, a bit dull, but there all the same.

The night those two had painted that, Riggs had been under the impression Jamie was going to meet him at the skatepark at midnight. They'd skated there at night once when they were fifteen, lit by the headlights from an older skater's car.

Riggs had loved it. The cool night air rank with the stench of the nearby creek, their long freaky shadows chasing their tails across the concrete, the thrill of skating amplified by the terror of darkness. When he'd told Jamie there was a full moon, a perfect opportunity for a repeat performance, Jamie had said yes. Let's do it.

Riggs was stoked: he'd been missing Jamie something chronic. Jamie was off with Penny a lot in those days. Riggs liked their graffiti, mostly for its flagrant violation of the rules, but he hated that for them it was all about the creation and the detail. Couldn't care less for their endless chatter about the 'work', their discussions about colour, shape, perspective that never reached a bloody conclusion. All that made him feel gross and excluded in some important way. So, if Jamie was willing to skate instead of spray painting with Penny, then Riggs was pleased. He missed his friend, and he resented that the girl he fancied seemed to prefer the company of someone else.

Riggs arrived at the skatepark a few minutes before midnight. Moonlight skittered over the obstacles. Shadows menaced. A lone ruru called. He sat and rolled his board with his hands and waited. No Jamie. Ten minutes, twenty. He did a few half-hearted ollies, skated over the pyramid with a furious laziness. It wasn't as fun by himself. Less of a thrill, more a kind of humiliation, as though he had nowhere better to be in the middle of the night. After half an hour, thoroughly fucked off, he headed home.

The night's quiet was eerie. Every few minutes the sloshing boom of a wave on the beach rose up loud. A scraping noise came up from near the shops, and he paused. The sound was human. Someone was there.

He crept nearer. At first he saw nothing. Then, from the dark end of the shops, a flicker of torchlight. He walked slowly towards it, kept his feet slipper soft. He saw them soon enough, their faces in and out of view as their headlamps bounced around.

Riggs stood twenty metres away, obscured by the night, and watched. The metallic clink as Jamie shook a can, the wet sound of paint releasing. Riggs felt his whole body gather fist-like and hard. That dick was painting when he said he'd come skate.

A few minutes he watched them, and they sat after a while, looked up at their work. An enormous phoenix rising from a bed of fire on the side of the butcher's shop. It was cool, he'd give them that. The bird's feathers looked soft, a technical detail he would have thought impossible with the blunt instrument of the spray can, and the flames were geometric and bold. He saw Jamie turn to Penny, say something, his light playing on her face. Riggs could almost see her freckles, her green eyes. He was about to run up to them, scare them, hassle Jamie for standing him up, put his arm around Penny and try to win her over. He was going to tell them how cool the phoenix looked. He took a step — and froze. Penny leaned in, pressed her face to Jamie's and kissed him.

Jealousy pulsed in Riggs's neck, thick as blood and hot with shame and a punishing desire. All the way home he cursed them both, and himself, and the world and the stars — all of it. No one woke when he got in, despite his carrying on. He carried the phone to his room, closed the door and dialled the number for the local cop station. Hello, he'd said, yes, there are some kids vandalising the shops at Rocky Bay. Yes, they are there now. Two of them. A boy and a girl.

He'd run off in such a rage he didn't see what happened

next. He missed seeing Jamie move his head from hers, didn't hear Jamie say to Penny, No, we can't do this to Riggs.

He didn't see Penny touch her hand to her lips, her cheeks dark with humiliation. Didn't know how cold she felt then, despite her thick woollen jersey.

He didn't see the cops arrive. Didn't see them taken to her house; didn't see Damian break her finger. He never knew that Jamie pushed Damian, and that the older man fell and cut his head. Never heard Damian shouting, telling Penny and Jamie he would press charges if he saw his daughter hanging around with him again.

Riggs didn't know, and he never knew. If he had known all this, maybe he wouldn't have let Jamie ride that board at the Alley-Oop. Maybe he would've said, Mate, the screws are loose. Maybe he would've even tightened the screws himself.

Eyes back on the road, Riggs presses his foot on the accelerator, leaves the butcher's shop behind. He sneaks a look at Penny. She must be thinking about him too. She must be. Lord, it's all he can think about. He says, voice hardly more than a whisper, 'Where do you want to go?'

'Anywhere,' she says. 'I don't care.'

Riggs rubs his chin, grips the steering wheel tighter and says, 'Let's go see Jamie.'

JAMIE

JAMIE PLACES HIS CLOTHES in the bedroom drawers. Slips a sheet onto the bed, smooths out a duvet, hangs a towel on the rack in the bathroom. He potters around the house, the dog shadowing him. In the kitchen cupboards, Trish has stacked Maggi noodles and biscuits and chips and baked beans and canned tomatoes in two neat rows, and she's stocked the refrigerator with boxes of cheap beer, more than Jamie would normally put away in a month, maybe two. As darkness falls, a hammering rain kicks off, and an icy wind pierces the bach's many weak spots. He turns on the small heater, only it can't keep up, ticking away without pause, and the house grows ever more frigid. With numb hands and a pink nose, the dog sitting calm at his feet, Jamie looks at the fireplace. That would do it, he knows it would, it'd keep him and the dog warm. There might be firewood in the shed where Trish had told him the wetsuits would be, so he says to the dog, 'What do you reckon? Shall we go look?'

He hurries through the driving rain to the shed. The dog scampers on the pine needles, stopping to shiver the wet from her fur before they've even made it into the shelter. Jamie spies the wetsuits hanging from a nail in the far corner and, where the feet would be if the wetsuits were to walk, a pile of dry, dead pines. Wouldn't take much to get a bit of wood, set it up and set it alight, have a nice little bit of heat. The dog twists her head and her ears flip up, erect, as though she's curious as to why Jamie hasn't yet made this a reality. There's an axe on a bench mottled with paint the same berry-red as the house, and Jamie, cautious as a rabbit after dawn, picks it up, feels the weight of it in his hands and runs it along the side of one of the pine trunks. It's sharp and mean: a slice of wood peels where he's dragged the blade. He hesitates. What if he misses the wood and hurts himself? He chews the worry over until it's tender and raw. Would it be better to keep his hand and freeze his balls off? Or lose his hand and bleed out toasty and warm beside a roaring fire? He loves the sound of flames, the curling lick of them, the hypnotic dance of them, but in the end he sets the axe back on the bench. He can't trust his eyes, and if he can't trust them, how can he trust his hands, his arms, his legs? He can't, and that's the truth of it.

He leaves the hearth hollow and dark, and that first night he lies awake in bed for hours, the dog curled into his side, shivering in the cold, listening to the column heater click on and off at regular intervals as though to mark the end of the world.

He wakes before the sun to the sound of the ocean. The cold

front has moved on and the day is still. He climbs stiff-legged from the bed, watches the dog run on ahead. Jamie fills the jug, sets it to boil, makes a coffee. Drinks the coffee on the deck, his legs extended into the scrubby sand. The dog sniffs around the dunes and watches the birds. The air is crisp but not cold, the remnants of winter sharpness met with a hint of summer's warmth, and it's so beautiful. In just a few minutes, the sun has drifted up over the horizon, dropping a chain of light across the rippled silk of the water. Small waves rush to the shore, rolling over into bubbling wash that simmers on the sand and then eases backwards into the ocean once more. Three dark birds fly near the northern end of the beach, heading toward the cliffs, and when a larger wave rises up, the result of a swell originating much further out in the water, Jamie's sure he sees fish wavering in the clear-green face of the wave. Near his feet small grasses sprout and tiny insects crawl over the grains of sand. Looking closer, he sees each grain is singular. No two alike. The colours of the grains merge to form a tan-gold carpet further down the beach, and, in the space between tides, mounds of curling moss-green seaweeds and small logs of intricately battered driftwood mix with scattered shells of various hues: cream, mauve, stone, amber, grey and moonstone blue. There's almost too much beauty — the sun rises more, and the colours of the sky around it shift from lemon to peach, from peach to an arctic blue. Jamie doesn't want to, only he can't help himself: he starts to imagine a world where he might sit here and not see a thing.

There are plenty of things Jamie doesn't mind if he never sees again. Crocs. Fireworks. He can live without watching basketball, won't suffer the loss of computer games. The list of what he would miss is much longer. Movies at the IMAX, intense colours drilling into your brain. His mother's eyes — deep brown with an ever-growing navy ring around the iris. The extraordinary splendour of stars sprinkled over the dark sky. A desert, the rippling ochre and orange dunes shifting in the breeze. Clouds, every type: striated, fibrous, wispy, towering, mackerel, buttermilk, contour-less, rounded, puffy, domed. A waterfall. Macaw parrots, giraffes, the skeleton of a T-Rex. Crowds of people crossing at Shibuya Crossing — even if only on video. The flick of power poles out the car window when you're driving at speed. Views, any views, out any window, from any vantage point, across any vista. Colours. He can still see colour in all its varied shades, but in the grips of anxiety he's starting to fantasise about the day he'll forget the delicate hue of Iceland's Blue Lagoon, or the dappled sandy grey of his mother's horse when he was a child, or the flamboyant bursting of pink peonies, his favourite flower.

He'll miss watching surfers sliding on perfect waves, the grace of their bodies and boards as one. The ocean. The magnificent power of it in all weather. And skateboarders. Someone swooping in the bowl, a hand on the coping, the other hand on the board, legs in the air, a magical trick where the rider is inverted for the longest time, an impossible amount of time. He'll miss doing it, but Christ, he'll miss watching that bewitching dance on four wheels.

Then come more devastating thoughts. What if he never sees another face in his life? He'd forget his own face, wouldn't he? Given enough time. He'd forget the exact shape of his own eyes. The curve particular to his own smile.

His body. Someone else's body.

Her face. Her smile. Her body.

And, for the first time in his life, he thinks about killing himself.

Now the thought is in his head, it's hard to get it out. Maybe it has been there all along, lurking, a genetic inheritance from his dad. Madeline must have sensed it inside him and got out of there as fast as she could. Can't blame her, can he. Turns out she was right on the money.

Dr Sobhani has warned him not to catastrophise. Yet without test results, no news does not feel like good news. He showers in the mornings, procrastinates on starting work in the kitchen by repeatedly measuring the same benches, then, in the evening, he listens to the column heater ticking in the corner. Despite his attempts at busyness, a dismal quiet lingers in the house. The dog sulks, inheriting his mood. Jamie walks around heavy-footed, and though his sight remains for the most part intact, he keeps his hand on the wall to guide him. He's alone out here. If something dreadful were to happen ...

Soon, the dismal quiet moves within him. Thoughts of death become louder and more difficult to ignore. The thoughts find voice, and it speaks of the nothing that is coming. The nothing, the darkness, the blankness, the void. The voice tells him there is another way, and that his father, his father Paddy, understood this.

The man named Roy Avery his mother mentioned arrives in a beat-up brown Ford Sierra wagon and drops off some supplies so Jamie can begin work on the kitchen renovation. He figures he should make a start on it, for no other reason than to keep his mind occupied. Simple things, safe things. No sharp tools. In the evenings, bored to tears, he sits with the dog on the couch and gazes at the shelves of books. On the third night, he goes over to look more carefully at the titles. He's never found reading that interesting, but recognises some of them: *Brave New World, Moby Dick, Things Fall Apart, To the Lighthouse, Dracula, Middlemarch, One Day, The Shipping News.* A slim orange spine catches his eye. Maybe that's why he chose it — there's a chance he might finish it. Before ...

As it is, the words drift and pitch. He turns on another lamp beside the couch and, with the dog warm against his leg, he finds the milkiness lifting and words coming easier. It's a good distraction, the world of the book. The instant he puts the book down, the bad feeling creeps back, so he starts reading every second he can. In only a couple of days, he finishes two books and starts on his third. *The Sea, The Sea* by Iris Murdoch. At the end of page thirty-two he looks up, and there, out beyond the breakers, he thinks he spies a pod of dolphins.

Jamie stands to get a better view. In the flickering blue and white of the sea, he's not sure now whether he's seen dolphins or if it was a trick of his mind. The last dying kicks of two eyes refusing to give in. The dog stares at him with a doleful expression, and Jamie wishes for the first time since he's been at Desire that there was someone else to share this with, someone to confirm they saw it too, that it is real, that it's all real.

It's only midday, but he figures there's no medal for delaying the inevitable. He cracks his first beer. He holds the can tight and looks out to see if the dolphins, if that's what they were, are still there. There are just shafts of light on waves, dark pines looming on cliffs. He takes a sip. That first beer, he has to chew it down. Makes quicker work of the next two, though. Waves slash the shore and a rustling wind sneaks through the pines and above it all the voice rages in his head. Iris Murdoch sits neglected. He drinks the fourth beer, the fifth, looking for the number that might dull the urge to do something he might regret. He loses count before he gets there.

The next morning, after an hour with his head over the toilet bowl, he goes to the fridge to get another beer. Hair of the dog and all that — and, as though she can read his mind, the dog comes to him and drops a pine cone in the hope of him throwing it.

'Sorry, girl,' he says. Too hungover to play with his dog. What a useless, stupid, disabled piece of shit he is. Vomit pushes up and he's back on his knees. He's still there in the bathroom, head resting on the linoleum, when he hears his phone ringing. It takes him a moment to stumble through the house to locate it. The screen shows one slim bar of reception and a number Jamie doesn't recognise. He isn't sure he wants to take the call. The only person he needs to hear from is Dr Sobhani, and even then he's not certain he wants to talk to him. The phone goes silent.

Only ten seconds later, same number. Jamie grabs the phone, mostly to shut the damn thing up.

'Is that Jamie?'

Cautious, he says, 'It is.'

'Jamie, my man.' A short lull, then: 'It's Riggs.'

Riggs. The name hits him like a bullet to the brain. He'd thought he'd never forget that laid-back, almost monotonous voice, the intonation distinct to the entire Riggs family, and now look at him, he hasn't recognised the sound of his oldest friend's voice. What a shit friend he turned out to be.

'Riggs!' he says. 'Wow, it's good to hear from you.'

The dog lifts her ears.

'Of course, of course,' Riggs says. 'I mean, after all this time, a phone call is the least I can do, right?'

'Right,' Jamie says aloud, then, to himself: Riggs. Fuck.

Riggs doesn't hear his panic. He carries on yarning as if they'd seen each other only yesterday. 'So, you know, I'm back in Auckland and I figured, man, 'bout time I saw my old mate Jamie and what's her name, Marilyn?'

'Madeline,' Jamie says. 'And we've broken up.'

'You broke up? Man, sorry to hear that.'

It was three years ago, he is mostly over it. 'It's fine,' Jamie says. 'We weren't meant to be.'

Riggs says, 'I saw your mum.'

'What?'

'I talked to your mum. She said you were in the Coromandel?'

A peculiar sinking sensation tugs at his chest. The tendrils indicating his hangover headache is transforming into the start of a migraine lick at his temples. He needs a painkiller. 'Yeah,' Jamie says. He pinches the brow between his eyes. 'She's right.'

'Bro, where are you? I want to see you.'

Jamie says nothing until the silence becomes awkward. 'I'm in Pākarukaru. My uncle has a bach here.'

'Where the fuck is Pākarukaru?'

'North of Opoutere,' Jamie says. 'South of Pauanui.'

'Right,' Riggs says. 'That's a pretty nice part of the world.'

There's an even longer pause.

'Do you want to come out here?' Jamie says.

Riggs's response comes quick: 'Oh yeah, that'd be incredible. Perfect weather for a bit of beach time. You got room for Penny and me to crash?'

'Penny?' The sinking feeling increases and he's straining for breath.

'Yeah, man, she's here too. Thought it had been too long since we'd seen our folks, you know. They ain't getting any younger.'

'No, you're right,' Jamie says. 'There's room for you both. When do you think you will make it down here? I heard Penny had an exhibit planned?'

Riggs lets out an acidic laugh and says, 'Don't mention the exhibit, bro, whatever you do. You'll get yourself skinned. We could come down tomorrow?'

'Tomorrow,' Jamie says. 'Great.' In front of him, the waves are curving perfectly, holding up under an offshore breeze. He can make them out in rippled variations of clarity and opaqueness. Not one thing clear or easy in sight. There's something desperately wrong with him; no dog, no book, no glorious sunrise can change that. Despite his earlier desire for company, he wants no one to bear witness to this undoing of his life. He doesn't want them to come.

Riggs says, 'Do you need us to bring anything?'

'Just some food, what you want to drink. Whatever you want.'

'Great, bro, great,' Riggs says. 'I guess we'll see you mañana!'

'See you soon,' Jamie says, and Riggs disconnects the call.

Tomorrow. They will be here tomorrow. Riggs and Penny.

Penny. Christ. He's barely ready to see Riggs. He definitely isn't ready to see Penny Whittaker.

PENNY

THE WAIHEKE FERRY IS delayed, and when they finally leave Kennedy Point wharf, the boat churns brutal in the rough sea. For most of the trip Penny rests her head between her knees. How could she have been so naive?

Riggs ignores her. He's still bent out of shape from their argument about having another kid, and about her behaviour at his parents' house. 'Maureen had set up a room,' he's said several times, and though it upsets her to be fighting once again, she has no immediate plans to placate him, to make him feel better. Let him be angry.

Her phone's maps app tells them it's not much more than two hours' drive from Auckland to Pākarukaru. They stop once for petrol and a can of Coke for Riggs just after the Shri Guru Ravidas Temple, and continue on without speaking. Later, as they cross the Kōpū bridge, she starts to drift off to sleep, and in this dozing state pretends she hadn't made a fool of herself accepting the invite from Sally Trubridge, and that Rose hasn't died, she's instead sleeping in the back seat of the car. If Penny doesn't turn around, it might be true. And if she turns her head towards the window, she can no longer see Riggs either; she can see only the reflection of her own face in the glass. Looking away, it could be anybody driving the car.

The spell is broken when Riggs picks up his Coke, the can crinkling in his grip. Who is she even joking? There is nothing else, just this moment. Rose isn't sleeping in the car behind her, there is only this road, this country, this journey. Nothing more than mile after mile of twisting roads, red-roofed sheds and rusted-out car wrecks, glossy sorrel horses and ragged sheep awaiting their yearly shear, busted farm fences, flattened possums, dozens of wild goats grazing on the highway verge, valleys giving way to sneak peeks of the ocean, hillsides cleared of pines beside pockets of lush native bush. The sky low and blue, edged with skeins of cloud. Adam beside her, taking the corners too fast. No one in the back seat.

'Gonna be so good to see Jamie,' Riggs says. 'Been a long time. I bet he hasn't changed.'

It has been a long time. Bit more than twenty years.

She remembers the first time she saw him; the first time she saw Riggs. She'd been living on Waiheke for nearly a week, and she'd hated every minute. The narrow roads, the backward rural kids. School had started at the local high school but her parents hadn't enrolled her. They were debating whether to send her there to finish her final year or get her a place at

Elam art school in Auckland. Damian was convinced he could pull some strings and get her into the next intake. The idea made her skin crawl: art school with a bunch of people who'd assume she was only there because of her surname and would discount her work on principle? The idea of starting at a new high school was no better, but she waited, powerless, for her parents to make up their minds.

She saw the boys first at the skatepark, of course. She'd left the house to go for a walk, heading down the steep driveway to the small collection of shops that lined the coast below her parents' new build. It was four o'clock on a Sunday afternoon and most of the shops were closed up for the day: a butcher's shop, a dental clinic, a bakery called Simple Delights. Only a hardware store and a fish and chip shop, Catch of the Day, were still open. Across the road, an overgrown field bordered the primary school. She heard the sound first, then made out in the far corner a skatepark frothing with boys in baggy pants, oversized tee-shirts and baseball caps.

It didn't take long for her to note two boys who stood out from the group. They were talented, far more talented than all the others combined. Around her age, maybe a bit older. One of them was so tall he looked out of place on a skateboard, looming over it with a slight hunch, knees bent, arms loose at his sides. Blond hair sneaking out from under a navy Yankees cap. He pushed with his right foot, gathering speed. Then he stopped stamping his foot on the concrete and placed it on the deck of the board, rising and falling on the curves of the park, and she was struck by his delicate grace, how he lifted himself into the air and almost magically lifted his board too, landing on a smooth rail higher than his hip, then sliding down, arms outstretched for balance. When he dropped, he flicked out his heel and the board spun in a lateral pirouette. He saw her watching, his face broke into a wide smile, and she was ready to admit she should reconsider her estimation of him — he was a natural. Made it look easy. He wasn't too tall. He was a bit unkempt, wearing ridiculous clothes, a typical skateboarder, only she could see he was more than that. On the board he was a magician. A dancer, a rock star.

The other boy was almost the complete opposite. Dark hair, olive skin, thickset. This guy muscled his way on the board, each motion rough and square, like a grater through water, nothing smooth about it. Threw his chest around and ground his feet into the turns. Everything done with an insouciant swagger. He'd mastered many of the same tricks as the lanky boy, executing them with a defiant lift in his chest, as though daring anyone to judge him inferior.

It was clear they were both striving for the same thing, yet the results were night and day. The shorter boy was inelegant, and had no sense of how to fake it, though Penny thought there was a certain dignity to his obvious determination. You couldn't see the work with the blond boy, even when he fell. It felt fluent even when it was failure. Every time he dropped, every time he floated, her breath caught in her chest. When he flew past her, she saw curves, colours, energy, movement. Inspiration.

And there was something else there even more compelling than the boys on their boards. Graffiti. She'd seen plenty of it tagged on derelict buildings and motorway underpasses in Auckland, but this was different. It covered the entirety of a long brick wall bordering two sides of the park, and there was more on the skatepark itself too. All bright colours and dark outlines.

It was the antithesis of what her father had taught her to paint. It was expressive, bold, relevant. She walked slowly around the perimeter of the park to see it all. There were tagged initials and names, a pastel-coloured scarecrow lying on its side along a curved edge. The half-pipe was edged in lavender tulips. On another line of the park a tiger curled around a mermaid; next to them, an astronaut swam in an ocean with bright-green and fuchsia seahorses. All the while, the two boys were skating in and out of her vision.

They didn't properly meet that afternoon. That happened later. She left the skatepark, and on her way home stopped at the hardware store. Bought five bottles of spray paint — red, yellow, blue, white, black — and that night, after her parents were in bed and the clock had ticked over ten thirty, she carried the cans of paint down to the skatepark.

The park was deserted. All the kids had gone indoors to play Tony Hawk's Pro Skater 2 or something even more boring. She held a torch in one hand, the black spray can in the other, and started to outline her work.

It wasn't painting the way she was used to. Which is to say, it wasn't Damian's way. For him, there was one way to paint and one way only: realist landscapes, never abstracts, because, as Damian constantly said, abstraction was the type of art people made when they couldn't paint well enough to create truth: on canvas, with oil paints. Her father insisted she paint only with oils — he claimed they showed the true measure of an artist — so she'd never used acrylics or watercolours, and she'd certainly never created anything with spray cans. She wasn't sure what it was about the graffiti art that appealed to her. It was brave and loud, unapologetic about interrupting the world. Anyone could do it, even if no one was allowed to do it. No one was gatekeeping, there were no museum opening hours to keep viewers away from the art. She loved what she made with her father, and she loved traditional painting, but she was aware now that this wasn't all she could do, it wasn't all she could love.

She swung her arm, depressed the nozzle and let loose a spray of black. It came out in an uncontrolled mist. Maybe she was too far from the surface she wanted to work on; she moved closer. She was hoping to do a scorpion, but as she stood back to assess what she'd drawn she saw the shape was wrong. The proportions were out of whack. This was so much larger than anything she'd ever worked on, and the paint was coming out too fast. Fat drops ran down the curve of the half-pipe as though the scorpion was deflating and sinking to the earth.

'You've got to hold it more upright,' someone said. 'And don't press down too hard. Then it won't drip so much.'

The tall blond boy was beside her, holding his board under his arm. He wore a backpack and the same navy baseball cap.

'Shit,' she said. She took up the lid and attempted to put it back on the can. It fell to the ground and rolled away near the boy's feet.

'You're not in trouble,' he said. He knelt down, picked up the lid, came closer and held it out.

Penny stepped back in surprise, tripped over her bag and fell onto her arse.

'I'm not going to hurt you,' he said. 'Promise.' He held out his other hand.

She took it, and he pulled her back to her feet.

'What are you trying to paint?' he asked.

She grimaced and gestured at her work. 'A scorpion. I know. Bad.'

'It's cool,' he said, tipping his head from side to side. 'That's what we're all trying to do.'

'What do you mean?'

'We're all trying to take something bad and make it better.' He set his board on the ground, rolled it with his foot. 'Have you done this before?'

'No,' she said. 'Never.'

'Wow. How come that's so good then?'

'It's good?' She felt her cheeks flush.

'Really good,' he said. 'Shit, it's better than anything I've ever done, and I've been doing it for a few years.'

'I paint,' she said. 'You know, the normal way.'

'Cool,' he said. He swung his backpack off his shoulders and stuck his hand inside. 'Guess what,' he said.

'What?'

He pulled out a can of black spray paint. 'I can help you,' he said.

They worked together for two hours, the night air cooling until their breaths were coming in short, warm clouds in the torchlight, until their fingers were stiff with cold. The scorpion glowed white with a thick black border, rising out of geometric red, yellow and blue triangles. Penny painted a lot, finished a lot of artworks, and nothing felt the way this did. Was it the illicit nature of the work? The immediate and bold effect of it? The night, chill and dark around her? Or was it working with someone else? With him?

'It's amazing,' he said. 'I love it.'

She looked down at her feet. No one really complimented

her art. Her mother ignored her work, on the whole, and Damian offered criticism veiled as advice. 'Someone's going to paint over it, aren't they,' she said.

'Probably,' the boy said. 'Like my mum always says, good things come, and good things go, but at least they come.'

They packed up their cans, and he took the skateboard up under his arm again. 'What you doing tomorrow night?' he said. 'You want to meet again, do something else?'

'Yes,' she said quickly, too quickly.

He smiled and walked away, and he was partway across the field when he turned and shouted, 'I forgot to ask your name!'

'Penny!' she called to him.

'Penny,' he said, 'I'm Jamie.'

He walked away in the direction of Rocky Bay. The tips of her fingers throbbed, unused to the effort needed to depress the spray can. She watched him melt into the night, navy cap almost as dark as the world around them, the blond hair sneaking out the sides catching the last of the light from her torch, his skateboard under his arm, backpack slung over one shoulder, and her body buzzed as if she was intoxicated. She wasn't sure if it was from the smell of the paint, or the strange, slightly askew scorpion they'd created on the curving half-pipe, or the plain fact of him, but the truth of it was, she understood she'd underestimated this island.

When she arrived the next night, Jamie wasn't alone. He was with Riggs.

She glances over to Riggs now. The interior of the car is close and warm, and his cheeks are flushed a pale pink. He looks much the same as he did then: wide across the shoulders, thick arms, definitely attractive in a rough, thoroughly masculine way. Only he's not quite his old self: he's not on a skateboard. He's sitting ramrod straight in the driver's seat, with his chest pushed forward at an awkward angle. A muscle in his lower jaw tightens and loosens in a manic rhythm; he's clearly in pain.

'I could drive,' she says.

He swivels his head to look at her and then turns back to the road. 'No,' he says. 'Why?'

'I thought you might want a break.'

He licks his lips and readjusts his grip. 'You enjoy being in control of everything, don't you?' he says.

'I don't,' she says.

Riggs laughs, and the sound is distorted by a bitter edge. 'I can be trusted to get us there safely,' he says. 'I'm not a total fuck-up.'

'I never said that,' Penny says.

The car smells strongly of some chemical cleaner and a headache flirts at the sides of her head. Surely this bach can't be too far away.

'You don't have to say it,' Riggs says. 'I already know what you think of me.'

Brutally confident in his own opinion, hyper-inflated in his belief in himself: that was Riggs. Honestly, it drives her crazy. He was exactly the same the first night they were introduced.

'Penny, this is Adam, but everyone calls him Riggs. Riggs, this is Penny, she's an artist.'

Riggs grabbed her hands and held them tight in his two,

and he stared directly at her, unblinking, his mouth open. After a minute he said, 'Hello, sexy.'

'Give her a break, Riggs,' Jamie said.

'No,' Riggs said, 'I think I'm in love.' He leaned forward to kiss her, and she ducked away.

Riggs had laughed and said, 'Joking, I'm joking.' Only then his face had straightened, and he'd said, fully serious, 'I'm not joking.'

He didn't come with her and Jamie every night they went out to paint. She knew it wasn't exactly painting, only that was what she called it. It wasn't graffiti to her. It was art. Street art, a modern mural. Riggs referred to it as 'their hobby' in a way that suggested he thought it was juvenile and asinine. When he did come, he stood very close to her, at times too close, peppering her with questions. Did she want to go skinny-dipping, what was her middle name, were her parents rich? He'd seen the house, he said, on the hill. She had the impression he was jealous, though whether it was of Jamie or of her she couldn't tell. He was supremely assured, in a way she wasn't, and although she found Jamie more attractive, there was something about Riggs, she had to admit it; there was something magnetic. She'd not known then that this charismatic quality of his was unstable, unpredictable, flammable, and that if the chemistry faded she'd be left with nothing.

It was his confidence that persuaded her that having a child would be okay. She'd said no kids for years. She'd seen what it had done to her mother's career. Meg Novak had been a 'promising artist' too, or so the profiles of her father in *Artforum* and *Art World* explained. 'Meg Novak, once a promising artist in her own right, disappeared into obscurity after the birth of their only daughter, Penelope.' The reporters never failed to make this point, and it haunted Penny that a regret, or at least one as big as a child, could never be reversed and would end your burgeoning career.

Her mother wasn't totally forgotten. She had a small cult following in niche corners of the New Zealand arts community, but that was it: no fame, no fortune, no influence, no power. She'd stopped painting altogether after Penny was born, and though she never let on that it bothered her, Penny knew she must hold it against her. If that was the price you paid for having a child, Penny knew it was one she would never accept.

So that cool April afternoon when she sat on the side of the bathtub, waiting for the result of the pregnancy test to show itself, her only thought was no, please no. She'd imagined she'd never love anything more than she loved art. Her father certainly loved nothing more than his vocation — not her, not her mother. Not even any of the women he formed short-lived but combustive affairs with. When she moved to Los Angeles with Riggs, she assumed that her art would sustain her and had no expectation he would be the love of her life. She'd left with him because she needed to leave, because he offered her the life she wanted. Because he loved her with a power she'd never felt before, and because he was fun.

And it was fun. Honestly, it was. They travelled, he skated, she painted. Her broken fingers healed and for a long time she put Waiheke Island out of her mind. Didn't want to think of those sparkling waters between rising hills, the lush green bush, the winding roads, the bonfires on the golden sand, the moonlight on rising tides, the softness of sand dunes, the skatepark, the phoenix on the side of the butcher's shop. Didn't want to think about it, and it wasn't as hard as she'd thought it might be to block it out.

Their life together was good. She wouldn't have stayed with him otherwise. He started winning competitions, lots of them, sponsors flooded in, he was on the cover of a skate magazine. She was painting, and she could see her style developing, improving, even if she had none of Riggs's success. She liked working at Sketchy's for the friends and the cheap art supplies. Riggs loved her, was proud of her, and he made her laugh. He liked to take her out for margaritas and tacos on Friday nights. Took her to galleries in Paris, Florence, Buenos Aires, and listened while she talked about the art she loved and the art she disliked. Didn't force her to make nice with her father when they visited, allowed her to take over the wardrobe with her shoe obsession. There were always people around Riggs; they were drawn to him, and for good reason. They had enough money to live and enjoy themselves. For so many years, Penny had no responsibilities to anyone or anything except her art and to Riggs. All he asked was that she was loyal to him, and she was. She was, in a way, happy. And then, without meaning to be, without planning it, she was pregnant.

When the two lines appeared strong and instant, she didn't feel joyous. She didn't want kids. Had never wanted kids. And then Riggs came into the bathroom.

'What are you doing?' he asked, but she didn't need to answer. The test in her hand gave the game away. His face went red, and he knelt in front her. 'Fuck me,' he said. 'Penny, we're gonna have a kid?'

'Riggs,' she said. 'Come on.'

‘I’m being reasonable,’ he said. ‘A little Riggs. Maureen’s gonna flip.’ He took the test from her and stared at the lines, a man in love.

‘You know I don’t want kids,’ Penny said. Even she heard how selfish and strange it was to say such a thing when she was pregnant. It had seemed sensible and mature to be so self-aware, yet she’d never anticipated how it might feel to say such a thing when something, someone, was growing inside her. An immediate unsteadiness came over her, and she pressed the heels of her hands into her eyes.

‘It’s gonna be all good, babe,’ Riggs said. ‘I’ll help, I’ll help you, it won’t mean the end of anything.’ He squeezed her knee. ‘We’re not your parents. I’m not your dad, and you’re not your mother.’ He laughed. ‘I mean, fuck, could I be any more different to your dad?’

It was only Riggs’s buoyant optimism that helped her believe it would be okay. His assurances, his promises, his total faith that this wouldn’t mean the end of her career — she wanted to believe it.

He bought the Woodland Hills house a few days after the pregnancy test.

‘Here,’ he said, leading her to the studio beyond the pool. ‘Here you can work.’ It was funny, she thinks now, how fervently they’d imagined property could make a dream life come true.

Rose was born after a punishingly long labour, her umbilical cord wrapped around her neck like a pulsing necklace. The glimpse of her moments after birth made Penny’s heart skip a beat, two. The tiny body the colour of Winsor & Newton’s Purple Lake, yet unmistakably a baby, a real baby. The hospital staff, faces hidden behind their masks, had glinting disquiet in their eyes. They rushed around with the newborn, their loud voices fake with a pretend calm, and Penny wondered if she'd carried this child all these months to lose her. When she heard the baby scream for the first time, a feeling relative to relief rushed through her, but when a nurse handed her the baby wrapped in a soft white towel, it wasn't love at first sight. Not the way you read about it. She held the squirming, slippery body that was her Rose, and understood she wasn't good enough to do this. It was beyond her. Sure, she was exhausted after a thirty-eight-hour labour, but her first thought was: All that for this? And then guilt consumed her, a guilt so pure and profound she knew she'd spend the rest of the child's life attempting to erase it.

The first few weeks were a hellish blur. Rose wouldn't sleep and Penny struggled to breastfeed. No matter what she tried, and she tried everything anyone suggested — lactation cookies, nursing more often, herbal teas, pumping after every feed, smoothies full of oats, flaxseed, fennel, fenugreek, blessed thistle, brewer's yeast — there was never enough for her insatiable daughter. She was a failure. And always there was this rage. She didn't want to worry about optimising her milk production; she wanted to think about her work. She missed her work in a severe and personal way. She missed the person she had been.

The forest-green shit staining Rose's nappies reminded Penny of Phthalo Deep Green. Rose's creamy pink feet were an exact match for Pale Rose Blush. She couldn't admit it to anyone, not even Riggs, but she resented the child for her intrusion on her life. Exactly what she'd feared would happen had happened. Her daughter didn't deserve that kind of mother.

She deserved a mother who never doubted. A mother who could hold it together, could let go of everything else and be present for her. A mother who never felt torn to be somewhere else, doing something else.

Until slowly it changed. When Rose was nine weeks old, the longest nine weeks of Penny's life, she slept during the day for longer than forty minutes. Penny showered, had a nap, and still Rose was sleeping. Instead of another round of feeding, changing, stimulating play — but not overstimulating! — and then putting her down for another sleep, there was a quiet pause in the house. Penny felt refreshed. Alive in a way she'd forgotten she could be. She took out her sketchbook and began to plan out a new painting. By the time Rose woke, Penny was looking forward to seeing her. She bent over the bassinette and, for the very first time, Rose smiled at her mother.

That smile. It wasn't gas. It wasn't a facial tic. It was a real smile. Her mouth opened wide, her bare gums shiny and pink, her cheeks swelling to peachy dumplings so chubby a tiny dimple appeared on the left side of her face. It felt like a cliché, the suffering mother won over by the baby smiling at them for the first time. Only it was true for Penny.

She felt transformed. It wasn't easy, or painless. Frustration and weariness plagued her. She bucked against the new boundaries of her identity, lost in a mire of wet wipes, blood, tears. Mastitis burned in her breasts, and her paintbrushes lay untouched for weeks and then months. Woven through it all was the question: is this worth it? And then she swiftly moved on. There was no point in dwelling on what might have been. Her daughter must never know that Penny was uncertain, that she wavered almost every day. Her beautiful baby girl, smiling in her bassinette, the clear, mellow Californian light pouring in through the window — she would know she was loved.

We could have another baby. Do it right this time, he'd said. The suggestion was as compelling as it was repulsive. She wants another child, and she doesn't. They tried it once; she took a chance and look how it ended. And what she didn't say to Riggs, because she can't yet say it to herself: she doesn't deserve another child.

Rose died because she, her mother, hadn't taken her to see a doctor earlier. Who cared what Riggs had said about bruises and skateboarding and what it meant to fall. If she'd been alert, if she hadn't been so distracted by her own desires, she would have taken her to see a doctor. She wants another child, and she desperately doesn't, and the two opposing desires seem impossible to reconcile.

Without indicating, Riggs slows the car and swings right. For a flash she sees Rose in the trees: her small face hovering, the impish smile, the long, shimmering hair glittering in the green. The car takes the turn and the face is gone. Penny holds her hands in her lap and stares out the window, unblinking, breathless. Only it's hopeless. The face doesn't return.

'We're here,' Riggs says.

They leave the road and roll slow down a long driveway. There's nothing to see but dense pine forest. No house, no ocean. Not yet, at least. They're there somewhere, and so is Jamie. Light flickers through the trunks in long panels, yellow and somehow tangible, and she winds down the window to feel it on her face. A heady, piney scent fills the car, and on top of it the fresh, salty bite of the ocean. Over the car's engine, the faint pummel of surf. She pulls off her beanie, toys with the ribbed edge, and then returns it to her head again. They've arrived.

JAMIE

THEY HEAR THE CAR a few minutes before it pulls up. The dog lifts her head from sleep, ears pricked high. It's not long after four in the afternoon. Already the light is stealing away from the day, though there are plenty of hours left before true darkness. Jamie sets his book down on the deck. Dylan Thomas now, *In Country Sleep*. He stands slowly. The dog jumps down from the deck and runs around ahead of him. Jamie pauses at the corner of the house where he can't be seen, letting the dog do the hard work of breaking the ice.

'Oh, hello there, sweet doggy.' Penny. Her voice is deeper, stained with a Californian drawl. When was the last time he saw her? Would've been Riggs's eighteenth birthday party, a week before they left without telling anyone she was going with him. He sees her now as he saw her then: Penny standing by the front door, holding a beer, laughing at a story Riggs's sister Belinda had told her. Later, dancing to the music in the lounge, hips sliding to a tempo just off the beat of the music. Later still, hours after midnight, kissing Riggs in the carport, where they thought no one could see, her face with his face and his hand on her arse, Jamie's heart dropping to his feet.

The dog lets out one sharp bark and scarpers back to Jamie, flicking its gaze to the new arrivals.

'It's all right, girl,' Jamie says. No use delaying the inevitable. No promises were made; no promises were broken. He'd said what he'd said, so who could blame her? He steps around the corner of the house.

There they are: Riggs, hair buzzed to the skull, leaning into the boot of the car, pulling out the luggage. A tattoo on his forearm, a red flower: Rose. And Penny. She's brushing pine needles from her jeans, looking around at the trees, the house, the beach, her face wide open and curious as ever, as if she notices things no one else could ever hope to observe. The reason he'd liked her, the reason he said she seemed like an artist to him when they met. It was as though she understood the world had shapes and colours and meanings that connected in ways he wished he understood too. She's aged, yeah, though it's subtle. Softer around the face. But that mouth that edges up to a smile. Eyebrows thick over those enormous green eyes. She's plain-faced, no make-up, in black jeans and a striped tee-shirt, a red fisherman's beanie. Her hair is shorter, the ends curling out from the edge of the hat. Still beautiful. Still goddamned beautiful.

'Hey, guys,' Jamie says, chill, unperturbed. No reason to let them know what's going on with him. They don't need to know he's falling apart. Christ, look at them. Grown adults.

They've got it all sorted out. Clear, tanned skin. Matching silver suitcases. American accents. A diamond ring glittering on her left hand. Shit.

Penny runs around from her side of the car, calling his name. She rushes in close. Her arms light around his back, though her embrace is strong and right, and he holds himself coiled, wary of what might be let loose. It's been months since he's been hugged. Years. Jesus, the last person to touch him was Madeline.

'Jamie,' she says, pulling her head back to look at him. 'How are you?'

'Penny.' He steps out of her embrace. 'You've met the dog.'

'Your dog? He's gorgeous.'

'She's a she,' Jamie says. 'Though I don't think she's particular about her pronouns.'

'Does she have a name?'

'I just call her Girl.'

'What kind of man doesn't name his dog?' Riggs calls from the far end of the car.

'I'll just call you Girl too, then.' Penny buries her face into the dog's long fur. 'What a sweet girl you are.'

A tightness in his chest at the sight of her with the dog. He says, 'Didn't know you were a dog person.' She glances up at him and says so softly he knows Riggs can't hear, 'Plenty of things about me you don't know.'

There's no time to reply, no time to figure out what she might mean — Riggs is there beside them, dropping the bags with an exaggerated huff and pulling Jamie to him with one arm, leaning halfway to a hug.

Jamie leans in. The thick, hefty intensity of Riggs. They'd

never been friends who hugged, although the day after Jamie had found his dad, Riggs had flown into Jamie's temporary bedroom in the basement, leapt towards him with his arms extended, tucked Jamie into his chest and held him there, kissing his head and his forehead and near his ear, whispering, 'I got you, bro, I got you.'

Here in the pine trees Riggs pats Jamie's back, and there's a long pause before either pull away.

'Jamie,' Riggs says. 'How long's it been? Fifteen years? Mint spot you've got here. Bit of a drive but woo! Sick, bro, sick.'

It hasn't been fifteen years, he wants to say, it's been twenty, only he's shocked into silence by his own harshness. Get a grip, ya finicky bastard. It's Riggs, for goodness' sake. Who cares how long it's been? Enjoy it, they'll be gone again soon, thank Christ.

'It's pretty nice, now it's getting a bit warmer,' Jamie says. 'When do you go home to LA?'

Riggs and Penny look at each other and Riggs says, 'Don't know yet. Playing things by ear.'

'Right,' Jamie says.

The three of them stand watching the waves through the trees. There's an awkward, electric tension between them. The dog, sitting between Jamie's feet, appears to feel it. She shivers, then takes off down the dune onto the sand, chasing a handful of seagulls bathing in a pocket of light at the water's edge.

'You gonna show us round, or what?' Riggs says.

Jamie, feeling stupid, says 'Right' a second time and leads them in through the back door.

'This is your room,' he says, gesturing to the bedroom at the far end of the hall. He'd made up the bed with thin sheets and the spare blankets from the linen cupboard. It had been an effort to forget who'd be in there together, and he looks over at them now, a couple who've built a life together. They are lucky to have found each other, and to make it work for so long. He isn't nasty enough to begrudge them that.

He stands back out of their way, lets them stick their heads into the tiny bathroom and grimy laundry, the old dunny, then follows them to the kitchen with the dusty windowsill. He'd spent the day tidying up, but the place still looks shabby: the grotty couch, the mildewed curtains. He picks up his dirty socks from beside the couch and balls them in his fist. All the cleaning in the world can't hide the fact he's a middle-aged loser living in squalor. Inviting them here was a mistake.

'Like what you've done with the place,' Riggs says. 'Real bachelor pad.'

'It's my uncle's bach,' Jamie says. 'He's letting me stay here while I fix his kitchen.'

Riggs takes in the entirely unchanged kitchen and nods. 'Looks like you've been real busy.'

'Riggs,' Penny says. 'Don't be mean.' She stands in front of the sliding doors. 'What a view,' she says.

Riggs jabs Jamie in the stomach. 'I'm joking, man,' he says. 'I wouldn't be working if I was living here either. Bet you're too busy surfing.'

'Not much surfing going on,' Jamie says. 'Mostly I've been reading.'

'Pull the other one, mate. Come on, let's sit out here and have a beer and you can tell me what you've really been up to.'

Riggs opens a box of pale ale from a craft brewing place

in Motueka that Jamie hasn't heard of and takes two out to the deck. Riggs leans his bottle to Jamie's.

'Cheers,' Jamie says.

'To friends,' Riggs says.

'Right,' Jamie says.

The dog scampers up, sandy and wet. Penny sits down next to Jamie. 'Where's my beer, then?' she says.

Riggs's back straightens. 'You drinking?'

'Yeah,' she says. 'Get me a beer too, please.'

'You don't drink,' Riggs says.

'Not for a while, no,' Penny says. 'But tonight I feel like a beer.'

'I only got enough beer for me and Jamie. Why don't you have a glass of the sav I got? You used to enjoy the vino.'

Jamie can't quite make out Penny's expression. Whether she's genuinely put out. Whether Riggs is truly surprised. He's out of the loop here, twenty years out of it, and he's at best the useless third wheel. Everybody knows you can't skate on three wheels.

'No thanks,' she says. 'I'd like a beer.' She pauses. 'Is it such an inconvenience when I change my mind?'

Riggs raises his eyebrows and says, 'Come on, don't give me that. You haven't drunk in years. And I mean, if we're going to start trying again ...'

'Fine,' she says, her shoulders dropping ever so slightly. 'I'll have a glass of wine.'

Jamie's starting to get it, or thinks he does: the oppressive weight of other people's expectations, the feeling that those closest to you have the hardest time accepting that you've changed. He says, 'I'll have the wine. You have my beer, Penny, if that's what you want.'

'Whatever,' Riggs says. 'Both of you have a beer, for fuck's sake, let's not be pussies about it.'

Penny prods Riggs with her foot and says, 'Can you grab me one then?'

'Get it yourself, babe,' Riggs says. 'You got two legs.'

The atmosphere stiffens.

'I'll get you one,' Jamie says. He stands quickly and turns. Doesn't see the door frame until he's right on it. No time to stop or twist out of the way, and he slams into it with a heavy, brutal collision. Penny yelps, a squeal not unlike the dog's whining to be let out in the mornings.

'I'm fine,' Jamie says. 'Got a bit of a head rush and couldn't see.' It's rotten to lie, but he doesn't want to tell the truth. Blood pools in his cheeks and his face grows hot.

Penny hovers beside him. 'Sit down,' she says. 'Riggs was right, I can get my own beer. Are you sure you're okay?'

'Fine. I'm fine.' But he lets her lead him back to where he was sitting. Riggs gives him a look that's equal parts quizzical and suspicious, and Jamie tries to smile. Penny goes into the house and Jamie touches his face. It's tender and swollen right beside where he hit his head at the Alley-Oop. Soon it will be sore as hell.

He calls into the house. 'Penny, would you bring some ice?'

She comes out with a beer under her arm and a few ice cubes wrapped in a butter-yellow tea towel.

'You getting soft in your old age?' Riggs says. 'Once upon a time we didn't ice our injuries.'

Jamie feels like laughing or crying, maybe both. Icing his injuries is the least of the things that has changed about him. Penny sinks down onto the deck between them and drinks from her beer. Jamie looks at her hand, the one her father hurt.

Her pinkie finger is still crooked, bent inwards in an unnatural curve. The sort of damage you would have to break again to properly heal.

Riggs and Penny. Blink and it might actually be the same as Riggses' eighteenth. The three of them sitting on the deck of the Riggses's house waiting for the party to begin, Spiller's 'Groovejet' on the stereo, mosquitoes swirling around their ankles. Jamie shifts the ice against the throb. He can't believe she's sitting beside him. The aching in his head blends in with the strangeness he feels, and he takes two Panadeine from his pocket and swallows them down with his beer, hoping they will ease both his nerves and his pain. He clears his throat with a thin cough and says, 'When did you guys fly in?'

Riggs presses his hands together and clicks his knuckles, rolls his head on his neck. 'Got in last week,' he says. 'You're not working?'

'I'm not working right now,' he says.

Penny picks up the Dylan Thomas book. 'You're reading this?'

'Yes, I'm reading that,' he says. 'It's really good.'

'And they say people don't change,' she says. 'You weren't much of a reader back in the day. And now *poetry*.'

He rubs his chin and says, 'They're not always right. People change plenty.' He isn't certain about this, even if he's made it sound as if he is.

'Bro, I thought you were joking when you said you were reading. I thought reading might be code for something else.'

'Code for what?' Jamie says.

'I dunno. Porn, maybe. Weed.'

'Nothing that exciting going on out here,' Jamie says.

'That was before I arrived,' Riggs says, and they both laugh, because he's right: Riggs is the fun. The big ideas were his. The night they camped out in the reserve when they were eleven, a cat prowling at midnight sending them into terrified hysterics; the tree hut they built in Jamie's backyard with no parental oversight and dodgy technique; at fourteen, stealing Trent's beers and getting smashed in the hollow behind the half-pipe. Jamie rubs his chest and feels a strange new warmth flood through him. Been a long time since he's laughed. Feels good.

The sunlight shifts then and picks up a glimmering set of waves stacked out as far as you can see. Riggs sets his beer down and peels the label off, placing the shreds in a neat pile. He never stops moving. Peeling, shredding, setting the strips in the pile, his leg bouncing around. He plunges into a detailed list of all the things he's done since he left New Zealand, leaving no space for Jamie to talk or ask questions. He talks about comps in Barcelona, Cape Town, Guangzhou, Lyon. Tells Jamie about that one time he made the cover of *Slap* magazine. July 2006. Then he starts on explaining his YouTube show, the X Games, competing at the first Street League Skateboarding comp in Glendale, Arizona: 'I think some people thought I was in with a chance to win but I mean, come on, when Nyjah is there, what chance does anyone else really have?'

Riggs doesn't stop talking for a long time, prattling on at a frenetic pace that Jamie can't keep up with. He's listening with only half an ear, to be honest. Part of him is bitter with unexplored envy of his friend's life, the life he'd wanted for himself. The travel, the skateboarding. But there's something else distracting him from Riggs's long-winded history. The ice helped numb his forehead but it can't dull his body's keen awareness of Penny, right there, no more than a footstep away.

RIGGS

WAS NEW ZEALAND ALWAYS this fucking beautiful? Maybe he appreciates its natural charms more now he's older. Age changes you, sneaky-like, even while you strive desperate to stay the same. It modifies your priorities. You begin to treasure things you never had time for when you were younger. Like birds. Nature. Sunsets. Even the air in Aotearoa is thin and clear and perfect. He's so used to the haze and smog of Los Angeles, he'd forgotten about this. Penny told him how the European painters arrived on these shores and freaked out, not understanding how to paint the quality of light here. They tried to reproduce the landscape using their old techniques and it didn't do the place justice. He sees it now; he truly sees it. The magic of this place. Waves curl in, clouds bunch exquisite on the horizon, sunset falls in a sweet pastel radiance. It's bloody heaven. And here, beside his oldest, bestest mate and his missus, taking it all in. He's certainly one lucky bastard.

Riggs brushes scraps of beer label from his leg onto the pile he's made on the deck and sets his last empty beer bottle — number six, nice even number — with the others, jiggles his legs in the sand. He's full up and jittery on the beauty of the place and the prize of these people beside him and he feels like jumping off a cliff or something. Maybe he should get another tattoo. Maybe they should all get matching tattoos. Or maybe they should go skinny-dipping. Why not, look at it, that sublime swath of ocean. It would feel great right now to ease into it, water slick on skin. Maybe later. Penny might join him if it's dark enough.

'You know what we should do,' he says. 'We should have a bonfire. Like the old days.'

What he means is a bonfire like the last one at Rocky Bay. What a night that was. Drunk out of his skin. Last exam done and dusted and freedom in sight. His birthday mere weeks away, and then it was Christmas. He'd won the Alley-Oop a week before and he was high on the thrill of it all. He'd lit the bonfire, kissed that girl, what was her name, Mallory, kissed her until she squealed, and then he ran naked down the beach into the starlit water. God, he missed being young.

He doesn't remember Penny or Jamie at that bonfire, but that's no surprise. He doesn't remember everything that happened to him growing up. Only the fundamentals. The rest of it — hell, if he doesn't remember it, it can't be important.

Jamie says, 'We're not allowed bonfires on this beach.'

Riggs taps out a drum-roll beat on his knees. 'Rules,' he says, 'are only made to be broken. Is there any dry wood around, bro?'

Jamie nods, biting on his lower lip. So cautious.

'There's a few dead pines in the shed,' he says.

'Sweet.' Riggs is off to the shed, then begins dragging the trees, one at a time, down to the sand. His back snaps and rattles. Pain you wouldn't believe running over him with gravelly spikes. Doesn't bother saying anything about it to Penny or Jamie. He's found it's near impossible to explain to people the way the pain feels. What it does to you, nibbling at your brain. Bumping into you when you're trying to be someone else, pulling you back to the place of misery. His temples pique; he's holding his jaw clenched so hard the muscles throb and grouse.

Jamie helps him pile the trees together, and Penny carries down some smaller sticks and pine cones.

'Is there any diesel in that shed?' she asks Jamie.

'I spied a can of petrol,' Riggs says. 'That'll do.'

'Mate,' Jamie says. 'Not petrol. You want to blow your head off?'

Riggs shuffles, throws a few fake punches at Jamie and softly rounds one off his shoulder. His back is howling. 'You know me, bro,' he says. 'Not scared of anything.' Not true. He's scared of pale little bodies. Of caskets so small they should be illegal.

He races up to the shed, the dog at his heels, running fast to lose his breath and the fear inside his exertion. There, in the corner, a rusted-out petrol tin. Gives it a shake: half full, he'd say, if he were a betting man. Which he is. He unscrews the lid and takes a sniff, rich and dense, better than any cologne. And he is right. The light from the setting sun sparkles on the splashing remnants in the tin. Half full. No one can deny he's an optimist. There's a box of matches too, on the shelf above. A dozen matches, the red tips still bright. They'll do.

Back down the dune, the petrol can sloshing in his hand, the setting sun melting the air orange. The dog takes off down the beach to tease the incoming tide, and Riggs strides around the circumference of the fire, the lid of the can removed, petrol soaking into the straggly pile of dead pines. Careful not to get any on his feet or body. He's not that much of an idiot. Or is he? He takes the box from his pocket, swipes a matchstick down the red phosphorus. It doesn't take. He shifts his hold on the match and curves his wrist to strike again.

'You want me to try?' Penny says.

'I don't,' he says. 'I'm good.' Does Penny roll her eyes? The sun lingers at eye level and she lifts her hand to shade her face. Maybe he's too quick to judge. Hard to break those habits of thinking about someone once they set in. Hard to break a habit when you mistake it for who you are.

A second attempt. Match down the box. Sparks flare but don't hold. The match snaps, useless, and he tosses it into the pile of wood to burn. Tries a new match, his movement twitchy with frustration. One lone white-blue spark springs out — small at first, a circle of heat, then it rears up and swells to a flame.

'Careful,' Jamie says.

'Nothing great ever comes out of being careful, bro,' Riggs says, and he stands away from the wood and flicks the burning match into the petrol-soaked bonfire. Flames sweep up, engulfing the entire pile of wood in mere seconds. Amazing, one small action, to create such a devastating reaction. He likes the feeling it gives him to be so powerful and destructive. Nothing can touch him. The flames rage, and he watches them lick upwards, hungry for air. The heat and the smoke and the sound of the waves: it's as if he's hallucinated the past into being, the Rocky Bay bonfire round two. He picks up another heavy log from the sand and throws it into the white-hot heart of the fire just to watch it burn.

'Come sit down,' Jamie says.

Riggs drops to the sand and drapes his arm around Jamie's narrow shoulders. 'I've missed you, bro,' he says.

He'd had mates in the States, plenty of them. He was a minor celebrity at one point. Skating royalty, almost. Invitations to parties pinged in constantly, and these weren't any old parties: they were packed dense with cool people, beautiful people, famous, rich people. Skateboarding was no longer a crime; it was now desirable. He was desirable. The invitations flowed as generous as the cocaine. It was easy to say yes to the drink, to the drugs, to the women.

It was fun, and he still likes to have fun. Only in the end it was hollow. They weren't true friends. His accent confused people, and every once in a while he took a joke too far. He knows he alienates people, freaks them out. He's missed Jamie. Jamie understood him. He hadn't realised how special that was. And now, here they are. Together.

'I missed you too,' Jamie says. 'I missed both of you.'

'You should've visited us in LA,' Riggs says, squeezing Jamie's shoulders. Feels good to hold him close and hard. 'I could've taken you on a skate tour of the city. Done our thing in Dogtown.'

Penny makes a snorting sound, and Riggs says, 'What?'

'Nothing,' she says. 'He's right, Jamie, you should have come.'

Why does she always have to make him feel like he's making a fool of himself? He cracks open another beer. Cool it, cool it.

No need to get into it right now: not now, not when everything's so good and so right. It's like no time has passed. He can almost pretend they have their whole lives ahead of them and their mistakes are yet to come.

'Now it's great here, I'm not denying it,' Riggs says. 'But I don't know how you've done it, Jamie.'

'Done what?'

'Stayed living here,' Riggs says. 'Why didn't you ever leave New Zealand? I mean, it's nice and green and all, but—'

'But what?'

Riggs shrugs. 'It's a rite of passage, bro. The big OE.'

'I've travelled,' Jamie says. 'It's not as if I've never left New Zealand.'

'It's not too late, bro. You could come back with us, live in LA for a while. We got a sweet place up in the hills, swimming pool, spare bed.'

'Maybe,' Jamie says.

'Moving away and living somewhere else opens your mind to other cultures. Makes you grow up a bit.'

'Riggs, you've been living in the States,' Penny says. 'What massive cultural learnings are you going on about?'

'I've travelled,' Riggs says. 'Extensively.'

'I'll get us another drink,' Penny says. 'Leave you two to your deep and meaningful.'

He watches her walk up the sand, the shift of her arse in those jeans.

'Just because I've stayed doesn't mean I'm a loser,' Jamie says. 'I'm curious about the world and interested in other cultures. I guess I wanted to stay near Mum. I owe her that.'

Riggs snorts. 'You don't owe your mum your whole life.'

'Well, there's a few ways to look at it, I suppose. I mean, man, your parents are nice people, Riggs. Funny, caring, kind. I don't know why you wouldn't want to hang out with them more.'

'If you love them so much, why didn't you go and say hello when you were staying with your mum a few weeks ago?' Riggs's voice is broken-glass sharp.

Jamie stares over the fire to the beach where a pair of pitch-black oystercatchers wander on the wet sand, beaks the same colour as the wicking flames. After a while he says, 'You're right. I should've gone over and said hello. I owe them that.'

'Stop saying that,' Riggs says.

'What, that I owe people in my life attention and love?'

'You don't owe anyone anything.'

'You see, Riggs, I disagree. I think there's plenty of things we owe the people we love, only we no longer live in a society that prizes the community over the individual. After my dad died, I needed her and she needed me.'

'That was a long time ago, bro. She'd be okay if you went off and did something else now.'

Jamie shakes his head. 'It was a long time ago,' he says. 'But it was also yesterday and it's also right now. It's tomorrow too. Thought you might understand that now, given all you've been through.'

The words stroke in Riggs's chest a twinge of memory. It is every moment, every moment happening in every moment; he understands, except he doesn't want to. He needs at least another beer, at least.

'I was sorry to hear about your daughter,' Jamie says. 'I imagine the past few years have been really hard.'

'It's been something all right,' Riggs says.

'If you ever want to talk about it,' Jamie says, 'you know I'm here, right?'

Riggs stands. He can't sit any longer. He takes up the petrol can and pours more accelerant into the fire. It whooshes ferocious-strong, and orange sparks threaten to envelop him. It would take it all away, wouldn't it? Quick, too, if he used enough petrol.

'Careful, Riggs,' Jamie says. 'You don't want to burn yourself.'

'You're only half right, bro,' he says softly.

Penny stumbles down the dune from the house, beers in hand.

'Let's swim,' Riggs says.

'I don't have my swimsuit,' she says.

'You have your birthday suit.' He sticks out his tongue. 'Even better.'

He kicks off his clothes with a flourish. Butt naked, firelight hitting the shadows of his arse-crack, the breezy clean clear air of New Zealand slapping away the cobwebs of his coddled Americanised body, he streaks into the water.

The cold shallows don't slow him down. He slams into the breakers. Whitewash swirls around his head when he surfaces, gasping. Holy hell it's good. The shock of the water reverberates down his limbs and he pulls his arms in a breaststroke, his legs frog-kick, his body a fish — until a spasm of pain shockwaves down his spine. Almost bites the end of his tongue clean off from the brutality of it. What he wouldn't do for an oxy right now. Two of 'em, washed down with a syrupy single malt. He spins in the water to look back at the bonfire, the sole spot of colour against the forest and the darkening hills behind. Penny and Jamie, they look like dolls from here. Their bodies and faces in miniature. Jamie's blond hair almost yellow from this distance. Her red beanie hiding her dark hair. What are they talking about? Her face turns towards him — does she smile? Is his body shifting closer to her, or is Jamie simply being polite?

It isn't the first time he's watched them from afar. That was a lifetime ago, though, wasn't it. She's his girl now, his fiancée. Maybe they'd kissed that one time, so what of it? Nothing more came of it. A few weeks later she was on the plane with him, drifting over continents to a new life. She was a woman who wanted more from life than a New Zealand accent, and he was the one who'd given it to her.

'Hey!' he shouts. 'You guys getting in or what?'

The tiny faces look up, though neither makes a move to get in. Those little fuckers. He swims to shore, waves sweeping around him. They can't get away from this. Can't sit there chatting, when there's living to be had.

He races up the beach. The dog yips and Riggs shakes his head and arms, flicking water to where they sit.

'Stop it,' Penny says. 'You're getting me all wet.'

'Exactly my plan,' Riggs says. 'In more ways than one. You two are getting in with me right now.'

'I have to get me gears off,' Jamie says.

'Too late,' Riggs says, and he picks Jamie up from around the waist, hoisting him firefighter-style over one shoulder, stumbling back towards the water.

Jamie shouts and wriggles free, stepping hot-foot away on the soft sand.

'Can't get away from me that easily,' Riggs says. They're both laughing, a sound better than a bird call, better than the suck and the splash of the waves, better than any of the birds populating this little country way down on the bottom of the earth. Hell, he's missed this man, this mighty beast of a man. Jamie. The dog shoots around and skirts their legs, and Riggs swarms Jamie once more, arms around him in a bear hug, lifting him from the ground and staggering to the shallows. He drops Jamie in the water, fully clothed.

'Get your gears off, bro,' Riggs says. 'You'll never regret it.'

He turns to see Penny. She's smiling, that smile he's yearned for, and it sparks in him like fire. Hope — that's the burn he feels inside, hope that there's love there still, that he hasn't lost her, that he hasn't failed at this like everything else. And there, to accompany it, that scratching in his mind. That aching for a pill.

Jamie kicks off his wet jeans and his underwear and splashes back into the water. 'Come on, Penny!' he calls, and Riggs watches Penny stand. She discards her jeans and tee, her beanie. Riggs's heart flickers in his ear. He senses he's not the only one watching her walk down the sand to the water. Dark-burgundy bra and underwear, the last of the faded pastel sunset glow on her skin.

'Hello there, sexy,' Riggs says when she paddles near.

'I'm not sexy,' she says, and she lifts a glistening arm and points towards the horizon. 'Look!' she says. 'Dolphins!'

In a flash the water around them is alive with movement. Must be fifty dolphins massing around them. The sun is resting right on the horizon, so the water is rippled gold, and the glossy grey dolphins dip and rise amid the glittering wash. Riggs's body is stippled with goosebumps, either from the cold or the thrill, or both. Both, it's both. The cold water is tight around his dick, and the dolphins, strong and magnificent, surge around him. His whole body feels inflated by a soaring bliss. He feels connected to the water, to the animals ducking around him, connected to Penny and Jamie. The others seem to be feeling the same way. Penny's grinning in a way he hasn't seen in a long, long time. And Jamie's face, hell, it's bright with joy.

'I knew it,' Jamie's shouting. 'I knew it!'

The dolphins are almost entirely silent. The only noise is the water subsiding and washing over their bodies, and in this there is some intense, quiet potency. Riggs thinks he spots a baby in the crowd of swirling grey bodies: 'Look! There!' The three of them cluster together, legs curling in the water to stay afloat, gathering close to look where he points. It's there, a smaller dolphin, tucked in beside its mother.

Magic, that's what it feels like, paddling there among the dolphins. The baby slips around the mother and appears again, playful and boisterous. The animals are all instant: this moment matters and no other. It makes him feel as though the dramas of his life, the pain, his guilt, the anger, the shame, are all imaginary. Made-up stuff for people with brains too big for their own good, who have lost sight of how to be and need to create stress for their brains to chew on. Cows with cud. If only he could tie himself to this moment. But the pod begins moving toward the southern cliffs, the water dimpling in their wake. As he watches, the dimpling vanishes, all evidence that they were there gone.

'Holy hell,' Riggs says. 'That was incredible.'

'Did you see how close they were?' Penny says. 'One of them brushed up against me, I thought I was going to have a heart attack.'

Jamie doesn't say anything. If anything, he looks close to tears.

'Cheer up, bro,' Riggs says. 'Once-in-a-lifetime dolphin

encounters aren't meant to make you weepy.'

Jamie rubs his eyes and shakes his head. 'I'm not sad,' he says. 'I guess I'm a bit overwhelmed right now.'

'Well, don't stop crying on our account,' Riggs says. 'If that's what you need to do, we're not going to judge you. Sob at your leisure.'

Slowly, slowly, they swim to the shore, jostling with each other to talk more about the dolphins, exclaim about what they'd seen. Riggs's head buzzes, and Penny lets him wrap her in one of the towels Jamie brings from the bach. He rubs her shoulders before she takes the towel and moves away — only incrementally away. Still close. She gives him that smile one more time and says, 'Thanks, Riggs.'

They huddle around the bonfire to warm up. The night is still, not a jolt of wind. The fire is pumping and the tide is coming in for them wave by wave, sliding and slicing and crashing out there in the oily darkness. The beers have gone to Riggs's head. Direct, no mucking around in the guts, so he is woozy but great. Oh, he is great. Stars whirligig above him and he pitches around the edge of the bonfire, picking his way to where Jamie is sitting.

An hour, two hours must go by, the three of them drinking, joking, talking about Waiheke and people they'd known back when they all lived there, about Riggs's sisters in Australia — one married, one widowed; debated the merits of smoking versus vaping, Novak Djokovic winning the US Open final and whether tennis was more difficult than skateboarding, the war in Ukraine, the upcoming general election, whether Auckland is better than Los Angeles, Trish hanging on in the family home, Trent and Maureen still in the house next door, Damian and Meg high on the cliff above. When Jamie gets his guitar from the house and starts to play, Riggs leans back on his hands, satisfied that right now there is nothing else he needs. His stomach muscles are tender from laughing, and it's years since he felt this good. Fuck the pills. Everything he needs? It's all here.

PENNY

PENNY'S SUITCASE STANDS IN the corner near the bedroom door; beside it, Riggs's skateboard. Moonlight filters through the crooked blinds and, over the staccato stutter of Riggs's snores, crickets work their music outside in the pines. A strange bird call haunts the night. Try as she might, she can't hear a thing from the next room. It's one-thirty in the morning, and she can't sleep.

It isn't the moon's glow keeping her awake; it's not the crickets. It's not her worry about Riggs — he's there beside her, swaddled in the bedclothes. Nor are thoughts of Rose keeping her awake either. She can't sleep because an electric warmth reverberates down the side of her leg. It feels alive with memory: of the dolphin that brushed past her, and of where Jamie's leg pressed into hers momentarily, accidentally, while they trod water together, marvelling at the juvenile dolphin diving with its mother.

Technically, today is her birthday. She swipes on the screen of her phone, though there's no point. It's ridiculous to expect to have heard from anyone, especially her parents, especially this year, especially in the middle of the night, especially here in the middle of nowhere, but people do ridiculous things all the time. Why should she be the exception?

It's tempting to blame the lack of messages on the patchy reception, but she's not that deluded. It's something else entirely.

For most of her adult life she's had a lot of friends — Rachel, the watercolour genius from Sketchy's; her best friend Caroline, whose son Otis was born the same week she had Rose. She used to get along well with some of the partners of other skaters who had the same board sponsor as Riggs, and there was the architect Veronica who she met at a Pilates class in El Segundo. Sometimes they'd get a juice together after class, and Veronica once took her to MOCA Grand Avenue and the Geffen Contemporary. They were her friends. Good friends. They came to Rose's memorial. Dropped off casseroles in those first few weeks.

Penny gets that it was hard for everyone when Rose died. Like Caroline. She found it impossible to be around Penny, overcome by some bizarre remorse that her child hadn't got sick and died. 'I don't know how I'd survive if Otis died. You're so much stronger than me.'

The others? Well, they grew apart. Penny could tell they couldn't truly comprehend how it was for her. They'd cried with her for a while, then they went home to their real lives and their own families. Moved on. They didn't have to traverse the wreckage. They didn't understand she could no longer live the way she had before. The old way was gone.

Riggs snuffles and turns over, and Penny climbs out of the bed. She can't lie on that shitty mattress and think anymore. She creeps into the lounge. Through the glass doors is a smudge of deep orange, the bonfire's embers smouldering. 'A bonfire,' Riggs had said, 'like the old days.'

Like the old days, down in Rocky Bay. When he suggested it, a hot feeling came over Penny, a blood-rush to the face. Thank god Riggs didn't seem to notice.

The last bonfire had been only a couple of weeks after she'd painted the phoenix with Jamie, a week after the disastrous Alley-Oop. She remembers that night: the lick of flames against the indigo sky, the laughter of the other kids, the sound of Riggs telling jokes, water lapping at full tide. How could she forget the night when everything changed?

All day, a thin, insistent drizzle had fallen. Then, an hour before sunset, the rain had eased off, the clouds dispersed, the protective tarp was stripped from the pile of wood, and the bones of the bonfire were set up under a clear cool sky. Pōhutukawa trees lined the beach, drooping down onto the sand, and their deep ruby-red blooms were visible even in the low light of late evening. Stars flickered on in the eastern sky, more sparking up as the night set in proper. Penny sat with Jamie in the spiky grass dunes on the far side of the fire, separate from the others. He had his skateboard and his moon boot; she had her broken finger and two cans of beer. It was the first time they'd been alone together since the night they'd been picked up by the cops. Both of them were thinking about it, she knew. The phoenix, the kiss. His excuses, her father.

Down on the beach, Riggs squatted at the base of the fire. When the first flames sparked up, he leaned back and fell on his arse in the sand. All the other kids laughed, though the sound was soon lost in the crackling and blistering of the fire. Penny didn't know most of them. They were school friends, Jamie told her. None of them paid her any attention. They were fizzing and excitable – their final exams were over. School was finished forever. Ahead of them were endless possibilities – they were free to be the same, free to change.

She wasn't confident what she felt was envy, but it was definitely close. She didn't feel that same freedom. It had been fourteen days since she'd last painted, with either brush or can, and her prospects felt more constrained than ever. She hadn't finished high school. She had no back-up plan. It was her father's way or no way. Art school or nothing. She didn't know if she wanted to paint anymore, not if it meant resembling him in any way, but she had no better ideas. And the one thing she'd thought she was certain about? She'd kissed Jamie and ruined it all. Her broken finger throbbed, and the thin white tape she'd used to strap it to her other fingers made it impossible to open her can of beer. She fumbled as she tried to pull the tab.

Jamie said, 'You want me to open it?'

She held out the can for him, and when he took it their fingers touched. His cheeks reddened and he wouldn't look her in the eye.

'How's your hand?' he asked.

'Could be worse,' she said.

'He shouldn't be allowed to get away with hurting you like that.'

Penny shrugged, and her voice felt small when she spoke. 'It's not the worst thing he's ever done.'

Jamie groaned.

'Are you okay?' she asked.

'It makes me feel funny when you say that he's hurting you. Like I want to go and punch his face in or something, and I'm not usually, you know, a violent person.'

'It's okay,' she says. 'I'm going to leave.'

This was a silly thing to say: even though she meant it, she had no way to make it happen.

One of the kids near the bonfire tossed something into the flames, and it burned and scuddered brighter into the darkening sky.

'I don't want you to leave,' Jamie said.

She should have asked what it was he did want, only she was seventeen, and fearful of what he might say, so she simply nodded toward his foot and said, 'How's your ankle?'

'The swelling's gone down a bit,' he said. 'The doctor said I've got another couple of weeks in this thing. Should be back skating after Christmas, I guess.'

'What about your head?'

'It's epic. Can't you see the bruising?'

'No,' she said. 'It's too dark.'

'The cut's starting to scar,' Jamie said, and he tilted his head towards her.

She moved closer. Long strands of blond hair had fallen over his forehead. She moved the hair with the tips of her fingers and wrapped it behind his ear. In the dim light she could make out only the soft violet edges of the bruising, a hint of yellow, a touch of red and shining-white at the cut. This was the moment she should have explained to him what Riggs had told her about the Alley-Oop, but when he closed his eyes and moaned softly at her touch, she knew she would never tell him.

'Did I hurt you?' she said. 'Sorry.'

'No,' he said. 'It didn't hurt.' He dipped his head and looked at his feet. In a small voice: 'It feels nice, actually.'

She held her hand to Jamie's cheek, felt his skin hot and dry on her palm. He closed his eyes, let the weight of his head fall onto her hand. Then, so quietly it was almost drowned out by the sound of Riggs shouting and the other kids laughing, he said her name. And then he kissed her.

Everything happened fast after that. Hands and legs around each other, bodies pressed together, her hands in his hair. The hot feeling bursting through her skin and out the centre of her brain. He touched her stomach under her sweatshirt, and he stopped when he felt the wire of her bra, though she said it was okay.

'Are you sure?' he said.

Yes, she told him, she was sure.

'Not here,' he said, 'not with everyone so close.'

He meant Riggs. Riggs was too close.

Nobody noticed them slip away down into one of the hollows of the dunes. Nobody saw him lay his jacket on the rough grass. Nobody saw her take off her top and unclip her bra. Nobody saw his face, saw them kiss again. Nobody saw them.

Penny turns away from the beach but doesn't go back to bed. The house clicks and creaks. There's enough light seeping in from the moon for her to make out the titles of the books on the shelves. There's no sleeping to be had right now – not with Jamie so close. She slides out one of the books. The blurb bounces, won't stick in her mind, so she returns it to its place.

On a lower shelf there are a couple of snapshots in burnished metal frames. In one of them three men stand on the deck of a boat. Behind them is a washed-out glint of ocean, and the man in the centre holds an enormous snapper. In the second photograph she recognises Jamie and his mother, Trish. The snapper man has his arm around Trish, and there, slightly off to the side, is Jamie's father, Paddy.

She only met Paddy a couple of times. He'd told her that while he didn't approve of the vandalism aspect of the art she was making with Jamie, he did cherish the fact his son was showing some interest in the arts. 'I teach art up at the high school, you see,' Paddy had told her. 'And Jamie's never wanted to take any of my classes. You should come to the school sometime, Penny, show the other kids what real painters do. You'd blow their socks off.' Paddy was unfailingly polite with her. He asked only a few questions about her father, although he undoubtedly knew who Damian Whittaker was, as though he understood she wanted to be an artist in her own right and not sheltered within her father's shadow.

Paddy himself wasn't a painter. 'A photographer,' he'd said to her on another occasion. 'I find ways of seeing the real and turning them into more interesting versions of themselves.'

Higher on the shelves are two paintings she hadn't noticed earlier. God knows how – even in the low light she can see they're exceptional. The composition is unexpected, the eye drawn along unanticipated lines to find surprising detail.

Whoever painted them knew what they were doing. She studies them more closely and each time finds something new in the perspective and the framing. The painting on the left is made up of bold, gestural marks: a man in a dark suit strides towards the viewer, his face turned down. He's in a city street, or alleyway, and soft white light filters between the towering buildings on either side, and the light hits the crown of his head in a way that's almost angelic. The second work is more colourful and impressionistic, of a woman from behind, sitting on a bench, long dark hair down her back. Her body is fluid and erotic, even though she's fully clothed. The paintings look out of place in the shabby old bach. They are heady and arousing; she feels them in her gut, deep beyond her eyes. How empty her paintings are in comparison, how devoid of perspective. It's clear to her that all she's been creating are mere mimics of her father's work, and for what end? To impress him?

'Are you okay?'

She cries out in fright, but it's Jamie, spectral in the pale light, wearing nothing but boxer shorts. A cool breeze chases around her ankles and she feels colder than she had only seconds ago. She's assailed by the same feeling she'd had that afternoon when he appeared from around the side of the house, the dog skipping ahead of him, and she is glad of the room's dim light.

Before they'd arrived, she hadn't been worried about seeing Jamie, so the feeling when she first saw him — it was a shock. She'd moved on a long time ago, put aside her pathetic devotion to him, forced herself to forget the things he'd said to her the morning after the bonfire, and tried to make a life.

No one could say she didn't try. When they'd left for Los Angeles, she'd imagined that greatness awaited her. Riggs believed she was destined for a life of grandeur too, and if a man like Riggs believed then it was destiny. And when it didn't happen straight away, that was okay, she was still young. Even when she turned thirty, she was still young. Maybe no longer a prodigy, or a media sensation, but still respectable. And then, suddenly, she was mid-thirties and pregnant, and now forty and grief-stricken, and she can see that while she'd left to become something great, all she'd become was someone lost.

'Are you okay?' Jamie says again.

'I'm fine,' she says.

'You looking for something to read?'

'Not really. I was looking at these incredible paintings.'

'Thanks,' he says. 'I didn't know my uncle had them.'

'You painted these?'

'I did.'

'I thought you were a builder.'

'You're not wrong. I was a builder.'

'You're an artist,' she says.

'I'm guess I am,' he says. 'Or I was at least. I mean, it is possible to be both those things, a builder and an artist.'

'Sorry,' she says. 'I suppose I'm being judgmental.'

He rubs his neck and says, 'You know, if I'd never met you, I probably never would have painted these.'

'What?'

'Do you remember the time you showed me how to mix paint?'

She did. It was only a few weeks after they'd met. He'd asked to see her work — what he called her 'real work'. While he looked, she stood, hands clasped behind her back, hardly breathing.

'What colour is that?' he asked, gesturing to a bluebell.

'It doesn't have a name. I mixed it.'

'How?'

'How do you think?'

'Blue and white?'

Well, she said, sometimes it's not that simple. Depends on the blue and the white. 'I'll show you what I mean,' she said. She took up a palette and a knife, three tubes of paint. Two different whites that appeared almost identical, and a third, a blue.

'Mixing isn't a perfect art,' she said. 'It doesn't always work the way you think it will.'

With a careful hand she opened the white paints and put a small amount of each onto the palette, two white dots, one above the other. Then she opened the other tube and added two dots of blue next to each white. 'These two whites look pretty much the same, don't they,' she said, 'and even if I tell you they're different, it's hard to see the difference by looking at them. I'm going to add the same amount of Ultramarine Blue to each. What colour do you think we'll end up with?'

'Well, light blue,' he said.

'That's what you would expect. White plus blue equals lighter blue. Only this isn't maths. It's art.' She mixed the top dots of white and blue with swift, sharp movements of the palette knife. It combined quickly, making a bright, light blue. She tapped at the colour with the knife and said, 'That's the colour of my bluebells.' She wiped the knife clean on a rag and started to cut the bottom dots of colours together with the same twisting movement of her wrist. The difference was immediate. The white disappeared into the blue, and the colour became a vibrant, darker blue. She pressed the knife through one last time to ensure the colours were evenly mixed, and said, 'Do you see?'

'It's about more than calculations, and about the chemical reaction when certain things are brought together?'

'I guess it's about that,' she said. 'It's also about how you thought you could see one thing and it turned out to be another.'

It hadn't felt like a big deal. Nothing but the mechanics of a palette. She hadn't taught him to see the world in the way he obviously did. She hadn't shown him the things that actually mattered.

'It meant a lot to me,' he says. 'Especially after Dad died. He'd wanted me to be more interested in art, and you'd taught me enough to start.'

'You're very good. He would be proud.'

'I'm an amateur,' he says. 'You're the real artist.'

'I'm not an artist.'

Jamie pulls at his hair and says, 'What happened with your exhibition?'

She doesn't answer straight away. 'It wasn't what I wanted, I suppose.'

'Why not?'

She stretches her neck long and looks up at the ceiling. 'Ah, well,' she says. 'Long story.'

'Sorry,' Jamie says. 'You don't have to answer that if you don't want to. Riggs told me not to bring it up.'

'Then why did you bring it up?'

He shrugs with one shoulder and says, 'I thought it said more about what Riggs didn't want to talk about than you. But I mean, if you don't want to talk about it, we don't have to.'

She stares out the sliding doors. The gristle of orange in the black. His body on hers.

'The short answer,' she says. 'I wanted something, and I didn't get it.'

Jamie smiles wanly. 'I know that feeling. A real banger, isn't it.'

He's thinking about the bonfire too. The one in Rocky Bay.

The dog creeps into the lounge, weaving around her legs. Jamie says, 'I saw the dolphins the other day. I thought I was imagining it. Or worse.'

'I can't believe that actually happened,' she says. 'I didn't want it to end.'

'I felt the same,' he says. 'But, you know, good things come and good things go, but at least they come.'

She remembers the first time he'd said that the night of the phoenix. A glib little saying holding such a large philosophical truth.

'It's been a long time since we saw each other,' she says.

It's hard to tell in the low light but she thinks he is blushing.

'A long time,' he says.

'You look older,' she says. 'But you're still beautiful.'

Jamie laughs. He is definitely blushing now. 'Right,' he says. 'Well, you're still beautiful too, and somehow you don't really look any older.'

'Now you're lying,' she says.

They both stare out through the doors at gasoline-black waves rolling in, at low-lying cloud shuddering over the thin sliver of moon. An awkward, intimate silence settles over them. Jamie steps back and knocks into the armchair, tumbles to the ground. In the quiet house, the sound is loud. Jamie presses his hands into his eyes and moans.

An urge to touch him rushes through her. To comfort him, to comfort herself. To take him in her arms and tell him everything will be okay. Instead, she holds her hands against the front of her pyjamas and says, 'Are you okay?'

He drops his fingers away from his eyes and nods. 'Not really.'

Her voice doesn't sound like her own when she speaks next: 'If it's any consolation, I'm not okay either.'

'I'm truly sorry to hear that,' Jamie says. He takes a breath. 'What about Riggs?'

'What about him?'

'Is he okay?'

'No,' she says. 'He's not okay either.'

A wave crashes onto the sand, a peculiar bird call rings out, and she feels as though any second she will start crying.

'I guess that's good,' Jamie says. 'I wouldn't want him to feel left out.'

She can't help herself — she laughs. It feels good.

'I owe you an apology,' Jamie says. 'What I said to you about my father. I was wrong. I know it's not much after all this time, but I am really sorry I said that. I didn't mean it. I was angry.' He's quiet for a few seconds. Then he says, 'Mostly I was scared.'

The morning after the bonfire, he called her. She thought he'd want to talk about what they would tell Riggs and what they would do about her father. Only their conversation went in another, backarseward way. For the longest time, he said nothing, though she could hear his breath coming shallow and fast. When he did speak, the implication was clear: if he hadn't been with her in the dunes, he might have been at home.

If he had been at home, his dad might not have climbed in the car.

He might not have turned on the engine.

It was her fault he'd died.

Jamie said he didn't want to see her again. What had happened was a mistake.

Over the next two weeks she didn't see him. He'd hidden out at the Riggses' house, and he spent the night of Adam's eighteenth birthday avoiding her. So she never had a chance to tell him that she'd returned home after the bonfire to find her father too.

Only hers wasn't in the garage. He was sitting in the lounge. Waiting for her.

'You've been with that boy again, haven't you,' he'd said.

'No, I've been at the bonfire,' she said. 'He wasn't even there.'

It wouldn't have mattered what she'd said. Damian was perked up and ready for a fight. He staggered towards her, shoulders sagging. When he drew close, he raised his arm above his head the way he did when he was paused between brushstrokes, when he was contemplating the next sweeping movement. The impact took her by surprise, the palm of his hand solid against her ear. She made a choked, animal sound and landed on her side on the floor. Penny thought she heard a soft inhale of breath from the staircase and she wondered if her mother was there, watching.

Damian lowered his head to hers: 'Don't waste your talent on these no-hope skateboarders, darling. I will not stand by and watch you throw your lot in with these lowlifes.'

'I'm not wasting my talent,' she'd said. 'I'm using it to do something else.'

Damian laughed. 'I've made inquiries and there's a place for you at the Royal College of Art. A lot of people would kill for this opportunity. You'll fly to London after Christmas.'

Of course, before Christmas she was long gone. She was in Los Angeles, following Riggs around for a decade of parties and travel and skateboarding competitions, wasting whatever talent she might have had exactly as her father had predicted. She thought she was proving him wrong, when all she'd done was swap one man who thought he knew what was best for her for another.

RIGGS

IT'S THE SOUND OF the kettle jumping and bubbling that wakes Riggs from the worst sleep of his life. He's freezing cold, board-stiff, his spine jangling with razorblade pain, and for a minute he's unsure where the hell he is.

When he sees Jamie in the kitchen, pouring boiling water into the coffee plunger and then leaning down to pet his dog, it all comes back to him. He's on that piece-of-shit couch in the living room, not in the bedroom with Penny where he started the night. And it isn't just the temperature causing him to feel so bloody chilled: it's also humiliation. Jamie would've heard everything that went down last night.

He swings his legs around and sits up. Jamie turns and says, 'Morning, mate. You want a coffee?'

'Hell yes,' Riggs says. He grips one hand in the other and twists it to crack his knuckles, only he stops smart at the white-hot shock in his fist — fuck, he'd forgotten about that punch to the wall. Clever move, dickhead. His knuckles are swollen and scraped raw. Maybe he should take a hint from Jamie, put some ice on it. The fist, that is. Maybe the temper too. How does that man stay so zen?

Riggs watches his friend shuffle in the kitchen, hands running along the edge of the bench. He'd listened like a priest at confession to Riggs's bullshit last night, to his rambles about skating comps and lord knows what else. Jamie had made Penny laugh, too. Actual real laughter. It had turned him on to see her so happy: cheeks flushed, lips pink and wet. He made everyone happy, didn't he. He was good-natured, generous to a fault, with a fucking good sense of humour. To top it off, Jamie takes every knock like a true man. Like the Alley-Oop — took that fall, cracked his head, fractured his ankle. Did he whine, make a fuss? Nope, resilient as a bull ant. If Jamie knew the truth of it, maybe he wouldn't be so nice to him. He doesn't know, though. Riggs can tell.

Jamie hands him a coffee in a small blue mug, smiling as though he'd heard nothing in the early hours of the morning, like there's nothing strange about his mate sleeping on the couch instead of in the bedroom with his missus.

'Thanks, bro,' Riggs says.

But Jamie hovers, as though he can't quite find the place to be. He looks everywhere but at Riggs's face. 'Did you sleep all right, Riggs?' he asks, and Riggs can tell from his voice that there's something else going on with him. It isn't only the nonsense from last night, Penny telling him to stop, and Riggs, idiot that he is, not listening. His mate is harbouring a secret of some kind. You can't be that close to someone all those years and not know when they're keeping things from you.

Riggs doesn't hold that against him. Honesty is overrated: we put too much stock in knowing everything about everyone. Privacy is more important than we give it credit for in this age of social media. Isn't that the point of *1984*? Not that he's read it. But he gets the gist.

He himself has plenty of things to hide. Penny, too — she is probably the person he knows best in the world and it's plain she has things she's never told him. Riggs looks around at the bookshelves, the windows, the kitchen bench. What a small house. Far too small for all the things they are keeping hidden from each other.

'Terrible sleep,' Riggs says. 'This couch is about as comfortable as a bed of nails.'

Jamie picks up another cup of coffee from the kitchen bench and moves towards the sliding doors. He pauses on the threshold, and says, 'I think you should say sorry, mate.'

'What's that?' he says.

'I think she's owed an apology. That's all.' Jamie turns away and disappears from sight.

Riggs moves the coffee mug to his other hand and wipes his forehead with the hem of his tee-shirt. Is it hot in the bach or is he still hungover? Does he owe her an apology? For letting her know he finds her attractive, even now when they're both middle-aged and saggy? For trying, in spite of it all, to stay close to her? Who the fuck is Jamie to say he needs to apologise to his own fiancée?

He'd thought they'd made peace — a truce of some sort. A promise. She would let go of the art thing, chill out a bit, and he'd get clean. And he is clean! It's been weeks since he's taken anything, not even a Panadol. Not even a fucking herbal remedy.

It was the sound of them laughing in the lounge that had woken him up. He liked the sound of her laughing – it made him believe that goodness can still exist in this world. He'd woken, his mouth dry from the beers and his dick hard as all get-out. When she came back to bed, he'd tried it on, and she'd said no. He tried again, as any horny man would, and again she said no. He couldn't figure it. They'd had such a good night. Laughing together on the beach, a bonfire, swimming with the dolphins. Pretty bloody idyllic. So, when he woke with a hard-on, getting her naked seemed like a natural thing to do. He missed the shape of her, the familiar dips of bone, the softness of her thigh, the delicate skin of her ear. She would've wanted it too. It's been years since they've been together in that way, and she's only human. He tried to persuade her. He'd said, 'You're saying no but you're so wet.' And then she'd kicked him out of the bed. Made him feel like a criminal for wanting a fuck with the woman he loves. He'd punched the wall on the way out, almost proving her point.

The last time they'd tried, not long after Rose passed away, in the desperate months in the middle of the pandemic, he couldn't even get it up. Penny had been polite about it, but they hadn't given it another go since then. Then he'd left to film the show in Portugal and he'd hurt his back. When he got back, they started fighting like it was an Olympic sport and life started to unravel for real. The pills helped, until they became impossible to resist, and soon after that it was clear she dead-set detested him. Last night he was trying to fix it and, guess what, typical overreaction.

Riggs can hear Jamie talking to Penny outside the bach, and he stands to look out the window. They're by the shed, close together, Jamie's voice low, his body turned to hers. Her cheeks are pink in the morning light, her engagement ring sparkles as she moves her hand, and she's got that look on her face.

Well. Fuck them. Fuck them both. He clenches and unclenches his fists, the sore one complaining at the movement. He takes down a slug of hot coffee, sets the mug on the table. Doesn't want to think.

In the bedroom the blinds are still drawn, but he can make out the shape of where her body had been in the rumpled bed linen. She'd overreacted last night. In typical Penny style. He's her fiancé, and she needs to lighten up. If anyone deserves an apology, it's him. She has humiliated him. He sits on the end of the bed and unzips his suitcase. Several hot pangs of pain zing through his back and into his chest. It's too much to take, too much for one human. He's doing what she asked, and she isn't giving anything in return. Nada, nothing. He toys with the zipper. He could take two. She never needs to know.

He rifles through his clothing, tossing aside jeans and beanies until he finds his old brown suede shoes. The last time he'd worn these was at a competition a few months before the pandemic where he'd bombed out and didn't make the finals, and he wore them for the episode of *Roll With It* he filmed in Poland. They used to be his good-luck shoes. He'd worn them when he'd won the Street League Skateboarding event in Atlanta, and when he'd skated in Barcelona. He slides his hand into the shoe, fingers crawling in the toe cavity. There they are: Meg's tramadol.

He turns the blister pack over in his hands and melts at the sound of the silver backing crinkling at his touch. His promise to get clean is still valid if these are kept only for moments of true desperation. Such as: right now. He's pretty bloody desperate right now. His missus doesn't want him, and his best mate thinks he's a rapist.

Only the slightest touch of pressure with his thumbnail is required to cut into the silver backing. He presses out two pills and swallows them down without water. He returns the blister pack to the shoe and hesitates. It would be prudent to keep these with him for the day. Who knows how he might feel in a few hours' time? He might be desperate then too. He pulls on a clean tee-shirt and his jeans, and slips the pills into his front pocket.

He wanders through the house and out onto the deck. The beach is brilliant in the morning sun. There's that clean, clear air. A white bird dashes over the water. The waves stream towards the shore in perfect sets, and it seems possible right then to forgive Penny for kicking him out of their bed. It takes two to fight and two to fuck, and he isn't an innocent in any of this. He could be magnanimous, show her he's a good Christian boy, ready to turn the other cheek.

He walks slow around to the shed. There they are. Jamie's head is alight in the sunshine like an intergalactic halo and Riggs is transported right back to the days before Penny arrived, before the Alley-Oop and the skating, before all of it. When it was the two of them, and the world was their oyster, and together they strove to swallow it up, pearl and all. Lord, if only he could go back. Not to change anything, simply to feel the wondrous freedom and possibility of youth. How he's missed that feeling! He grabs Jamie's angelic head and kisses that blond bastard on the mouth.

Jamie smiles, though it's hard to tell if he's pleased or alarmed. He puts his arm around Riggs's shoulder and asks, 'You all right?'

'Never better,' Riggs says. 'Never better.' He squeezes Jamie's shoulder. 'You know what we should do?'

'I don't know,' Jamie says, 'what should we do?'

'We should drive to Whangamatā and hit up the skatepark.' Riggs can see it now. They don't need to go back in time, they can relive their youth rolling on four wheels together. Plus, he's a better skater than he was when he left New Zealand. This is a chance to show Jamie he's not a loser; he's not a wanker who forces women to sleep with him. Riggs is a winner.

Jamie looks down and shuffles his feet.

'Come on,' Riggs says, trying not to plead. 'It'll be sick, bro.'

Jamie nods slowly. 'Yeah,' he says. 'We should do that. One last skate.'

'One last skate?' Riggs says. 'What the hell are you talking about? Bro, we're gonna be skating when we're in the old folks' home. We're gonna be skating when we're the oldest farts in the village. That'll never change.'

Penny says, 'What about your back?'

He shrugs. 'What about it?'

'I thought you said it was too sore to skate.'

'Feels okay to me,' he says, and jumps around and lands squat-footed, as though he's surfing, knees bent, arms extended, a wide grin on his face. The tramadol is working. There's a loose rush in his head. A rinse of guilt too, but he doesn't need to feel guilty. He learned pretty early in life that feeling guilty won't get you anywhere. He won't be taking any more, so the best thing to do is forgive himself and move on.

'Must be all this restorative sea air,' he says. 'Why don't you come with us, babe. Cheer us on.'

'I'll stay here,' she says. 'Read my book.' She keeps her eyes on her coffee cup. Won't look up at him. She wants him to grovel. Hell, she's a tough bitch that Penny Whittaker.

'Give me five minutes,' Jamie says. 'I'll have a quick shower and then I'll be ready to go.'

The dog follows him into the bach and Riggs is alone with Penny. Her hair blows back in the wind and her face is bright and ruddy from the cool salt air. It suits her here. Maybe they never have to go back to LA. They could make a fresh start. Jamie would be cool with them staying on for a while. They'll keep him company. It was better when the three of them were together. Last night, the way they felt with the dolphins around them, they could have that every day if they stayed here.

'Hey,' he says. 'Sorry about last night. I just thought ... I don't know what I thought. I guess I thought we were here for a second chance and that this, us, was what you wanted.'

'Hm,' she says. 'I said no.'

'I know, I know.' He takes her hand, and she lets him, her fingers limp, the pinkie finger bending around unnaturally. The hands that held their daughter when she passed. They have that. They'll always have that. He squeezes her fingers tight. She looks up at him, as though waiting for him to say the one very specific thing that might make it better. He says, quietly, desperate for this to be the words she's waiting to hear: 'I'm trying.'

'Okay,' she says, her downcast eyes telling him what she doesn't say aloud. He's got it wrong. Yet again.

PENNY

WHEN THE CAR HAS disappeared and there's no sound but the waves and the dog's paws clicking on the thin carpet, Penny walks to the bedroom at the end of the hall. What happened last night is thick and resonant in the musty room: You're saying no but you're so wet. Her mouth feels gritty and sour at the memory. She picks up Riggs's suitcase, dumps it on the bed and unzips it. What is she looking for? Loose white pills, or a medicinal brown container with a white lid? Maybe a plastic bag filled with unidentified white powder?

Something secret. Something that shouldn't be there.

Maybe she's paranoid, or maybe she's upset about how he'd behaved last night. Maybe she's angry he forgot her birthday. But it isn't only that. It's the way he'd been outside before they'd left. The exaggerated movements, the silliness. The unsolicited apology. The sudden relief in his pain. He's taken something;

she's almost certain of it. She stares at the jumbled mess of Riggs's things and feels rotten in her stomach at what she's about to do.

A strange noise clicks in the pines, and she glances out the window. Have they come back? Will they catch her, furtive and duplicitous and hypocritical? On her birthday too. What a bitch. But it's only the wind, shaking through the trees.

She feels as though she is standing on a very narrow precipice, and she will tumble down no matter what she does. If she searches through his bag, if she carefully sorts through his clothes and feels inside the pockets of the trousers, if she opens his toiletry bag and investigates the pockets, she might be vindicated. She might find what she suspects he's hiding. Or she might find nothing. Either way, she's fucked. She will have to live knowing she's the sort of person who would sneak through someone else's things to find them guilty.

She surveys the lumpy mess of his suitcase. Lying on top is a copy of *Outside* magazine he'd brought with them from Los Angeles, and underneath that a pair of jeans tangled around an Icebreaker merino top. Unpaired socks nestle inside the legs of his corduroy shorts. So far, so innocent.

There had been a time when she'd welcomed the drugs, it's true. At the beginning they were a godsend. Chronic pain made Riggs irritable and nasty. She gets it. Chronic anything will do that to you. He would explode over the slightest inconvenience, and she wasn't capable of helping him: Rose had died only months before his accident. When the doctor first prescribed the pills, Riggs was reluctant to take them. 'Don't be afraid,' she'd said. 'The doctor can see you need them.'

The pills, they made him float. He was happier too, when he

could skate, and he could only skate when he was on something. And where was he right now? At the skatepark. He had been in such a rush to get on his board, he hadn't even remembered her birthday.

She pushes the clothes around and smells him rising up: everything in the suitcase is deeply infused with that musky, slightly sweet smell of Adam Riggs, and each item is a vivid reminder of another time. That light-blue tee-shirt with COLORADO printed on the front? He'd bought it at the shop in Boulder the year she turned twenty-four. And there, at the bottom of the suitcase, the old black and white Element baseball cap he was given at the Temerario competition, three weeks after they'd arrived in Los Angeles. You could barely read the Element logo now, the years fading it almost beyond recognition, and the size adjuster at the back is broken. Nothing, it seems, can last forever.

She pulls out a pair of khaki canvas trousers. She excavates the two front pockets, the two rear pockets. Nothing. Her heart is hard in her ear and her tongue feels too big for her mouth. She drops the trousers to one side and continues her search, picking up items of clothing one by one, methodically, clinically inspecting them. The dog races into the room, jumps up onto the bed and sniffs the pile of discarded clothes, then, as though certain there's nothing of interest, she curls up on the pile and settles to sleep.

The suitcase sits empty. She has found nothing more sinister than a receipt from In-N-Out Burger and the clear plastic lid from a bottle of water Riggs had bought at the airport. No painkillers. She opens his toiletries bag and takes out each item: toothbrush, nail clippers, a condom. Dental floss, a razor, three Band-Aids. Whitening toothpaste and some out-of-date antihistamines. Not one shred of silver foil, not one stray white unidentifiable pill.

Penny puts both hands to her mouth and makes a strange sound. She's unfolded every sock, scanned his boxers and briefs, checked every pocket of every bag. She even touched into the toes of his sneakers. He has hidden things in his shoes on previous trips — car keys, his driver's licence, cash, his pills — but not this time. This time he has nothing to hide.

He hasn't lied. He's clean. He's clean, and she's a prying, pathetic psychopath. The promise she's made to give him another chance feels comically insincere when, here she is, hunting for an excuse to leave him.

She takes the clothes out from under the dog, folds them back into the suitcase. The trousers, the shorts, the tee-shirts. Sets the shoes beside the baseball cap, zips the toiletries bag shut and places it on the top, and gently closes the suitcase.

When she'd decided to leave with Riggs all those years ago, she was too young to understand what she was doing. She hadn't planned it. Hadn't even known about his birthday party until she'd bumped into him outside the bakery on a Friday in the middle of December. Her finger was less painful but still taped up and bent. Riggs was standing on the pavement, his skateboard under one arm and a cream donut in the other hand, and when he spotted her, from the way he smiled, and the way he ran his tongue along his lower lip, she knew he had no idea she'd slept with Jamie at the bonfire.

'You're coming to my birthday,' he said.

'Birthday?'

'This weekend, at my house. My birthday party. Everyone's coming.'

Jamie would be there.

'I'll come,' she said. Then, after a pause, 'How's Jamie getting on?'

'He's pretty gutted,' Riggs said. 'He's been staying with me. His mum's not doing too good.'

'Right,' she said. And then: 'He'll be at the party then?'

'He certainly will,' Riggs said. He leaned over her, casting his shadow over her face, and said, 'You haven't told him, have you?'

'No,' she said. 'You should tell him.'

Riggs shook his head. 'Never. See you Saturday.'

The party was crawling with people Penny didn't know. Maureen and Trent stalked the hallways, attempting to dissuade anyone from joining in anything too crazy. She couldn't see Jamie anywhere, but felt his presence in the house, as though he was just out of sight, and she drowned her nerves with bottles of pre-mix vodka. She talked to Adam's sister Belinda for a long time, laughing like an idiot at all Belinda's lame jokes. Later, Riggs turned up the volume on the stereo, so that the music thumped inside her chest, and she danced to it, afraid to stay, scared to go home.

Much later, when the world started to swirl and she was having trouble keeping upright, Belinda asked if she wanted her to walk her home. Most of the guests were leaving: the party was over. 'Not yet,' Penny said. She might have been drunk, or stupid, or both, but she didn't want to leave until she'd asked Jamie to leave Waiheke with her. They could go to

Sydney. Melbourne. Paris. Anywhere. She had money, enough for flights, and they would figure it out. He couldn't have meant what he'd said. Could he?

Penny crept through the house, whispering his name. But Jamie had vanished. His bed in the Riggs's basement was empty and untouched. Riggs's sisters were asleep in their bedrooms.

She found Riggs in the carport. She tripped on a skateboard someone had left out, and he rushed over and caught her.

'Careful, gorgeous,' he said. He held her until she was steady, and even then he didn't let go. He was warm and solid and smelled of smoke and eucalyptus oil.

'Where's Jamie?' she said.

Riggs brushed some of her hair out of her face. The gentleness of his touch surprised her, and he smiled. Their faces were so close she felt his breath on her lips.

'Last time I saw him he was with Holly McIntyre,' Riggs said.

'Shut up. Where is he?'

Riggs shook his head. 'I told you. He's with Holly.'

She jerked away, and Riggs tightened his grip. She said, 'What do you mean?'

'You know what I mean.'

He was right. She knew what he meant.

'I like you, Penny. I think you're amazing.'

He pulled her closer and touched his mouth to hers, his tongue rough. Penny's knees went slack. She kissed him, she did, and she regretted it as much as she liked it.

He said, 'I'll give you whatever you want, Penny Whittaker.'

She didn't hesitate: 'Take me with you to Los Angeles.'

He didn't require any convincing. They agreed they shouldn't tell anyone they were going. No one would understand, and she knew they'd try to stop them. They booked flights for the following weekend, and after that, she made more choices, each of her own volition and of her own preference. It isn't until now that she understands that each of those decisions tallied up to an outcome very different from what she'd thought she'd wanted, and now, on her fortieth birthday, she can see all the lives she could've lived instead, if she'd been a bit braver, or taken that risk, or said yes to that opportunity, or said no to that other one, and how her choices narrowed with every year, the paths not taken vanishing until it was inevitable that she was here, in a bach with Riggs and Jamie, in the middle of nowhere, with the knowledge that whatever she did next she would hurt someone.

In the bathroom, she washes her hands, scrubbing at her fingernails and palms until they sting. Is it possible to wash away the deceit? Her reflection stares back at her, and she wipes her hands on the towel. Forty years old today. It feels to Penny as though she's been entirely forgotten.

She looks at her face until it becomes strange. A nest of fine lines is etched on her forehead and thin narrow lines dart from the corners of her eyes; dark spots of discolouration are scattered along her cheekbones and around the edges of her hairline. She pulls at her cheeks until the whites under her irises show: she's old.

She liked being young. Somehow, she thought there'd be more time to be young, that she'd have more time to choose, more time to play, more time to make mistakes that weren't of the irrevocable variety. Of course, Penny understands old is a word that has meaning through comparison; she's young compared to Jonathan, the one hundred-and-ninety-year-old Seychelles giant tortoise. Young in comparison to the universe, young even compared to her parents, but she isn't young really, not anymore, not for a human.

Penny doesn't mind ageing, not in itself. She has no real desire to cling to youth the way her mother does, with her Crème de la Mer and her strict diets and her Botox. It's the smaller, more everyday things that hit her hardest. Every time she clips her nails, or cuts her hair or notices a new grey flashing in her brown; every time a scab dries and heals over with new, sheeny pink scar tissue: these incremental reminders of time passing swamp her with a fresh wave of grief. Another chunk of time without Rose: gone. Soon all the parts of her that held Rose will have gone.

She releases her cheeks and gathers her hair into a short ponytail, reassesses herself. If no one else is going to make a big deal about the wasted life of Penny Whittaker, then she will have to do it on her own.

In the bottom drawer in the kitchen is a round cake tin. It's battered and well used, with blackened remnants of long-ago cakes around the rim. She retrieves a bag of plain white flour, two eggs, a half-kilogram bag of caster sugar, and the tiniest dregs of vanilla essence in a bottle half-hidden in the pantry. There's even an unopened bag of icing sugar and a floral-patterned teacup filled with remnants of birthday candles. In another drawer, an ancient electric beater, a spatula; in the fridge, a slab of butter; in the furthest corner of the pantry, a jar with spidery black writing on the side: *Baking powder*. Except the jar is empty, the sides dusted white with the faintest smear of powder. She takes her phone from her pocket and types out a text message to Riggs, asking him to pick up some baking powder at the supermarket before they come back. The message sits undelivered, and she lifts the phone to the window, tries to send it again. No dice. She presses the screen again and, miraculously, the message goes through.

When she puts her phone away, she thinks she sees, out the corner of her eye, Rose — the lilac, the glittering golden hair — though on second glance there's nothing; she's alone.

The first time she believed she'd seen Rose, Penny thought she'd finally succumbed to her grief. Lost it completely. How else to explain the visions? It wasn't a ghost, exactly; Penny didn't feel haunted, not in some spooky, unsettled spirit kind of way. Sometimes it seemed as though it was a sixth sense, like the movie, where she felt the past emerging, every moment hovering in the present. When she told Riggs about it once, he'd found it absurd and told her she might need to have her eyes checked. He seemed to think she wanted it to stop. She didn't mention it to him again.

The oven buzzes while it gets up to heat and the dog saunters from the bedroom to the couch, where she sits and watches Penny with a wary eye. When Riggs comes home with the baking powder, she will make a cake. A decadent cake with a perfect soft crumb, topped with the thickest layer of icing and as many candles as she can fit. If necessary, she will eat the entire cake herself. Until today, every time she's blown out her birthday candles, she has made the same wish. To be a great artist. It is the exact definition of stupidity, isn't it, doing the same thing over and over and expecting a different result? She greases the tin with a smear of butter. Perhaps it's time, she thinks, to do something different.

JAMIE

THE RUGBY FIELD BESIDE the skatepark is dry and dusty and empty, the sky above so bright the blue tinges on the edge of electric. Several young kids stand on the edge of the skatepark near a low green cinderblock fence, cackling and kicking the base of their scooters. Riggs parks the car, takes one look at the kids and says, 'Bloody scooters. Too scared to try the real thing.' He grabs their boards from the back seat and gives Jamie a sharp grin, eyebrows raised. 'Ready to throw it down, bro? Let's show 'em how it's really done.'

Jamie follows Riggs into the park, holding his board under his arm, readjusting his grip every second step. The scooter boys race up towards them at speed, chasing off the edge of a lip, and, in the air, a foot spins the scooter base in a full 360, then they land both feet on the thin pad and roll away. It's pretty impressive. It's actually beautiful. He wants to say he doesn't mind the scooters. He likes kids on the park, prefers it to be busy than abandoned, but he says nothing.

He stands beside Riggs on the edge of the quarter-pipe while together they survey the obstacles, the opportunities. In this severe bright light, Jamie can see pretty clearly. Can see the cracks in the concrete working through like veins. He works to hold that clarity, not let it drift away. Without it he's destined for nothing greater than a concussion and some broken ribs.

They are standing so close Jamie can feel Riggs's tee-shirt grazing his arm. The air between them is warm from the heat of their bodies, and in that space he feels the weight of the years they've lost pulling at him. He looks at Riggs, takes in what he can. Only yesterday they were wee slips of things, young kids holding boards too big for them on Waiheke; look at them now, with grey in their beards and joints that smart. That's the way of it, isn't it. Time passes and you feel the same, only everything about you changes.

Riggs taps his board on the ground and says, 'Don't see a lot of these snake runs anymore.' He drops his board down, holding it with one foot, and without any flourish or warming up he pushes and drops down into the park. His shoulders relax, knees soft and angled, body low on the board. Picks up his foot and pushes at the ground, moving at pace. He takes the turns smooth, letting his body remain loose and easy, arms slack at his sides. It looks so natural in the way he gathers speed, his leg moving strong, and then he's up to a high handrail, hoisting his body and board into the air with a flippant ease — no wavering, just commitment. The scooter boys are trying not to show it, but Jamie can tell they are watching Riggs too. Compared to them, even with their tail whips and their bunny hops, Riggs is in another league.

'The years have been kind to you, bro,' Jamie calls out to him. 'Those are some sick moves for a middle-aged stooge.'

'I'm no stooge,' Riggs says. He taps down on the tail with his foot and catches the nose when it lifts to his hip. 'You going to play or what?'

Jamie sets down his board and looks out over the skatepark. Dr Sobhani would not be impressed. He'd told Jamie no skating, not for love nor money. Well, Jamie isn't risking everything for anything as basic as that. It's for something much more important: lifelong rivalry.

His foot holds the board, and it wobbles, indecisive. Clouds swim over the sun, casting a momentary dark shadow. He freaks. Could swear his heart stops beating. He blinks, and once more everything is crisp and defined in the morning light. Is this the last time he'll ever skate? Is it better to know the end is coming or be aware of it only after the fact? He isn't sure.

'Get on it, bro,' Riggs says.

There's nothing else for it. Foot on the tail, pressing down into the coping, Jamie tips in and skates away. He curls around the snake run, body soft and supple. The wind on his face, the board under his feet, his body in motion. Christ, it feels good. He pushes his foot to pick up speed and pitches up and down the side of the pyramid. There it is — that feeling he's been missing. No space to think about anything other than the present. All that exists now is clarity and a freedom from the terror he's been holding at bay and from the ceaseless urge to kiss Penny.

The sun drifts overhead. Jamie and Riggs roll past one

another from time to time, failing to land flips and attempting rails. Jamie feels high on the thrill of knowing each manipulation might end in disaster and then flirting with the possibility come what may. Scooter boys leave and are replaced with nearly identical versions, bigger boys and some smaller ones, tiny tackers with bulbous helmets strapped tight, anxious mothers watching from beneath the shade sail.

After over an hour of skating, Jamie's ragged and tired. He pulls up in the crook of the shade sail. Somehow Riggs still looks fresh on his board. The man is indefatigable. But he's always been able to push himself on and on, never seeming to tire even when they'd spent countless hours practising punishing tricks, rail slides and shuvits and frontside 180s. A hard worker, that's what he was, all grit and determination. Maybe that's why he'd succeeded when Jamie had not. Maybe Jamie hadn't wanted anything badly enough.

Riggs speeds by and carves around a corner and then up to a ledge. He lifts his body and board into the air. Shoulders rotating, nose of the board coming back 180 and then grinding along the coping, his torso spinning and flinging the tail to the front. At the end of the ledge, he attempts a switch flip to exit, and the board lands on the deck, the wheels spinning. The scooter boys hoot and laugh. Riggs keeps moving, and jogs his arms a bit, his shoulders up by his ears like he knows he's failed but sees the humour in it.

'Couldn't quite stick the landing,' Riggs calls. He skates back up to the deck of the quarter-pipe and claps Jamie on the shoulder. 'Your turn, Flannery.'

Jamie makes a small grunting sound and says, 'A back 180 nose-grind switch flip? I don't think so.'

'Mate,' Riggs says, his voice low. 'Come on. Show me what you're made of.'

Jamie shrugs and squeezes his board.

'We'll take turns,' Riggs says. 'See who can get it first. See who can win.'

Jamie drops his board and glances at Riggs. A hard lump sets up in his throat and he feels some strange crackling pressure sparking up between them. This back 180 nose-grind switch flip is a fool's errand, complete dumb-shit territory. He can't do it. He isn't Riggs. He hasn't spent the last twenty years riding with the best skaters in the world, learning from them, sponsored by great companies and attached to incredible coaches and teams to do more, fly more, skate more. He's probably going blind. It's a stupid idea, and of course he is going to try. It's idiotic, but maybe he is an idiot. This time he wants to win.

He presses his foot onto the board and his breath drops to his feet when he rolls down into the park. There's a rancid stench in the air and there are patches of concrete where someone without taste or style has done some of the ugliest graffiti he's ever seen. Under his feet, the board feels too soft and uneven. It is old, too old. Probably been sitting in the damp carport for years. It was probably there when he watched them kiss, her hands on his face. Christ. He pushes on.

The ledge is getting closer. He considers the angle, what speed he'll need, the energy of the jump. Getting this trick is the only thing that matters right now. The wheels on the ground. The feel of the deck under his feet, the microscopic variations in footing that could determine it all. Who cares that he'd stayed behind, found a quiet job; who cares that he hadn't got the girl. Who cares indeed. Maybe he's dying, maybe he's not yet truly started living. Doesn't matter right now. The past is no longer real, the future can't be guessed at, so this is it: make it worth it.

The ledge comes up sooner than he expects. A milky haze lours his vision. Panic swarms. Forget it. Focus.

The ledge, closer, closer. He's doubtful he has the speed to swing his body around to get the nose behind him. Sweat prickles on the back of his neck. He swallows a few times, lets his mind slip away, drops his foot to push — and the ledge is there. It's time.

Up: his body moves with an elegance that no one would expect from a man who looks the way he does. He twists his shoulders. Torso torqued. Arms bent upward, face to his feet. And, in the motion, he swings his right leg around in a quick, fluid snap.

He's on the ledge. Sliding. Precarious. Heart in mouth, mind buzzing. He presses his toes into the nose, grinding it, and wipes along at a solid pace. The board teeters beneath him. He shakes his left arm to create some balance, and he's at the end. Time for the fireworks. He pushes down with his toes, flicking his back foot up, and the board spirals. Afloat for only a split second, he watches the board rotate. There isn't a thought in his head. Not a sight in his eye. It's empty space, muscle memory, and when he hears the wheels scrape onto the ground and his body pulled by gravity back toward the board, he's consumed by one thought: land it. Land it, goddamnit. Could go blind tomorrow and never touch a board again, but I can have this in my pocket and Riggs is there to witness it.

He lands it all right, bent in half like a sandwich, heavy on his toes. He's beaten Riggs to the trick. He's seized by a satisfaction he can't quite hide.

The joy, though, is short-lived, a mere half-second, no more. He's overcooked it.

The distribution of his weight is wrong, only a touch, but enough — he's too far forward on the board, his feet not quite aligned. He jumps from the deck, and the board rolls away from him.

A hollering shout rings out, and he turns in time to see Riggs coming full tilt towards the ledge, his tee-shirt whipping back on his body in the breeze, arms humped at his sides. He's going for his second attempt. He twists, hops up, grinds along the ledge, movements swift and hard, until he reaches the end and comes down severe in the switch flip, his face tight in a sneer.

The landing is smooth, simple and classy. He sweeps past, two arms in the air. His hands in fists, pumping up and down, exposing a gleam of silver poking from his pocket. He looks at Jamie, his face bright with triumph.

Riggs isn't the skater he used to be. In Jamie's memories, Riggs was clunky on the board. Good, but the goodness was spoiled by the obvious effort required. He's not that skater now. He's a superstar. It's there in every slight movement to rebalance his weight, in every tack of the board, in the finesse he applies to every trick.

For all these years, Jamie's believed that if he hadn't fallen, if his board hadn't failed, then he would've won the Alley-Oop. He would've gone to Los Angeles with Penny, and he would've had everything that came with that. Skating in Portugal, China. The X Games. A family. A life.

But now, watching Riggs skate, Jamie wonders if he's been wrong. Deluded, even. It'd felt good to cling to the idea that he was a better skater than Riggs and it was only bad luck that kept him from success, a moment of misfortune thieving away all that he was rightfully owed. He can see now that Riggs is a great skater. An incredible skater — brave, savage, relentless. And if he's been wrong about this, what else does he need to reconsider? What else is he deluded about? Everything, anything; all of it?

The boy comes out of nowhere. No more than six years old, careening on a three-wheeler scooter, his little twig leg pumping quick. Jamie calls to Riggs, 'Stop, mate!' but already it's too late. Riggs is soaring at top speed, and even with a carving turn there is no way to avoid a collision. The impact knocks the boy to the ground, there's the sound of his helmet hitting the concrete, and instantly the mothers come running. Riggs, unsteady on his feet, trips on the scooter and tumbles down nearby.

The shattered scooter lies on its side near the funbox. The kid is still flat on the ground, his face beet-red and tear-streaked, knees cut open and bleeding. Riggs's board freewheels, unattended, down into the bowl.

Riggs starts nutting off, cursing at the boy, yelling about etiquette and street rules and watching out for others. The other scooter boys cluster in a far corner, heads together.

A woman rushes up and pushes his chest with both hands. 'Hey!'

'He rode out in front of me, lady,' Riggs says, hands up beside his head, innocence personified. 'I didn't do anything wrong. There are rules. He needs to learn.'

'He's five years old! As the adult it's on you to be mindful of the children.'

A strange expression takes over Riggs's face, and Jamie

hears the unconstrained rage when he speaks: 'Be mindful of the children? You think I'm here waiting for an opportunity to hurt little kids?'

Jamie hurries to his side. Wraps his arm around his shoulder and says, 'Everything okay, Riggs?'

'This bitch thinks I'm bashing up little kids for the hell of it.'

Jamie smiles at the woman. This is the way it goes: Riggs riles people up, Jamie swoops in to make amends. It is uncanny how easily they slip back into these roles.

Riggs has never been able to keep his cool, especially when he thought he'd been wronged. Jamie remembers what he'd heard through the paper-thin walls the previous night. Riggs hadn't, in the end, done anything but punch the wall. They'd all had a bit to drink and it was late. He wouldn't hurt anyone, especially not a woman, and not a kid. Would he?

'I'm really sorry about all this,' Jamie says. 'He wouldn't have hit your son on purpose. We're getting around on our boards quite fast and it's difficult to stop.'

'I should call the cops on you two creeps hanging out at the skatepark watching kids.'

She releases the clip on the boy's helmet, brushes dirt from his bloodied knee. Riggs watches them, the mother and her child, his fingers curling and uncurling, his body almost vibrating.

Jamie says, 'You ready to go?'

Riggs rubs his face with the heel of his hands then says, 'Fuck, mate, I'm more than ready.'

He ploughs ahead of Jamie, vaulting over the wire fence to Martyn Road. He opens the car passenger door and climbs in. Jamie puts both boards into the boot and stands back on the pavement. He hasn't driven a car since his accident. The ophthalmologist has told him not to. Anyway, he doesn't even want to drive. Never wants to feel the weight of another vehicle barrel into him, never wants to be in the position to feel that sick shock of blood in his mouth. Less likely to happen if he's not behind the wheel. He taps on the passenger window. Riggs clicks the window down.

'What, bro?'

Jamie pulls his hair and says, 'Can you drive?'

'What d'ya mean? You can drive.' Riggs shakes his head and sets the window to wind back up.

Jamie glances behind him. The mothers of the scooter boys are watching. Jamie's chest tightens. There's nothing else for it. He climbs into the driver's seat. Shifts the seat back, shifts it forward again, adjusts the rear-view mirror, clips in his seat belt, hands shaking. He turns on the engine, and he and Riggs sit there, the engine idling, Lil Nas X interspersed with static on the radio. Jamie turns the station dial, softly, softly, to find the clear signal.

'What the fuck you waiting for?' Riggs says, though there is no venom in his voice. He has reclined the seat and his eyes are shut tight.

Jamie puts the car in gear and leaves the skatepark behind.

The streets are quiet. He takes it slow towards a roundabout, his hands slick on the steering wheel. The vehicle feels too large and unwieldy for him. Riggs shifts in his seat and takes something silver from his pocket, rustles with it, then puts his hand to his mouth and swigs from a half-empty bottle of water.

Jamie takes the left, and is passing Breakers Motel when something small and brown streaks across the road. He slams on the brakes.

A couple of birds flit by. That's all.

'Holy shit,' Riggs says. 'Give me a bit of warning next time you think you're gonna do that, okay?'

Jamie guides the car to the car park near an enormous sea elephant statue and turns off the engine. Lil Nas X goes silent. There's a jagged, strained quiet in the car. Riggs leans forward, elbows on knees, fists balled into his eye sockets, and starts to cry.

Jamie has never seen Riggs cry. Not once, not even as kids. Riggs was too tough for what he called 'weepy shit'. Left the weak stuff, such as feelings and crying and empathy, to Jamie — or at least that was what he'd said: 'You cry enough for the both of us.'

Jamie squeezes the steering wheel. 'Are you all right, mate?'

Riggs drags his hands down his cheeks and says, 'I didn't see him. Honest. I'd never hurt a kid, you know that.'

'Who cares whether she thinks you did it on purpose,' Jamie says. 'She's just some lady.'

Riggs starts pounding his hands on the dash, shouting, 'I care! I care!'

'All right, all right,' Jamie says. He lays his hand on Riggs's shoulder, feels some of the fight go out of him. The tears slow, and Riggs stares out the front window. 'I should've listened to her,' he says.

'You did, we did,' Jamie says. 'She made it clear we should leave, and we did.'

Riggs shakes his head. 'I don't mean that. I mean Penny. She told me something was wrong, and I didn't listen. It's my fault Rose is dead.'

Jamie tries to imagine Penny pregnant, the wide curve of her stomach. She'd told him, when they were younger, that she didn't want kids. Clear evidence of how natural it is that people change their minds. You can choose one thing and then you can choose another. That way, it's never too late to make another life — or is it? Or does there come a time when it's too late to make another choice?

'She doesn't blame you,' Jamie says. 'Don't say that.'

'Yes, she does. And she should,' Riggs says. 'My fucking fault. And she won't forgive me. I can't forgive me. And I miss her, mate, I miss that kid so bad I can't breathe, and when I see Penny I think about our sweet girl and I want to hurt something just to make it go away.'

Riggs slams the dash again, softer this time. He says, 'What do I do? What on earth do I do now?'

Jamie lets out a long breath and says, 'I think you pick yourself up and you try again.'

'Sounds easy.'

'I never said it was easy. None of it's easy, mate.'

'Listen to you. So old and wise,' Riggs says.

'Don't know if anyone would describe me as wise,' Jamie says, and laughs. 'I'm not sure I'm getting anything right. Making a mess of it all no matter how hard I try to turn it around.'

Riggs turns to face out the side window. His skin is still covered in a sheen of sweat. 'How do we handle it, bro?' he says.

'Handle what?'

'All this,' Riggs says, waving his hands around, as though to indicate this precise moment, or maybe the past or the future — perhaps all of it. Maybe he means all of the hard parts. 'It knocks me down when I least expect it, bro. I think I'm doing okay and then, hell, I'm all over the place.' He presses his hands on his legs and his chest sags. 'I didn't use to be so angry all the time,' he says. 'I used to laugh a lot, you know? Found things funny. I was interested in things. Now I spend most my time thinking, is this really my life?'

'I know how you feel,' Jamie says. 'I guess we're all taking it one day at a time.'

'Aren't you ever scared?'

'Scared of what?'

Riggs shrugs. 'I dunno. That everything's falling apart around you and you don't know how to fix it?'

Jamie doesn't say anything; there's too much he could say, there's nothing to say. He unfastens his seat belt and tells Riggs he has to drive.

'Why can't you drive?'

'I've got no licence.'

He's decided he will tell Riggs about his eyes. If he asks. He braces himself, waiting for the questions, the interrogation. But Riggs is too consumed with himself. They swap seats, and Riggs revs the engine. Doesn't even look at Jamie, not so much as a glance. Without indicating, he pulls onto the road, roars up to the bend. Takes the corner too fast. He presses down on the accelerator and starts driving even faster, the speed pulling up deep in Jamie's chest.

'I don't think I can do it,' Riggs says.

Riggs's meaning isn't clear, but Jamie says, 'You can mate, you can, Penny needs you.' He hopes that will help, though he isn't sure that it does, because Riggs makes a low, painful noise, then says, 'Bloody Penny.'

Riggs gives the car another surge of speed and, with a sudden jerk, crosses over the centre line to overtake a Suzuki Swift on a blind corner. At a hairpin turn, Riggs holds at 75, way too fast, and Jamie, thoroughly spooked, clutches the handle above his window. For the first time in his life, he's scared of his friend.

The outside world passes in flashes: a dead possum on the verge, a broken sign for real fruit ice cream 150 metres ahead, the rusting skeleton of a car frame pushed into the ditch beside the road. Every time Jamie looks over at Riggs, his mate's holding the steering wheel like it's a lifebuoy and he's a drowning man.

Jamie can hardly speak for relief when they near the driveway to the bach. Riggs eases into the space where the pines open and slows the car to a stop.

'I'll drop you here, bro,' he says. He takes one hand from the wheel and presses it to his side. His skin shines a sallow grey. 'There's a few things I need in Whangamatā,' he says. 'I'll be back soon.'

'Nah, man,' Jamie says. 'It's been a long day. Let's go inside and have a beer.'

Riggs won't look at him. A vein in his neck pulses bluish and fat.

'Get out,' he says coolly, so Jamie gets out. The wheels skid in place and then the car takes off back in the direction they've come. Jamie feels a twinge in his ankle. Rain is coming.

PENNY

THE BACK DOOR OPENS. Penny lays her book on the couch beside the sleeping dog and waits, tense and tight-jawed. It will be Riggs, back from skating, hot and bothered and pitching for a fight. He'll go into the bedroom and see the suitcase and he'll know she doubted him. A true betrayal of trust, he'll shout at her, and he will be right.

Heavy footsteps come down the hall. The dog wakes and her ears straighten, alert to both Penny's fear and the new arrival. What will Riggs do when he finds out she went through his things? When he is angry, she often has this weird feeling he is going to hit her. Because, although he hasn't hit her yet, the threat is there. He smashes things, and every so often, like last night, he hits the wall. Many times he's threatened to hurt himself if she leaves him, which feels worse somehow than being hurt herself. To be the reason someone would do that to themselves — how could she live with that? Probably the same way, she thinks, we live with all the other burdens of being alive in a world with so much suffering. With a bit of ignorance, a bit of distraction and plenty of necessary, disgusting, unavoidable self-absorption.

The dog leaps from the couch and runs down the hall. It isn't Riggs. From the way the dog is yelping, it must be Jamie. Penny knows it's wrong, but she is glad he's home.

He comes into the lounge, hair tousled, the dog dancing at his feet. A dark flush fills his cheeks when he notices her sitting there. He rubs at his head and says hi.

'Hi,' she says. Then, hesitantly, 'Where's Riggs?'

'He dropped me off,' he says. 'Said he was going back to get a few things.'

Penny's chest twinges sharp. She has no right to be suspicious. After this morning. But still. She asks, hopeful: 'To get baking powder?'

Jamie shakes his head. 'I don't know, sorry. He took off in a bit of a hurry.'

'What did he say, exactly?' He'll have met someone at the skatepark. Someone who can get him something.

Jamie walks to the kitchen sink, fills a glass of water and drinks it down. 'Not a lot, actually,' he says, and places the glass down on the bench. 'He was a bit worked up. Why do you need baking powder?'

'I'm going to make a cake.' The idea now seems both ridiculous and absolutely essential. A cake, of all things.

'Right,' he says. 'Why not.'

'It's my birthday.'

'You're joking,' he says.

'No,' she says, 'I'm not joking.'

'Oh Christ,' he says. 'It's a big one, isn't it? And I forgot?'

'You did, you bastard.'

He laughs at that. How good it feels to make him laugh; she's almost embarrassed.

'Forty, eh,' he says. 'Happy birthday, Penny.'

'Thank you.'

'Well, of course we should make a cake,' Jamie says. 'We need to celebrate. Tell me what to do.'

'We don't have any baking powder.' She goes over to the kitchen bench and wipes it down with a tea towel.

'Ah, she'll be right without it,' Jamie says. 'Sometimes we need to stop waiting for the perfect conditions and just get started.'

'You sound like my mother,' she says, and flicks at him with the tea towel.

'Better than being like your father,' he says.

She lets the towel drop.

'Sorry,' he says. 'That was out of line.'

'It's true, I suppose,' she says. 'Anything is better than being like my father.' She clears her throat, pretends she's fine, takes up the tattered, stained copy of the *Edmonds Cookery Book* and starts to read. 'Cream the butter, vanilla and sugar, and then add the eggs and beat until combined.'

Jamie sets the electric beater into the bowl. The muscle in his forearm contracts, and she feels too warm all of a sudden, though the day is cool. She toys with the hem of her tee-shirt and her eyes move to the back of his neck, the tanned skin, the swing of the shoulder muscle. She shouldn't notice him in this way, she knows this, but still, she notices.

'I think it's ready for the eggs now,' he says.

'Yes,' she says. 'Sorry.' She cracks the eggs, one at a time. The beater starts spinning and wet, eggy batter whips from the bowl and splatters, Pollock-style, over their bodies, the bench and the walls.

'Christ,' Jamie says. 'It's everywhere. Can you pass me the cloth?'

'Easier this way,' she says, and she wipes batter from her forehead and licks it from her finger.

'I don't think I want to do that,' he says, spreading his hands, palms up. The skin is rough and pricked with small dots of blood and raw skin.

'What happened?'

'Took a fall off the board this morning.' He takes the tea towel from her shoulder and wipes the batter from his wrists and fingers, taking extra care on his palms. 'When you've got a large appetite for risk, from time to time you're going to fall down.'

She looks at her own hands, soft and undamaged. Not even a lick of paint on them. 'I don't have much of an appetite for risk,' she says.

Jamie holds the towel in one hand and leans forward. He smells of grass and sweat and she feels the warmth of his body strong on her, like sunshine through the window. For a second, she's certain he's going to kiss her. Instead, he gently wipes batter from her forehead and her cheek, and says, 'You've been in love, haven't you? Pretty certain that's one of the biggest risks of them all.'

While the cake is baking, Jamie suggests they go for a walk on the beach. The high tide is beginning to drift away, leaving only a thin, crusted wake of seaweed debris. The dog skips along with them, sniffing and inspecting sticks of driftwood. Jamie shuffles along, shoulders rounded, wind in his hair.

'Did you have a good time at the skatepark?' she says.

'Bit jealous you stayed here with a book, actually,' Jamie says. 'I've been getting into reading these past couple of weeks.'

'Really? I never thought I'd hear one of you say you'd rather do something other than skating.'

Jamie shrugs. 'Don't get the wrong idea,' he says. 'I still love it.'

'But?'

'What do you mean?'

'I thought you were about to say but.'

'You know,' he says, 'I'd forgotten that about you.'

'Forgotten what?'

'That sometimes it feels like you can read my mind.'

Jamie stops walking when they near the northern cliffs. Rock pools dot the coastline, and they watch as waves rush into the hollows and suck out to re-form anew.

'What a world,' Jamie says. 'I mean, look at it.'

Oh, yes, what a world: from the horizon, long frilled strands of white clouds fan out over their heads. Over the bay, a large bird swoops, a flash of white against the steel blue. The bird reminds her of Don Binney's paintings, and she thinks how he might have arranged the canvas, wings fat and feathered, curving up around the bird's body, the blue strident and pungent and unapologetic. She could never make an artwork so striking. Never.

'Tell me how you'd paint this,' he says. 'Describe it to me.'

Where to start? What does she have to say about a scene others have conveyed with such brilliance? What does she have to offer?

'No, I mean, I can't,' she says.

'Please.' He closes his eyes. 'I want to imagine how you see it.'

'I would start with the water,' she says, hesitant. 'I would layer up the colours. Lots of grey, blue, white, some green. A touch of yellow in there at certain points, you know, where the light hits. Edges of white. Lacy, almost. There's a lot of movement in the ocean today, so I'd use some fine brushes to create that same energy and shape. Little triangles, with this sweeping motion.' Her hesitation has vanished. 'Then, I don't know. The sky? It's really dark at the top and then the value drops as you get to the horizon, so I'd work on getting that right. The clouds, I'd do maybe a white with some really pale-pink undertones, light grey in the depths, sort of Vanilla Sky-esque, but a lot less beautiful. A lot less.' She doesn't say the greatest difficulty will be in imbuing the painting with the startling tension she feels, standing there with him. Without it, the image would never accurately represent this moment in time, and isn't that, in the end, the point?

The dog sniffs at a pile of seaweed further along the beach, and a cloud passes over the sun, dampening the light.

Jamie opens his eyes. 'Why wouldn't it be as beautiful?'

'I paint the way my dad taught me,' she says. 'Don't paint what you think you see, paint what you actually see. And I don't know, I can do that, and so what? Anyone can open their eyes and see the water. My paintings don't make them see the ocean in a new way. I'm a good painter, but I'm not a great one. I don't know, that probably makes no sense.'

'I think what you see is already great,' Jamie says. 'But maybe the problem isn't what you're seeing but how you frame it.'

'Okay,' Penny says. 'What do you mean?'

'Well, you say you see the water. And I see the water. But

the way we think about the water is different. The way we feel about the water is going to be different. That's what you need to paint.'

He kneels, picks up a small stick and draws four identical triangles in the sand, each about three inches from the others. Penny kneels beside him.

'What do you think about this?' he says.

'I don't know,' she says. 'Triangles.'

'Right, exactly. Like you said the waves would be,' he says. 'Not much else to this, is there? Just four triangles in the sand. But when we do this—' he pauses, draws a large box around one triangle, situating the shape dead set centre inside an almost perfect square — 'we start to make sense of the triangle in a different way.' He draws another box around another triangle, smaller this time, with the shape pressed into the bottom right-hand corner. 'When I do this, it's the same triangle, but the feeling is different again.' Around the third triangle he sketches in a long rectangular frame, and, on the final triangle, a frame so small it can't capture the entire shape within it. 'Do you see?'

The identical triangles are no longer identical, no longer meaningless. In the way he's framed them, Jamie has transformed them. One is grandiose, another suspect. Yet another is overwhelming and the last is classical. The lesson is simple and effective. Four identical things rendered dissimilar through perspective. She knows that Damian would say that if you are serious about composition, then you would want to look at Newtonian physics and evolutionary psychology, but Penny thinks Jamie's explanation is perfect in its simplicity and intention.

'And you think I'm the artist?' she says. 'I could listen to you talk about this all day.'

His cheeks flush and he hastily rubs away the triangles.

'Well, you forget I was raised by a photographer, so I'm not completely clueless,' he says, tossing the stick for the dog. 'I remember him teaching me this when I was a kid, but it wasn't really until he died that I understood what he was really saying.' The dog drops the stick at his feet, Jamie picks it up, repeats the game. 'A long time after he died, I realised that the triangle is death. And we will all have this triangle come into our lives at some point. Sometimes sooner, sometimes later. But not one of us can escape it. I couldn't choose to avoid it. I couldn't erase it or pretend I didn't see it. But I could choose the meaning of it for me. I could choose how I moved on from it. I could choose my framing. It doesn't need to be that deep for you, though. I was literally just meaning maybe you think about how you approach your work in a new way.'

'How did you get over your father's death?' she says. 'I mean, how did you get your grief to go away enough so that you could keep living?'

'I don't know if I ever got over it, to be honest,' he says. 'The grief didn't go away. I just got on with things. And in the living, in all the good things — well, all the things that happened to me kind of nestled around the grief. Like some sort of nest. It sounds strange, I know. Every now and then the grief tips and comes out, the same as the day he died, but that sort of thing happens less and less as more experiences and joys wrap around it.'

'That doesn't sound strange,' she says. 'It sounds lovely.' She imagines a rose, the petals never dying, instead multiplying around a glowing red light where the hurt is, cushioned and held by the petals. And it's living that makes the petals grow — in the joy, not in the hiding away in the studio, in waiting at home alone for Riggs to come back.

They start walking back to the house. Waves fizz to nothing on the sand and far off behind Slipper Island Whakahau is the faintest line of dark-grey cloud.

It's well after five in the afternoon. Riggs still hasn't returned. The cake is miserable. The middle droops down in a sodden crater and the edges are burnt crisp.

'I can see why you wanted baking powder,' Jamie says. 'Don't worry. I'll still eat it.'

'I want to ice it first. It might make it more appealing.'

She spreads pink icing an inch thick on top, presses twenty candles in a spiral pattern around the hard edge. The icing is garish, the candles are burnt to stubs, but it is a cake. She carries it, a box of matches tucked under her arm, to the deck where Jamie is sitting with a book he isn't reading. *Normal People*.

'I'm reading that too,' she says, sitting beside him. 'Are you liking it?'

He nods. 'I watched the show, with Madeline,' he says. 'She didn't like it. One of the many reasons we weren't compatible.'

The cake is too warm and the icing has started to soften and drip. She sets it down between them.

'Wow,' he says. 'That's a really pink cake, isn't it.'

'Pink was the only food colouring in the cupboard,' she says. 'It's only a bit toxic.'

He watches her light every single candle. A bird calls from the pines behind the house, and the dog's ears pitch. The tiny flickering candle flames shimmer in the breeze.

'What are you going to wish for?' Jamie says.

'I can't tell you, or it won't come true.'

'It depends, I suppose,' he says, 'on the wish.' He's staring at her with a very intense look in his eyes, the same way he'd looked at the world earlier and said how beautiful it was, this wonderful world. His eyes wide, as though to let more of the beauty in.

It's the first time he's looked at her directly since she's arrived, and he's smiling. Perhaps it's the sunlight, the sea breeze, the hard beating of her heart against her chest, or perhaps it's the feeling of being watched by someone who seems to take some pleasure in it, but a strange feeling comes over her, fills her head. A good feeling.

And — nothing bad is happening. No divine retribution has been set upon her. No karmic reckoning. In fact, there's a distinct lack of godly intervention. How pointless it's all been, this shunning of delight. How stupid and ridiculous and selfish. It hasn't brought Rose back to her. It hasn't done anything at all. It says nothing about who she is if she feels joy. This feeling makes her wonder if she's been wrong. That life isn't meaningless after all. Maybe feeling like this is the whole point.

She smiles back at him, brushes her hair away from her face with one hand, dips her head toward the cake, summons her wish, and blows out all the candles in one long breath.

Penny slices the cake, twice, three times, and lifts two large pieces out onto plates. 'Here,' she says, handing him one. She takes a bite of her slice. The icing is too thick and too sweet, almost gritty, the cake hard and dry.

'Hm.' Jamie nods, and swallows. 'Interesting.'

'I should've used that baking powder in the jar, even though it's probably too old to work,' she says.

'Bit like me,' he says.

'If you're old, then I'm old,' she says, gesturing to the cake. 'Over the hill.'

'Middle-aged, come on. You're not old yet,' he says. 'Just prepare for your mid-life crisis.'

'Too late.'

'Is that what's going on?'

The dog barks, the sun emerges from behind a cloud. She says, 'You know he lost his job?'

'Riggs?'

She nods, takes another bite despite it all.

'I didn't know,' Jamie says. 'He never mentioned it.'

'Burned it all down,' Penny says. 'He always does.'

He hesitates just for a second. 'Has he burned you?'

'Oh yeah,' she says, 'he's burned me many times.'

Jamie looks at the cake in his hands. When he speaks, his voice is hoarse. 'Have you ever thought about leaving him?'

Does she ever think about leaving him? Does Jamie mean her shameful, intoxicating dream of freedom? She could lie. It is easier to lie in these situations, she's found. To answer questions like, 'Do you have children?' with a cheery no. To tell Riggs he's forgiven, when he's shouting and telling her he's doing his best and could she please, please give him a break.

She says quietly, 'I think about leaving him all the time.'

He says, Fuck, under his breath.

'Forget I said that.'

'No, no,' he says quickly. 'It's not that, I mean, I'm glad you can be honest with me.' He sucks air in very fast, as though he's been winded. 'It's just ... you know.'

'Yes,' she says. She knows he means what he heard last night, and her head feels light and sore. 'That's not all, you know. He's gone cold turkey.'

'Right,' says Jamie. 'What's he been doing?'

'Painkillers, mostly. He's been doing other things too, but I don't know the details. It sounds awful but I don't want to know.'

'Wow. Okay.' He coughs. 'Has he been to rehab or anything?'

'No,' she says. 'He refuses to go. He's promised he'll get clean, but I don't know if it will stick.'

'How long's that all been going on?'

'A couple of years,' she says. 'Since Rose died.' She extends her hands over the sand and rubs them together to brush away the crumbs, and she finds she can't stop, she can't brush it all away.

Jamie stares at the remainder of his cake. 'You know, Riggs thinks you blame him ...'

Her jaw tightens and her voice comes out all strange. 'You want to know the really sad part? I don't really blame him. I blame myself.'

'Please,' Jamie says. 'Don't do that.'

'Why not? I was her mother. I should've taken care of her.'

Jamie lets out a long, audible breath. 'I've found,' he says softly, 'that all these years of blaming myself for my father's death achieved very little except making myself miserable. I thought for so long if I'd been there that night, he might not have done it. It took a long time to forgive myself, a long time. But you know, I wasn't responsible for what happened to him, and I know you weren't responsible for what happened to your daughter. And Riggs wasn't either.'

'How do you know?' she says. 'How do you know I wasn't an awful mother? That it was some punishment from God?'

'I know you, Penny,' he says. 'I know that you wouldn't have been able to stop yourself from loving her. I also know you don't believe in God.'

She wipes her eyes and nods. 'I did love her. I did.'

'It hurts because you loved her. I promise you. The pain reminds me how much my dad meant to me.'

'Is love supposed to hurt like this?'

Jamie shakes his head. 'No one wants it to. But it seems to be true whether we want it to be or not.'

Penny removes the candles from the remaining cake and lays them in a neat line on the deck. There are so many of them, yet they're only half the number she really needs. She looks up at Jamie and says, 'Do you want to know what I wished for?'

The wind picks up and gusts around them, and strands of her hair fly in her face. He drops his uneaten cake into the sand, and even though his fingers are tacky with the residue of the icing he reaches out and brushes it out of her eyes.

'Tell me,' he says, and she leans to him and whispers in his ear.

RIGGS

RIGGS FANGS IT ROUND the coast back to Whangamatā. Must be pollen season, because his hayfever is acting up. He can hardly see the road through these damned weepy eyes. He swipes at them with his wrist to clear the view, yet the weeping returns instantly. A white ute pulls around the corner, heading towards him. Its horn blares so long Riggs eventually figures it's for him. And it surely is: he's over the centre line, heading direct into the oncoming traffic. A black Mercedes behind the ute almost comes dinging into a head-on with him, and he can't help but laugh.

Wouldn't have been all bad to kick the bucket in that fashion. Speeding through the warm spring afternoon, hills out the window speckled in the greens of New Zealand bush. Sun sprinkling on the ocean. Window down, wind rushing in. Didn't happen, though, did it. He's still here. Besides, he doesn't really want to die, does he? At least not like this? Not now?

He slows only when he is deep in the quiet streets of Whangamatā. It's a ghost town now. A bunch of seagulls clot around a split rubbish bag on a street corner. The wind brushes an empty McDonald's cup across the road, and he guides the car so his tyres flatten it on the way past. He presses the accelerator and his knee pings. Gives the kneecap a rub. Disgusting – his jeans are stiff with blood. Must have roughed it up when he'd collided with that kid. He can still feel in his bones the sound of the helmet hitting the concrete. Even now, hours later. Won't ever stop hearing it, will he, it will merge into the sound of Penny crying, of Rose retching that poison, her frightened whimper. The helmet crack is one more song added to the soundtrack of his guilt.

His phone buzzes and he picks it up, trying to look from the road and the screen and back. Two messages. An email notification from Verizon letting him know his internet bill is overdue back home, and a text from Penny she'd sent earlier, presumably while he was skating. Baking powder? Hell. If only that was some sort of code for another, more desirable white powder.

He eases the car into a parking space near the entrance of the New World, then spends ten minutes meandering in a daze, uncertain where exactly baking powder would be shelved, memories of that woman yelling at him at the skatepark coming to mind, her face inexplicably similar to Penny's when she told him: I said no. Get out of this room right now.

Rows and rows of beers are stacked in tidy rows in the chiller. Reminds him they'd drunk most of the IPA he'd bought last night. Best get some more. He stares at the beers for an inordinate amount of time. There's almost too much choice for someone in his state of mind. All the cans decked out in obscenely bright and colourful designs. Reminds him of the graffiti Jamie and Penny used to do. Same graphic shapes, same bold contrasting shades of neon and pastel. Maybe she should have got into product design. Maybe she would have been happier if she had been less ambitious. Maybe he would have been happier too, if he hadn't wanted so much. Or if he'd expected less from what he'd got. What would make him happier? He's tried chasing pleasure, he's tried chasing pain, figured out they're mostly the same thing. Confusing, that's what life is. He's a simple man in a big world; he can't make sense of it.

A pack of beer, some sour worm lollies, a box of Marlboro Red 20s, a box of baking powder, and he's back in the car. Cruising the streets. Cigarette smoke thick. At the next corner he takes a left and he's at the skatepark once more. The curves of the snake run are blinding in the mid-afternoon light. Only a few kids are there now, trash talking on the lip of the bowl. No mums huddling in the corner, thank the lord. The last painkillers are still working their magic; his back pain is dull. He flicks his cigarette butt out the window, grabs his board and a beer, another for later in his pocket, and kicks down into the park with a nonchalance he wishes he truly felt. When the world is falling apart, why not skate?

The beer is cold and fizzes on his tongue, only it doesn't taste as good as he had hoped. The kids at the bowl take off as he approaches, and he has the park to himself. Usually, he would relish the serenity. He can be king. No one to wait for. Every obstacle his to tackle at his own speed. Only now the echoing sound of his board seems empty. It had been a lot of fun skating with Jamie that morning. The two of them together again. This doesn't feel the same at all. He ollies up onto the rail, grinds along 50/50, swigging more from the bottle as he falls from the rail in an acid drop. Be mindful of the children. As if he was keen to hurt as many little fuckers as possible. He lazily rolls to a half-metre drop and kickflips down, knees bent deep, bottle in his mouth like a hairy baby. Heart drops out: there's a blue mark on the concrete where the kid's helmet smacked the ground. The way it smears and the unique shade of blue reminds him of Rose's legs. Those bruises. Her stick-thin thighs mottled navy and purple and yellow. He drowns himself with the beer, trying to get the entire bottle into his gut as fast as possible.

'You're pretty slick.'

Riggs turns to look over his shoulder. A kid in his early twenties, chin shaded with stubble, hands inside the pocket of his hooded sweatshirt, rolls towards him on a roughed-up eight-and-a-quarter-inch Quasi Crockett board.

'Thanks,' Riggs says. 'Nice board.'

'Nice beer,' the kid says.

Riggs gets the spare beer from the pocket of his jeans, hands it to the kid and asks, 'You old enough to drink?'

The kid laughs. 'Bro, you a cop or what?'

They skate for an hour. Kid is good — not as good as Jamie, but sufficient. His company gives Riggs the illusion that this is where he's meant to be. He's meant to be slightly drunk, body ticking through the tramadol; he's meant to be skating here with this dude barely out of adolescence. He isn't supposed to be anywhere else.

The kid applauds when Riggs does a trick, and although Riggs wants to tell him to stop kissing ass, he kind of likes it. Been a while since anyone has complimented him.

'I've never seen anyone do a fakie bigger triple flip before,' the kid says.

'I'm Adam Riggs.' The boy's expression remains unchanged. 'You know, *Roll With It*?'

'Nah, bro,' he says. 'I'm Brad, but everyone calls me Booger.'

'Nice to meet you, Booger.'

They skate on as the afternoon wanes. Riggs grabs another couple of beers from the car. A blustery easterly picks up and adds a bit of kick to the skating. In the middle of the field a man tugs furiously on the string of a kite, and Riggs watches as he tries to manage it, control it, no matter how the gusts attack or what the kite might think it wants to do.

Booger rolls past, lumpy on his heels. Riggs skates hard to impress, throwing himself around with minimal restraint. He wants to skate until his skin peels off from mucksweat and exhaustion and a new Riggs can emerge. Fresh and clean and ready to return to his real life, ready to control his kite. He takes the pills from his pocket and washes a couple more down with the last of his beer.

Around five, two of Booger's mates turn up. One of them carries a small speaker that he sets up on the edge of the coping.

'What is this crap?' Riggs says as the music blares out.

The two new arrivals glance at each other. 'You don't like Kid Cudi?'

Riggs shrugs.

'You want us to play some Pearl Jam, old man?'

Booger makes a noise, a loud honking sound. Riggs gets the

distinct impression the kid is laughing at him. He kicks up his board and looks at the car. Might be time to go.

'Holy shit,' one of the newcomers says. 'You're Adam Riggs. I have your copy of *Slap* at home somewhere.'

Booger looks confused. 'Who?'

'Adam Riggs, you know. 2005 X Games bronze medallist in the vert.'

Not entirely true, but Riggs is not going to correct them. They got his name right — all that matters, really. He grins and asks the kid, the one who recognised him, a few questions about himself. When did he start skating, etcetera. The kid's face glows with pride. Riggs has missed this. Used to be he couldn't spend a minute at a skatepark without someone wanting his autograph. And hell, he loves chatting with people. This is what made him so good on the show. He can get a conversation going with anyone. Bet Alex Alexsson or whatever his name is can't do that. What the hell is Riggs going to do now, anyway? What do you do when your current plan has worked its way to a natural conclusion and you're still alive?

'You're prehistoric skating royalty,' the other one jokes, and the good feeling Riggs had felt a second ago seeps away.

'He's joking bro,' Booger says. He lights a joint. 'You wanna smoke?'

Riggs holds the jay to his lips, pulls a breath deep into his chest. He takes another drag and passes it back to Booger.

'You should watch this.' Booger gets his phone out of his pocket and swipes to a video-sharing app. He holds out his phone so Riggs can see. The video, uploaded under the username HillBombersSanFrancisco, shows a squad of four guys in graphic tee-shirts and cargo jeans floating 50 ks an hour down Quintara, their boards wobbling dangerously close to one another. Near the base of the hill, one of the boards slashes sideways from under the skater's feet, and he falls. His body rubs on the tarmac something vicious, and he comes to a stop only when he spins into the side of a car. The other three skaters, two of them crouching low, one standing, arms outstretched, Christ-like, carry on. The sequence ends with a quick interview with one of the men: 'I'm howling, man, I'm howling.'

Riggs's heart is all over the place, thundering up and then missing a beat. It might be the drugs, it might be contrition, only he thinks it is inspiration.

'Play it again,' Riggs says, and Booger taps the screen to make it play.

'Pretty gnarly, right,' Booger says.

Riggs notices that one of the guys rides over a manhole cover, setting the board to swing, and he has to bend his knees and extend his arms to recover his balance. There's an art in recovering from disaster. Continuing on in the face of ruin. Some do it with grace, others less so. Riggs wants to be someone who does it in a blaze of glory.

'It's gnarly all right,' Riggs says. 'You ever done that?'

'Nah,' Booger says. 'No hills like that round here.'

'There's that street in Dunedin,' Riggs says.

'Baldwin Street?' the other boy says. 'People have tried. But you gotta have big fucking fat balls to hill-bomb Baldwin Street.'

'I'd do it,' Riggs says, and he ain't bullshitting. It seems to make sense to him. He swipes on Booger's phone — and the men race down one more time, in control and out of control, risking it all, certain they'll be fine, knowing if they let in even a half ounce of doubt they'll be too scared to even start. He wants to feel it. The wind against his face. Incremental muscle movements to hold yourself upright, to keep the board steady. The incredible danger of everything collapsing yet shooting for the glory, living as though you've only got the one shot. Living as though every day you're dying.

'Someone got killed going down that street in a wheelie bin,' Booger says. He fiddles with the sleeves of his hoodie so they cover his hands. 'You serious about hill-bombing it?'

'As serious as I ever was.' Riggs keeps a straight face. Lying comes easy if you do it often enough. 'I'm going to do it.'

'Make sure you video it,' the kid who recognised him says. 'I'd watch it even if you fucked yourself. You'd probably get more views if you do fuck yourself.'

More views if you fuck yourself. How true. He'd become more famous if he died doing it, probably. Former professional skateboarder dies in stunt gone wrong. Much more interesting than man succeeds and doesn't fuck it up.

'Let's go, Booger,' one of the kids says.

'Where are you guys going?' Riggs picks up his board.

The three of them look at each other. Freaking out. Riggs knows that look. He's embarrassed for himself right then, though he's not sure he understands why.

'Got a party at Ella's place,' Booger says. 'We thought, you know, you'd have other stuff to do.'

'Yeah,' the one who recognised Riggs says. 'I mean, aren't you a bit old? Don't you have a family?'

Aren't you a bit old for a party? Maybe, Riggs thinks, maybe not. When do you get too old to party? Do you ever get too old for living?

'I didn't want to go to your lame party, ya dickhead,' Riggs says. 'I wondered if you boys needed a lift somewhere, or if you needed me to change your nappy before you go.'

'Sick burn,' Booger says, and the three of them laugh, and they're still laughing, the noise of it echoing back across the pale rugby field even when they are pretty much out of sight.

Riggs parks the car behind the bach. He doesn't get out straight away. He takes up his phone and swipes the screen on. There's one bar of reception: enough, hopefully. He scrolls, looking for the video, only the reception fades out and he can't retrieve it. If she could watch it, Penny would understand his plan. When she sees these guys flirting with the edges of possibility, living right at the brilliant edge of death, she will get it.

The bloody dog appears from the side of the house, stares at Riggs and then starts to bark.

'All right, all right,' Riggs says. He opens the car door and tells the dog to give it a break. She stares, hostile, and skips to the deck out front. He follows, board in one hand, the remaining beers in the other. The sun is bright on the beach but out near the horizon enormous bursts of charcoal-grey clouds flare up like castles. An onshore wind prickles in cold squalls. Pretty soon those clouds will swamp the bay, he reckons; they'll take this pretty day and make it nasty.

Penny is sitting on the deck with Jamie, her body turned towards him. She's flushed in the face. Riggs's racing heart skips another beat.

'What are you guys doing?' he says.

'We're having some cake.' The colour drains from Penny's face. 'Where have you been?'

He keeps his eyes on his feet, scuffing in the sand. 'I had some things to do,' he says. 'Catch.' He tosses the box of baking powder to her, and it lands on the ground near her feet.

'Thanks,' she says. 'Better late than never.'

'Too late for what?' He cannot figure what she means. Thoughts won't run straight. His mind's a little foggy. His hands tremble and he's aware that he's giving off that qualmish stink of dried sweat, marijuana and beer. If Penny smells him, it's all over.

'The cake,' Jamie says. 'Are you okay?'

'I'm fine, bro,' Riggs says. 'Never better, in fact. What's the cake for?'

Penny ducks her head.

'What's the secret?' Riggs says.

The cake they're both going on about is flopped between them. Bright-pink icing melting down the sides in unattractive gloops. Crumbs litter the plate where a large section is missing. There's icing in Penny's hair, on Jamie's hand, around her mouth.

Jamie says, 'It's her birthday, mate.'

Oh, holy hell. Her birthday. He looks at the time on his phone. Six-thirty. He's forgotten her birthday, and it's pretty much over. His tongue is furry with a bitter tang, and he swallows it down, nearly gags on the taste, shifting from foot to foot as though unsure where he should go, as though the earth beneath him is shifting. He's fucked it up properly this time. If he sits down, she'll know in an instant he's been using. Truth, it's only a few pills and weed, couple of beers, but he's pretty certain she won't be happy with that explanation. If he goes off to shower, to rinse away the long, dirty day, he'll look even more hopeless than he already does. There's no winning here, and that infuriates him no end.

'Babe,' he says. 'Happy birthday.'

There's a silly look on her face and she says, 'How old am I, Adam?'

He wants to unfurl his fists and count the years off. He used to have a good memory for things — faces, birthdays, anniversaries, phone numbers, historical events — but after Rose died, these sorts of details have drifted from him, unimportant somehow in the face of it all.

May as well take a punt, though. 'You're forty,' he says.

Her lips turn at the corners — an infinitesimal amount, no one but him would notice the change — and he feels it, deep in his chest, that he's got it right and he's pleased her.

'Good guess,' she says.

'Don't malign me with those baseless accusations,' he says. 'I didn't guess. I knew. I know you.'

'Where have you been, really?' Penny asks.

'Went back to town,' he says. 'Got your baking powder.'

'It took you four hours to get baking powder?'

The dark clouds heave up and over the sun, and the day dims. The temperature bottoms out, and Riggs shivers.

'I had another skate,' he says. 'Went down the beach. Ate a burger. Took a shit in the public toilet. Is that enough information for you? What do you think I was doing?'

She flushes red again. A scattering of raindrops blows in on the wind, cold on his cheek, and the pines thrash in the gust.

'Nothing,' she says. 'I was worried, that's all.'

'Well, you don't need to worry. I'm here now.'

The rain intensifies then, dropping down in thick silver sheets. Jamie picks up the cake, and the three of them rush inside. Wind slashes raindrops and pine needles against the windows. The dog runs to Riggs, jumpy at the sound of the storm, lifts her front paws onto his legs, and the painkillers crinkle in his pocket. He glances at Penny. Oblivious. Too busy with Jamie in the kitchen, examining the cake for rain damage.

He knocks the dog to the floor and says, 'So, is it party time, or what?'

Penny shakes her head. 'I don't know about a party. Maybe we could play a board game?'

'There's Scrabble,' Jamie says. 'Or Trivial Pursuit?'

Board games. What in the blazes. Cup of tea at eight o'clock and off to bed by nine? Don't you have a family, they said. Don't you have a life? He doesn't want to sit around. Leaves too much room for thinking.

'Fuck that,' Riggs says. 'We aren't old yet. Let's have some drinks, celebrate together, the three of us.'

'Three people, what a party,' Penny says. 'Let's not go too crazy.'

A tease of thunder rumbles in the distance.

'What's the saying?' Jamie says. 'Two's company, four's a party. Three's a — what is it?'

'It's a crowd,' Riggs says. 'Three is a crowd.'

JAMIE

RAIN HEAVES WITHOUT PAUSE and soon a leak sets up by the back door. By the time anyone notices, the puddle has soaked through the carpet so that even the floorboards feel soft and rotted through. Jamie pokes around in the laundry, hunting for a bucket or old ice-cream container to catch the drips. He doesn't want to be responsible for everything falling apart.

Back in the lounge, kneeling in front of the hearth, heaps of dry wood from the shed at her side, Penny places balls of newsprint into the belly of the fireplace. Such care she takes, burying them beneath a pyramid of kindling before she sets it all to ignite.

The first flames light up her face, and in that instant she looks much like she did earlier that afternoon, her head lowered to blow out the candles on her cake. The candlelight played on the sharp line of her cheekbones in the same way.

The hair growing soft and short at the nape of her neck. He had been sitting so close to her he had smelt the lavender-fresh shampoo in her hair. So close, he'd had ample time to study the exact shape and colour of her eyes. So close, he could've pulled her close and kissed her.

Kissed her, yes, hard and true. Looked at her while he did it, and burned the image into his memory, cradled it deep in a place where it wouldn't ever fade or change, somewhere safe from whatever witchcraft turns memories into unreliable fictions.

Would he forget what she'd whispered in his ear? 'I want the good things to stay.' Her voice soft and papery, her breath hot on his neck, even if it still isn't clear to him exactly what she meant. Oh my god, what a loon he is, like some love-sick teenager with a hopeless crush.

'Are you okay? You look like you've seen a ghost,' Penny says, and in that instant, her face changes. Is it his vision causing her face to blur? Or is it merely trails of smoke drifting up around her face? Because she looks like she did twenty years ago. Unburdened, fresh. Happy. The room wavers, and he can't tell what is real. It is like seeing a ghost, like his past come to haunt him. He sits on the couch and presses his hands down into the cushions, tethering himself to the world. She repeats herself, asks if he's okay. What to say, what to say? There are too many things he wants to say. Too many things he wants to ask, though in the end they boil down to one specific thing: does she regret leaving with Riggs?

Can't ask her that. Can't ask her that. He pulls at his hair and sits on the couch, jiggling his legs. Beneath the rain, the sound of Riggs singing in the shower. Riggs's shoes by the doorway. Riggs's sweatshirt hanging over the back of one of the dining chairs. Can't ask someone if they regret their whole life.

All he says instead is: 'Do you believe in ghosts?'

She bites her lower lip and lifts her head. Her eyes are a startling green. 'I see Rose,' she says. 'Every once in a while. I mean, I suppose it happens to a lot of people.'

Jamie has read about this phenomenon. Visions of lost loved ones in large crowds. Mistaking the stranger walking down the street for someone else, for someone it could never be. A mirage of loss; a hallucination of bereavement. When he was younger, he'd yearned for that momentary illusion. Wanted to see his father one more time.

'Of course, I know it's not her,' Penny says. 'But, you know, sometimes it is.' She puts another log of wood into the fire as the kindling burns down. 'I can't explain it. I know it sounds crazy.' Quieter: 'I thought you might understand.'

There's no time to gather an answer. Riggs comes in, cropped hair still shimmering wet from the shower. He perches on the couch next to Jamie, his leg bouncing, his foot jiggling, an unsettled body in constant motion. Jamie remembers suddenly: Riggs taking a silver sheet from his pocket, pressing something to his mouth, swallowing on a dry throat.

He's promised he'll get clean but I'm not sure it'll stick.

Jamie rubs at his eyes. The blurriness remains, and for a brief second they're in the calm of the storm. In the sudden quiet, he can hear the leak dripping into the bucket, rhythmic and steady. Jamie thinks he can hear a message in the sound, like Morse code. It is a signal, a heartbeat. A warning.

The storm builds once more, rattling the windows and setting the dog on edge. Riggs drags a box of records between his feet and says, 'Now then, what should we listen to?' The rose tattoo blinks in and out of sight as he flicks through the box. He pulls one out: 'Aha! This'll do.'

Piano chords ring out: 'Bridge Over Troubled Water'.

'This reminds me of those potluck dinners at your place when we were little tackers, Jamie.'

'My dad loved this song,' Jamie says. 'My mum hated it.' His mum did hate Simon & Garfunkel, but she loved a potluck. Chicken drumsticks and chocolate chippie log covered in cream. Later, the adults drunk, the kids running around unsupervised and on the verge of hysteria. Later still, he'd wake on the floor of the rec room, Riggs and his sisters asleep beside him, the sound of his parents talking with Trent and Maureen in another room, voices like bells.

Riggs slaps his hands on his thighs: 'That was a real childhood. We should do that,' he says. 'Have a ton of kids, live next door to each other, let the kids run wild.'

Jamie imagines it: a house full of children; he and his partner, whoever she might be, chatting to Riggs while he turns the pink sausages and the bloody steak on the barbecue. Spiral pasta salad on the table, iceblocks for dessert. Later, the kids watching a movie under duvets in the lounge, the adults drinking on the porch, him meeting Penny's eye across the table and feeling awkward and unbearably aroused.

In the pause between songs, Jamie hears the pines creak in the wind, and the slow, tentative, magical intro of 'El Cóndor Pasa' fills the silence. He has always liked this song. Not many songs have a feeling about them the way this does, a feeling of both future possibility and of a past that has slipped away, childish and sinister at the same time. To hear it now, with these two, it's almost too much.

Riggs stands up, sways his hips and extends his hand to Penny, but she shakes her head. Riggs won't take no for an answer. He doesn't let up; he takes her hand and yanks her to her feet. The hand that punched the wall is wrapped around her waist. They move in and out of Jamie's vision, their bodies spinning, her green eyes one moment, Riggs's tattooed arm the next, the fire crackling behind them. Three's a crowd.

Riggs slows and bends his arms, forcing her to dip down from her hips. Penny hesitates, only for half a second, then she allows her weight to drop into his arms, lets herself be caught. Except that Riggs stumbles, and she falls clumsy and heavy to the floor. Christ.

'Sorry,' Riggs says. 'I wasn't expecting you to be so heavy.'

Jamie's skin hikes to up to crawl. What a thing to say. Riggs isn't bothered: he doesn't stop dancing. He twists around with his arms outstretched. Penny rubs at her cheek and sits on the floor at Jamie's feet. He can feel the heat of her body on his legs, or perhaps it's the fire? Jamie can't tell what's what anymore. Riggs spins and spins, and knocks into the small wooden cabinet on the far side of the bookshelves. There's the unmistakable twinkling of glass. Riggs hears it too — he stops dancing and tugs on the cabinet's handle.

'It's locked,' he says. 'What's Uncle Martin hiding in here, eh?' He turns the rusted key. 'Oh yeah. Motherload. There's no getting around it now, babe, you're definitely having a party.' He holds up an unopened bottle of a pale-yellow tequila. 'Single estate agave. Aged in a single barrel, limited edition. Jackpot, baby!' With a theatrical flourish he tears the sticker from the corked lid and pops it open. 'Smells good. Minty, quite tart, a bit of cocoa, some earthiness too for good measure.'

'Cecilia' ends and the next song begins. Jamie bends down to look inside the cabinet beside Riggs. A dusty bottle of port and a half-empty bottle of Tia Maria are tucked into the corner, along with four shot glasses, tall and slender with cut-glass engravings on the sides. As Jamie reaches for them, his wrist knocks something that has been balanced against the wall, hidden from view. A pack of cards: *Say It or Shot It.* He turns the box over to read the back. *Answer a question or drink a shot: your call. Discover the secrets your friends are keeping and unearth your enemy's worst nightmares in this best-selling party game.*

He draws out a card at random: *What's the movie you've seen the most times?* Another: *Describe your secret sexual fantasy in detail – don't forget to include your fetish!*

'What's that?' Riggs says. He grabs a card from Jamie's hand and reads aloud, 'Do you believe in monogamy?' Riggs lifts his eyebrows. 'Well, do you?'

'I don't know,' Jamie says. He suspects Riggs will laugh at his answer. 'I like the idea of trust and commitment, so in a way, yes, I do. But if monogamy is simply a construct of capitalism and the patriarchy, and there's only the expectation that the woman is faithful because she's considered the property of a man, then the answer would be no.'

'Christ,' Riggs says. 'I'll definitely need some tequila if you're going to answer every question like that.'

Wind rushes the pines and shakes the house, followed quick by a solid lashing of rain. All the lights in the house flicker.

More gusts pile in, and light and darkness alternate as the lamps flicker — and then blink out. The music stops and the dog barks once, twice. The only light now is from the fireplace. From far in the distance, a faint rumble of thunder rolls in.

'Shit,' Jamie says.

'You got any candles?' Penny asks.

'I think there are some in the bottom drawer by the stove.'

Penny makes her way to the kitchen and returns with a set of ten white long-wicked candles and a supply of empty jars. She dips each candle into the fire, sets them in the jars and places them on the table, and when she leans over him — there, one more time, the fragrance of lavender — he feels outside himself somehow, the world around him smudging and his head tingling, as though Penny was still whispering in his ear that she wants the good things to stay. Christ, he needs to pull himself together.

'It's like a seance,' Riggs says. 'Come on. Let's play.'

A seance? That might be the last thing they need.

Jamie sits at the table, facing Riggs, Penny to his right. Riggs shuffles the deck like a card sharp, his hands flashing. The house groans around them as a solid blast of wind batters from the south.

'So,' Riggs says. He sets the cards in a pile in the middle of the table. 'I'll pick a card and read for Penny, then she will pick and read for Jamie, and last, Jamie, you read for me. We good with that?'

Penny shifts in her seat. 'If I don't want to answer—'

'No answer, you drink,' Riggs says. 'Where are those shot glasses?'

'I'll get them,' Jamie says. He moves slow and careful in the darkness, wary of hidden sharpness. He can't see a damned thing in the low light. But there they are, the four glasses in his hand. A shot of tequila might do him good. Help him relax a bit. He stands one glass before each seat, and Riggs pours tequila right to the rim.

'Let's go,' Riggs says. 'I'll start. Penny, what was the last thing you searched online.'

'Stonewall Gallery.'

'What's that?' Jamie says.

'The detritus of broken dreams,' she says.

Riggs shakes his head. 'Don't ask, bro, don't even ask.'

Penny takes up a card. 'Jamie, who was your first celebrity crush?'

'Winona Ryder,' he says, and he lets a quiet whistle out through his teeth. '*Reality Bites*.'

'It certainly does,' Riggs says. 'Viciously.'

Jamie reads to Riggs from the next card: 'Have you ever fallen asleep during sex?'

'Mate,' Riggs says. 'So many times. What, you haven't?'

'Can't say I have. Are you doing it right?'

Riggs laughs. 'Touché,' he says. 'Now Penny, what's your go-to karaoke song?'

'"Wicked Game",' she says. 'Chris Isaak'.

'Well, go on then,' Riggs says. She tugs at her sleeves and starts to sing. Jamie has never heard her do that. Her voice is clear and bright. But she's interrupted by a hard smattering on the sliding doors, and they all turn to look.

'That's hail,' Riggs says. 'It's hailing.'

Jamie stares at the candlelight. 'You have a lovely voice,' he says.

'Not a bad voice but the song is boring,' Riggs says. 'Mine would be Sublime's "Santeria". Guns, women. Great song.'

Penny turns to Jamie. 'What's yours?'

'Hm. Maybe "Linger" – you know, The Cranberries.' It was his favourite song as a teenager, back when he too thought nothing would go wrong. Still loves the song.

'What the fuck, bro. Far too soppy. Anyway, this is not how the game goes. Too much chatter, not enough drinking. Penny, pick a new card for Jamie already.'

She reads aloud: 'What are you glad your family doesn't know about you?'

'I hate my mother's cooking.'

Riggs says, 'It's true, Trish can't cook for shit.'

They all laugh. Jamie's uneasiness has faded. He's enjoying himself, despite it all. Been a while since he's played a drinking game, been even longer since he's had fun like this. You get to a certain age, and everyone you know is coupled up, with mortgages and no other plans for the weekend other than a coffee, a croissant and a visit to the local playground so their toddler can go mental and run themselves down for the midday nap. Too busy, they say, when you ask them out for a beer. Your friends fall away into this nuclear-family black hole and you're alone, with a job you hate, in a house you don't own, maybe going blind, and dreams of another kind of life haunt your sleep.

So, to have this: friends, laughter, a bit of banter? It's so good he can almost forget the throbbing headache and the increasing shadows in his vision. Because these aren't any friends; they're his oldest friends. Christ, they're not perfect, but nobody is perfect. If he has to be with anyone right now, then it should be with people like this, the kind of people who know you deep down, who know your mother's cooking is bad. People who remember how you got that scar on your forehead, the ones who can see through the changes of age and see the person you wanted to be, even if you missed the mark and became someone else entirely.

Jamie takes the top card from the pack. 'Have you ever broken the law?'

Eyes on the table, Riggs spins his shot glass faster and faster, somehow without spilling a drop of tequila. 'Of course,' Riggs says. 'But I mean, not like murder.'

Without any probing, he details his crimes: stolen chocolate bars and Doritos from the dairy on Waiheke — 'Both of these crimes were with you, Jamie, if I'm not mistaken'; class C drugs; class B drugs; class A drugs; driving under the influence of all drugs; skateboarding in places it's prohibited; skinny-dipping in Dubai, which he does not recommend.

'There are other things,' Riggs says, 'but they're morally wrong, rather than legally wrong, and I believe I'm not compelled to list those sins right now.' He stands and goes to the kitchen. 'All this talk's making me thirsty. I cannot imagine there'll be a question I'd refuse to answer, and I'm thirsty.' He takes a beer from the fridge, pops the top and drinks solidly for a few moments, then he sits again, the bottle of beer hanging lazily from his grip, and slides a card from the pack. 'Tell us, Penny, about the time you lost your virginity?'

Riggs is grinning as though he knows the answer. Christ. Jamie almost feels embarrassed for him.

Whatever Riggs thinks the truth is, he's wrong. Jamie remembers it like it was yesterday. His hand on her stomach, the sand cold under her back, the pale cream of her underwear. He risks a glance at Penny, and in the dim light, and through his failing eyes, she looks exactly the way she had that night: like someone worth taking a risk for.

PENNY

THE QUESTION HANGS IN the air between them. The asinine, juvenile humour Riggs has always prided himself on has now become grotesque. He leans back in his chair. Smirking, quiet, waiting for her to recount the night they arrived in Los Angeles.

That cheap motel near the airport. The room smelt of instant ramen, and Penny had heard a tap dripping somewhere nearby, a bit like the insistent sound from the drip down the hall. It was awkward sex, elbows in faces and teeth clashing when they kissed, and though a part of her wasn't convinced she wanted to be doing this with him and a part of her was wondering how she had ended up there with him, it was fun. Riggs knew how to make things fun. She'd run away from her parents, and the person she thought she loved had blamed her for the death of his father: all she craved was fun. She could tell that story, embellish it, make the awkward parts sound hilarious.

Only it wouldn't be true, and Jamie would know it.

She takes up the shot of tequila and holds it to her lips. There's no answer she can give, lie or otherwise. In one movement she tips the glass and drinks. The tequila is creamy, with hints of vanilla and caramel, a bit of pear. She coughs and wipes her mouth and sets down the empty glass. Riggs hollers and says, 'Don't know what you're so shy about. Greatest night of your life, you told me.'

That rank smell of beer on his breath. The leering broken tooth. He uncorks the bottle of tequila and refills her glass. 'Anyway,' he says, 'your turn to read.'

She takes the top card from the deck, turns to face Jamie. 'Do you believe in fate?'

Jamie rests his elbows on the table, his face expressionless. 'I don't think so.'

The rain lumbers down harder and the steady beat of drips in the bucket by the back door increases. She shivers, though she isn't cold.

'Why not?' Riggs says. 'I mean, I don't either, but as you're the philosopher around here, I'm curious to know your reasoning.'

'Ah, I'm too bitter,' Jamie says. 'If fate is real, then she's truly a bitch.'

Maybe it's the tequila rushing golden through her veins, but he's right. If fate is real, then she's truly a bitch. Why put everyone through such misery? Penny starts laughing at the absurdity of life. Look at the three of them, worn down with so much tragedy. Riggs looks at her oddly and then taps his hands on the table in a drum roll to match the rainfall.

'Well, she is,' Jamie says. 'I mean, we all get told we have "one precious and wild life", or whatever it is. I feel like it would be impossible to feel so hopeful if there was only one path and one outcome predetermined for us. I'll make mistakes and I'll learn from them, and when I choose the wrong path, I'll find my way to a new one. Every day I like to think I can choose to make a new ending, even if I can't do anything about my beginning.'

Riggs lifts his eyebrows. 'Well, I respect your thoughts, Professor Flannery. Now, shut up and read one for me. First though, Penny has inspired me.' He holds up a hand to pause all play. 'I cannot continue this game without a bit of fire in my belly.' He picks up his shot glass and slams back the tequila with his eyes screwed shut. He shakes his head. 'What the hell are we thinking? Where's the salt and lime?'

'Salt is on the bench,' Jamie says. 'Don't think we have any limes.'

'Fine, no salt, no limes,' Riggs says. 'Just straight liquor. Before you read for me, Jamie, you must also drink. Get it in ya, mate!'

Jamie raises his eyebrows and downs the shot. 'Right,' he says, setting the glass down. He picks up another card, but holds it for a bit before reading aloud: 'Riggs, have you ever had romantic feelings for someone of the same sex?'

Riggs grins. 'You all know me as a raging exemplar of heterosexuality, but I've had a plethora of sexual experiences. So, yes, the answer would be yes, and Jamie—' he looks serious for a moment — 'I have a confession to make.' He leans over and he kisses Jamie on the side of the head, pulling him into his chest. 'My brother, I love you.'

Jamie's cheeks flush bright red. He leans into Riggs for a moment, eyes closed. Riggs pulls away first and refills Jamie's shot glass. His hand is trembling ever so slightly.

A confession to make? Penny doesn't know how Riggs can say that with a straight face. She thought he was going to say something else.

Just then, a slashing wind hurls itself at the bach and the room seems to Penny to slide sideways, as though she's slipping off her chair. But she is seated still, safe and straight.

'Now we all drink,' Riggs says, and the three of them lift and drink in unison.

Penny sets her empty glass on the table again and glances at Jamie. The scar on his forehead from the Alley-Oop accident glints like danger in the candlelight. It's her turn to read to Jamie, and her voice sounds to her thin and clear, though her heart is thick and fast in her ear: *What is your biggest regret?*

'My biggest regret?' Jamie says. 'I try to avoid regret, on the whole.' He presses his hands together, puts the tips of his fingers on his lips and doesn't speak for a few seconds. 'There was this girl, a long time ago. And I don't know. I regret pushing her away.'

The room slides in the opposite direction. A log in the fire cracks and crumbles into the ashes. She holds the sides of her chair tight.

'Hell's bells,' Riggs says. 'I swear to god you're the most romantic bloke I know.' He imitates Jamie's voice and intonation: 'I thought I was falling in love, and for whatever reason I told her to get lost. Where is she now, bro? Maybe we should call her, tell her how you feel.'

Penny says softly, 'She's your biggest regret?'

Jamie leans back in his chair and tips his face up to the ceiling. 'Well, there's plenty of things to regret in my life, that's for sure. But she's ...' He sighs, pulls at his hair. 'I know, it's kind of lame.'

Riggs picks up his tequila and drinks it. He cracks his knuckles, eyes locked on the candle's gentle glow, and says, 'What are the things they say you think about when you're on your deathbed? The people you love, bro. Love is never lame.'

Rose in her final moments: her body, so ephemeral and pale, small, too small, eyelids thin as waxed paper. Penny, in bed beside her, the small feather-light hand in hers. Riggs collapsed in a chair at the side of the room, snoring so quietly it could have been moths beating at the window, trying to get to the light. The purple tutu hanging from a clothes hanger, the Minnie Mouse doll propped in the toy basket, Rose's heartbeat fluttering strong and then weak, pulsing in her wrist. What did Rose think about in those last moments? Penny hopes she was thinking of something peaceful. Something that made her feel safe, and loved, and that she was not in any pain. Had she made her daughter feel safe? Had she made her feel loved? She wasn't sure, she would never be sure. Her own turn will come, at some unknown point in the future, and who, or what, will be in her thoughts?

Wind races through the pines and the house shudders once more. Riggs pushes his chair back and tells Jamie to read for Penny. 'I need another beer,' he says, and he stalks to the kitchen, humming and rubbing at his head. Jamie picks up the top card from the deck.

'Are you happy?' he reads.

Penny smiles. 'Of course.'

Jamie looks at her. She rocks her chair onto the back legs and hovers. He says in a low voice, so low she knows Riggs won't be able to hear: 'I don't believe you.'

Riggs is standing in front of the open fridge, asking if Jamie wants a beer too. Jamie says he's all right. His cloudy grey eyes on her.

Her chair teeters. 'What makes you so confident about that?' she says.

'I can tell when you're lying.'

She tips her chin to her shoulder. 'He can't tell when I'm lying.' The chair tilts, wobbles. Riggs is still in the kitchen, fiddling with a bottle opener.

'Well,' he says, 'he doesn't want to believe you're capable.'

'And you do?'

'I think you're capable of anything,' Jamie says. 'And I mean that in a good way.'

Her chair jerks and tips backwards. The room twists, and she makes a small noise, not a shocked sound, no more than a small oh, as though still surprised that what she's been waiting for has happened. Without taking his eyes from hers, Jamie reaches out and catches the back of the chair. Pushes her back to solid ground. Only she feels more unsteady than she has ever before.

'Thank you,' she says.

'Penny,' Riggs says, seating himself beside her. 'Get a card for Jamie.'

She reads quickly: 'Do you want kids?'

'Easy,' he says. 'Yes, I would like kids. Not sure fate has them in store for me, but.'

'That bitch,' Penny says.

'Biggest bitch I ever met.'

'Not too late,' Riggs says. 'Maybe call that girl you were talking about earlier, she might be up for it. We're thinking about having another one, aren't we, babe?'

Penny keeps her face expressionless and says, 'Riggs.'

'All right, all right,' he says. The new beer is almost finished. His eyes are glassy and feverish, staring off into the middle distance. 'Let's all do a shot. Then Jamie, you read for me. Go, go go.' Another shot is the last thing Penny needs. She drinks it anyway. Why stay sober in this shitshow? The tequila runs hot to her gut like a first-degree burn. Jamie asks Riggs a question she can't follow and then Riggs is holding a card and saying her name louder and harsher: 'Penny.'

'Yes?'

Riggs reads from the card: 'If you could only do one sex act for the rest of your life, what would it be?' He flicks the card with a twist of his hand, and it flits across the table and hits her in the chest. She takes it and reads it silently, hoping he's joking and the card has another question entirely. It's not a joke. Of course, her answer doesn't have to be serious. She can say something ridiculous, make them laugh. Because what she needs is to laugh more, live more, not take everything so seriously.

Riggs turns to Jamie and says, 'It'll be missionary. Something boring like that. That's what happens when you marry a virgin, eh?'

She places the card on the table and sets it under the deck. The room spins, drifts southward, and the rain is loud and terrible on the tin roof. How can she make a joke now? She should let it go, forget about it, take the shot and make the question go away as she did earlier. Instead, she says, 'Excuse me?'

He has the decency to look a bit humiliated, but he says it again, louder this time: 'I said you're so vanilla you'll choose missionary.'

Vanilla. Simple. Unsophisticated. Penny plain. He means timid, maybe. Mediocre. Boring. The opposite of a risk-taker. The opposite of a person who wants to fill their life with pleasure and joy, the opposite of a hedonist. The opposite of the person she wanted to be. Her skin tingles as though scorched. What he's said hurts, mostly because she is frightened it's true.

'We're not married,' she says quietly. She spins the ring on her finger, slides it closer to the knuckle.

'I'm being honest!' he says, hands raised as though surrendering to her. 'Nothing wrong with missionary. It's just a bit, you know.' He shrugs.

'Honest?' Penny says. 'You're being honest?'

'Don't do this, Penny,' Riggs says. His eyes are turned down at the corners, the way they do when he's tired, or high. 'Don't be crazy.'

Jamie picks up his shot glass, drinks it down. 'Don't call her crazy,' he says.

'I can call her whatever I want!'

'If you're going to be honest, you should tell him about the Alley-Oop,' Penny says.

'Tell me what?'

Riggs sits motionless, cheeks sallow and thin. 'There's nothing to tell,' he says.

The drink and the sorrow hit her, and she's talking before she can think: 'He knew the screws were loose on your board.' As soon as she's said it, she regrets it. *What is your biggest regret?* Everything. All of it. None of it.

Jamie's voice is small. 'You knew my board was fucked? And you let me skate on it? Bro?'

'I mean, I didn't *do* anything to your board.' Riggs lays

his hands flat on the table. 'You have to understand, I didn't ... I never thought it was going to come apart. I thought it would hold.'

'Shit,' Jamie says.

'It's all good,' Riggs says. 'I mean, it was a long time ago! You're fine! Look at you! You've had a good life.'

'I'm fine?' Jamie says. 'If my wheel hadn't come off, I would've won. If I had won ... My whole life, in that one moment.'

'That's nothing but a hypothetical,' Riggs says. 'Maybe I would've won anyway. Can't live your life clinging to what could've been.' His voice is stiff and strange when he speaks again. 'You wanna live in some dream world of what if? That's pathetic. Live in the real world, bro.'

'I might be going blind,' Jamie says. 'Because of that head injury. That's the real world, Riggs.'

Riggs squirms. 'You're full of shit, mate. I mean, look at you. You're not blind.'

A flare of lightning pulses through the house and ghostly versions of their faces are reflected in the glass of the sliding doors. She can't see Riggs's chipped tooth. She sees him as he was. Light-hearted, daring, fiercely in love with her: there, in the turn of his head, the flash of his smile. The reflection seems to offer a glimpse of another life, another world. All sorts of things could be different there. If only she were brave enough to take a step, she could be in it. Then Riggs extends his arm to pick up the bottle of tequila and she spies the Rose on his arm, the spidery inky name, and her stomach drops. There is no other life, no other world. There is only this world, and the only thing left is for her to understand how to live in it.

A clap of thunder chases the lightning. The dog runs full

tilt down the hall and starts barking, a series of short, sharp, frenzied yaps louder than the storm.

Jamie turns to Penny. A muscle in the side of his face twitches. He says, 'Adam's been taking something. Some kind of pill.'

Riggs slams his hands on the table. The candles in their jam jars bounce and the two full shot glasses tip onto their sides. The dog, in one of the bedrooms, starts barking, barking, barking. Riggs clutches Penny's hand. The bones in her hand twinge and hurt and her pinkie finger zings. She tries to pull her hand away, and he holds it tighter, pulling her towards him.

'Penny,' Riggs says. 'I've been trying, I promise, I have. I mean. Hell. I don't think anything I do will make you happy. You've always been jealous of my success. I've tried to help you. I give you a studio, all you do is complain that what you paint is shit. Give you a child, then you blame me for every single thing that goes wrong. Get you a gallery invite and you fucking turn your back on it.'

The candlelight flutters. Her hand begins to throb.

'You asked Sally Trubridge to invite me?' she says.

Riggs drops her hand and stands up.

'So what if I did?' he says. 'I thought it was what you wanted. I asked your bloody father, who hates me, you know. I asked him for a favour, 'cause I thought it would finally make you happy.'

Jamie says, 'Riggs, sit down.'

Riggs points at Jamie. He's mad as a bit snake, grimacing and hostile. 'Shut it. I'm warning you.'

Jamie stands too. When he speaks, his voice is barely audible over the wind and the incessant barking of the dog. 'Let's calm down, eh?'

Another flash of lightning flares over the house. The dog bolts back down the hall and stands pawing at the doors, her reflection scattered and erratic in the firelight. There, behind the dog, in the reflection, an evanescent head of strawberry blonde. Penny's heart is in her throat, punching, punching. Tequila rising up into heartburn. Thunder rolls through loud and punishing, and the head vanishes.

Riggs moves around the table towards her, rolling his head on his neck from side to side until the vertebrae click. His dark eyes are sunk deep, the tattoo stark and ugly on his arm, and there is a wild look on his face that Penny doesn't like.

'Adam,' Jamie says. 'Leave her alone.'

'Mate,' Riggs says, strangely calm. 'With all due respect, would you kindly fuck off?'

'We're drunk,' Jamie says. 'It's late. We should go to bed, sleep it off.'

'Why are you so keen to stand up for her? Eh? What's she to you?'

'Riggs,' Penny says. She rotates the ring around her knuckle, sliding it off her finger. The prongs of the diamond setting dig into her palm. The threats no longer matter to her: he can do as he pleases. She never wanted to leave the last thing to connect her to Rose. To keep going, to make a new life, she never imagined it would mean burning her old one down to the ground. The only thing she wants right now is never to see him again.

Riggs smiles, a big toothy grin, and he nods his head real slow. 'You two been going at it behind my back, have you? You have, haven't you, you've been fucking, haven't you?'

He steps forward, raises his hand, knocks her across the

head. She gasps at the pain, the memory of it the same, as though both moments are happening at once, forever and ever. Again, he hits her, so hard she falls to the floor. He loses his footing and knocks the table with a solid thump. All ten candles waver, jam jars dancing on the wooden top.

Much later, she will recall what happened next as though in slow motion: the candles, one by one, toppling to their sides, the spilt tequila bursting into flame, the space between the three of them burning up, blazing bright with fire.

RIGGS

THE FIRE BURNS OUT as swiftly as it started. All that's left is the pungent stench of smoky rubber, and the sound of Jamie coughing. Without the candles, the room is darker and dingier than ever. He can't see much, and the feeling makes his skin itch. What he needs is a lungful of that wild, stormy air — yes, hell yes, a bit of fresh air and some time away from these two idiots — so he picks up his beer and heads to the doors. He opens them a crack and, before he can stop her, the dog races out in front of him. A wet wind blows in at Riggs hard as a brick wall, and he steps outside without so much as looking back.

Rain shimmies down in thick sheets and the ocean churns and rages. Riggs follows the dog down onto the sand. The cold smacks him sober and he thinks of the look on their faces when the flames consumed the table. Shit. Nearly enough to make him laugh. Nearly. They looked like they thought the whole place was going to burn down around them. That fire was never going to cause any real damage. What was burning was nothing but vapours.

He heads south along the beach. Could just as easily be heading north. He has no idea where he's going, what he's doing. Dog has disappeared, and since he doesn't want to go back to the house, he takes it one foot in front of the other, slow-going, pushing against the wind. Going blind, Jamie had said. What the hell was that all about? From the Alley-Oop? The dog comes back into view, skirting the surging tide, and Riggs downs the remaining beer in one long gulp. Glances back at the house, spits out the last bitter mouthful at his feet.

He thought it didn't need saying but clearly it did: he didn't sabotage Jamie's skateboard. He'd noticed the screws were loose! That was all! It shocks him that this requires such direct clarification. He didn't tamper with the damned thing. Tampering is not his style. He'd considered the rickety wheels and truck a potential problem, but he'd thought it would be fine! Never would have given Jamie the board if he'd thought it would end in disaster. Or would he? In hindsight, on this beach in the middle of the night, his hand still ringing with the sensation of slapping the one person he loves more than anything, he's no longer certain of what he has done or what he might do in the future.

Far off over the southern cliffs the sky sparks with silver lines of lightning. The rain eases off; the storm is moving on. Riggs shivers. In his pocket, the last of Meg's pills and the keys to the rental car, his wallet, a lid from a bottle of beer. Everything else — his passport, his shoes, his cell phone, his whole bloody brilliant life — is back in the bach. Fuck, who cares? Doesn't need any of that. Not now. He tosses his empty bottle into a pile of driftwood, hopes it smashes. What did they want him to say, huh? Admit that he'd deliberately messed around with it so Jamie wouldn't win? Hell, how was he to know when the wheel would actually ping off? He'd done nothing, he'd simply failed to recognise the true danger. People do that all the time. We aren't fortune tellers. He isn't a psychic. We can't predict when terrible things are going to happen. Can't pin the blame at his door when all he's done is exist with all his ordinary human failings.

Could've been his board come undone. Whether you tanked or not was nothing but luck. It was destiny, fate. The world had played out as it did and there isn't anything anyone can do about it now, not twenty bleeding years later. He'd seen it in their faces, in those frozen moments before he'd fallen onto the table, that they were contemplating a world in which it hadn't happened, the world in which he, Riggs, had lost. The world where Jamie won, and Jamie took the girl, and he ruled the skateparks, and they had the child, and the child hadn't died.

Well, fuck them both. That isn't what happened and there's no use getting all twisted up about it.

He tracks off the sand and into the pines, looking for the car. He feels good but he has had a lot to drink. Still, when has that stopped him from doing what he wants? And right now he wants to go to Whangamatā. Or Auckland. Find someone to talk to, someone who might know someone who has what he craves. Driving there at this hour of the night, in this sort of weather, there'll be no one else on the road. The only person he could hurt is himself. And who is going to stop him? No one alive on this good Earth gives two shits about whether he's all right.

He weaves through the pines. The car must be close. A glint of light washes over the windscreen and he's there, keys in hand. Gets the door open, key into the ignition and, in the seconds before he closes the door, he pauses, listening. He won't admit it, but he is waiting for someone to stop him. Except no one calls out. No one is at the door, begging him to stop. He wrenches at the ignition. The engine grumbles to life, and he backs the car around and leaves the bach behind.

The driveway seems longer than it should. Light and shadow flicker through the pines and Riggs thinks the trees are moving, walking perhaps, shifting in place, and though he refuses to feel frightened his mouth is full of a horrid taint.

At long last, the end of the drive, and he's spat out onto the road. The car skids slightly on the greasy tarmac, enough to get his attention, so he readjusts his grip and picks up speed. The forested hills loom on both sides, and he turns on the radio. Red Hot Chili Peppers' 'My Friends' fades in and out. He can't remember what the song reminds him of, only he knows he used to listen to it all the time, and then it comes to him: he and Jamie sitting on the grass near the half-pipe, sharing headphones plugged into Jamie's Discman, a whole life and world ahead of them.

He swings around a tight bend and the car's headlights spotlight a possum ahead. The animal pauses in the glare, red eyes like lasers. Riggs guns the accelerator. Funny how something so treasured elsewhere can be a damned pest here. One man's garbage, another man's treasure and all that. The car's leering down on it, and the possum doesn't even try to move. Stupid animal. When the tyres roll over its body, the bump is so minimal Riggs could be convinced nothing happened. It seems not every terrible thing makes much of an impact.

A gentle tap on the brakes and the car lurches — his feet are blocks of ice. He regrets not bringing shoes, or another beer. Tricky to gauge the pressure on the pedals with feet this cold. A push on the accelerator jumps the car forwards. Who cares. He was right, the roads are empty, abandoned to the storm and the night, so he doesn't have to worry too much about how he's driving. The entire road is his. He swerves the car over both lanes, starts deliberately speeding up and braking hard for the hell of it. A stroke of lightning, closer this time after all, hits — and for a second the sky is seamed with white as though the universe is breaking apart.

Red Hot Chili Peppers cut out and another song starts, filtered with static. Watery-sounding chords, string instruments, a humming voice. The Cranberries' fucking 'Linger'. What are the fucking chances of that? A damp tightness pulls at his cheeks, and deep in his guts a bad feeling sets in.

Going blind. Is that true? And it's his fault? Of course it is. It is all his fault. He can tell himself all he wants that he wasn't able to predict the future, can protest as much as he wants that he's only human and that he did nothing wrong. He can do that all day until the cows bloody come home and moo their heads off, and it wouldn't change the truth, would it. He'd known the truth from the instant Jamie landed the impossible ollie from the rail, known it as soon as the front of the board had softened and his friend had plunged headfirst into the ground. When Jamie lay prone, and blood, so much blood, was seeping from his skull, the board with Penny's design cracked and broken beside him, his ankle bone snapped at a horrifying angle, Riggs had known he could've prevented it.

And then, the true burn, worse than giving Jamie the board, he'd turned away from the scene of the crime. Instead of going to his friend, instead of accompanying him, his brother, to the hospital, he'd turned away and prepared for his turn to compete. His mind on the prize. He couldn't face the truth, not then, not in any of the years since. He'd told himself, waiting for his turn to zip down and win the Alley-Oop, that there was nothing he could have done. He wasn't a bloody doctor. He wasn't a nurse. He was merely a guy who desired more than he had, and who wasn't going to waste his chance to get it.

Rain again. Riggs hits the wipers. Wind buffets the car, and he grips the steering wheel tight. He wants to be out of his mind now; he doesn't want to think about any of this. He was never Superman, he was never tough, he can see that now. Maybe he didn't cry as a kid, maybe he never let his emotions get in the way, but it's obvious that doesn't make him stronger than anyone else. He was weak; he is weak. Penny will leave him and what will he have? What is there, when everything is gone?

He accelerates into a hairpin turn and the car's weight rests in his stomach. It slides and takes him with it. He can't go fast enough because he can't leave the trouble behind. It's inside him. He pushes down on the accelerator a bit more, and he's amazed at how quickly it happens, the car responsive to his control, then, two seconds later taking on a power of its own, veering from the road, swerving into a ditch on the far side.

In those few precious seconds between the crash and falling into unconsciousness, Riggs remembers a long-ago day with Jamie. They're nine, ten maybe, children still, playing down at the creek behind the school. Sunlight dappling through the leaves and brown air. Another moment: the two of them meeting Penny, her hand in his and him kissing it. It seems unbelievable that someone as stupid as he is has had such a good life. He's had his hard times, but that's life, isn't it, suffering? He's been a fool to think it was ever going to be anything other than that.

Thoughts race and hurl after each other, and through them he can hear the engine hissing. His head pounds and his chest burns where the seatbelt grips him solid. An odour fills the car — shit and blood and the smell of the bush after rain. What a serious clusterfuck of mistakes have led him to be here! All his, no one else to blame, really. His mistake was to tell Penny what he'd done or failed to do at the Alley-Oop. His mistake was giving the board to Jamie. His mistake was thinking Rose would be all right. His mistake was believing that Penny loved him. His mistake was believing he would never hit her. His mistake was thinking he didn't need to forgive himself. His mistake was believing he could change.

Before he closes his eyes, he's certain he sees Rose in the darkness beyond the window, her strawberry-gold hair aflame in the flash of lightning. There, he sees her pointed chin and widow's peak, that purple tutu, her thin, bruised legs. This is what Penny had spoken of. How could he have laughed? The sight of his daughter is sunshine, and he feels warm all of a sudden. A rinse of bile washes over his tongue and he swallows, blinks twice, and she disappears before he's ready to say goodbye. What was it his father said to him the other day? Sometimes you'll hold on to something so hard, hold it tight so it stays there with you and stays the same, and you can get all worked up about it when, really, you have no choice but to let it go.

Let it go.

JAMIE

DRUNK AND FUELLED BY rage, Jamie staggers down onto the sand and shouts to Riggs, over and over: Adam! Adam! Adam? *Adam*!

Where is that arsehole? Where has he gone? Jamie shouts again, but it's pointless: the split second his voice leaves his mouth it is whipped away by the wind. There's a spattering of rain, and he slips on a pile of slimy seaweed, cutting his hand on a broken shell as he falls. Kneeling on the sand, jeans soaked through, cut palm stinging, he wonders why the hell he is even out here chasing Riggs. He gave Jamie a crook board at the Alley-Oop and stood by while Jamie ruined his life. He took Jamie's girl and didn't love her the way he should. Now, ego-bruised, he's stormed out of the house, and Jamie is out in the middle of a storm, cold and wet and angry, too angry to think straight, trying to stop Riggs before he does anything stupid.

Jamie carries on further along the beach. What will he even say to Riggs when he finds him? That he's forgiven for what happened at the Alley-Oop? He can't say that, because he hasn't forgiven him. Hell would have to freeze over before he could forgive him. All this was Riggs's fault, the motherfucker. Maybe he could forget talking; he could curl up his fist and lay it on his friend instead. Christ, that would feel good, wouldn't it, a smack to the face. He must be drunk, if he's considering hitting Riggs. He's never hit anyone in his life. Never even been tempted.

There, movement on the beach not far away. Riggs! He runs towards it, but it is only the dog, sandy and wet and wild. She scooters near and then in a flick of sand she's off into the night.

Jamie pulls at his hair and looks around. Is the bach over there, or over there? He takes a few steps and pauses, his heart faltering. In the darkness the world is completely lost to him. He is marooned in the nothingness.

He's felt this way before, as a kid. Six he was, maybe seven, out alone after a game of spotlight in the fields beyond Rocky Bay. Waiheke was pretty quiet in those days. Away from the lights of the houses and the small strip of shops, it was black as pitch and completely isolated. He doesn't know how he got left behind, why the others left without him, but he remembers the feeling when his torch batteries flickered and cut out. How he nearly cried when he called for help and no one answered and he understood he was alone in the feral emptiness of the farm. He sat, huddled on a small hump of hill where the grass grew long and glossy, cradling his knees to his chin. It wouldn't be long before someone came to find him — his mum or his dad would come. They would never abandon him to the darkness.

He hadn't had to wait long. Soon, a bouncing, pale torchlight could be seen winding over the field. Someone called his name, and he knew the voice: Adam had found him.

Only Riggs won't save him now: he's gone. Fucked them all and taken off into the night, as though he was the victim and he needed to leave before they hurt him anymore. Jamie curses his friend under his breath just as the world cracks with a slash of lightning. There! He spies a shadowed figure, hunched and wide-shouldered, twenty or twenty-five metres south, moving away from him down the beach. Must be Riggs. Jamie has to stop him. Who knows what that maniac might do? The dazzling silver light vanishes, a roll of thunder grumbles in the distance, and Jamie sets out in the direction he believes Riggs has gone. He can't let him leave. No matter what's just happened, he can't let him disappear out into the night drunk and breakneck wild.

The wind blasts sand over his legs and his face, and he hears the dog barking somewhere to his left. He moves quick and shouts Riggs's name again. An enormous log of driftwood blocks his path, and he steps around it. He's certain he's going in the same direction as the figure he'd seen ... or is he? No, no, he's not certain, not at all. Soon the shallows are puddling around his ankles, tingling cold water biting at his toes, and he turns, trying to find the dunes and the forest. A few steps more, yet the water's no shallower. Waves push against him from all directions, slashing at him in wet unruly slaps, and he swallows hard and moves the opposite way. Too much drink, too little sense, and he shouts to the nothingness. His teeth clam together, and now the water is up to his chest.

'Penny!' he shouts instead. 'Penny!'

'Jamie? Where are you?'

Her voice warm in the wind. Too far away though. Can't see anything in this darkness. He moves sloppy in the water towards where he thinks the sound of her voice carried from, only there's just more water, nothing but choppy waves popping up and splashing his face, pooling around his chin. 'Penny?' His throat is dry and hoarse. 'Penny?'

Before he has a chance to shout once more, he is underwater.

He should have heard the wave coming. Should have heard that telltale sound of sucking and building, the water pulling away from him to build into the swell. Only he didn't, and the wall of water hits him and knocks him to the ocean floor. He can't stand. Is held hostage by the whitewash billowing overhead. The water seethes around him, sand thick in the crush. Saltwater floods his nose, and he's frantic. He paddles with his hands, flailing in the water, and he's up, up, up in the holy air. He takes a long, sweet inhale and shouts for her. Penny.

Another wave surges through, more powerful than the first, and he's under again, spinning and tumbling for an eternity. It must be an eternity because soon he's craving another breath. But he's still underwater, rolling, rolling. His elbow and knee graze the sand. Still underwater. His brain and lungs scream for a breath. A hard pressure pulses in his chest, and he swims up, surely this is up, only the surface eludes him and he begins to feel a real terror. He is down still, held down, kept under the churning wash of the waves, alone and for too long, the pressure growing stronger and more urgent.

He isn't as frightened at the thought of drowning as he might have expected. He won't have to worry about his future if he drowns. Won't have to consider the consequences of what has happened tonight, or what will happen tomorrow, or the day after that. Will never have to contend with a life without seeing, won't have to try to understand how he got to this place that he can't find a way out of. A total abdication from life — what other idea could bring such agony and such sweet peace? Is this what his father craved? A peaceful retreat from it all? What would the harm be if he let the ocean take him? At least he, Jamie, wouldn't be leaving anyone behind. His mother would understand; she'd get it. He was poisoned, just as Madeline foresaw, fated to follow his father down this path.

He is scared, by Christ he is scared. Maybe this is not what he would choose, but he can live with it. He isn't dead yet: he exists in this moment, in the blistering cold water, floating in a darkness, alone in the universe, and for now that is enough. Any moment, he knows, any moment he will lose control and his mouth will open and the icy water will rush in and he'll sink and it will be over.

PENNY

PENNY STANDS ON THE beach, waiting to hear Jamie's voice. She has no idea where he is. She has no idea where Riggs is either. She heard Jamie call before, she's certain of it, the sound of it thin and unsteady, though loud enough to know it wasn't a trick of the night. He's out there, somewhere, in the mayhem. She takes another step, listening, trying to hear anything, anyone, above the waves and the wind in the trees.

The rain has mostly eased, but the wind is incessant. From somewhere in the pines behind the house she hears the sound of a trunk cracking, a tree falling to the ground. She shouldn't be out here, none of them should. It's two in the morning, and she's exhausted and drunk on tequila.

A snap of silver lightning dazzles the sky for the briefest of moments: she can't see Riggs or Jamie anywhere. The dog rushes by, kicking sand up behind her paws. Driftwood and seaweed and a stingray tangled in fishing line lie on the beach. The pines on the crest of the cliffs rise like jagged teeth against the silver sky. Then she sees a pale shape, tumbling in the waves. A body. Only darkness envelops her again, and the shape, the body, is gone.

There's no time to think. She races toward the water, pulling her sweater over her head and unbuttoning her jeans as she runs, kicking them off with the next few steps and leaving them where they lie. She feels the bite of the southerly on her bare legs. Murky water swirls around her ankles. Is she heading in the right direction, or is this a mistake? Who knows, but she doesn't hesitate. She rushes into the waves, wading deeper and deeper. A bigger wave leers up, and she dives into its guts, the cold hitting her harder than a heavyweight. Her hands paddle to bring her to the surface, and for a moment seem to make no headway, but when she does re-emerge it's raining hard again, thick glinting sheets undulating in the wind. She dives under, eyes wide, arms swinging. The ocean is too vast, she will never, never ...

Up once more, a gasping choke of an inhale. Is she crying or is it the rain? Her brain pounds from the drink and the cold. Can't think straight. Can hardly register her engagement ring is lost. She dives. Kicks down beneath a wave and is dragged along the beach by the swell and the current.

Then, her leg touches something.

Something solid.

She reaches out and wraps her arms around the solid shape — and yes, it is a body. It's Jamie. The wave has pushed them near the shore, and she finds she's able to stand. She holds him upright and his head rolls slack and heavy. Up through the mess of waves, her breath catching from the effort. She drops him awkwardly onto the sand. His arms lie floppy and loose by his sides, and her first thought is of Rose, the weight of her when she died, and she takes Jamie's hand and presses it tight between her own as though she can bind him to this world through her grip. Stay, stay here with me. The tide rushes up and around his head, and she sweeps at the water to keep it away from his face.

His chest is still. His lips are faintly violet, his skin chalky. She places two fingers into the crook of his jaw. There, feather-light, a pulse. The dog sits only a few metres away, quiet and watchful, almost as though she knows what is happening. Penny tips Jamie's chin to the heavens, opens his mouth with a cautious finger. Pinches his nostrils closed, presses her mouth to his lips and begins, slowly, to exhale.

Two long deep breaths, and then she leans back, waits to see if Jamie's chest lifts. The moon moves into an opening in the clouds, and his face is burnished with a sheen of glorious light. Penny was raised an atheist. Her father's idea of spiritualism was a good review in *Art News*, and if her parents ever mentioned organised religion, it was to ridicule followers of such things for their naivety. And that has never shifted for her. But with Jamie's face as bright and perfect as a Caravaggio angel, she finds herself longing for the existence of a god. She craves someone with a power greater than her own. She wants to beg mercy. This isn't a new feeling, and it hasn't ever worked before — not even when she'd bargained with her own life in exchange for her daughter's — but the yearning returns to her nonetheless. Please, please, let him live. She lowers her head and breathes into Jamie again. His mouth is cold and tastes of brine, and his body remains unresponsive. The prayer moves with her, lifting up in her chest with her inhale and moving from her mouth to his.

Still nothing. She almost laughs at the absurdity of it. What is the point? She isn't so special that a pleading prayer will make any difference, even if there is a god. And still she keeps breathing, moving life from her body into his, aware it is probably too late. The dog shifts in the sand beside her, the waves land heavy on the shore, and she understands with a sudden certainty that if he dies or if he survives, none of it is to do with her, and that Rose's death was not her fault either. People come, and people go, and all she can do is love them fiercely while they're there. Good things come and good things go, Jamie had said. Aren't we lucky they come at all? He is one of the loveliest things, it's clear to anyone. She grips his hand and starts to cry.

A spluttering then, and a cough. She tips him to his side, and he heaves water up onto the sand.

'You're okay,' she says. 'You're okay.'

Those were the words she repeated to Rose as well. She'd said it every time a phlebotomist had taken bloods, every time that flinty-looking chemotherapy nurse injected the poison that might save Rose's life, every time Rose felt such pain you wanted to sell your soul to the devil and scream to the gods: Take me! I'm the one you're looking for! That was what she'd said. You're okay. Those inane, meaningless words: You're okay, my darling. You're okay. She knew it wasn't always true, what she'd said, but it had always felt kind, and it had always felt necessary. For Rose, and for her. She says it now for the same reason, and this time, like every other time, she fervently hopes it might also be true.

A bluster of wind covers them both in a shimmer of sand. They need to get inside the house before hypothermia, or worse, sets in. She stands and pulls Jamie up, resting his weight on her hip, and very slowly walks him to the bach.

The fire in the hearth has dwindled to ash and the rooms are dark. The floor is sticky with tequila. She lays Jamie on his bed, easing a pillow under his head, brushing the hair from his eyes. He needs to be warmed up, but how? The room is shockingly cold. She flicks the light switch a few times. The power is still out, so the column heater is no help. They say get skin to skin to prevent hypothermia, only she can't, she shouldn't, so she searches in his drawers for dry, warm clothes. She peels off his wet trousers and top. Carefully, slowly, she towels his body dry. His legs, his stomach, his chest, his arms — she touches him gentle and tender — then she re-dresses him. Pulls his arms through sleeves of a woollen knit. Gathers socks into her fingers and eases them over his feet. She rubs his wet hair with a new towel, covers him with a duvet and several blankets, smoothing out the creases in the bedding until it is immaculate. Through all this he is quiet on the bed, breathing slow and calm. He is alive, he is safe. Everything is all right. Only a leaden heaviness bears down on her; a sense the worst is yet to come. She peers out the window: the car is gone.

She dozes for a while, a fitful half-sleep, and when Jamie moves in the bed she wakens fully. The room is almost completely silent and dark; the wind and rain have eased. 'Is that you, Penny?' he says faintly.

'Yes,' she whispers. 'Sorry.'

He moves his arm to prop up his head. 'I don't mind you being here,' he says. 'It's nice, actually, to wake up and not be alone.'

She looks up at the ceiling and says, 'I thought you were going to die.'

'So did I.'

Neither of them speaks for a minute.

'Funny,' he says. 'A few weeks ago I think I would have been okay with that.'

'You wanted to die?'

'Yeah. I thought maybe my dad had the right idea after all.'

'I'm glad you changed your mind.'

'To be honest with you,' he says, 'I don't know if I have.'

'If you'd killed yourself two weeks ago, you wouldn't be here with me, would you? And who knows what you could be doing in two years' time, what you might be feeling? You might lose some things, but there will be other things yet to come. I promise.' She can't promise, of course she can't, but what else is there to say?

'That reminds me of this graffiti I saw yesterday at the skatepark,' he says.

'What was it?' She thinks of their phoenix, their last great masterpiece together.

'It wasn't a picture,' he says. 'It was more like a tag, I suppose. It said, Hurting now does not mean your future holds pain.' She can tell he is trying not to cry. 'I suppose it makes me think about my dad. If my dad had waited, maybe life could've been okay for him. I don't know. Or maybe I'm selfish. I wanted him around for my own selfish reasons. Maybe what he did was really brave, because he was true to himself.'

'I don't think it's selfish to wish you'd had more time together.'

He takes her hand, runs his thumb along the side of her crooked finger, and her heart pounds in her ears. 'Your bloody father,' he says. 'Our bloody fathers.'

'When we grow up, let's not be like our bloody fathers,' she says.

In the deep indigo of the room his face is hazy, indistinct, but she believes he is smiling.

'You know,' she says, 'when I thought of you, I imagined you'd be happily married, three kids, good job, nice schools, big house in the suburbs.' This was what she'd wanted for him. A lot of love. A good life. A happy life. An ordinary life.

'You thought about me?'

'Every now and then,' she says. 'Did you think about me?'

'Every now and then,' he says. 'Every now and then.'

RIGGS

IT'S THE CHILL THAT wakes him, the biting, damp chill of dawn. Every inch of his body rages and hurts. For a few hours he drifts in and out of consciousness — psychedelic dreams, freaky shit he's not keen to dwell on — and when the sun rises the air in the car grows foul. When his back starts to spasm beyond endurance, he knows it's time to get out and figure out what in the hell he's going to do now.

He stands in the ditch not far from the road's edge, shivering and grotty, bare feet stony cold on the wet ground. His mouth is sour with hangover and his skull crackles with a ten-tonne headache. Thick bush closes in on him on both sides of the road, and he waits to see if a car will pass and pick him up: either direction, he's not that finicky. No one comes. He starts to walk back the way he came, back to the bach.

He has no clue how far he drove in the night. His memory of

leaving — after the fight, in the middle of the storm — is full of gaps, and even after what he supposes must be twenty minutes of walking, he is still in the middle of nowhere. In a few ways, it's quite impressive how far he managed to drive under the influence of tramadol, weed and a whole lot of alcohol.

Tramadol. A hand to his pocket, and a tingling jolt down his lumbar spine. He's lost the last of the pills, as well as his wallet and the keys to the rental car. All that remains in his pockets is the lid of a beer bottle. What a bloody disgrace. What a stupid, stupid, stupid piece of work he is. The mere thought of what happened last night makes him stop and vomit into the scrubby road shoulder.

The night before. Enough of it is there, skulking. He knows how devastating it was. How disgusting his behaviour was. Maureen would have him exorcised if she knew. He hears the beer bottles falling from the table and the bach rattling in the storm. He sees the bright warmth of candlelight on Penny's face when she realised he had asked Damian to arrange the solo show, her green eyes flashing in the knowledge that he'd undermined her so viciously. He sees too, and feels in his gut Jamie's expression when he understood his board had failed because of Riggs, the person who dared call him a friend, a brother. The shame of his betrayal flares up and he stops to chunder again. More and more gorges out until all the good stuff is gone and he's down to the thin scrapings of bile. A car drives by. He can barely lift his head to see if it might stop to pick him up, though it turns out there's no need. The driver passes without even slowing to check he's okay. Turns out he's not the only arsehole on the Coromandel.

The sun rises directly overhead; the day drags on. He

hobbles along, getting nowhere fast — the worst speed for a day like this, leaving far too much time to wallow. His left eye is brutally tender to the touch, and his feet are worn raw and bleeding. A shower and a soft bed, that's all he wants, though it's far more than he deserves.

A step, two steps. Grinding pain in his back, his body cold and hot in sweeping shifts. A dead possum lies in the middle of the road, pink insides in a dainty pile beside the body. Did he hit it last night? That very possum? The memory is hazy but what is certain is that the thing he's been dreading all these years — basically since the night he first kissed her — has happened. It's over between him and Penny. He'd be a moron to think otherwise, and while he can't deny he's a blockhead dope, a part-time sociopath, an exceptionally loose unit, and occasionally the world's biggest dickhead, he's no fool. He gets it: there's no coming back from this. She's put up with a lot from him, and he's tried his best to keep her, only this is next level. He accused her and Jamie of having it off, didn't he. He did the one thing he's always considered the worst of the worst. He hit her. Holy mother of god. Well, he wouldn't blame them if they got together. Even a blind man can see Jamie would be better for her than he is.

A red Suzuki Swift blazes past, and he lifts his thumb in its wake. The brake lights dash on and his heart lifts. The car takes the corner without stopping.

'Fuck you too!' he shouts into the emptiness; he walks on.

Three goats startle in the bracken above him and he stops to watch their retreat. He spits again, runs his tongue round his mouth, buries it into the hole where the missing tooth should go. Can't help it, can we, as humans, prodding deep into the places where things used to be? A mass of cloud rises up and blots the sun. The heat drops away and he walks in the glorious shade for almost an hour.

A white van rolls around a tight bend, headed in the opposite direction to Riggs. But it slows and pulls over into a thin strip of shoulder. The driver winds down the window and beckons him to cross over.

'Where ya trying to get to?' A man with long hair leans from the open window, and a Phoebe Bridgers song wafts from the radio. Penny loved that woman, sang her sad songs over and over and over, drove Riggs near crazy.

'You need a ride?' the man asks. 'I'm on my way to Whangamatā but don't mind a detour.'

'Great,' Riggs says. 'I'm staying at a bach this way.' He notices how the man flinches when Riggs comes close. Whether it's the blood or the swollen eye, the shit-stained pants or the missing tooth, there's no way to tell.

'Didn't know there was anything around here,' the man says. He pushes aside some McDonald's burger boxes and tells Riggs to excuse the mess.

'Mate, look at the state of me,' Riggs says, and the man laughs.

'You certainly look as if you've had a rough time of it.'

The driver does a U-turn and heads north. 'I Know the End', that's the song.

'Nice ink,' the man says.

Riggs spins his forearm. 'Yeah,' he says. 'Got that for my daughter.'

'Nice. Not a father myself. Not for me. It's good to know that about yourself, right?'

He turns the radio volume up a tab, right when Phoebe is going on about not being too scared to disappear. The trumpets or whatever the hell they are start blasting and the man taps the steering wheel and Riggs feels sick rising in his throat. The song ends and there's Phoebe heavy breathing, and he's pretty sure he's going to throw up.

'I'm not feeling so good,' he says.

'What's that?'

Too late. He thought he'd thrown up every single particle held in his digestive system. Turns out he was wrong. Vile spew coats his legs and feet, the dashboard, the gear stick.

'Fuck me,' the man says. In an instant he's pulled the van half off the road and he's shouting at Riggs to get out.

'I can't keep walking,' Riggs says. 'It's not that far now. Come on.'

'Get the fuck out, man. Look at this.' The guy covers his mouth with his hand. 'One of the reasons I didn't have kids, man. Can't stand all this sort of bodily fluid shit. And now look what you've done.'

Riggs glares at him with his one open eye. 'You going to leave me here?'

'Sometimes the only person who can help you in your hour of need is yourself,' the man says. 'Now piss off.' He laughs. 'I hope you make it where you want to go.'

It must be an hour at least before another vehicle passes by, a truck this time, winding around the narrow bends. The driver leans on the horn, presumably to punish him for meandering on the shoulder, so Riggs lifts a middle finger. He keeps it there even after the truck has turned and disappeared. It feels good, he thinks, to tell the world he doesn't give a shit. Because he doesn't, not anymore.

A bank of dark clouds presses close and a thick shower of rain soaks him thoroughly. At least, at the very least, he won't stink so much now.

The clouds break apart when he's nearing the bach and a watery sun takes the chill from his bones. With each step, his mood lightens, his hangover lessens, and soon he's wishing he had his board so he could float down these roads, take the corners with a wide arc.

Only a certain kind of person enjoys skateboarding. Someone who doesn't mind pain. The simple act of standing on the board is too much for many people. What should be supportive and steady is anything but. A skateboard isn't transportation, although you can use it that way. It's a dare, a promise, an invitation. To go somewhere and not just forwards. Up. Around. Over, under. There's danger in every second. The goal is control of something outside your control.

Plummet. Get up. Come a cropper. Try again. Trip; begin again. He's that sort of person. Someone who won't stay down. Yeah, he's lost it all. He's lost his best mate, his missus, his only child, his career. He's plummeted to the bottom. Fallen as far as it's possible to fall. But he is a special kind of person, despite all his flaws. He is someone everyone wants to be deep down, someone who is willing to risk it all, to live fully and thoroughly, someone who will never sit back and think what if. Someone who will get up and try again. Someone who acknowledges that bad times are gonna come, and that you can choose if you want to be tough or if you're gonna lean into that weepy shit.

It's late in the afternoon now. The horizontal shadows through the pines across the road appear golden. A car passes in the opposite direction, a brown Ford Sierra wagon, and he thinks he sees someone in the back seat wave to him. He turns off the road and heads down the long driveway to the shabby old bach. He knows exactly what he's going to do.

A plan has come to him, formed full: skateboarding will save him. He will make a skateboarding video. Not just any old video full of nasty falls and the same old tricks. No, this will be much more ambitious. He'll contact one of the producers from *Roll With It*. They'll come on board. They'll see the big picture, how truly epic this could be. It will go viral, without a doubt. He's not going to rehab, even if that's what people think he should do. He's not going to have surgery. No hospitals for him. Can't stand to be inside hospitals after everything with Rose. Can't abide that disinfectant smell, that specific sound of shoes on the hospital floor, the curtains on their rails opening, shutting, the children with their dark eyes. Who would he be getting better for? Huh?

Doesn't deserve it anyway.

Nah, he's going to do better than all that. He's going to hill-bomb Baldwin Street.

If he survives, everyone will know his name. New contracts, new sponsors, new fame: he'll be sorted. If he dies, and that is not an unlikely scenario, what will it matter? He won't know if it all goes to shit. That can be someone else's mess to clean up.

JAMIE

EARLY THE NEXT MORNING, in some miracle of coverage, Jamie's phone rings. His first thought is: Thank god, he's alive. Beside him, Penny rolls over and wipes her eyes, and Jamie swipes the call, hands damp with anxiety. Christ only knows what they'll say to each other after last night. Only it's not Riggs.

'Is this Jamie Flannery?'

'That's me,' he says.

'Hello, I'm Deirdre, I'm calling from Dr Sobhani's clinic.'

The skin around Jamie's neck tightens.

'He'd like you to come in to see him as soon as possible.' She stops, and he can hear the click of fingernails on a keyboard, the drone of a printer in the background, the white noise of office life. 'We have an appointment tomorrow afternoon?'

'That's going to be difficult,' he says. He glances at Penny, wrapped in the bedding like a gift. 'I'm out of town.'

He gets up and wanders to the lounge. It looks as though the storm happened inside the house. Empty beer bottles dot the floor. Hardened wax speckles the tabletop. Riggs's chair still lies toppled over. Jamie doesn't stop to pick anything up. He opens the doors and goes outside.

'Would Friday work for you?' Deirdre says. 'He has a two o'clock or a four-thirty?'

'Sorry,' he says. 'I'm out of town for a while. Could I talk to Dr Sobhani on the phone?'

'I'll see if he's happy to do a phone consult. Hold, please.'

Kiwiana holding muzak drifts down the line. A cold wind still blows from the south, and dark clouds loom over the southern cliffs. Despite his reduced vision, he can see a small, white bird drift over the sea. It has long pointed wings, and from this distance is not much more than a speck against the harsh steel blue. In a sudden jerking movement, the bird lifts upward, tossed by a gust of wind. Then it battles on undeterred towards the northern cliff face.

The song cuts off before the chorus and Deirdre is back. 'Dr Sobhani will talk to you now. Normal consult fees apply.'

Jamie licks his lips and lets out a juddering breath. Why does he feel as though he's going to be sick? There's no mystery here. He knows what the doctor is going to say. You're going blind and it's Adam Riggs's fault.

'So, Jamie, hello, it's Dr Sobhani. I've got all the results of your tests. I do prefer to do this face to face, for many reasons.' There's a slight break in the line, and Jamie's stomach stings acidic and sharp. 'I'm sorry to be the bearer of bad news. Your tests have come back positive for a genetic disease.'

Sobhani says a long word then, a few of them, and it takes

longer than it should for Jamie to realise he's been given a diagnosis. Eventual blindness. Six weeks, six months — the doctor says he can't be certain when it will happen, but it will happen and there is nothing they can do to stop it. Jamie finds himself opening his eyes as wide as he can get them, drinking down the world, letting light slip in. Light, and colour, and shape, and shadow. The distinct types of cloud over the water, swollen and pale; the way sunlight hits a wave in a spectacular glitter. Slipper Island Whakahau hovering a translucent ghost-grey. The whole world in all its glorious beauty.

'Are you aware of anyone else in the family who has suffered from this or a similar condition?' the doctor asks.

'I don't think so,' Jamie says. The name of the syndrome slips around, hard to catch. He's never heard of it before. Can't hold it straight. He keeps losing it, and an image of Riggs walking from the bach into the storm replaces it. 'So,' he says slowly, 'this isn't because of the concussion?'

'That is correct,' Dr Sobhani says. 'This is unrelated to the concussion you suffered. I can see no long-term neurological or visual damage from that incident.'

Unrelated. Jamie scratches the back of his neck, grasping at something that isn't there.

'You'd be surprised at how life will continue much as it does now,' Dr Sobhani says. 'There are adaptations that didn't exist even five, ten years ago. You can still use your iPhone, for example. Though in truth I can't underplay it. This will of course, be a significant life change. Our team will give you the names of some organisations who can help you prepare, and we have an in-house psychologist we recommend you begin talking with as soon as you feel able.'

The doctor doesn't notice Jamie's silence; he talks and talks, his voice increasingly smarmy. Does he charge by the minute, like a lawyer? Jamie has no idea how he's going to pay for this phone consult. And what the hell is the guy even saying? A genetic disease? Blind? Christ. What is he going to do now? His only skills are hammering nails, lifting wood, skateboarding, and painting very badly, and these all need him to be able to see. He couldn't make money from the last two things anyway, no matter how much effort he put into them, no matter how perfect his sight. And now the doctor's suggesting a psychologist? Money, money, money, your health, your dignity, your humanity — it all takes money, and he is running short.

When Dr Sobhani ends the call, Jamie tries phoning his mother. Damn — no reception again! He pulls at his hair, vicious and desperate, then walks down the beach, near to the water. Driftwood and broken shells and coloured plastic junk have gathered in piles. He lifts the phone into the air and the reception bars notch up. It might be a mistake, talking to her when he is so worked up. Only he needs answers.

'How are you doing, love?' Trish sounds pleased to hear from him.

'I'm not sure, Mum. I'm not really sure how I'm doing.'

'Has something happened? Is everything okay? What's going on?'

'Yeah,' Jamie says. 'I guess something has happened.'

'What's going on, Jamie?'

He lets out a long breath and says, 'I'm going blind, Mum.'

A pause. 'Who told you that?'

'The specialist.'

'An eye doctor? Or some quack at the local medical centre?'

'An ophthalmologist. In Auckland.'

'They're one hundred percent sure? How on earth? What else did they say?'

'I'm going blind, Mum. They said it's been going on for a while. Probably since I was a kid. They said ...'

Trish says softly, 'What else did they say, Jamie?'

He repeats the name of the condition Dr Sobhani had told him, his words slow and clear. He hears her gasp, and he wonders if it is too late to stop talking now. If he should take it all back. Then, so quiet he almost doesn't catch it — the sound of her crying.

'They said it's an inherited disease,' he says. 'They asked me if anyone else in my family has had this.'

She doesn't say anything. It doesn't matter. He doesn't need her to say it. He knows.

The sound of footsteps on sand along the beach. Penny. Her hair is wet, and she's wearing a grey sweatshirt. She gives him a small smile, and a thickness clamps at his jaw: he's convinced he's about to lose sight of her this second, about to lose sight of everything, when she's only just returned. If there ever was a time he wanted to believe in a god, so he could ask him, Please, please, don't take this from me, don't take this from me the way you've taken everything else, then that time would be now. It's time to let a lovely thing stay.

'I didn't know how to tell you,' Trish says. 'There was such a huge chance you didn't have it. I really thought you didn't.'

'You should have told me.'

'I know, I know.' Trish sounds manic. 'Your father was so

afraid of losing his sight. He wouldn't listen to anything I said. He couldn't bear it. Didn't want to be a burden on anyone, but I said so many times, "Paddy, you'll never be a burden, not to me, not to anybody." He wouldn't listen to me, he never did. He thought he was doing us all a favour.' Trish sobs uncontrollably now, her voice breaking in her chest on the peak of each cry. 'He said he felt right about it, because he knew we'd all be fine without him, and I told him that wasn't true. He wouldn't listen to me. We needed him, you needed him. It's never been right without him.'

'You should've told me, Mum,' Jamie says. He can almost feel her flinch at his words. 'You should have told me a long time ago.'

'You're right. I should've told you. I'm sorry, I'm so sorry. Do you want me to come out there? You shouldn't be alone.'

'I'm not alone, Mum. Look, I'll talk to you soon, okay?'

He takes the phone from his ear and ends the call. He's going blind, and it isn't Riggs's fault. There is no doubt about it now.

Jamie gets obstacles, he gets them all right: when he's skating, he knows what to do with an obstacle. He knows they aren't only things that get in the way of forward momentum — they're an offering. When you're skating, you don't only want to overcome the obstacle, to stay upright as you go over or past them, you want to use them, because the obstacle is an opportunity to make magic. But, hell, what an unwanted challenge this is — to his way of life, to how he understands himself, to the way he thought his future would unfold.

Penny comes towards him down the beach and he wants to

stay right there forever, never having to know whether he can learn to live with this or whether he won't. He doesn't want to encounter this obstacle and see what magic he could possibly create. He wants to pause and hold this moment, always. No one would blame him. Look at all the good things: the golden strip of sand dirtied with debris, the white lines of waves lacing the edge of the shore. The tussocky dune grass flickering in the breeze, the looming dark of the pine forest around the house. Penny perpetually walking towards him, the arching blue sky above her, the daylight never fading into night.

It doesn't last long enough. Nothing good ever does! Soon she's beside him, shifting her feet in the sand. A lone magpie chortles in the pines behind the house and the dog scampers nearby. Jamie wipes at his eyes with the back of his hand and hopes she doesn't know he's crying.

'Was that Riggs?' she asks.

He shakes his head and laughs softly. 'You know, I wish it was. It was my doctor. And then my mum.' He tells her then about his diagnosis, the prognosis, the whole damned thing. 'A gift from my father,' he says. 'Mum said he killed himself because he didn't want to go blind.'

'Oh, shit, Jamie, that's terrible. I'm so sorry.'

'What am I going to do now? All this, Penny. I'm losing all this.' He gestures around him to the ocean, the forest, the sky, to her, to everything. 'What am I going to do without all this?'

'Nothing has to change,' she says. 'All the big things won't change. Who you are. What you mean to people. And I know that whatever you want to do, you can still do it.'

'Everything will change,' he says. 'I don't know what sort of life I'm going to have.'

'No,' she says. 'Don't act like you haven't got a choice in what happens next. Remember? You don't believe in that bitch fate. You make the decisions.'

'Everything that made me who I am is going to go,' he says. 'I can't work. I can't skate. I can't paint. Pretty soon I won't be able to see any of this.'

'Close your eyes,' she says. 'Come on, humour me.'

He's reluctant to shut out the world when so soon it will be robbed from him, but he does as she asks. Sunlight pierces his eyelids, and everything is bathed pink and gold and warm. Still, he clenches his fists.

'I don't like it,' he says.

'I'm right here,' she says. 'You're okay. What do you feel?'

'What do I feel?'

'Yes.'

'The sun on my arms.'

'What else?'

'The salt spray on my lips.'

'Anything else?'

'The sand on my feet, the slipperiness of it. The sun.'

He stops talking. He knows what she's doing. He stands there, letting the glow permeate his eyes. His whole body feels as though it's on fire, as though it's some sort of burning antenna, alert and conducting new transmissions. There's the day's temperature ready on his skin. The cool breath of the forest on his neck. The thrumming of the waves inside him. The dog around his legs, the occasional touch of fur on his ankles. Penny's body, even if he can't feel it directly, he can sense it somehow. He can sense how close she is. He feels her hand on his chest now, and he places his hand over hers, the ceaseless drum of his heart vibrating beneath their palms.

'Do you feel that?' she says. 'You're still alive. Not everything can be seen, Jamie. Sometimes the most important things can only be felt.'

When he opens his eyes, there's a sudden onslaught of colour and light. Except he can't focus on anything other than her. They are standing closer now, too close, her face almost touching his collarbone. He is sure they can both feel his heartbeat getting faster, faster. And now his other hand is holding her head, and she smiles. When he leans forward, she doesn't back away. His lips on her lips, her hand pinned between them on his chest. She closes her eyes. She doesn't know that he keeps his eyes open. Neither of them knows that watching her face as they kiss will be one of the last things he ever sees.

But — not quite the last thing: there's a short period of clarity as everything around him crystallises into crisp lines and colours. The pines waving tall in the wind, the dunes rising up to their feet and vanishing beneath the needle carpet. Her cheekbones, the lightest wash of freckles across her brow, her curved ears like precious shells, the small pearl earrings. A magpie sitting in a tree, a dotterel scampering along the sand, a work-up of birds far out to sea, their bodies a swooping, diving white flash of life. A sweeping wave lifts up and a gust of onshore wind lifts its tip and covers them in salt spray. Her wet, lavender-scented hair is now on his face. He kisses her again, more urgently. Her mouth tastes of salt water and honey, and he's so turned on he thinks he might erupt.

'Let's go inside,' she says. 'I'm cold.'

He follows her in. His whole body blazes hot as though she's cast a spell on him and now every nerve of his body is alight. She stands in the middle of the lounge, dripping wet and sandy.

'I'll get you a towel,' he says, and he goes down the hall to the bathroom, hand on the wall to guide him. He takes off his wet tee-shirt and drops it into the washing machine. His hands shake and he holds the side of the machine to steady himself.

He kissed her. Deep breath, Christ, take a deep breath, but he can't, he can't. Last night, the fighting, the fire, the near-drowning, the news from the doctor, the conversation with his mother, the kiss — he's overwhelmed by it all. The feeling of her hand on his chest. What's a man to do with all this? A cup of coffee, he will make them coffee and they can talk, figure out what in the hell is going on.

The jug settles down to boil and he settles at the small table, his knees bouncing. He rubs his hands on his legs simply for something to do. He tries to focus on the details he can make out, to bring himself back down to earth. The bright green of the Milo tin. The red of the Bell tea box. The toxic yellow of the liquid dishwash. He doesn't think about what will take their place when he can no longer see.

The jug clicks and he pours water into the plunger. 'You want a coffee?'

There's no response. 'Penny?' Still nothing. He makes his way down to her room.

She's not in there. Riggs's suitcase is propped against the far wall and the duvet is pulled up. He calls her name again, heading back down the hallway, though he stops short after only a few steps. She's in his room, in his bed.

Lightheaded, he leans on the door frame, and she smiles. 'You okay?' he asks.

'I don't know,' she says. 'I actually think I've never been better.'

'Right,' he says. 'That's good.'

'Are you going to join me, or what?'

Her smile is so wide he could fall into it. She sits up in bed and the duvet slips down from around her and he can see she's naked. 'Oh lord,' he says quietly, and his whole life melts down to this moment. Doctor Sobhani and his diagnosis is gone, Trish and the horror of their phone call is gone, the death of his father and all his guilt are gone. Riggs is gone, fucked off somewhere. He owes Riggs nothing and everything, and Jamie knows that whatever happens after this, he will never regret Penny Whittaker.

He dips his head and says, 'I thought you said you didn't have much of an appetite for risk.'

'Turns out I do,' she says.

He goes over and kneels on the bed. She holds his face and kisses him, and the blood rushes from his head to his dick to his heart. He kisses her lips, her cheek, her neck, her breasts, her stomach. Moves around her body, taking in every inch of her, and he won't blink. He's so hungry to see her, he won't even blink if he can help it — he won't blink, he won't — though even as he thinks that, he knows what she said is true: the best things are the ones you can feel. He puts his hand on her leg, and her skin is warm. His hand trembles and he moves it between her legs, spreading them wide, and he touches her first with his hand, lightly, then he presses one finger inside her. She moves under him, then takes his hand up and slides his fingers into her mouth. An involuntary soft moan escapes him, and he brings his mouth to taste her, and even though he doesn't blink, he knows it wouldn't matter. It would be as good with his eyes closed.

PENNY

THEY LIE TOGETHER IN the bed. Arms and legs and skin entwined, his thigh pressed so hard between her legs her entire body hums.

Thin morning light slants through the window, slowly deepening toward midday. Jamie kisses her, and she lets herself be kissed. The events of the previous day feel a long time ago. Then the dog starts barking. Riggs is home. Jamie's body stiffens; he is thinking the same thing. But the dog is quiet again, and there's nothing but silence, their breath warm between their faces.

She knows she should feel guilty. But she doesn't. What she does feel is uncommonly alive and full and vibrant. Does this make her a bad person, the worst kind of person? No — how can something this good be wrong? A warm palm on her cheek, on her chest, a finger tracing the edge of her nipple. Doesn't she, doesn't every person, deserve some joy? And it has been so long since she's felt this way. It isn't entirely the sex, although it's been a long time since she had sex with Riggs; even longer since she's had sex that feels like this. It's more that she's living. And in the living, in the experience, she's creating a petal to wrap around her grief.

She does wonder where Riggs is. The last thing she wants is for him to be hurt and alone. She would never want that. He's probably fine — falls on his feet, that man, always does — but she can't help feeling a twinge of anxiety when she thinks of the last time she saw him, walking out of the bach into the storm.

She turns her face into the space between Jamie's jaw and his chest, her chin tucking into his collarbone. Coffee, some sort of spice and the smell of something burning. She inhales deeply. She has always loved that smell. He holds her hip and pulls her closer. It's true: she hopes Riggs isn't hurting, and at the same time she hopes she never sees him again. If he never returns, then he has left her. She cannot be blamed for what he chooses to do after that. All those threats over the years about what he would do if she left him: they're null and void if he is the one who abandons her.

Jamie leans back on his pillow. He clears his throat and says, 'Being here with you is the best thing that's happened to me in a long time, to be honest.'

'For a long time I thought only selling a painting would make me happy,' she says. 'Turns out I needed this.'

'What? A beach holiday?'

'No,' she says, laughing, pressing herself against his chest. 'This.'

'Oh right,' he says, 'this.' He cups her breast and kisses it.

She feels so good she can't help imagining she'd not left with Riggs all those years ago. A pointless endeavour – what did Riggs say last night? Can't live your life clinging to what might have been? – but it's as if she at last has permission to dream. Maybe her father wouldn't have sent her to London, or maybe she would have gone there as he'd planned. She wouldn't have lived in Los Angeles. She wouldn't have had Rose. If she'd not had Rose, and lost her, she would be someone else entirely, a person so different from who she is now, she can't even begin to conceive of that version of Penny. Someone who doesn't know about bone marrow biopsies and chemo ports. Maybe someone who eclipsed Damian's fame and talent, maybe not.

She says, 'Do you ever think about what life might have been like if you'd chosen different things?'

'There have been times I've thought about what it might have been like if I'd won the Alley-Oop, for sure, or if my dad hadn't died. I think about if Madeline and I hadn't broken up.' He looks at her. 'I think about if I hadn't blamed you for my dad. But, you know, I don't think there's some magical, happier life that I could've had if I'd done anything differently. I mean, maybe my dad wouldn't have killed himself in another life, but I bet something else just as devastating would've happened.'

He's right, of course. She's lived long enough to understand the truth of it: there is no avoiding the bad things in life. It's the price you pay for living, and for loving. You have to endure sorrows so great no words can explain them. No one is spared those things. The person she might have been – the one who knows nothing about acute lymphoblastic leukemia – wouldn't be miraculously untouched by pain.

'Did you know,' he says, 'our phoenix is still on the side of the butcher's shop?'

'I saw it,' she says. On the drive away from Riggs's parents' house, the sight of the phoenix taking away her breath: the glorious upward sweep of the wing, the flames biting at the feet. How hard it was to keep a straight face in the car when what she wanted to do was run back and touch the painting, to marvel at its durability.

'It's a bit worse for wear,' Jamie says, 'but still rising up from the flames. A bit like us.'

'What, a bit weathered and old?'

'Yes,' he says. He runs his finger along her lips, along her jaw, careful not to touch the bruise from Riggs's palm. 'A bit older, a bit tattered. Been through the fire, maybe, but forever rising.'

She showers for a long time. Shampoos her hair, watches the suds congregate around the plughole and slowly dissipate. The feeling of Jamie's hands on her body still on her skin. Doesn't think of Riggs, or at least not too much. Doesn't think about what might happen later, or tomorrow, or next week. When she stands on the bathmat, drying herself with an old towel, she hears Jamie in the kitchen. He's singing a Taylor Swift song; getting all the lyrics wrong. She puts on some jeans and a tee-shirt in the bedroom, ignores Riggs's suitcase at the foot of the bed, unconcerned now about what is or is not inside it, and goes into the kitchen. Jamie turns, puts his hands on her shoulders and steers her outside.

'Where are we going?' she says.

He turns her off the deck and guides her toward the shed.

'I've got a surprise for you.' One hand moves from her shoulder to cover her eyes, and she walks cautiously to the shed. 'Here,' he says, and then releases her.

On the workbench is a box, and inside there's a set of old paints, two brushes that have seen better days, a palette knife and a stack of paper. Familiar friends, yet her hands grow cold and a sick panic sets in. Jamie takes up one of the brushes and hands it to her. Numb fingers can hardly keep hold.

'Where did all this come from?' she says.

'It's mine,' Jamie says. 'I haven't used it in a while. Mum wouldn't let me leave it behind. Go on, paint.'

'I can't,' she says. 'I have artist's block, or something.' She rubs the dry brush end with her fingertips. 'I haven't painted anything since Rose died.'

'What are you afraid of?'

'What, if I paint?'

'Yes.'

'That it will be awful. That it won't be good enough.' That it won't be good enough to justify her child's death.

'Well, don't worry about that,' he says. 'Your only task right now is to make it as terrible as you can. No, I'm not joking. Make it horrible. Completely ugly.'

Her hand moves, uncertain, but doesn't touch the paper.

'Don't overthink it,' he says. 'Why don't you try closing your eyes? Don't judge what you can see. Paint what you feel.'

'Why?' she says.

'I believe in you,' he says. 'You're the best artist I've ever met.'

In his own way, her father must have believed in her. So many hours he'd poured into her, and Sir Damian isn't the kind of person to do all that for generosity's sake. Riggs had humoured her, but he wasn't that interested in her art. He wasn't invested in it; he didn't care about it. But Jamie. He'd believed in her. Still does. What a feeling it is, when someone has faith in you.

Penny lifts the brush to the paper. For ten minutes she lets the heart guide her to what's essential.

'I can't really see it,' Jamie says, 'but you can. What can you see?'

She can see all the problems. There are so many of them, too many of them — the angle of the horizon is wrong, the shape of the pine tree at the left edge, her early interpretation of the ocean's movement. Colours are off, that brushstroke too heavy. But it is the first thing she's painted in years. She puts her hand to her mouth and her face feels feverish. It's terrible but—

It's something. Rose is gone, Riggs is gone, and she's able to paint.

'It is pretty bad,' she says.

He gathers her into him, his arms tight around her back. 'You need to let go of the idea of making the perfect thing,' he says. 'Not only is it impossible, but you're limiting yourself. If you let go of that idea, you have an opportunity to create something more meaningful.'

'You're saying I should take a bad thing and make it better?'

'Yeah,' he says, and he sits on an upturned crate, his legs crossed at the ankles. He leans against the wall and closes his eyes and says, 'Do that.'

JAMIE

HE MUST HAVE SLEPT, leaning against the dirty wall of the shed, cobwebs in his hair, his arse sore against the wooden crate. Long shadows fill the room, and beside Penny are piles of discarded paper covered with brushstrokes. The piece she's working on now is heavy and wet with paint. She moves her hand over the paper, adding more paint to the top left corner, violet on top of black, the wet paint shifting and glinting in the light. Through his misty eyes, the texture ripples like velvet.

'You've been busy,' he says, his voice not betraying the panic he feels. The painting she is working on is in plain view and he can only see parts of it. This is his new reality. He's not ready. He won't ever be ready for this. The edges of everything are dark and caving in, and in spite of himself a small, scared noise escapes him.

Penny turns. 'Are you all right?'

'I'm not sure,' he says.

'Wait a minute,' she says. She puts the brush down, wipes her hands on her jeans and picks up one of the discarded paintings. 'Why don't you try touching this.'

'What do you mean?'

'I mean what I said. Touch it.' She holds it closer. 'You can feel what I'm doing.'

He hesitates. It seems to go against everything he knows about paintings: look, don't touch. 'Won't I wreck it?'

'It's mostly dry,' she says. 'Besides, it's not like it's a van Gogh.'

He places his fingertips to the page. The paint is brittle yet also spongy. There are lumps and dips and grooves and smears. Maybe it's the fourth coffee he drank after they'd made love, or maybe it's the wonderful feeling of being in the shed in the late-afternoon light, so close to her, the smell of her hair filling the space between them, but for some reason his hand feels terrifically sensitive. He can feel the ridges of the brush's bristles in the paint strokes. Can sense the energy and direction of her movements — what came first, what came next, where the eye might be directed.

'Tell me about the colours,' he says.

'Right now,' she says in a very quiet voice, 'you're touching a dark red. Like blood.' His hand moves. 'Now, a really bright green, a mix of yellow and cyan.'

With every pass of his fingers she tells him the colour: mauve; forest green; mustard; a mix of yellow and orange that she calls magic tangerine.

He drops his hand, and when he opens his eyes she's looking at him with a pale, solemn face.

'My mum texted me,' she says. 'While you were sleeping. The

paintings I had shipped over for the cancelled exhibition have turned up. I said I'd go pick them up.'

'You're going to leave?'

'Yeah,' she says. 'I'll pack up my suitcase.'

'Right,' he says, and then there's a pause, a quiet that's quickly filled with the wash of a wave, the squawk of an oystercatcher overhead, the blurred swish of the wind in the pines. 'Are you going to come back?'

'I don't know,' she says.

He looks down at his feet, or where he imagines they might be. 'I'll call someone,' he says. 'Get them to pick you up. They might take you to Whangamatā, and you can hire a car from there.'

It only takes her a few minutes to gather her things, and he sits in the lounge, unable to read, or look at her, or concentrate on anything but the sound of her moving through the house. He doesn't want the silence back, that dismal silence. The dog presses in beside him, as if she also worries how things will be without Penny, or Riggs, in the house. Who will tell him if what he sees are dolphins or if it's a trick of the light?

Roy Avery arrives a half-hour after Jamie calls him, pulling his wagon up under the pines like he did not even a week ago. He knocks with a sharp rap, and Jamie answers the door.

'Roy,' he says.

'Jamie, you're looking well,' he says. 'I'm here to pick someone up instead of dropping something off, am I?'

Jamie opens the door wider and Penny walks down the hallway, wheeling her suitcase behind her.

‘Leaving him here all alone, are ya?’ Roy asks her.

She blushes and says she might come back.

‘You don’t have to say that,’ Jamie says.

She kisses him while Roy heaves her suitcase into the boot.

‘I’ll think about you,’ she says.

‘Only every now and then,’ he says.

‘Every now and then,’ she says, and he’s still standing in the doorway, shocked and heartbroken, twenty minutes later when Riggs comes stumbling down the drive.

Quails scurry into the shadows of the trees at the sound of Riggs’s footsteps. The dog, beside herself at the new arrival, circles his legs and barks incessantly. Riggs ignores her and staggers closer to the bach.

‘Mate,’ Riggs says. ‘You didn’t have to wait out for me.’

‘Christ, Riggs, are you okay?’ Jamie’s eyesight is wretched and milky, yet even he can see the state of the man: stains on all his clothing, his eye swollen shut, the skin meaty and purple, the crusted blood from a gash on his forehead. His feet, red and sore, the eyes bloodshot and half-closed. The rose tattoo is nearly completely obscured by blood, and when Riggs comes nearer the stench of him makes Jamie recoil.

‘Totalled the rental car,’ Riggs says. ‘Bloody hell, what a day. Took me fucking hours to get back here. I’m sick as a dog. Hadn’t planned on coming back so soon but got the feeling I was a bit underdressed to rock into Whangamatā.’

Jamie gestures for Riggs to follow him into the house. ‘Come in, come in,’ he says. ‘Let’s get you cleaned up.’

Riggs screws his face up. ‘Is Penny inside?’

'Nah, man,' Jamie says.

Riggs's face falls, and he nods.

'She take off, did she?'

'You just missed her.'

'Did she say if she was coming back?'

Jamie pulls at his hair. 'I don't think so, mate.'

While Riggs showers, Jamie can't sit still. The sound of Riggs retching unsettles the dog, who follows Jamie from room to room, her nose on the back of his calves. Jamie strips his bed sheets, certain Riggs will see the bed and somehow know what had happened there only hours before. He can still feel the sensation of Penny's body on his, the swell of her ribcage, the taste of her on his lips, and he wonders how long this might sustain him, how long the memory of this day will reverberate through his body when he thinks back on it. A long time, he hopes, a very, very long time.

They sit on the deck together in the early-evening chill. Jamie picks up a pine cone for the dog and tosses it out onto the sand. He doesn't know what to say about anything that's happened.

'Penny's gone, then,' Riggs says. Jamie nods. He braces himself for an outburst, but the only thing Riggs says is, 'Well, I suppose that makes it easier.'

'You're not mad?' Jamie says.

'Bro, if I wasn't so incredibly tired and sore, then maybe I'd be burning the house down again. But I'm too fucking tired.' The dog drops the pine cone at Riggs's feet and he kicks it down the dune. 'But all is not lost. I have a plan.'

'A plan?'

Riggs fiddles with his phone, cursing the shitty reception,

and after a moment he holds it out. 'Watch this,' he says. 'Hurry, before the thing cuts out again.'

Jamie blinks a few times. He can see most of the screen when it's this close: four men skating incredibly fast down an impossibly long, impossibly steep street. Bodies erect and wraith-like on thin skateboards. They've timed the streetlights at the intersections to perfection, yet the threat of a car skipping a red and ploughing them down is unavoidable. One of the skaters' boards dips — is it into a manhole cover? — and for a second it seems he will fall. He lurches, arms out and knees bent, and, miraculously, he recovers and continues.

It's clearly insane, what these men are doing. Beyond dangerous. Putting themselves and others at risk. Still, it's impressive. Like mountain climbers triumphant at the peak of Everest in the thin air of the outer atmosphere, or free divers who sink a hundred metres deep in the Bahamas with no oxygen tank. Like astronauts teetering in the cosmos, or anyone, really, who lives on the extreme edge, pushing against the limits of physics. Their bodies vulnerable and open. Daring the universe, daring themselves, living exactly in that moment and nowhere else. Haunted by nothing — you couldn't allow a thought in your head, skating that fast down a hill, no helmet, no protective gear, no nothing. Only things keeping you upright are your muscles working by the guide of intuition and memory. Jamie doesn't necessarily want to skate down that hill. But he wants to live in a world where he could still make that choice. Take a risk. Live.

'So, what do you think?' Riggs asks.

'Looks incredibly dangerous,' Jamie says. 'And I say this is as someone who doesn't mind a bit of danger.'

'Yeah, but it would be fun, right?'

Jamie shrugs. Fun isn't the word for it.

'I'm gonna do that,' Riggs says. 'I'm going to skate down Baldwin Street. Steepest street in the world. We'll make a documentary. It'll be massive, I mean, it will definitely go viral.'

'Baldwin Street in Dunedin?'

'Fucking brilliant, right?' Riggs says. 'I can't say I've done a lot of hill-bombing but it can't be any harder than Burnquist's Mega Ramp at Dreamland.'

'You'll have to slide,' Jamie says. 'You'd go too fast if you hill-bomb it.'

'Sliding is for pussies,' Riggs says. 'If I'm going to make it worth something, I have to hill-bomb. First person down Baldwin Street. Gonna be fucking sick.'

Jamie shakes his head. 'You're crazy.'

'I'm not crazy,' Riggs says. 'I just want different things than you do.'

Sand shimmers along the beach in a gust of wind. Different things. Do they want different things? Or do they merely have different ideas about how to get them?

Riggs looks up at the sky. 'So, do you want to come with me? I'll need people to help me out.'

'I'm going blind, Riggs. I'm not sure how much help I can be.'

'Nah, man, I need you to hold my hand when I get scared.'

'You might hurt yourself,' Jamie says. Doesn't want to say what he really thinks.

'That's sweet,' Riggs says. 'I'm not gonna die, bro.' His voice is strong and clear, but his hands are trembling. 'And if I do, you should know that I'm sorry.'

'Are you?' Jamie says.

'Of course,' Riggs says. 'I've made mistakes, plenty of them, but I know when it's time to apologise. I did you bad, bro. I should never have let you ride that board.'

The dog races down the beach and into the water. The setting sun flickers on the gathering waves as they roll in one at a time.

'It doesn't matter now anyway,' Jamie says. 'The past is what it is.'

'Spoken like the true wise man you are.'

They sit in silence for a minute. Riggs kicks his foot towards Jamie's and says, 'I'll head off tomorrow. Before I go, what you reckon, one last skate?'

'I can't, mate,' Jamie says. 'I can't see well enough.'

Riggs shakes his head. 'You don't need to see, bro. That's why you've got me.'

They stand, thumbs out for a hitch, early the next morning. Riggs, suitcase in hand, complains about the fact the first car they saw picked them up and that it must be Jamie's blond hair that made the difference. 'No motherfucker on the peninsula wanted to give this old fart a ride, even in my hour of need,' he says. 'But you — boof, easy. Everyone's always loved you best. Suppose I shouldn't be surprised that hasn't changed.'

The Whangamatā skatepark is empty. Too early for the scooter boys. Jamie holds his board close and follows Riggs to the edge of the quarter-pipe. The first time Jamie touched a skateboard, it was both heavier and lighter than he'd imagined it might be. He was seven, sitting with Riggs on the grass, watching the older boys hoon around the decrepit skatepark on boards that looked ready for retirement. One of the boys took a dislike to Jamie's shoes or hair or name or face, he was never sure what it was that convinced this tall boy on the cusp of manhood to saunter over, say *I dare you* and hand Jamie his board. He was surprised at how heavy the board was, because these skaters were flipping them up and flying on them, spinning them around, lifting them up – *levitating* – and sliding down rails. It was lighter than he thought it should be as well, because how could this featherlight slip of wood ever keep you safe? Later he'd come to know everything about the board. Eight layers of sweet maple wood, four plastic wheels, connected by two chunky hunks of metal they call trucks. All he saw was the sticker on the underside of the board. *Skate with caution. Injury, disability or death may result from improper use.*

'All right,' Riggs says. 'You good?'

Jamie presses his weight down on his right foot, holding the tail hard on the edge, and nods. It's not going anywhere until he's ready. There's a sweetness in the air, almost as though he can smell the eight layers of maple plywood, sugary and tangy, just like the syrup. He shifts his foot slightly to keep the deck straight, his shoe rough on the grip tape, the board grinding on the coping. Next to him Riggs, the strong aftershave, the hefty warmth of his body. He's telling Jamie, in a careful way, as if he's just chatting about the weather, about the drop, leaving Jamie to parse the key information for himself: the drop's not vertical, about a metre deep. Then, once he's got his bearings, Jamie wants to focus. He needs quiet.

Jamie clenches one fist and then the other. Tingles cascade down his legs, through his feet. He feels the nerves in the deep hollow of his gut. The nose of the board dips slightly and he jerks back. Riggs puts a hand on his shoulder. The warmth comes through his tee-shirt onto the skin over his collarbone.

'You got it, mate,' Riggs says, his voice like gravel. Jamie's glad he can't see Riggs's face right now. Bright eyes full of pity. The last thing Jamie wants is for anyone, especially Riggs, to pity him. That would mean they are only seeing what he cannot do. He wants them to see all the things he can still do.

He nods again, more vigorously. 'I'm good,' he says. He shifts his right foot, feeling for the twist of the board under his weight, under his control. It's time, he knows it's time to commit, to lean forward onto his left foot, tip the bulk of himself into the drop. Any hesitation and it's lost. Without seeing, it's anyone's guess if he can keep his foot under the eyes of the board. It's anyone's guess if he's straight. He doesn't dare ask Riggs. He needs to do this on his own.

Shoulders first, slam the left foot, push the nose down so the four wheels touch the ground and roll down the incline. He's falling, once again, falling down, and there's no guarantees about what might happen next.

PENNY

THE SIDE DOOR TO the garage of her parents' house is unlocked. Penny lets herself in. It's better this way: she's not in the mood to see either of them.

Her mother had told her the paintings were in the garage, only she didn't explain where, and Penny can't find them. Unlike the rest of the house, the garage is jam-packed: plastic storage tubs are stacked high along the back wall, along with black rubbish bags full of dried-out brushes, emptied paint tubes, scraps of canvas, stained clothing. Worn Nike sneakers sit beside mud-splattered gumboots, piles of wood lean against a dusty black stereo system. No sign of her paintings.

Beyond the wheeled rubbish bins is the door to the back room. Her parents had stored their fake Christmas tree in there when she was young. Meg had been explicit in her instructions: Penny was not to go in that room because that's where she kept her gardening supplies. 'Keep out, darling,' her mother would say. 'I don't want you going near pesticides or getting Legionnaires' disease either.' The paintings are unlikely to be in there, but Penny pushes the door handle and the door opens. She goes in. The unannounced visitor can do what the obedient child cannot.

The room is exactly what she'd imagined: more gumboots, set in neat pairs against the wall. An open bag of potting mix. Under the south-facing window an array of umbrellas and gardening implements, along with empty seedling pots and a set of well-worn leather gloves. The Christmas tree awaiting the upcoming Yule.

Against the far wall is a trestle table. Its surface is covered in tubes of Winsor & Newton paints, ProArte brushes, Sennelier oil pastels, cut-off pieces of canvas, odourless solvent, paint-crusted rags. Hundreds of dollars of art supplies on a table in a room with terrible lighting and the particular aroma of dog kibble. Penny touches one of the brushes: it's still soft. Kept clean by someone meticulous. Someone who cares.

At the end of the table there's a hoard of finished artworks of various sizes. The pieces are similar, yet distinct in their own way. She sifts through them, a series of colour blocks in varying shapes, overlaid with shifting stripes, short lines in wavering patterns. There's a brightness and a textural rhythm to the work that isn't her father's usual taste. He favours a more natural palette, even more so as he's aged, and there's an abstraction in these works that she knows he wouldn't approve of. Echoes of Aboriginal artwork that he wouldn't abide, that Penny finds seductive and compelling. 'I'm a realist,' he always said to Penny, 'and I won't apologise for it. I know it's fun to splat the paint on, willy nilly, but it takes more discipline to paint the world as it is. More honesty.'

Besides, he works upstairs, in the room at the top of the house, with the best light and the best view. His studio was, and presumably still is, a private space even Meg can't enter without his permission. No, this isn't her father's work. And it isn't hers. She'd remember painting like this. There are similarities to the work she'd done in her teens, if you look closely and carefully at the contour and shadowing, only this is more alive. Too technically advanced, as well, if you examine the brushwork and the style choices. She extracts one of the works from the stack and sets it on the table.

The artwork reveals its secret: the lines of stripes on the surface of the paintings are deliberately creating a noise, a disturbance, to cloud another image underneath. Up close the colours behind the stripes appear random and insignificant, though she suspects they aren't. The shapes and the intricacies of the paintwork are not accidental. She steps back, allowing a distance between her and the work, and the image beneath the short lines rises forward.

Her mother's face.

They are all her mother. Behind the lines, her face. The face looks youthful in some; in others there is a sadness, displayed mostly through the shapes and paint strokes used for the eyes, for the set of the mouth. Penny places them one by one on the table, leaning against the wall, and the hidden portraits shine forth, almost glowing. There is her mother. She was there all along, camouflaged behind the tumult and the fuss of her father and her own selfish ignorance.

At the bottom of each painting is a slight dark mark. MN.

Meg Novak. Then, in dark numbers, a year. The earliest she can find is 1999, the year before they'd moved to Waiheke. Then 2001, 2005, 2008. Her mother completed a painting every few years.

Penny feels like the ground has given way. Her mother never stopped painting; she'd simply stopped telling the world she was painting.

'I looked at yours too, so I suppose we're even.'

Penny turns. Her mother is in the doorway, white hair damp on the sides, her rain jacket in her hand, a look of slight irritation on her face.

'Sorry,' Penny says.

Meg lifts her jacket to a hook on the wall and says, 'Hm.'

'I was looking for my paintings, and I thought they might be—'

'They're not in here. I've told you not to come in here.'

Penny feels her cheeks grow hot. 'I know that, yes, I just—'

'Never mind. What's done is done.'

'You looked at my paintings?' Penny says.

'Yes, I have. And I assume you want to know what I thought of them.' Meg walks over to stand at the work table beside Penny. 'Although you'd probably prefer your father's opinion.'

'No,' Penny says. She wants the person who had toiled so diligently in this quiet room at the rear of the garage that smells of dirt and exhaust and cobwebs for nothing more than the glory of painting to approve of her work.

'Well,' Meg says. 'Before I begin, why don't you tell me your thoughts about my work?'

Is this a trick question? Her mother has habitually taken delight in creating situations that unnerve the people in her life, and it strikes Penny for the first time that perhaps she does this not to hurt people, but as an act of self-preservation. She uncrosses her arms and steps forward to examine Meg's paintings in closer detail.

'What do you think about this one, for example?' Meg gestures toward a canvas coated only with a first layer in a shade Penny guesses must be Raw Umber. There are darker and lighter marks, a map of the composition to come. A bottle of solvent stands next to the canvas, two hard brushes as well.

'Well,' Penny says. 'You've blocked in too tight.' She can see the proportions and shapes created and how the painting might progress: she looks at it as if she were a fortune teller, able to foresee the future of a work from an early stage. But as soon as she hears the words, she regrets saying them. She sounds like her father. 'Sorry,' she says. 'But you haven't left much room for any positive space, for light.'

'There's space for light,' Meg says. 'Without doubt.' She places one long, elegant finger on the artwork, tracing down a sharp angle that might eventually be the forehead, or nose, of the final work. 'Your father taught you to do things his way, as if that was the way God intended, written in stone in the time of Abraham. He doesn't use solvent, though it might improve his work. I prefer it this way. I change my mind. I let my mood each day shift the work. I'm more fluid. There are thousands of ways to paint, many of which I suspect have never crossed your mind. Underneath all of these—' Meg points to the completed portraits — 'is this—' She points to the work in progress. 'You can't tell what's gone on before when you look at what's going on right now. You can't look at what's going on right now and know what it will look like in ten minutes, let alone ten years. You and

I could both take this piece and work on it, starting from this exact same place, and they would be foreign to each other within seconds. The same past can create a very different future. The picture behind doesn't limit the picture that it can be. Damian likes to believe in this strange theory that the first brushstroke dictates the success of the final outcome, but that man has no bone in his body for spontaneity. He has no clue about how to let real life into his work, doesn't know how to start over, would never consider painting over something that's not working and creating something new in the shadow of failure.'

Meg pauses then, and they stand looking at the portraits, avoiding the other's gaze.

'I thought you'd stopped painting,' Penny says.

'I never stopped doing what I loved, creating a life I loved,' Meg says. 'I simply stopped showing anybody. Your father can't understand it. He cares more about what others think than I do, you see.'

'Easier said than done,' Penny says.

Meg tips her head. 'I suppose it is,' she says. 'Now, Penny, what are you going to do next?'

'Next?'

'Yes, next.' She sighs. 'What are you going to paint next?'

'I don't know.' Penny scuffs her shoe on the concrete floor. 'I don't know how much art I have left in me.'

'Don't give me those theatrics,' Meg says. 'Your work, from what I could see, was proficient, and charming. Your talent hasn't necessarily faded. But I must say I was surprised to see what you'd done. You completed these when?'

'In the months before Rose died.'

'Right.' Meg turns to look at her. 'Then why don't I see any of that in the work? I see pretty beaches and lovely coastal trees and some excellently captured cloud work, a cleverly executed point of view. I see landscapes you could've painted when you were sixteen. They're hollow somehow, darling, I don't think I can put it into words more eloquently than that.'

'You've made the case for me then,' Penny says. 'I should give up.'

'You're being ridiculous. You don't have to stop painting. I wonder whether you give yourself permission to want other things. You might be a good painter, you might even be a brilliant painter, if you can get out of your own way and let the good stuff out. Less talented painters than you might have more glittering careers and get all the spoils you've dreamed about, but such is the way it goes. Don't ruin the rest of your life by narrowing it down even more. Take it from one who knows: sometimes not getting what we think we want is the better option.'

Penny picks up a fan blender brush and sweeps the bristles against her palm. 'After Rose got sick, I put everything into my art, but I've failed, and it's so pointless, all of it.'

Meg places her hand on Penny's shoulder. It is hard and hot. 'I know we've never been close,' her mother says. 'Partly that is my fault, because you are so unlike me. I have never quite known what to make of you. You've been your father's daughter in many ways, and perhaps I should have done more to give you another perspective. It is one thing to want to paint, to want to create. It is another thing altogether to desire the "artist's life". The interviews, the splashy opening nights, the glory. When I see your paintings, I see someone trying to paint towards that life. You're painting from up here—' she points to her head — 'when the good art comes from down here.' And she presses her palm to Penny's collarbone, above her heart. 'You have greatness in you,' she says. 'You need only allow yourself the grace to be human, and to allow that humanity, that ugliness, that pain, the whole lot of it, into your work.'

'Mum,' Penny says. Her eyes are wet, and she wipes them with the side of her hand. 'Do you regret having me?'

'Regret?' Meg takes her hand away and places it now on her own chest. 'Goodness, no. Whatever gave you that impression? Those stupid journalists? I was one of the lucky ones. I could have a child and have my art. I know people assume that I'm jealous of your father, that I "gave up" my career when I had you, but that's simply not true. I gave up wanting the trappings of a creative life, the adulation, the things that happen when your art becomes a product. The process is the thing for me. What I get from the creation is the thing, Penny. The rest of it is just noise – and why did I need more noise when I had you in the house?' A small smile crosses Meg's face. 'No, darling. I don't regret having you. Not once, not ever.'

Penny says, 'I guess I should get going.'

'Back to Adam?' Meg gazes at Penny's cheek. 'Is he responsible for what happened to your face?'

'I'm not going back to Riggs,' Penny says.

'Good. Then you start anew. There are no medals in heaven for loyalty – there are only the days of your life. Reinvention is a good option, love. I don't think enough women are given the opportunity to reconsider themselves when they get to your age, and that's an unfortunate thing. You don't owe anyone the same person you were at twenty. The Russian revolutionist Alexandra Kollontai believed women spent too much time and energy on matters of the heart. She said if women were forced to choose between love and their work, they must always choose the work.'

They walk together from the room, through the garage, and out onto the driveway. Long, thin streaks of cloud trail off towards the ridged hump of the Coromandel, and Penny's immediate thought is that Jamie is there, just over that hill.

They stop beside the rental car. Penny fishes her keys from her pocket and lets out a long breath.

'I guess you can bin those paintings, then. The ones I had sent over.' There seems no point in taking them if she's going to start anew.

'What, waste all that good work?' Meg pulls in her chin. 'No. I've taken a shine to one or two of them. I think they'd look good in the dining room. You don't mind, do you? I'll pay you for them, handsomely.'

Penny can't speak. All she can do is nod and swallow past the lump in her chest as she gets into the car. Her mother hates it when she cries. 'Say goodbye to Dad for me,' she says.

Meg takes her hand through the window and holds it tight. Penny's misshapen pinkie vibrates in her grip. 'You know, he's so proud of you. I don't think he's every truly told you how proud he is. And, Rose, well. We wish we'd had the chance to really get to know her. After a loss like that, you don't simply go on as you did before, do you? Most things work out eventually, but not everything. I know that.' Meg squeezes her hand ever tighter.

'And before I forget,' she says, 'that phoenix you did on the side of the butcher's shop, the one you did with that blond boy?' Meg leans in closer. 'It's really very good,' she says. 'The composition, the choice of colour. You two were very good collaborators. It's a miracle it's survived all these years. Your father makes such a fuss when we go by, but I don't mention how much I admire it.'

'Sometimes good things stay,' Penny says. She lets her mother hold her hand for a minute. 'I should go,' she says at last. 'The ferry will be leaving soon.'

'Right. Wouldn't want to miss the ferry!' Meg moves back from the car, her fingers over her mouth as though holding in a laugh, or tears. A short wave with the other hand, and then she is nothing more than a small figure before the looming house, growing smaller as Penny drives down towards the coast, smaller still until she can no longer be seen.

Penny looks up at the phoenix as she drives through Rocky Bay, at the faded feathers and the geometric curved beak, the flames curling up, threatening to bring the bird down but never once succeeding.

The girl who painted that phoenix, she'd wanted a big life. She'd wanted an extraordinary life. In this half of it, she hasn't got what she wanted. Instead, she's had a life with loss and hardship, a life without any great success or great achievement. Maybe it hasn't been what she'd wanted. But perhaps she's had a good life so far, perhaps the very best kind of life: an ordinary life, with its ordinary happiness and its ordinary sadness. Good things came and went and isn't she lucky she's still so young. There's plenty of time left for more.

That night, in a motel near the airport, she picks up two tubes of paint, considers them for a long moment. A fresh, unblemished piece of paper sits on the table. That strange, paralysing sensation floats up in her at the sight of the emptiness she's supposed to fill. When Penny was twelve, possibly thirteen, Damian told her value, the lightness or darkness of a colour, was by far and away the most important colour principle of all. He said value was the same thing as visibility, and that without a distinction of value, you have nothing but blindness. 'When you don't have value, there can be no hope in the painting, no hope at all,' he'd said. 'You have nothing but the blank page. And when you're an artist, you don't want a blank page. You want it to be filled with meaning.'

But Damian was wrong. She believed him for so long, railing against the blank canvas as though it were evidence of her failure. But the blank page has value. The blank page is perhaps the most exciting thing of all. The start of everything, the start of anything at all.

She closes her eyes and sees Jamie as she'd seen him only days before, the sunlight blessing his face with a warm, yellow halo. Damian always liked to say that when you're an artist, you're never lonely. Art is essential, he'd told her. Lifesaving. And it is: but art is a cold bedmate when what you need is something much more alive. A warm hand to hold in yours, a body in your arms. Art alone won't save her.

Maybe she didn't have to choose between the work and matters of the heart. Tomorrow she might drive to Whangamatā to return the rental car, and then she might find a way back to Desire. For now, though, she's here, alone, a brush in her hand, Alizarin Crimson and Cerulean Blue by her side. She starts to paint.

Acknowledgements

THIS BOOK WAS MADE possible only with the help of many people, including the Sargeson Trust, for gifting me the Sargeson Fellowship in 2024, which provided me the time, space and income to work on this novel; also thanks to the Michael King Writers Centre, for the Emerging Writers Residency in February 2023, where I began this novel; and lastly to the University of Auckland for the use of an office in October 2023 and October 2024 to work on structure and voice.

Thanks to the readers of the terrible early, unfinished drafts: Nat Baker, Karen Holdom, Erica Stretton, and to Nicki Judkins for her feedback and especially to Sarah Ell: your enthusiasm for the project when mine was gone is one of the few reasons the book exists today.

An enormous thank you to my editor, the wonderful Jane

Parkin, who worked on this novel with such thoughtful consideration and clever suggestions, and treated my writing like it mattered: thank you. The book would be much poorer without your insight and knowledge.

I must thank the amazing team at Allen & Unwin Aotearoa New Zealand, including Michelle Hurley, Melanie Laville-Moore, Abba Renshaw, Leonie Freeman, Rebecca Simpson, Nyssa Walsh and Hollie Wilkinson, plus an extra thank you to all the team at Archetype New Zealand, and to the booksellers around New Zealand who championed my first novel.

Some readers might notice the small liberties I have taken in the novel, for instance the fact that Baldwin Street was successfully hill-bombed by Australian skateboarder Zak Mills-Goodwin in August 2022, much earlier than Riggs decides he will do it. All other errors I hope skateboarders and artists can forgive me for!

This book is also dedicated in memory of Nathan Smith, and written with love for my sister, Crystal Smith, and their children, Saskia, Ashton and Lucia.

Finally, the largest thanks to Lee Shapiro, for always telling me to keep going, and for allowing me the time to write, and for putting up with my intense emotional outbursts and depressive episodes when my expectations outstrip my abilities. And, to my girls, Willa and Marnie, for your patience and your love.

JOSIE SHAPIRO is the bestselling author of *Everything is Beautiful and Everything Hurts*, which won the inaugural Allen & Unwin NZ Fiction prize and was named one of the best books of 2023 by *The Spinoff* and the *New Zealand Listener*.

A graduate of the University of Auckland's Master of Creative Writing, Josie was a Sargeson Fellow in 2024 and was named one of the 2025 New Voices of Aotearoa. She lives in Tāmaki Makaurau with her husband and two daughters.